Francisco Goya – Self-portrait

MEMORY
OF
BONES

ALEX CONNOR

Quercus

First published in Great Britain in 2012 by

Quercus
55 Baker Street,
7th Floor, South Block
London
W1U 8EW

A CIP catalogue record for this book is available
from the British Library.

ISBN 978 0 85738 962 6 (PB)
ISBN 978 0 85738 963 3 (EBOOK)

10 9 8 7 6 5 4 3 2 1

Typeset by Ellipsis Digital Limited, Glasgow

Printed and bound in Great Britain by Clays Ltd, St Ives Plc.

Floating on the water at the edge of the canal, hardly visible, was a bundle, wrapped tightly in a soiled white blanket. It was small, benign, but eerie. Gently, it glided away and began its grisly procession down the middle of the canal, on an almost imperceptible current. Transfixed, they watched its progress, the bundle finally passing under the full glare of one of the restaurant's outside lamps. The beam illuminated the blood-spattered wrapping – and the place where the parcel had come partially untied.

From which a disembodied hand, fingers outstretched, clawed its way to the light.

BOOK ONE

1

Bordeaux, France, May 1828

Under a horned moon, two figures paused. It was past one in the morning in the cemetery, on a humid, early summer night, when even the insomniacs of the town were restlessly asleep. Both men knew that if they were caught they would be jailed. Grave-robbing, especially the plundering of the crypt of an important man, could result in a long imprisonment. Or worse.

Impatiently, the older man began to shuffle his feet, his companion breaking open the seal into the crypt. Together they entered, ivy leaves brushing against their faces as they hurried in. Shutting the door behind them, the younger man immediately lit an oil lamp.

'It's here,' he said, holding up the light to illuminate the crypt.

The interior was dark and clammy with damp, the smell of mould oppressive as the man shone the light around the chamber. In the centre stood a large stone casket with a sealed lid, a mottled spider casting an intricate web over the lock, the lamplight flashing on the sticky threads. Without speaking, the man reached for his hammer and then brought it down violently, smashing the seal of the tomb.

'Come on,' he hissed at his companion. 'We have to be quick.'

Pushing at the stone, they strained to move the weighty top off the sarcophagus. Grunting with the effort, they finally edged the lid open, the smell of decomposition hitting both of them and making the older man gag. Together they pushed the lid further. It shifted a little. Again, they pushed. It slid again. On the third try it crashed on to the floor on the other side of the sarcophagus. The noise was deafening in the confined space.

Losing his nerve, the older man hurried to the door and looked out. For a long, breathless moment they waited for the sound of someone raising the alarm. But the noise hadn't woken anyone. Not even the stonemason who lived by the cemetery gates.

'Help me,' the younger man ordered.

'I can't—'

'Shut up!' the first snapped, turning back to the tomb and shining the light into it.

Expressionless, he stared at the remains of the man who had been buried a month before. As the odour increased – suffocating in the cramped vault – the robber could see that the corpse's white collar and cuffs were stained with decomposition fluids, the face puffy and oozing, the crossed hands black on the underside of the fingers and palms where the blood had settled in death. Supposedly airtight, the sarcophagus had, however, leaked in enough oxygen and damp to begin decay. Sinkage in the ribcage and eye sockets was pronounced and the lips of the cadaver had shrunk, drawn back from the bared teeth like an animal about to attack.

Stooping down, he took out a knife and hacksaw from his bag and turned back to the sarcophagus. Leaning over, he pulled back the white grandee collar from the corpse's throat, the smell intensifying as he touched the slime of the skin. Then, savagely, he drew his knife across the throat, the skin and muscle giving way and exposing the bone beneath.

'Give me the hacksaw.'

Handing him the tool, the older man turned away, not seeing but hearing the repetitive sound of sawing. When he finally looked back, his companion had climbed into the coffin and was straddling the corpse. The cadaver's flesh pooled under his fingers, his hands slipping as he sawed frantically at the neck bones. Finally, sweating with effort, the man tried to lift the head off, hoping to wrench it free from the body. The sound of cracking echoed in the dark crypt, the shadows of the grave robbers looming vast on the damp walls, the oil lamp flickering hellishly as he yanked at the head.

With a sickening crunch it came away from the body, the grave robber losing his balance and falling back against the corpse's legs.

Slowly the horned moon sidled up the night sky, making chalk patches on the indigo earth. Moving furtively down a quiet road, the men kept to the shadow of the trees, then entered the Rue d'Arles, the younger man walking round the back of a large house and rapping on the door. Instantly a tall man appeared, putting his forefinger to his lips and ushering them into a shuttered basement room. That he had money was obvious from his clothes, his voice Parisian, at odds with the rural French spoken by the resurrection men.

'You have it?'

'In here,' the younger man replied, holding up the sack.

Gesturing for him to put it in a nearby sink, the man handed him a wedge of money. 'You must tell no one—'

'We never did before. Why would we now?'

Nodding, the Parisian showed them to the door, glancing out and then beckoning to the men. 'Say nothing to no one. Betray me and you'll hang.'

'And you?' the grave robber replied. 'They'll do worse if they find out what you've done.'

2

London, the present day

The sweating, grotesquely fat man checked the address twice, looked round, then moved into the building. From the street it had looked like every other shop, the words MAMA GALA'S painted in large red letters at the top of the window, a selection of herbs, breads, nuts and pulses set out in an alluring display. Inside, a heavy African woman was serving a customer, laughing as she wrapped some arrowroot, wind chimes tingling eerily by the open door.

Nervous, the fat man walked over to her: 'I came to see Emile Dwappa.'

Her smile faded. 'No one called that here.'

'I was told to come here.' The man leaned towards the woman, who took a step back. 'Mr Dwappa sent for me himself.'

Suddenly she relaxed, one fleshy black hand pointing to a door. 'Go through there, right to the back. Then turn

7

left and go up the stairs.' She looked him up and down, laughing. 'You're one fat white man. One sweaty, fat white man.'

Embarrassed, he moved on, opening the door and walking into the large back room beyond. Immediately an unfamiliar smell hit him, and he flinched as he saw carcass after carcass of dried meat hanging on butchers' hooks along one side of the wall. Flanks of dark red flesh, ribboned with yellow fat, swung in a breeze from the open back door; other smaller packages piled up on high shelves. As the man stared up at the butchery, a piercing screech sounded behind him.

Spinning round, he almost lost his footing as he stumbled against a large cage, a macaw flapping its wings at him, its yellow eyes fixed, hostile.

'Christ!'

Hurriedly he moved on, passing more cages. Some held snakes, others small, feral monkeys looking out disconsolately, one peeing between the bars. The urine hit the floor by the man's feet, its stench mixing queasily with the smell of dead meat and the ammonia of bird droppings.

Stumbling up the steep, narrow flight of steps, the obese man clambered into the darkness above. Grunting with the effort, he waited at the top of the stairs for his eyes to adjust to the dim light, wiping the sweat off his forehead with the back of his hand. Every window was covered by blinds, daylight almost obliterated, and against a far wall was a sofa with two figures sitting on it, barely discernible in the dimness.

As the man walked in further, he could see a table on the left, the overwhelming scent of oleander and musk making him retch. Sitting at the table, a wizened black woman was cutting some herbs, a pestle and mortar beside her. At her feet sat a small, silent child, its arms curled around its knees. From below, the man could hear the sound of jazz music, punctuated by the screech of the caged birds and a monkey banging its feeding bowl against the bars.

The atmosphere was rancid, his curiosity forcing him on towards the sofa and the seated figures. Palms wet with sweat, he peered into the gloom. Then suddenly a match was struck, an African face coming into full view as Emile Dwappa leaned forward to light the candles in front of him. He was no more than thirty-five, his narrow head unexpectedly boyish, his eyes light against the black skin. Beside him lounged a woman, naked from the waist upwards, her left hand resting on one uncovered breast.

Dwappa smiled. 'Mr Shaw . . .?'

The fat man nodded.

'Take a seat.'

Jimmy Shaw eased himself on to an uncomfortable chair opposite the couple. Uneasy, he wiped his forehead and his palms, laughing nervously.

'It's hot in here.'

'Central heating,' Dwappa replied. 'I like it hot.'

Listlessly the woman moved, her skirt falling open and revealing the inside of her right thigh. Running his tongue over his dry lips, the fat man stared, transfixed, his heavy suit damp under the armpits, his shirt collar rubbing his neck raw.

'You wanted to see me?'

Facing Dwappa, Jimmy Shaw tried to remember what he had been told. Emile Dwappa was a businessman, with a reputation so sinister even the hard cases in Brixton were afraid of him. Rumours abounded and followed him like a gaggle of black geese. In the three years he had been in London, Dwappa had built up a terrifying reputation. You didn't cross him – you didn't even go anywhere near him – unless you wanted something very specific. Or worse, he wanted something very specific from *you*.

'So where is it?'

The fat man wriggled in his seat. 'Spain.'

'I want it. Here,' Dwappa said. 'I have a buyer for the skull. How soon can you get it?'

Shaw shook his head, trying to think up a lie and wondering at the same time how Dwappa had heard about the Goya skull so quickly. The same skull which someone had already approached him about. In the criminal undercurrent of the art world, news always travelled quickly, but this speed had been even more remarkable than usual. In the last twenty-four hours two dealers, an Iranian collector and a museum curator had contacted Shaw. And one was offering a king's ransom for Francisco Goya's skull.

For over two hundred years the skull had been missing. All that was known for certain was that it had been taken around the time of Goya's death in Bordeaux. No other facts were confirmed and the famous skull – emblematic of artistic genius – had vanished. Until now.

A failed art dealer, Shaw knew that there was a thriving trade in art relics. In the past, various and suspect parts of the saints had changed hands for money. Sometimes the Church paid up, wanting to retain a relic or to purchase one for a cathedral in an area which had need of a spiritual revival. But as religion lost its grip, secular art dealing became big business. In the decades which followed, sales and auction prices exploded in an orgasm of greed, and third-rate dealers like Jimmy Shaw found themselves edged out onto the shady periphery of the art world. Forced away from the high-octane embrace of London and New York, for men with more greed than morals a greasy slide into crime was inevitable.

And so Jimmy Shaw had become a handler. At first he had fenced stolen paintings, but gradually his slyness – and his contacts – promoted him into the select rank of men who stole to order. Collectors as far apart as Paris and Bahrain called on him to either find or thieve works of art. Naturally Shaw did none of the actual physical work; he had minions to do that for him. Men who needed money or a favour. Or, more likely, men who had something to hide. Something Shaw had winkled out of one of his other contacts. With impressive connections to old lags, runners, and gallery assistants looking to supplement their poor wages, Shaw had built up a network around London, expanding into Europe and even the

USA. Physically repulsive, his sole companion was money and the whores it could buy. As his criminality had extended he had become bloated in body and amorality, normal life forever curtailed by his reputation and appearance.

But who needed respectability when they had a fortune? And Jimmy Shaw could see a *huge* fortune waiting for him. Goya's skull had been found – let the bear-baiting begin. Of course he realised that competition for the relic would be intense. Everyone would want to own the skull. Collectors, dealers, museums – all of them grubbing around in the artistic mire to pluck an opal out of the shit.

The power and fame of Francisco Goya had never waned. His paintings were reproduced endlessly, his pictures and etchings revered, the notorious Black Paintings as frightening and compelling as they had always been. Oh yes, Shaw thought, he would make a fortune out of Goya's skull. A fortune Emile Dwappa wasn't going to snatch out of his hands.

'It might be a rumour.'

'What?'

Shaw coughed. 'The finding of the Goya skull – it might just be a rumour. People have claimed that it was found before. But they were always fakes—'

'I want it.'

I bet you do. You want it to sell it on – and then what do I get? A handler's fee? Fuck off, Shaw thought to himself. The skull was *his* prize.

He could remember several years earlier when a supposed strand of Leonardo da Vinci's hair had come on to the black market. Within hours Shaw had contacted collectors overseas, whipping up a frantic auction. In the end the relic was purchased by an Italian connoisseur in Milan. Hair, fingers or other bones from such legendary figures rarely came on the market, which was why they were so sought after. But a *whole skull* – Francisco Goya's skull – would set a record.

Curious, Dwappa leaned forward in his seat. 'I'll pay you for bringing it to me.'

'I don't know if I can—'

'You said it was in Spain.'

Fuck! Shaw thought. Why had he said that? He was nervous, that was why, but he couldn't afford to be. Dwappa had a reputation, but so did he. A reputation for cunning. Perhaps he could outsmart the African.

'I'll ask around for you.'

'What do you weigh?'

Shaw blinked, wrong-footed. 'Huh?'

'What do you weigh?'

'Three hundred and forty pounds.'

'Heavy ...'

Shaw shifted around awkwardly on the hard chair. OK, so I'm a fat, ugly bastard, he thought – but I'm the one who'll end up with the skull.

'You have to get the skull for me. I have a buyer.'

Only one? Shaw thought, unimpressed. His confidence was beginning, slowly, to return. He knew that Emile

Dwappa had never dealt in art before; he was naive. Perhaps a lot easier to cheat than he had first suspected.

'As I say, I'll ask around. But it might be difficult.'

'I'll pay you well,' Dwappa replied.

Shaw allowed a glint of smugness to enter his tone. 'I've already got plenty of money.'

'I heard that.'

'And I don't need any more work.'

'I heard that too.'

Smiling, Shaw turned his puffy face to the woman, then glanced back at Dwappa, who was watching him avidly. He could recognise something in the amber eyes: a cold heat and a total lack of empathy. Be careful, Shaw told himself. Be careful and you can still come out of this the winner.

'Mr Dwappa,' he went on pleasantly, 'all I know is that the skull's been found in Spain. That's all the information I have.'

'Who has it?'

Shaw shrugged. 'I don't know . . .'

He was lying. The man now in possession of Goya's skull was an art historian called Leon Golding. An aesthetic intellectual who had lived and worked in Madrid all his life.

'I'm sorry, but I can't help you.'

Dwappa's expression was unreadable. 'You have to get that skull.'

'Look, even if I could, it would take time. It's not as easy as it sounds—'

'You've stolen before—'

'*But not the skull of Goya!*' Shaw whined, wriggling on his seat. 'Even if I *could* find it – which I doubt – I couldn't do it in a couple of days.'

'I'll give you time.'

Wrong-footed, Shaw took a moment to reply. 'Like I said, I don't know anything—'

In one fluid movement the African lurched forward and struck. Shaw felt the blow and reeled back, then screamed with pain – Dwappa had driven a knife through the back of his hand, pinning it to the table underneath.

'*Jesus Christ!*' Shaw gabbled, blood spurting out from the pale, fatty flesh. '*Jesus Christ . . .*'

'Get the Goya skull,' Dwappa said, leaning forward and twisting the knife around in the wound, ripping up the flesh.

Screaming again, Shaw felt tears come into his eyes, his fingernails scratching at the table top in desperation as Dwappa's hand moved towards the knife again. '*No!*' he shrieked. 'I'll get the skull. I'll get it!'

Leaning back in his seat, Dwappa watched the fat man's face, greasy with fear. Sweat was soaking into his expensive suit, his flabby legs shaking.

'You said the skull was in Spain?'

The fat man nodded. 'Yes! Yes! In Spain.'

'You know who has it?'

Despite his terror, Shaw's guile was automatic. 'I'm not sure. I think so . . . Anyway, I can find out.'

'Good. Get the skull. For your own sake.'

Shaking uncontrollably, Shaw flinched when he saw the African raise his hand again. But he was only beckoning to someone across the room and a moment later the old woman walked over to him. Without saying a word, she handed Dwappa a paper with a ground-up substance on it. Behind him Shaw could hear the little girl laughing softly . . . Quickly, Dwappa pulled out the knife, then poured the soothing white powder over the wound in Shaw's hand. His head slumped forward, the powder clotting and turning red as it mingled with his blood.

'You can go now.'

The words took a while to register in Shaw's brain, and then he stood up, swaying on his feet for an instant before he headed for the stairs. Holding his bloodied hand to his chest, he paused, but didn't dare look back. The room undulated with heat and the oppressive odour of herbs and sweat. From the couch came the sound of the woman moaning and from below echoed the scrabbling of the monkeys' claws.

As Shaw staggered downstairs, a sudden, hot burst of wind blew in from the back yard, making the macaw screech and claw at the cage bars and the snakes rise up and hiss. It shook the meat carcasses so violently that they lurched and jerked, swinging on their butchers' hooks like a row of skinned men.

3

The two Golding brothers stood beside the grave in a dry cemetery outside Madrid. The heat was building, the sun unhindered by clouds, the brass plaque on the coffin glistening like a lizard's eye.

'There's something I have to tell you,' Leon said, his voice so low Ben had to strain to catch it.

They were attending the funeral of the woman who had raised them. Head bowed, Ben could feel the sun burning the skin on the back of his neck and longed for the cool drizzle of London. He could sense Leon's excitement as his brother stood beside him, the nervous scuffling of his feet, the intermittent hoarse coughs. Was he taking his medication? Ben wondered, stealing a glance at Leon, who was gazing, unblinking, into the grave. He wondered momentarily how his brother would cope with the loss of Detita – if the old woman's death would herald another breakdown. But apparently Leon had something

17

else on his mind, something so important that it over-shadowed the funeral of a woman he had loved since childhood.

'We have to talk—' Leon said urgently.

'We will. Later,' Ben replied, looking down at the grave.

Irritated, Leon studied his brother. Tall and olive-skinned, any other man would have taken advantage of his appeal, but Ben had no vanity. He wasn't a player either. In fact, for the last six years Ben had lived with Abigail Harrop, disappointing many nurses – and a couple of female doctors – at the Whitechapel Hospital in London, where he worked as a reconstructive plastic surgeon.

They had met when Abigail had been admitted as a patient after a car accident badly disfigured the left side of her face. Having been a good-looking woman she was affected both physically and psychologically by the accident and therapy had been of little use. Withdrawing into herself, she resigned from her job as an advertising exec-utive and began to work from home, her only forays into the outside world being to the Whitechapel Hospital, or to visit her family. Depression didn't overtake Abigail but shyness did. The self-confidence she had once taken for granted disappeared with the accident, and she would keep her head averted if anyone spoke to her. It was not the first time Ben had seen a pretty woman lose her looks overnight, but Abigail was different. Her lack of anger surprised him; her composure unfathomable.

It took Ben many months to realise that what really affected Abigail was her loss of appeal, something she had taken for granted before. Believing herself repellent after the accident, she rejected the opposite sex. Ben was the only man she turned to, first as a doctor, then later as a friend. Much later still, when she had left the Whitechapel Hospital, as a lover.

Restless, Leon continued the scrutiny of his brother. 'We *have* to talk—'

'Later.'

Glancing down at the coffin again, Leon could hear the priest's monotonous litany of prayers and began to jiggle his left foot as Ben gazed at him questioningly.

There were only a few people at the funeral; the widowed Detita had had no family apart from a daughter who had left Spain long ago. Detita had been wealthy once – although she had never fully explained her background – but bad luck and widowhood had overtaken her. Coming to work for the Goldings, she had appealed to their cultured sensibilities, her breeding obvious and unusual for a housekeeper. Her Spanish hauteur, coupled with her domestic competence, ensured that within weeks she was indispensable.

Soon Detita found herself courted by her employers, who were only too pleased to have her take care of their sons during their frequent absences. Reliable and regal as a duchess, by the end of the first year Detita lived only for the boys. Taken into Miriam Golding's confidence, she slid, boneless, into the family. So when an air crash over the Atlantic killed the parents, it was no surprise that Detita had been nominated the brothers' guardian.

She took on the role like a Spanish grandee, and over the years which followed leaked tantalising – but measured – information about her past, enough to incite curiosity but never enough to satisfy. Indomitable, she ran the old ramshackle farmhouse, intimidating the gardener and shadowing the cleaner. She was a bully with her own people but the equal of her charges. For two Jewish boys growing up in the predominantly Catholic Madrid, Detita managed to straddle the gap between the heat and suspicion of Spain and the cool learning of the boys' Anglo-American parents.

Although the brothers had been sent to an English boarding school in term time, when they returned to Spain Detita continued their education. She taught them fluent Spanish and took them to lectures and museums, pounding culture into them like a cook over-stuffing a pair of quail.

Leon had loved Detita very much – perhaps a little too much – but even her death couldn't stop the overheated excitement in his brain. As the service ended, he grabbed his brother's arm, leading Ben over to his parked car. His face was a mirror image of his brother's in all but tone. Leon was a watercolour study, Ben a masterwork in oil. One paper, the other tempered canvas.

'They've found the skull.'

Slipping into the driver's seat, Ben looked at his brother and wound down the window. 'Whose skull?'

'I was thinking that you could get someone – a specialist – to look at it,' Leon hurried on, ignoring the question. 'You're a doctor. You know people who could reconstruct it, check out the measurements, teeth. Do whatever you have to do. Just find out how old it is—'

'*Whose head?*'

'Goya's.'

Ben smiled and leaned back in his seat. A sudden gush of hot wind made the leaves flap and sent dust eddies shimmying around the bonnet of their car.

'His skull's been missing for over two centuries—'

'*Until now.* Builders were digging up the foundations of a house in Madrid, somewhere Goya stayed for a while. They found the skull under the cement in the cellar. The foreman, Diego Martinez, brought it to me, knowing I'd be interested in the possibility that it might be the artist's. You remember Diego – we knew him as a kid, when he used to come to the house with his father. You must remember him.'

Ben frowned. 'I don't.'

'Carlos fixed the guttering and the pipework.' Leon sighed, irritated. 'Diego was always getting sunburnt.'

'How much did he ask for the skull?'

'*He didn't charge me for it!*' Leon snapped. His voice was picking up speed, but he wasn't manic. Not yet. 'Jesus, what's the matter with you? I thought you'd be interested. We grew up near to where the Quinta del Sordo used to be, for Christ's sake!' He paused, his tone coaxing. 'Think about what this could mean for me. If it *is* Goya's skull it would be world news – and it would make my reputation.'

'They thought they'd found the skull before. But it was a fake—'

Leon wasn't listening. 'There's an exhibition of the Black Paintings this autumn. What a coup that would be – the genius's skull found just in time to coincide with the show. I'd be the most famous art historian on the bloody planet.'

'*If* it's genuine,' Ben said calmly. 'If it isn't you'll look a moron.'

'But it *is* Goya's skull! Goya died in Bordeaux in 1828 and was buried there until the Spanish authorities brought him back home to Madrid and re-interred him in 1899. Seventy-one years later.'

Ben sighed. 'I know the story, Leon. God knows how many times Detita told us that Goya's head was missing. But all this is supposition, not fact . . .'

Pausing, Ben glanced out of the car window, his own composure rattled by memory. Detita had made certain that her charges understood Spain and Spanish art. In her eyes, Goya came next after God. Ben could almost see her alive again, sitting at the kitchen table. Automatically he loosened his collar, the heat swelling, her image filling the car.

'. . . Goya's home, the Quinta del Sordo, was only a little way from here . . .' she would begin, sitting down in the kitchen, her back straight, her eyes unreadable. Overhead, the old house would creak, water pipes banging, the sound of wild geese coming, mournful, over the river. It had been nothing like their school in England, where the trees grew rich and straight. It had been another country. Another country of location. And of mind. '. . . Goya was one of the greatest artists who ever lived.'

'What about Michelangelo?'

She had made a dismissive sound as she turned to Ben.

'No fire. Goya knew the dark side. He lived in that big old house, near the river, near enough to see Madrid, far away enough not to be a part of the city. In that house Goya painted his private pictures, the Black Paintings. In them he left a message . . .'

Pausing there, she had reached for her books, turning over the pages slowly, grotesque images oozing off the paper.

It required no effort for Ben to remember the queasy unease which had wept from the reproductions.

'Look,' Detita had said, her white forefinger turning over the page to expose the *Witches' Sabbath*. Not the earlier version, with its light blues and comic devilry – this was the image of Goya's later years. After the Inquisition and the Spanish War of Independence, after the murder and torture. When the indigo power of Black Magic had been not merely a superstition, but a possibility. The Devil was no longer comic, but a shadow which had followed many Spaniards. The End of Reason in the Age of Enlightenment.

Ben had been repelled, but *compelled* to look at the painting: at the stupid, animalistic faces of the cohorts crouched on the ground. Women, once beautiful, had been turned by Goya into salacious hags, monochromic heads cowled, eyes wide open and blank with cruelty. And while Detita talked of Goya, she also talked of Spanish history – and the unknown. Of the two boys, she had caught

Leon's imagination first because he was mercurial in temperament, needing constant excitement and stimulus.

Ben was never sure if their parents had understood Leon's mental frailty, but he had been aware of it all his life – that nauseous dance between stability and hysteria, between appreciation and obsession.

Still staring out of the car window, Ben remembered Detita. The Detita of the daytime, practical, intelligent, stern. And then the other Detita, the night woman, languid as candlelight. Duty had had no place after the light faded – then she had told stories, stories she said had been passed down by generations of Spanish grandmothers, by *her* Spanish grandmother. But the tales had never been benign. Always, like her, they veered between two worlds.

'. . . *When you need me, come at midnight to the Bridge of the Manzanares, clap your hands three times and you will see black horses appear . . .*'

Detita had smiled as she recited the quote, Leon leaning forward expectantly under the overhead lamp, Ben's dark eyes fixed on her. At once she had noticed his expression, the almost warning glance, and felt her power weaken. Many times in the years that followed she had clashed with Ben as her control over him lessened. And then, finally, Detita had shifted her attention from the two brothers to the one. From Ben's granite control to the soft slush of Leon's instability.

For an instant, Ben closed his eyes. But still the memories kept coming.

'. . . The Spanish people have a dark heart . . .' Detita had said, luring Leon in with her stories. 'When Ferdinand VII reinstated the Inquisition the purges began, the Church re-energised along with its greedy, mercenary priests. And among the pogroms, the Spanish developed an even greater appetite for pain, murder and death. Goya feared Ferdinand because he was a liberal, and after Ferdinand was reinstated the King's power was absolute again.'

A fly landed on the back of Ben's hand, throwing a stumpy shadow before he flicked it away. In the over-heated car, he wondered why Leon wasn't talking and glanced over at his brother. Was Leon waiting? Was he biding his time? Or maybe just sulking? Suddenly another memory resonated in Ben's mind: his brother waking, screaming, in the middle of the night. *Every* night throughout one long, dry summer as Goya's image of *Saturn* picked away at his sanity like a black rook. Relentlessly, Leon had insisted that the house was haunted, that their dead parents lived in the cellar and banged on the water pipes . . .

Pleading, Ben had asked Detita not to tell Leon any more stories. She had replied with a limp shrug, smile benign as a lamb's, eyes like a tree monkey.

'They're just old Spanish tales!' she had said. 'Children have to know about the world, not just the part they can see. Leon might be scared for a while, but then he'll forget. No one stays frightened forever.' She had been playing cat's cradle with Ben's emotions, unexpectedly tender. 'You're a good boy to worry about your brother. You must always look out for Leon – he's not strong like you.'

'So?'

Startled out of the memory, Ben turned to his brother. 'What?'

'So will you help me?' Leon went on, his skin translucent, pale after a lifetime of ducking the Spanish sun. 'Will you get someone to look at the skull?'

'Yeah, OK,' Ben said finally.

'Thanks . . .' There was an awkward pause. 'You're staying overnight, of course?'

'I've got a hotel room booked in Madrid.'

'*Madrid*? Why don't you stay with us?'

'I've an early flight in the morning. Why disturb everyone?'

'But I want you to meet Gina,' Leon replied petulantly. 'I want you two to be friends. I was never lucky with women before, you know that. But Gina's perfect. She understands me, my work. I want you two to get on.'

'I'm coming back next month. I can meet her then.'

'Why not now?'

'Leon, next time, I promise.'

'She's very supportive—'

'Good.'

'Really cares about me.'

'That's good.'

'Very understanding—'

'She broke up with you for nine months and then came

26

back without ever explaining why she went off in the first place!'

Ben stopped short, cursing himself. Leon's tone was prickly as he replied.

'Gina left because we had problems. It wasn't all her fault. We've sorted things out now ... She's good for me, Ben. She's interested in sport, health. She said I didn't need to take so much medication—'

His patience strained, Ben stole a quick glance at his brother. 'You need it, Leon—'

'Yeah, I do now, but in time Gina says I won't. She knows all these people who practise alternative therapies; they've had great results.'

'Perhaps you should talk your doctor about it.'

He was sharp. 'I'm not a child!'

'I'm not saying that, Leon. I'm saying that it would be a good idea. You could take Gina with you.' Sighing, Ben tried to break the tension by changing the subject. 'I'll pick up the skull on my next trip—'

'Why can't you look at it before you leave?'

'*You've got it?*' Ben asked, surprised.

'Of course.'

'Shouldn't you tell the authorities?'

'I have done. And I told the Prado that I'd organise its authentication for them. I'm well respected here, they trust me to do the right thing.' Leon's voice held a slight tremor of triumph. 'Gina said I should do what I've always wanted to do – to finally write that book about Goya's Black Paintings. God knows I've done enough work on them. I've the chance to solve the pictures. Just think of it – a book to coincide with the exhibition *and* the finding of the skull.'

'But you don't know if it's authentic—'

'*You don't know it isn't!*' Leon's pale eyes were fixed on his brother. 'It'll be the making of me, Ben. I'll be the only historian who can lecture on Goya *and* exhibit his skull at the same time. Think of it – people love the macabre.'

'Leon, about the Black Paintings . . .' Ben began anxiously. Memories of Detita, of his brother's instability, shivered inside him. 'I'll get the skull checked out for you, see if it's authentic. I know someone in London who can do that for us. But I don't want you to do the book.'

'Why not? I've been talking about it for years,' Leon replied, bemused. 'Why would you want me to pass up on it now?'

'Detita used to say that the Black Paintings were cursed. She said they were bad luck—'

'Since when did you believe in things like that?'

Ben sighed. 'All right, but I don't think it would be good for you.'

'I know more about the Black Paintings than anyone. Anyway, I've got a new theory—'

'No one really knows what they mean,' Ben went on. 'They don't make sense.'

'They do!'

'All right, maybe they do. Or maybe they're simply gibberish. I don't know if Goya was ill when he painted them, or smoking something. But I know those pictures, Leon, and they're disturbing. Detita was right about that. They've caused so much speculation: crap about codes, hidden messages, even—'

'A link to the occult.'

'Which is unproven,' Ben said emphatically.

'But suspected by a number of people. After all, Goya didn't just paint one or two satanic paintings, he undertook dozens. He was consumed with the dark side—'

'And you? Are you consumed? Because if you are, that worries me.'

Leon blinked slowly, his tone sarcastic. 'Paintings aren't dangerous. They can't harm people . . .'

Incredulous, Ben shook his head. Of all the people in the world his brother was the most likely to be harmed by the queasy allure of Goya's last works.

'They're beautiful and they mean something.' Leon continued. 'They *do*. Goya was fascinated with satanism—'

'*Everyone* was at that period in Spain. It was a fucking hobby,' Ben replied drily. 'There have always been theories about Goya's work, but no one can prove any of them.'

'What if I could?' Leon challenged him. 'In satanism, they decapitate their victims. When Goya died in France, no one gave a damn about his remains for over seventy years—'

'Which is when the head could have been lost. Or separated from the skeleton when the body was moved.'

'*Goya's head was stolen*. Think about it, Ben. Perhaps the head could tell us something. An expert could discover if it had been cut off, or just taken after the body deteriorated.'

Staggered, Ben stared at his brother.

'Even if it *was* cut off, that wouldn't mean anything. Goya was an old man; it was a miracle he lived so long.' He paused, staring at his brother questioningly. 'What are you trying to prove? *That he was murdered?*'

'He could have been! The Duchess of Alba was his mistress and she was poisoned. Goya had already suffered a very bizarre illness in his fifties and then he was sick again in his eighties.'

'He was old!'

'He was afraid.'

'Of what?'

Leon glanced away. 'There's a coherent message in the Black Paintings – something Goya had to communicate. But he couldn't put it in writing. That would have been too dangerous. He was afraid of Ferdinand, afraid that the Inquisition would come after him again. It's no coincidence that when he finished the pictures, he went to France.'

'And left a message behind?'

Nodding, Leon folded his arms, hugging himself. 'Yes.'

'For whom?'

'I don't know yet. For his peers. For his country. For posterity. I've not solved all the paintings but I'm close, really close. I don't think Goya was mad. He may have wanted people to think that he was, but he knew what he was doing. He was a patriot. He'd seen his country gutted, he'd witnessed numerous atrocities. To see Ferdinand back on the throne after so much bloodshed, to see Spain under the royal boot of a vicious, conniving idiot would have been intolerable for him. And dangerous.'

Wary, Ben studied his brother: the flushed face, the clammy skin, the intensity which might precipitate an attack. If Leon *did* solve the mystery of the Black Paintings he would be thrust into the limelight overnight and come under attack, not least from his peers. He would be feted – and berated – for his theory, and bring a welter of jealousy down on his head. The Black Paintings were on a par with discovering the real sitter for the *Mona Lisa*: an intellectual prize that many had sought. Who in the art world hadn't wanted to expose their meaning? It was a ticket to instant fame. And notoriety. But it was also an aesthetic cul de sac from which there would be no easy escape.

Leon's expression hardened. 'You think I'm getting too worked up about all of this.'

'I think you might be tilting at windmills—'

'Oh come on! What you *really* think is that I can't deal with it.'

There was a long pause.

'OK, you want me to be honest?' Ben said at last. 'Maybe I *don't* think you can cope. Maybe I'm worried it will all get out of control—'

'And maybe I don't like being in control all the time!' Leon retorted, flushed. 'Maybe, being medicated to the bloody gills, I might *miss* the craziness. Did you ever think about *that*?'

Crazy was one thing, Ben thought, but the fall to earth which followed was always an unnerving affair.

'Just take it easy, will you?'

'Well, thanks for the advice, brother,' Leon said, hurriedly getting out of the car and then bending down towards the window again. 'Now, piss off.'

'Before or after I've looked at the skull?'

Bordeaux, France, May 1828

Closing the door and locking it, the tall man lit another lamp, illuminating a laboratory of sorts. On the walls there were occult symbols, the pentacle and marked-out circles making swimming patterns in the half-light. Against one wall was a bench with a selection of medical tools laid on it, and beside that an oven. On top of the stove was a hotplate and a large stewing pan filled with water, a fire underneath. Rolling up the sleeves of his silk shirt, the tall man moved over to the sink.

The sack looked benign, with nothing to give away its ghastly contents, but he found himself momentarily unable to touch it. Pausing, he moved back to his desk and opened a ledger, making a few quick notes before returning to the sink. A moment passed and then finally the tall man opened the neck of the sack. The smell rose up and sickened him. Gagging, he put a cloth over his nose and mouth and reached into the bag. His fingers closed over a scruff of coarse hair. Then he gripped it firmly and withdrew the head.

The lamplight flickered, a vast, juddering shadow bouncing against the wall as the head became visible. Its sunken eyelids and rictus grin leered into the dim light as the man moved over to the stove and plunged the head into the warming water of the cooking pan. As he pushed it under, the skin of the face relaxed slightly, one eye opening, the cornea cloudy, staring up at him. Unnerved, the man slammed the lid down on the pan and moved away, rubbing his hands repeatedly to clean them.

At three o'clock in the morning, the clock chimed the hour sonorously. Now seated at his desk, the man waited. In front of him was a porcelain head, marked out in portions to indicate the parts of the brain which controlled the mind's workings: intuition, intellect, emotion. A book next to it was marked Phrenology, the new popular science by which men of reason believed they could read the character and ability of a person merely by studying the bumps and indentations on their head. It had become a cult all over Europe, a pseudo-medical curiosity, every adept eager to 'read' the skull of a genius to see if there was anything truly remarkable about its configuration.

Behind him, the man could hear the water simmer, the smell repellent as he lifted the lid off the large pan. Flinching, he could see that the skin was coming away from the bones of the skull, a sudden hissing noise startling him as one of the dead man's eyes popped out of its socket. Fighting nausea, the man pushed the head further down into the boiling water, the dark hair – ribboned with grey – floating upwards, loose flesh pooling greasily on the surface.

Slowly the night wore on, the man not daring to leave his watch. Outside, the darkness remained thick, the clock marking out the leaden heartbeat of the house. Exhausted, he fell into a nervous sleep: the cold, queasy sleep of the early hours. The temperature in the room dropped, the night owl stopped hooting, and the only sound came from the hum of the fire and the foul, simmering water.

Half an hour later the man woke, alarmed, sitting upright and then remembering where he was. Uneasy, he rubbed his eyes – and then stiffened in his seat. From behind came the sound of knocking. A steady, rhythmic knocking which was very close. Terrified, his limbs frozen, he slowly turned his head a little to the right. The sound intensified … Was someone knocking on the door? Did someone know he was there? Had the grave robbers betrayed him? The lamps had all but gone out, the shadows cloying as the man finally staggered to his feet. Moving to the door, he stopped abruptly. The noise was coming from the pan.

His gaze fixed on the gleaming copper tomb as he heard the steady, rhythmic knocking and watched in horror as the fire suddenly flared up in the stove and the water hissed and bubbled. It boiled so urgently that the knocking speeded up even more: increasing, manic, deafening. Transfixed with shock, the man realised that the noise was the head banging against the lid. Knocking on the lid, trying to get out … Then with one sudden burst of energy, the white-hot water tossed the lid aside, toppling it on to the floor, the skull bobbing to the surface of the searing, stinking liquid.

No flesh remained, only a few tufts of hair. The black eye sockets – blank and damning – staring directly at him.

4

Madrid

In the Spanish capital they were having a heatwave. It was 96 degrees in the shade, and rising. Even for Spain, that was hot. Outside the Prado a queue formed under the lemon-yellow sun: tourists in their new lightweight clothes, their feet pallid in gaudy sandals, their shoulders peeling and their necks rubbed raw by the sudden heat. Slowly, the front of the queue edged towards the Prado Museum entrance and the welcome shade. At the front, a red-haired man was reading a copy of the English *Telegraph*. Beside him waited a group of American students, talking in awestruck tones about La Quinta del Sordo. Tell a kid a ghost story and you have him hooked. Tell an old man a ghost story and you make him think of death.

Sweating, Jimmy Shaw made a path through the queue, a woman automatically pulling her child away from the bloated, unkempt man. Shaw was feverish, overheated, holding his bandaged hand to his chest protectively as fluid seeped through the dressing, a sticky yellow plasma which pre-empted infection. Jesus! Shaw thought. How could the wound be infected so fast? Another thought followed on immediately. Maybe Dwappa had put something on the knife. Or had the white powder – which had momentarily soothed – been poisoned?

Oh, Christ! Oh, Jesus! Pausing, Shaw breathed in with effort, his jacket slimy with sweat. He had told his cohorts in London and New York about the Goya skull – many had heard rumours already – and promised them a decent fee for stealing it. He explained all he knew – that the skull was in Madrid and in the possession of Leon Golding, although he suspected Golding – a part-time lecturer at the Prado – had already informed the museum and possibly handed the relic over to them for safe keeping. So far, so good. But when Shaw mentioned Emile Dwappa, everyone backed off. One look at his hand told them everything they needed to know. So Shaw had been forced to undertake the task himself. No minions this time, no remote orders – this time Jimmy Shaw was on his own.

Dwappa's words came back to him with added resonance – *Get the skull. For your own sake* . . . Shaw knew what he meant. He was being poisoned and the longer it took him to find the skull, the less chance he had to survive. His only hope was to find the skull and get back to Dwappa as soon as he could.

'*Hey, watch out!*' an American boy shouted at him as

Shaw lunged away from the wall. Curious, the lad looked at the obese grey-skinned man. 'You OK?'

'Fine . . .'

'What happened to your hand?'

'I shut it in a car door.'

The boy's eyes narrowed, two of his friends coming over and staring at the fat man.

'Fucking hell!' one said. 'You look like shit.'

Grunting, Shaw pushed his way past the boys, following the sign to the Prado staff entrance. His head buzzed with fever and sickness, his tongue felt thick and dry, his skin chafed with heat rash. Before he left London, and then later on his way over to Madrid, he had researched Leon Golding and the Prado. Apparently the staff and affiliates had an exclusive entrance at the rear of the museum, on the left. Well away from the tourists was a door leading to a pristine enclave, nesting among libraries and cool rooms.

As for Leon Golding, Shaw had found out quite a lot about the man. Apparently Golding was respected, but highly strung. A scandalous Spanish newspaper had reported a suicide attempt a few years earlier, which had been duly denied. There was also an interview about Golding's longstanding interest in Spanish art and about how he was trying to restore the family house outside Madrid, a rambling farmhouse that had seen better days. Perhaps he would like some money to help with the restoration? Shaw wondered. If experience was anything to go by quite a few of the art world's intelligentsia could be persuaded to exchange morals for money.

Taking a press cutting out of his inside pocket, Shaw stared at the photograph of Leon Golding: a handsome if delicate-looking man. Carefully he studied the face. He wanted to make certain he would recognise Golding, a man he was certain he could bully. Or buy off . . . Suddenly dizzy, Shaw crammed the photograph back into his pocket and moved over to a nearby water fountain. Leaning on the button, he bent down and felt the tepid liquid fill his mouth. In front of him his shadow fell, huge and bloated, as he wiped his lips and headed for the back entrance of the Prado. His plan was blindingly simple – he would seek out Leon Golding and offer to buy the skull. If he refused, he would increase the offer. If Golding still refused, Shaw would steal the skull.

His hand throbbing, the fat man looked at the stinking bandage and swallowed. Time was in short supply – both to find the skull and to get back to London. Shaw could feel himself getting weaker by the minute, his blood thickening with infection, every breath pumping bacteria through his heart and organs. Fighting panic, he tried to steady himself. He had been to the hospital in Madrid, but although treated and reassured by the A & E doctor on duty, Shaw didn't believe that the poison had been controlled, let alone dissipated. Instinct told him that his time was limited. Very limited. He *had* to get the skull. He *had* to get the antidote. Whatever it took.

Leon Golding didn't stand a chance.

5

'Abigail?'

As her voice came down the line, Ben could tell she was smiling. Could imagine the upturn of her mouth, the incline of her head when she was listening. She would be sitting at the table by the window, within sight of the over-grown garden that Ben had promised – every week in summer – to bring to heel. In the end Abigail had hired someone and Ben had come home to a memory, to a recon-struction of the garden he first remembered when he had bought the house seven years earlier. And she had teased him about it. Said it was her only little miracle of surgery.

'What are you doing?'

'Thinking about going back to work full time.'

He was surprised that her confidence allowed her to articulate the thought. How long it would take for the thought it be turned into action he didn't know.

'At the advertising agency?'

She paused before answering, but the pause told Ben everything he needed to know. She wasn't ready. And somehow, to his shame, he was glad.

'I was thinking it was time,' Abigail went on, feeling her way around the words and then changing the subject. 'Anyway, I was expecting you to call later tonight. Why are you ringing now?'

'Just to say I miss you.'

He could hear her smiling again.

'I miss you too. When are you coming home?'

'Tomorrow. I'm catching the last flight. I've got to do something for Leon first . . .' Ben paused, found himself waiting for some kind of response. But Leon's animosity towards Abigail was never reciprocated. 'You know something?'

'I know loads.'

'Smart-arse.' He dropped his tone. 'You're making a fool of me.'

'Don't give me all the credit – you did that yourself.'

He laughed, then became gentle. 'Every time I leave you I leave a part of myself behind . . .'

She rested her head against the phone, closing her eyes as she listened. For an attractive man, who could have manipulated women easily, his honesty was tender. And seductive.

'. . . you know how much I love you, don't you? Or *do* you?' He hesitated momentarily. 'I keep thinking that I know, but then I go away from you and realise that it increases, that what I felt before was nothing in comparison . . . How d'you do that?' he asked gently. 'How do you keep refilling my heart?'

How? she wondered. How could she not? After the

accident Abigail had seen herself destroyed, her confidence as bloodied as her face. In the first weeks the shock had obliterated all feeling, but then, finally, she realised that the beauty she had taken for granted was no longer hers. Reassurance did nothing to help her, and when Ben Golding had taken over her case Abigail didn't believe his encouragement either. He said he would remake her face. She doubted it. He said he would give her back her looks. She didn't believe him.

Throughout the painful months which followed, throughout operations, swellings and pain, Abigail kept mistrusting him. When the first procedure succeeded in recreating her left cheekbone, she did – for an instant – catch a vague glimpse of the self she had once been. But it faded fast. The operations went on. More injections. More stitches. More bandages were used, became bloodied, were changed. Drains were inserted into her face, then removed. Every time the procedures varied. Every time Ben told her she was making progress. She was sick with the anaesthetics; she cried in the side ward at night, on her own, because she had no family, only a father in France, too weak to travel. In the grim Whitechapel Hospital Abigail Harrop lost herself and turned to the nurses for support. Only gradually, slowly, did she begin to believe. Some little triumph of healing had restored her eye socket almost to its original. And for the first time in over a year, Abigail saw herself and began to climb back.

She had had only one moment of doubt after that. Overhearing two nurses talking, Abigail had heard one refer to her as Ben Golding's personal masterpiece. His creation. Jealousy had sparked the remark, but instead of being unnerved Abigail had felt unexpectedly pleased. Whatever his motives, what Ben Golding had promised her, he would deliver. This man – and *only* this man – would give her back what she had lost.

But she never counted on loving him. Grateful, in his debt, yes. But to love him? That had never entered her mind, even though it would have been an obvious response. What people didn't realise was that Abigail didn't expect anyone – least of all Ben Golding – to find her attractive. So when, long after she had ceased to be under his care, Ben told her how he felt, Abigail's shock was genuine. She withdrew, confusing him. She rejected him, making him all the more certain of his feelings. And in the end she accused him of wanting her only because she was his guinea pig.

And he'd burst out laughing.

Her thoughts came back to the present. 'Get back home, will you? As soon as you can, hey?'

He felt the pull over the line, the jerk of sensuality. 'Tomorrow—'

'Can't come soon enough.'

An hour later, as Ben left the hotel, the sky suddenly darkened to indigo, lightning following within minutes as a hot wind blew across Madrid. Looking out of the window of his hired car, he fought the temptation to return to London immediately. Having once been passionate about Spain, he now found the country oppressive. But he had promised he would visit Leon, and so, reluctantly, he turned in the direction of his childhood home.

A moment later he was crossing the familiar river, freckled with birds and drowning reeds, a heat haze making the road shimmer before him. It had been urbanised when they were children, but now the area was even more built up, unremarkable, almost down at heel. His childhood tap-dancing before his eyes, Ben neared his old home, the site of the Quinta del Sordo close by. Parking in the driveway, he stared at the weather-beaten white-washed rectangular house.

Maintained intermittently for over two hundred years, the place was mottled with patches of repair, like a face freckled with sun damage. The gable where summer birds had once roosted was now closed off with netting, the bay window on the first floor barred with ornate ironwork. Ben's gaze moved upwards to his childhood bedroom, separated from his brother's by a shared bathroom. Without even trying, he could remember the sound of faulty pipework banging at night, and the paper kites Leon and he had exchanged through the open bedroom doors, many landing in the chipped bathtub between. But more than anything Ben remembered the underlying disquiet of the house. The muted but ever-present melancholia.

'You came,' Leon said warmly, walking over to him.

Smiling, Ben got out of the car to find his brother accompanied by an athletic, deeply tanned woman in a white linen dress. Shielding her eyes from the sun, she smiled as Ben approached.

'I'm Gina. And I'm so glad to meet you.' Smoothly, she then moved between the two brothers as the three of them walked into the cool interior of the house. It smelt to Ben of memory, poignant and unexpectedly hostile. 'You'll stay for lunch with us?'

'I'd like that.'

'Nothing fancy, but your brother likes my cooking. Still, what would Leon know about food? He's an academic,' Gina replied, changing the subject deftly, her American accent barely perceptible. 'Apparently you don't think much of our other house guest. Leon said you thought it was unlikely to be Goya's skull.'

'Well, it's a long shot,' Ben admitted. 'Turning up like that, out of blue, when people have been looking for it for decades.'

She tilted her head to one side. 'But it could be *proved* for certain one way or another?'

'There are tests which would authenticate it,' Ben agreed, 'or not.'

'Leon knows everyone in the art world, and he's so well thought of in Madrid that the authorities have let him have free rein. Anyway,' Gina went on lightly, 'I'm going to get lunch ready and leave you two to have a talk. But no longer than half an hour, OK?'

Watching her walk away, Ben felt a sudden sharp tug on his arm, Leon hustling him towards the staircase. He was nervous, edgy, his unease obvious in the erratic movements of his hands.

'Before I show you the skull, there are some other things

I thought you might want to see,' he explained, hurrying his brother up the stairs to the shady narrow landing which led to the servants' quarters.

Fiddling with his shirt collar, Leon walked on quickly, finally opening the door which led to Detita's apartment. As though still children, both men hesitated for an instant before walking in, Leon immediately moving over to the window, his back turned to the room.

'I was going to sort out her things, but I couldn't get round to it. Gina said she would, but I thought you might like to have a look first. You know – see if there's anything of Detita's you want to take. To remember her by.'

Slowly, Ben looked around the room. A heavy wrought iron chandelier suspended from the high ceiling, wooden shutters open to let in some air, a carved bed draped with white muslin and a quilt the colour of water reeds. Pulling open the wardrobe door, he found himself face to face with the print dresses and jackets he remembered so well, a row of shoes lined up like piano keys. And the scent of something, somebody, well known.

'She had papers too,' Leon said, and Ben turned and walked over to a side table where his brother had laid out several notebooks.

Apparently Detita had left behind *parts* of missives, *parts* of photographs, *parts* of cards. Nothing whole – just portions, incomplete and unreadable. And in among the meticulous chaos were images of Goya, his self-portraits and a fragment of the painting of the lunatic asylum. Beside those was a drawing of the Quinta del Sordo and one other: a disturbing image of a skeleton, half alive, half dead, writing the one word on black earth: *Nada*. Nothing.

'Look at this,' Leon said, picking up a hairbrush from Detita's dressing table. Her scent bottles were still sitting in the shade, lying beside a copy of *The Manuscript Found in Saragossa* and a *History of the Occult*.

'She had strange tastes.'

'Never tried to convert us, did she?'

Ben looked up. 'To what?'

'Catholicism.'

'She tried damn near everything else,' Ben replied. 'All those bloody stories she used to tell us! When I was little I was always waiting for those horses coming over the bridge to get me.'

To his relief, Leon laughed. 'Remember when you came back from school when you were fifteen and you went out at midnight and clicked your fingers over and over again just to prove that nothing would happen? Detita went crazy, said you would bring the Devil.' He shrugged. 'I admired you for that. I'd never have dared.'

'It was just a story.'

'Maybe ...' Leon said finally. 'So, what d'you want to take?'

Ben glanced round the room and shrugged. 'Nothing.'

Together they walked back downstairs into Leon's study. It was conspicuously tidy but overheated, the windows bolted shut, flies buzzing against the glass. Frowning, Leon opened the nearest window as Ben stared at a small cardboard box on the desk. Carefully he opened it. Inside was an old skull, lying among some shredded newspaper. It was discoloured, with several holes in the cranium.

'So . . .' Leon paused, trying to hide his excitement as his brother picked up the skull. 'What d'you think?'

'He's dead, I can tell you that,' Ben said, trying to lighten the atmosphere. 'Can I take it back to London with me? I'd like Francis Asturias to have a look at it.'

'I thought he was dead.'

'His wife lives in hope. No, Francis is still working. Still the best facial reconstructor there is.' Ben studied the skull, turning it in his hands. 'Are you sure you don't mind me taking it? I might need to keep it for a while.'

'No, it's OK,' Leon said, adding hurriedly, 'to be honest, I don't like it around . . . Don't tell Gina though. She doesn't have to know you've got it. Keep that between us, will you?'

Nodding, Ben put the skull back in the box as Leon moved over to the window. 'So, what d'you think of her?'

'She seems nice.'

'*Nice*,' Leon repeated dully.

'And very proud of you,' Ben added, trying to avoid a semantical skirmish. 'It doesn't matter what I think, Leon, if she makes you happy—'

A flutter of malice entered his brother's voice. 'How's Abigail?'

'She's fine.'

Leon had always found Abigail difficult. Not as a person, but as someone faulted. Her facial scars, although faint, seemed to evoke some peculiar resentment on his part.

Almost as though his mental instability should have been as obvious to an onlooker – and provoke as much sympathy.

'Is she still having treatment?'

'Not at the moment,' Ben replied. 'She agreed to leave it for a while—'

'She agreed? Or you talked her into it?'

Ben refused the bait. '*We* agreed.'

'Poor Abigail could hardly argue with you even if she did want more treatment, could she?'

'She doesn't want—'

'You being her lover *and* her doctor. You being Ben Golding.'

'I'm not her doctor any more.'

'Whatever . . .' Leon's jumpiness was gathering speed, his brother the nearest target. 'You were never influenced by anyone, were you? I was. First with our parents, then Detita, now Gina. And always you. But not this time.' Leon paused. Then suddenly, unexpectedly, he embraced his brother, releasing him just as quickly. His pique had taken a sidestep, balance coming back sweet and sure. 'Stop worrying about me. I know you do – you always have. But this is the start of something important. This is my big chance.'

'Just take it steady, hey? And if you need me, phone.' Ben tapped the box holding the skull. 'As for this, I'll keep you posted.'

'Goya's skull will make my name.'

'You've already made your name, Leon. You're a respected historian.'

'Respected, but not famous.'

Ben wondered fleetingly how his brother would cope with notoriety. How press attention and any prying would affect him. All his life Leon had longed for attention – but on his terms. Attention which could be corralled, fenced in. But fame wasn't like that. Renown flicked its victim like a bagatelle ball from one pitfall to another. It could test a strong man, a weak one it could destroy.

'For your sake I *want* it to be Goya's skull . . .'

'It is,' Leon insisted. 'It is. *I can feel it.*'

'. . . I want it to be genuine because you want it so much. Because you think it'll bring so much. But if it isn't—'

'It will be,' Leon insisted quietly. 'It *has* to be.'

6

London

As it had done for centuries, the Whitechapel Hospital crouched disconsolately among the warren of East End streets. Slivers of alleyways dating back centuries snaked between the modern concrete smack of office blocks. Overhead, the bridge joined the separate wings of the hospital and straddled the road like a birthing stool. The oldest part of the building had been standing when Jack the Ripper was active, the Whitechapel streets housing some of the poorest of London. In among slums, the overcrowded hovels had paid court to prostitution, thievery and gambling.

It was a part of London overhung with its own grim allure, where part-time enthusiasts held murder tours and overseas visitors thrilled to the knowledge that the skeleton of the Elephant Man was housed in the hospital across the road. Time and progress had smartened up some of the area, but a few hidden warrens and alleyways still lurked. The names of the places where Jack the Ripper killed his victims had been changed too. There was no Miller Court, no Buck's Row any more, but the stubborn, unremitting atmosphere of gloom remained. And over this thick knotting of streets and memory glowered the edifice of the Whitechapel Hospital.

Pounding towards his consulting room in the oldest part of the building, Professor Francis Asturias paused at a door marked EXIT, then hurried on to the fire escape outside. Lighting a cigar, he drew in the smoke hungrily, pushing the half-empty packet back into his pocket. Smoking was forbidden in every area of the hospital, but Francis always managed to find somewhere to take his intermittent nicotine breaks. Well into his seventies, he cut an eccentric figure, straight, greying hair reaching his shoulders, his eyes slyly amused. Beneath his white coat he wore faded corduroy trousers and suede loafers, bending up at the toes with age.

For ten years various Principals had tried to fire Francis Asturias, but he wasn't going anywhere. His father had donated a large amount of money to the Whitechapel Hospital and Francis took care to remind everyone of the next legacy which would follow – after his own death. So they let him stay on, long after anyone else would have been retired, working in the Forensic Department on archaeological remains or reconstructions of the victims of murder cases.

'You shouldn't smoke,' a voice said suddenly as the Fire Exit door opened and Ben walked out.

Francis shrugged. 'Fuck you. I thought you weren't back until tomorrow.'

'I came back early,' Ben replied, helping himself to one of his colleague's cigars and putting it into the top pocket of his white coat. 'I've brought something for you.'

'Not one of those straw donkeys with a sun hat?'

'I thought it would go nicely with your plastic bull-fighter.'

'You spoil me,' Francis replied, amused. 'So what it is?'

'Something special. Well, it could be. I want you to reconstruct a face for me.'

Stubbing out his cigar, Francis raised his eyebrows. 'One of your patients?'

'No. This is a very old skull – possibly of world importance.'

'They burnt Hitler.'

'They didn't burn Goya.'

Francis blew out his cheeks. 'Where's the rest of the body?'

'Still in his tomb. The head went missing a long time ago, apparently stolen by the French. Look, to be frank, it's unlikely to be genuine, but I want to check it out for my brother. He's an art historian and it would mean a lot to him.'

'Wouldn't hinder his career much either,' Francis remarked mischievously.

'Can you do it?'

'Sure, I can date it for you too. What about DNA?'

'No point. Goya has no living relatives. No points of comparison.'

'So you're relying on the dating and the reconstruction of the skull?'

Ben nodded. 'Your facial reconstruction's important because we can see if it matches the known images of Goya.'

'I could cheat, mug up on his self-portraits,' Francis suggested archly.

'You won't do that, because if the skull is genuine, just think how much it would do for your career when we release the news,' Ben replied. 'Keep you here for at least another fifty years, however many Principals come and go.'

'Anything else?'

'Keep it quiet.'

'Don't tell me your brother stole it?'

'No, but news travels fast. I don't want people to start asking questions, leaking it to the press. If it got out, everyone would be after the bloody thing—'

Francis looked over, his expression dubious. 'What the hell for?'

'It's a relic. An artistic object of worship—'

'It's a lump of bone.'

'It's a lump of *famous* bone,' Ben corrected him. 'Because it's Goya's skull it would be worth a fortune on the open market. Or the not-so-open market. There's a big trade in art relics.'

'In that case, someone should find Van Gogh's ear.'

'Actually, they said they *had* found it only a few years ago. Said it had come down the family from the prostitute Van Gogh gave it to originally.'

'And they didn't want to keep it?' Francis replied sarcastically. 'Mind you, Napoleon's penis has been going the rounds for decades. Probably getting more action now than it ever did.'

Smiling, Ben tapped Francis on the shoulder. 'Seriously, keep it quiet. The art world can be a dangerous place. Collectors will pay people to find the skull. By whatever means.'

Trying not to show her nerves, Megan Griffiths walked into the Reconstructive Department of the Whitechapel Hospital, situated above the hospital kitchens. The patients in this particular ward were children, the most serious cases sectioned off in isolation wards to allow their wounds to heal in sterile conditions. Not that these areas were only for children. It was to one of the side wards that Abigail Harrop had been taken when she first came to the Whitechapel Hospital. And it was the reputation of Ben Golding – not the surroundings – which had kept her there.

Megan paused, listening. Outside, rain – its rhythm as persistent as a tin drum – scuffed the high windows and dripped from Victorian gutters and lintels. In private clinics around London the rich and famous paid for their treatment, their buttocks filled or noses straightened in privacy. But in the National Health sector burns were treated side by side with deformities and car accident injuries.

Still thinking about Francis Asturias, Ben was preoccupied when he arrived on the ward and surprised to see

Megan Griffiths there. Moving into the nurses' station he paused in front of the electric fire to warm his hands and thought of the heatwave in Spain, hardly able to reconcile the damp London chill with the smouldering dryness of Madrid.

'How long has she been here?' Ben asked the sister, jerking his head towards the window which looked out over the ward.

'About half an hour. Dr Griffiths often comes to see the patients. One of your keener registrars.'

Curious, Ben glanced back through the partition glass, watching Megan examine a patient. The child's injured head was encased in a metal frame, from which steel rods protruded into her cranium. The metal screws on the helmet were turned twice a day to gradually pull the features into alignment. Brutal. Painful. Necessary.

An old memory came back, unbidden. Of his brother falling out of a tree. Falling flat, like a sandbag, without putting out his hands to break his fall. Leon, bellyflopping into the parched Spanish earth ... He had broken his left leg, his jaw and two of his ribs and knocked out four of his teeth. In a Madrid hospital Leon's jaw was wired back into line and his leg put in traction – and all the time he joked with Ben about why he had fallen.

The tree told me to do it ...

What their parents had euphemistically referred to as 'Leon's accident' had determined Ben's future career. Throughout their teens he had gone through every operation with his brother, sat with him, listened to him,

57

watched him. Known how much the surgery hurt as he observed the slight body pulled back into shape, the face restored, rebuilt. Over a period of years he saw Leon turned from a disfigured misfit back into a normal child. Physically, at least.

Two decades later Ben had notched up over twenty years' experience as a reconstructive surgeon, treating both adults and children. Twenty years of facial burns, of careless playing with candles, of car accidents, of hit-and-run drivers. Two decades of womb injuries, of nature's vicious tricks, of hiccups in the DNA. Twenty years, two hundred and forty months, one thousand and forty weeks spent in the company of victims. While his colleagues had made fortunes from facelifts and liposuction Ben Golding had stuck to his principles. He wasn't interested in making someone perfect; he was interested in making them fit in.

Walking over, Megan interrupted his thoughts. 'I was reading about one of your cases. Harry Collard—'

'I've got a meeting in ten minutes. I've got to get back to my office,' Ben replied, glancing at his watch. 'Let's talk as we walk.'

Together they made their way down the main arterial corridor of the hospital, leading to the consulting rooms.

'Harry Collard's had over twenty operations, hasn't he?' she asked, almost running to keep up with Ben. 'Isn't that a lot for a child?'

'Harry's twenty-one now.'

'But he was a child when you started,' she persisted.

'And surely the risks of all those anaesthetics is serious? Research shows that they can undermine a person's resilience, even do long-term harm.'

Pausing, Ben opened the door of his consulting room and showed her in. The room was crowded with research books, piles of X-rays creeping inexorably across the top of the filing cabinets. On the wall, over a black-painted iron fireplace, was a painting of a landscape long gone, the chimney behind leaking a faint odour of soot.

'We both know serial anaesthetics are bad for a child,' Ben said evenly. 'And much as I commend your interest, I think it's a front.'

'*What?*'

'Let's be honest, that wasn't what you wanted to talk about, was it?'

She flushed, surprised by his perception. 'I've got to make a decision about my speciality.'

'You could do well in reconstructive surgery.'

'I don't want to do what you do. I want to go where the money is,' Megan admitted bluntly. 'The National Health's declining. If it was a patient, they'd turn the respirator off.' She gestured to the high walls, brown wood below the dado, dark anaglypta wallpaper above, the lampshade over their heads a cheap inverted bowl design from the 1930s. 'I don't like being poor. I want to get on to the reconstructive gravy train.'

'But there are a lot of cosmetic surgeons,' Ben replied evenly. 'Why don't you do something more worthwhile?'

'Maybe I'm not the worthy type.' She held his gaze, but

didn't pull her punches. 'That little girl, the one we've just seen – I don't think she should be alive. I don't think she'll ever have a normal life.'

'So what are you saying? We shouldn't try?'

Tactlessly, Megan blundered on. 'Whatever you do, she'll still look terrible. People will make her life a misery. I sometimes wonder if you're doing all this to help her – or to experiment.'

She had gone too far and knew it.

'Well, do continue to stand in judgement over me,' Ben replied coolly, 'especially when you're taking a litre of fat from some eighteen-year-old's backside . . . I don't experiment. God does that. Life does that. I just try to repair what's been buggered up.' He sighed. 'Don't try to provoke me, Dr Griffiths. We're *all* mechanics. Every surgeon is a mechanic, every body is a machine. What we do is brilliant and pedestrian at the same time.' He paused, looking at her. 'One day a doctor went to a garage to get his car fixed—'

'You're telling me a joke?'

'The mechanic repaired the very intricate fault. Then he said to the surgeon: "You couldn't fix the engine, but I could. So how come you're paid so much more than me?"

'And the doctor replied: "Have you ever tried fixing it when the engine's still running?" '

Despite herself, Megan smiled.

'I could experiment with you, Dr Griffiths. See how far a few well-chosen words on your reference could go to wreck your career.'

'Just because I disagreed with you?' She was down, but not out. 'I don't care what you say, you *can't* make these children normal. Not some of the cases you take on. They'll always be freaks—'

'Yes, there *will* always be freaks,' he agreed. 'But as time goes on you come to realise that not all of them are in hospitals.'

8

Madrid

Having completed the equivalent of three miles on a running machine, Gabino Ortega stepped off and wrapped a towel around his neck. He found the sensation comforting, his tingling leg muscles a smug reminder of his triumphant challenge to middle age. After all, the men in his family were recognised as being the most handsome in Madrid – and he was never going to be a disappointment. Showering, Gabino admired his toned stomach and impressive penis, and thought that although he might be the shortest of the Ortega males, he was the best hung.

His family was an old one, tracing their ancestry back centuries; a family with wealth and business acumen, together with a certain reputation for ruthlessness. But for all their cultured learning and devotion to the arts, the Ortega family had never managed to shake off a veneer of clammy rumour which had come to a head with the infamous Adolfo Ortega. Physically massive, prodigiously gifted in the world of finance and investments, it had been Adolfo who had cemented the family fortune by marrying the listless Fidelia. Knowing at the time of her wedding that the marriage was a union of business, not love, Fidelia had still accepted the deal. In return she was rewarded with a negligent husband – and two stillborn sons.

Becoming anxious that the Ortega line might die out, Adolfo had then acted with his typical ruthless and divorced Fidelia. Within eighteen months his second wife had given him an heir, but the rejected Fidelia was not so easily dismissed. Unbalanced by her abandonment, and jealous of the newborn, she hounded her ex-husband and threatened his new wife. At first merely irritated, Adolfo finally threatened Fidelia – something she made known to her friends. But no one took her seriously, and besides, Fidelia had lost her power. Desperate, she took to self-harming – that mental abyss that sucks the vulnerable in. No longer part of the Ortega family, she had become little more than an embarrassing outcast.

But the final outcome shook Spanish society. After Fidelia had been missing for several days, her body was found in the backstreets of Madrid. Rumours circulated like blowflies. Had Adolfo killed her? Or had he organised her murder? He had the money and power; he could easily have arranged it and got away with it . . . which he did. The Spanish police couldn't – or didn't dare – investigate the killing too deeply and the official conclusion was that the unbalanced Fidelia had wandered off from her home, been robbed and killed. After all, she had been wearing expensive jewellery at the time, Adolfo told the police, and nothing had been found on her.

From then on, the Ortegas were treated with fear as well as respect. Respected for their money but feared for their power which had always been suspect. With the death of Fidelia, Adolfo lavished his wife and his new heir, Dino, with affection and money. As a result, the boy became spoilt, truculent and prone to angry outbursts, by the time he reached his teens he was a drug addict, hell-bent on destroying the family name and fortune. An early marriage produced no change in Dino's character, but did provide two sons. By now old but no less ruthless, Adolfo disinherited his dissolute son and changed his will, so that the whole Ortega inheritance would eventually pass on to the elder grandson, Bartolomé.

The suicide of the rejected Dino proved it to be the wisest decision Adolfo had ever made.

Having dried himself off, Gabino dressed, finally combing his hair and thinking of his brother. It was tedious, but he would have to visit Bartolomé at his home in Switzerland that weekend to smooth over an unsettling matter with a banker who had reported Gabino to the police for assault. For once the Ortega money hadn't been enough, and the man had refused to be placated, instead reporting the whole sleazy episode to the press. Although he could hardly have remained ignorant, Bartolomé hadn't said anything to his brother. None of the usual frigid arguments, no admonishing telephone calls. No remonstrations. Just silence – which was why Gabino was worried.

He had no intention of letting his brother get the upper hand and was keen to protect his lifestyle. Bartolomé might have chosen the life of an ascetic, but Gabino liked the social life of Madrid. It amused him to see the frisson of recognition when he was introduced to a woman, that sliver of interest always tempered by the Ortega reputation; the whispering of business hard-dealing and the ever shimmering ghost of Fidelia, making her presence felt more in death than she ever did in life. Gabino frowned. But had he gone too far this time? Pushed his brother's patience too much? It was hard to read Bartolomé, harder still to see the workings of his mind behind the flawless face.

Although handsome, Gabino had none of his brother's elegance: instead he was lustful, greedy and daring. Bartolomé had managed to escape the worst of the calumny, but Gabino had actively courted controversy. So far his charm had prevented a freefall, the actions of his grandfather an ever-present reminder that he could be ousted like his father had been. So for years Gabino had danced on the edges. Always an inch away from disgrace, he had somehow managed to keep his seat at the Ortega table. Many suspected his actions, but only a few dared to call Gabino an outright thief.

But someone *had* called him a thug. And the papers were busy drubbing the Ortega name again, a fact that would be more than a little unwelcome to his brother's ears ... Aware that he had made himself vulnerable, Gabino thought of what he had heard that morning and smiled to himself. Luck had played him a trump card in the shape of a rumour which was circulating in Madrid. A rumour that – he was hoping – had not yet reached Switzerland. Apparently the skull of Francisco Goya had been found. The skull of the greatest Spanish painter who had ever lived. The skull Bartolomé would covet above anything ... But even with all his contacts and money, Bartolomé wasn't in Madrid. Wasn't on the spot, ready to grab the opportunity. In fact, Gabino mused, there was a risk that someone else might get the skull before Bartolomé had a chance to.

Unless someone got it for him.

Relishing his newly birthed plan, Gabino decided that *he* would get the skull. He would win over Bartolomé with a present which would outdo all other gifts. The skull of Goya. The relic with which Gabino would win back his brother's affection – and ensure his future at the same time.

9

The Prado, Madrid

Sweating in his suit, Jimmy Shaw felt his tongue dry in his mouth. Saliva wouldn't come, his lips cracking at the corners, a little blood running on to his chin. He looked – without needing the confirmation of a mirror – repugnant. The kind of man *no one* would want to talk to, or be seen with, let alone some respectable art historian like Leon Golding. Leaning back against the stone wall, Shaw glanced at his hand, sniffing it and wincing at the unmistakable stench of decay. Perhaps he should ring Golding instead, make his case over the phone . . .

A sudden movement made Shaw glance across the court-yard – Leon Golding was walking through the entrance gates towards the Prado side door. Erect but ill at ease, his long shadow seemed more substantial than himself. Dressed with no little elegance, Golding should have been an imposing figure, but his movements were cautious, almost like a man who had had a drink and was fighting its first effects.

Curious, Shaw watched him, then noticed another figure move across the courtyard. But there was no hesitation in this man's stride: he seemed confident, almost arrogant, and so handsome Shaw felt an immediate and intense dislike. Surprised, he heard him call out Leon Golding's name, the historian turning and automatically shielding his eyes from the sun as he watched his approach.

Straining, Jimmy Shaw could just make out what he said.

'Mr Golding, I'd like a word, if I may.'

The man spoke in English, but with a pronounced Spanish accent. Leon smiled the faint smile of the polite.

'Can I help you?'

'You don't remember me?'

Leon's recall was swift. 'Mr Ortega . . . How are you? I haven't seen you since the auction.'

Easily, they shook hands, Shaw watching and sifting through his memory. It didn't take him long to place the Ortega name. Or the reputation. He had lost out on several occasions to their money and their tactics. Fuck it, Shaw thought, don't let this be what I think it is. Just let them be talking, just talking . . . Please . . .

Gabino was intent, leaning towards Leon. 'It was a good auction.'

'You did well. Bought that . . .'

'Murillo.'

Leon nodded. 'Yes, Murillo. It was a fine picture. Good

price.' His voice changed gear. Even from where he was standing Shaw could see that Leon was keen to move off.

But Gabino had other ideas.

'I was wondering,' he went on, tucking his hands into his pockets. 'Have you heard the rumour about the Goya skull being found?'

Shaw swore under his breath, then wearily turned his gaze on to Leon Golding. He had expected a response, a giveaway movement from him, but Golding wasn't as naive as he appeared and the lie was glossy, almost rehearsed.

'Goya's skull?' He laughed, but the sound wasn't as convincing as the voice. 'They find one every few years.'

'I heard *you* had it.'

'Me?' Leon said, but his tone was losing substance as Gabino leaned towards him, encroaching on his personal space, pushing himself in.

'Yes, you. Someone was talking about it yesterday. I thought it was rubbish, but then I heard about it again, and I heard that *you* had it.' He smiled, veneers sunny, shiny. 'Have you?'

Shaw was holding his breath. He knew Leon had the skull, but he wondered how the hell Ortega had found out so soon. He also wondered how Leon Golding was going to answer.

'I *had* a skull . . .'

Neither man had anticipated the words as Leon continued.

'. . . but it was a fake.' He shrugged, almost dropping his papers as his shoulders rose and fell. 'I was hoping –

praying – it was Goya. You know my interest – as great as your brother's. It would have been a coup for me. But it wasn't genuine. I feel rather foolish about it, actually,' Leon went on. 'I'd be obliged if you'd keep this quiet—'

'How d'you know?'

'What?'

Shaw could sense Gabino's rage and disappointment. It came off him like a hiss, a noise so faint it was barely discernible. His hands left his pockets, clasped in front of his body instead. But what should have been a praying motion came off as curiously threatening.

'I asked how you knew the skull was a fake.'

'I . . . I . . . had it examined.'

'By who?'

'Mr Ortega,' Leon started, his nerves beginning to show, 'what's all this about?'

'The skull, Mr Golding,' Gabino said coldly. 'It's about the skull. Who examined it?'

'A colleague,' Leon replied, 'A man I trust implicitly—'

'He could be wrong. Where's the skull now?'

'Buried,' Leon said shortly.

'Where?'

Disconcerted, Leon blundered on. 'I gave it to the church to deal with—'

'*The church.*'

'Of course. So they could lay it to rest in consecrated ground . . .' Leon glanced around, as though anxious no one should hear what he was about to say. 'To be honest, I feel rather awkward about the whole matter. I was very nearly taken in, fooled. I should have known better after being in the business for so long. Should be used to disappointments. The art world's full of forgeries. But you keep hoping . . . I'm afraid I have to be getting on now. I have an appointment.' Leon ran his tongue over his bottom lip, his smile wavering. 'It was good to see you again.'

Hurriedly, he turned and walked off, his gait stiff because this time he *knew* he was being watched.

10

Shaking two headache pills into the palm of his left hand, Leon took a gulp of water and swallowed them. How the hell had Gabino Ortega heard about the skull? Ortega of all people. If he'd heard about it, Bartolomé would want the skull, and Gabino would want to please his brother. He was always trying to ingratiate himself, or get more money off him. And Gabino would do anything to placate his brother after that public brawl with the banker ... Jesus! Leon thought, panicked. He would go to any lengths to get hold of the skull. He was disreputable – everyone knew that. Besides, how easy would it be for Gabino Ortega to *steal* it?

But the skull was in London, Leon told himself. It was safe. Ben had it. Besides, Gabino looked like he had swallowed the story about it being a fake. He'd seemed shaken ... Leon sighed raggedly. Who was he kidding? By now Gabino would have recovered his cunning. He'd be trying to find out more, like who had examined the skull or which church had been supposedly approached for burial ... Leon found himself trembling, hardly able to hold the glass of water in his hand.

It was *his* find! *He* had been given the skull. It was his discovery, his stab at greatness. The Ortegas had no right to it. They had so much, why should they steal *his* triumph? Bartolomé Ortega had spent fortunes on trying to solve the riddle of the Black Paintings and failed – he wasn't the man who was supposed to succeed. It was Leon's triumph and his alone.

His anger was childish and desperate, the glass dropping from his hand and shattering on the floor just as Gina walked in.

'Are you OK?'

'Fine, fine . . .'

Puzzled, she glanced at the broken glass. Over his shoulder she could see the reproductions of Goya's Black Paintings. 'What are you doing?'

'I'm working on the book. You've been encouraging me for weeks.'

She slid into his lap, red hair falling over her cheek. 'I hardly see you any more, darling. And I could help, Leon – honestly I could.'

'I can manage,' he said, dismissing the idea out of hand. He didn't want anyone interfering in his work, not even Gina.

Although she had encouraged him, researched books for him, even obtained reproductions of some of Goya's more obscure works, as the days passed Leon had found himself becoming more absorbed with the painter and less with her. Reluctant to share his ideas, he cut Gina out. He realised he was embroiled, sliding in and out of the Black Paintings, reading them as if they were written works and then testing himself against the stack of research. But he wouldn't – *couldn't* – share his passion with her. Instead he consoled himself with the thought that he would present Gina with the solution, not the mechanics. That he would impress her with his insight, knowing all along that he was being selfishly, childishly, possessive. After all, Gina wasn't a competitor. She was his lover.

But still he cut her out. All his energy and passion went into Goya ... He had become convinced that he alone could solve the meaning of the paintings. Hadn't he spent most of his childhood living within sight of where the Quinta del Sordo had once stood? Hadn't Detita filled his mind with Goya's life and works? Hadn't the painter's shadow fallen over Leon's existence like Goya's own picture of *The Colossus*? It was fate – even Diego Martinez finding and passing the skull on to him. What chance was there of that happening, if it hadn't been meant?

For decades Leon had been rocked in a cradle of mental instability. He had felt like a man forever destined to float on a rolling tide, unable to stand, prone to every movement and tipping of the elements. But no longer. Suddenly he was in charge of something which could change the world and make him – and his memory – indelible.

'Come to bed,' Gina said softly.

'It's too early.'

'You're not getting enough sleep—'

'Stop nagging,' Leon retorted, pulling his notes towards

him. 'I have to work this out before someone else does.'

'The Black Paintings have been around for centuries, Leon. No one's going to pip you to the post now.' She stroked his narrow forehead tenderly. 'Haven't you got any results on the skull yet?'

He tensed. 'Nothing yet.'

'Who's doing the research?'

'Some Spanish doctor at the University,' he replied, wondering how the lie had come so easily to him – and why he hadn't told Gina that his brother had taken the skull back to London.

'So, *was* Goya involved in witchcraft?' she asked, nuzzling Leon's neck.

'Maybe. He was involved up to a point.'

'You think that's what the Black Paintings are all about?'

'Maybe.'

'Why are you being so distant with me?' she asked, her tone injured. 'You used to love talking about your ideas.'

His enthusiasm momentarily overshadowed his reserve.

'Look, Gina, keep this quiet but I think I might be close to solving what the Black Paintings actually mean. I think Goya was leaving a message behind, but he had to keep the meaning secret because otherwise it would have been dangerous for him.'

'My God,' she said breathlessly. 'When will you know if you're right?'

'I don't know. I have to keep on with it. I think there's an order to them. Goya didn't give the titles to the paintings – those were picked later by Yriarte, Imbert or Brugada.

So, if you take away the titles, you see the pictures from a totally different angle.' He looked away, uncertain. 'But I'm not sure. Not yet.'

A shiver passed between them, a frisson of unease, before Gina spoke again.

'Why don't we have a seance?'

'*What?*'

She smiled, shrugging. 'Why not? I know someone who's a medium.' Leon flinched. 'It's OK, nothing bad will happen. I've known Frederick for years. He's not weird, he's just gifted. I believe in these kinds of things. Anyway, what harm could it do? He might even help you with your work.'

Baffled, Leon stared at her. 'Help me?'

'Frederick knows a lot of different kinds of people. He's got a lot of contacts . . . Some are interested in satanism now. Right now.'

Transfixed, Leon listened. He was suddenly back to being a young boy, held captivated by one of Detita's stories. Outside he could hear a summer wind blow up, and wondered for an instant if it was blowing across the old site of the Quinta del Sordo. Maybe something *was* still there, he thought, manic with excitement. Maybe something that could be conjured up. His breathing rate increased, his skin clammy. It was almost within his reach – the respect he had craved for so long. He would be world famous; he would translate Goya's dying works, tell posterity what the Black Paintings really meant.

'Darling,' Gina whispered softly, 'if you got the skull back we could use that in a ritual. Call Goya up.'

Leon smiled, as though it was absurd. But part of him believed it. *Longed* to believe it. '*Call him up?* Christ, Gina, you're joking.'

'What if I wasn't?' she replied. 'If we could contact him, Goya might help you. Guide your work.' She stroked the back of his head tenderly. 'For centuries people have tried to contact the dead. Many believe they've succeeded. I've been to seances and visited mediums. When my father died I spent a lot of time trying to contact him.'

Leon's eyes were fixed on her. 'Did you succeed?'

She nodded again, smiling. 'Yes.'

A soft hot wind blew in from the window, sighing around them.

'How did you know it was your father?'

'The medium told me things only he would have known. I was in contact with my dead father.'

Unnerved, Leon shuddered. 'I don't think—'

'You have to get the skull back,' Gina went on hurriedly. 'This means so much to you, Leon. You have a chance to make your mark now. A chance to solve a problem no one has ever come close to. You would be the most famous art historian in the world. Think about it – why did the skull come to you? Maybe you *have* to use it to contact the painter. If anyone else hears about it, they'll want the skull—'

He thought of Gabino Ortega and panicked. 'I know, I know!'

'They'll try and steal it from you. They'll put it in a museum or some collection out of sight. They might even try to use it in a ritual—'

77

He turned to her. *'What are you talking about?'*

'Goya was interested in the occult. Present-day believers would long to get hold of his skull, just to see if they could prove a connection.'

'Detita said something like that once . . .' His mind shifted backwards, the old woman's voice echoing in his ears. *'In Black Magic people use skulls to resurrect the dead, to bring the Devil from underground. Goya's head was stolen . . .'* Leon turned back to Gina, his voice hushed. 'Detita said that witches made Goya ill, that they made him deaf. They stole his hearing.'

'D'you think it's true?'

'I don't know . . . Goya was dangerously ill. He nearly died in the Quinta del Sordo. No one knows what the sickness was.' Leon felt queasy, as if he had already gone too far and should back off now, while there was still time. But he knew he wasn't going to. 'Some said Goya lost his mind in that house.'

'You think he was mad?'

'No, I think he was desperate. He wanted to leave a testimony behind. But no one can prove it—'

'You might be able to. You know about psychometry? That a medium only has to hold an object that the person owned to contact them? Well, think about it, Leon – *if they had Goya's skull how powerful would that be?'* She stroked his forehead, urging him gently. 'Please, darling, don't let it fall into the wrong hands.'

He was confused, his thoughts jumbling. 'I don't know about all of this—'

'But I know something about the occult,' Gina went on, soothing him. 'Enough to fear it. Enough to know that I have to protect you. I love you, Leon – let me help you. We *have* to make sure that you keep the skull. That you keep it safe. It's common knowledge that Aleister Crowley wanted to find Goya's skull years ago. And Crowley was known as the wickedest man in England. You don't want someone like Crowley to get hold of the skull, do you?'

She was swaying his judgement, and before he knew it Leon was hypnotised by her, her body pressed against his, her voice low, enticing. Suddenly he *wanted* Gina to be involved. Wanted to be close to her, safe with her.

'Get the skull back, Leon.'

'But—'

Leon was just about to admit that the skull was in London when the phone rang beside them. In that instant the spell was shattered and Gina climbed off his knee and walked away into the shadowy back of the house.

When he picked up the phone, the line was dead.

11

Gstaad, Switzerland

Bartolomé Ortega studied his secretary calmly, then glanced away. He resisted an impulse to bite down on his lip, to draw blood, to release a tumour of rage which was threatening to seep out of his skin as sweat, or out of his lungs as one long protracted scream. His extraordinary face, fine-boned and impassive, betrayed nothing of his anger, his hands clasped on the top of his desk, the glass reflecting the top half of his body. Like an elegant island he sat in the vast, minimal surroundings of his office, two windows on his left opened to let in some breeze, the smell of hibiscus innocently irritating.

Having been ill for the previous week Bartolomé had had little time for business. In fact he had enjoyed his sabbatical and the indulgent attention of his wife, Celina. It had even made him contemplate taking more time off in the future, just to be with her and their son, Juan.

Bartolomé knew that his grandfather would never have

been as patient as he had been. Adolfo would have disposed of any barren consort within a few years. But Bartolomé loved his wife, and even though she failed to bear a child for many years, he never considered divorcing her. Instead he had made discreet enquiries through his lawyer about adoption. Previously Celina had always rejected the idea out of hand, but as she approached forty and the likelihood of becoming a mother had grown slight, she had finally become receptive to it.

Three months later she became pregnant. Just as their doctor had predicted – *take off the pressure and often the couple will conceive.* So it had been with them. Once they had turned their attention to adopting a child, Celina had fallen pregnant. And six months later, Juan, the most recent scion of the family, had been born. Darkly handsome, an Ortega in his pram.

Hands still clasped together, Bartolomé swallowed with effort. Perhaps a reminder of his flu? Or simple rage at what he had just been told? He swallowed again, feeling the same tightening of his throat muscles as he stared at the vast expanse of floor in front of him. He liked the emptiness of his office, the cool, chilling grandeur of possessing a room so large that its brilliant architecture and size required little adornment. With the formidable Ortega collection at his disposal, Bartolomé could have covered the walls with images, but he left them blank. When he worked he liked no distractions, nothing to clutter his mind.

His mind wasn't cluttered at that moment; it was processing the information he had received. Goya's skull had been found. It was in the possession of Leon Golding, the one art historian Bartolomé feared. The one man he believed might solve the riddle of the Black Paintings before he could. But that wasn't all – Bartolomé unclenched his hands, flexed his fingers, stared at the mute walls – *his brother had known*. The sly Gabino had known about the skull. Apparently he had even approached Golding about it, *and never said a word to his brother*. Never told Bartolomé the news about the greatest passion of his life. Never passed on information which would have been priceless.

Reserved and unemotional, Bartolomé struggled to maintain his calm. As a man of stunning beauty and exquisite taste, in his hands the Ortega collection had secured some magnificent works, including a Velasquez and several paintings by Guido Reni. But Bartolomé's real passion was for Goya. The Ortegas already owned two small works, but he was always ready to acquire more. Judicious in his financial affairs and kindly in his affections, Bartolomé was, however, obsessed by the Spanish painter. In fact it was the only area of his life which had the ability to unsettle him.

Relentlessly he hunted the internet, his personal sources and auctions around the globe for more works. Over the years he had also spent prodigious amounts of money trying to solve the riddle of the Black Paintings. A queue of experts had come and gone, offering up explanations, none of which were definitive and many derivative. Bartolomé had lost count of the times he had been given Goya's insanity, illness or fear of death as an explanation.

Even hints of a sadomasochistic relationship with his mistress, Leocardia.

None of the theories rang true, and Bartolomé, with unlimited funds, became personally infatuated with the solving of the Black Paintings. At first he had been willing to hire people and ask celebrated art historians for their opinions, but as his interest festered into obsession, Bartolomé realised that he *had* to win. It was only right that a Spaniard should discover the truth, only correct that the wealthy and powerful Ortega family should make this cultural triumph. And, in the process, finally overshadow the thuggish reputation of their past.

So why had his brother deliberately kept the news of Goya's skull quiet?

Because Gabino had no interest in Goya, in paintings, in heritage. His life was spent fucking and hustling, as he grubbed his way around Spanish society. As boorish and ruthless as their grandfather . . . Pushing back his chair, Bartolomé stood up. He moved like a dancer, light-footed, erect, a man who could feel the earth under his feet and was sure of his place on it. A man who had carried the Ortega name with pride, holding it aloft, demanding respect – not like Gabino, swaggering like a stevedore with his heritage tucked carelessly under one arm.

Surprised, Bartolomé could feel himself shaking and turned as the door opened and Celina walked in.

'Darling,' she said, moving over to him and kissing him lightly. She smelt of earth and Bartolomé glanced down at her hands.

'You've been gardening.'

She nodded, her youthful face tipped up to look at him, her eyes green and intelligent, her hair a shade lighter from the sun.

'You should come out – it's cooler now. It will do you good.' She reached up and touched his forehead. 'Are you feeling all right?'

'Fine.'

She wasn't convinced. Knew him too well. 'Bad news?'

'No,' he lied. 'I'm just tired.'

The lie was difficult for him, because he trusted his wife and normally confided in her. Unlike other Ortega consorts, past and present, Celina was not excluded, partitioned off in some harem, her purpose erotic or maternal. She was her husband's equal. Her family was French and liberal. Certainly not wealthy, but Celina had attracted Bartolomé for exactly those reasons. He wanted no organised Spanish match, no mating of business interests. He wanted love and sanctuary. In Celina he found it. And something more – a prodigious intelligence.

Their chosen exile in Switzerland suited them both, as neither was particularly social and both treasured their privacy. For all his appeal, Bartolomé was not a sensuous man and his sexual appetite was meagre. He watched his brother's seductions with puzzlement, having never felt such lustiness himself. In truth Bartolomé had welcomed his early marriage and removal from the Spanish social scene and had been fortunate in choosing a wife whose erotic appetites were also minimal. Theirs was a marriage of understanding and mutual trust.

But despite that Bartolomé wasn't going to tell his wife about Gabino. Too humiliated to confide, he reassured himself. At any moment his brother would tell him about the Goya skull. Gabino would phone or visit. He *would*.

He had to.

Le Quinta del Sordo, Madrid, Spain, 1820

Dr Arrieta was aware of flies buzzing around the bed, and flicked his hand in their direction. They scattered, settling on the nets over the window, then slowly began to creep across the ceiling, eyeing the two men below. Over the previous summer months yellow fever had crawled like a cripple over Madrid, eventually reaching the bridge over the Manzanares. But the water did not stop it. Instead the fever skimmed on the surface and hopped with the gadflies in the miasma of heat and emerald slime. Fish which had populated the river had now gone, finding the further reaches where the disease hadn't polluted the flow. And around the Quinta del Sordo the dry earth gave up its ailing weeds to the city's sickness.

Sweating, Dr Arrieta leaned over the bed and stared into the invalid's waxy face. He was, he thought helplessly, already expecting to see a corpse. Surely Francisco Goya couldn't survive another critical illness at his age? Arrieta had not been in attendance before, but had been told of his patient's long illness in

1792. Some said it had been due to a fever, but although that was a possibility, Arrieta had his doubts. He wondered instead if Goya had a serious inflammation of the brain, his blood pressure rising high enough to cause a profound stroke. A stroke which might well have resulted in deafness, depression and even hallucinations.

But even after he recovered Goya had been – and remained – profoundly deaf. And after his first illness his whole life had changed, his court existence closed off, communication hobbled, music silenced. For a man with a great libido and prodigious energy, Goya had been cruelly cowed. In silence, he had gone back to painting; had grown older, more impatient, his deafness alienating him, driving him onwards.

And inwards.

Arrieta stared at his patient. He had a queasy feeling of dread that he might be watching a great man going slowly and irrevocably mad. The steaming, red heat of the Spanish summer clotted with the guttural, unintelligible sounds the painter made in his delirium and hung, clammily, about the plastered walls. Night shadows thick with the smell of drying paint and the stagnant water outside curdled around the high altar of the restless bed. At times Goya would reach out, grasping the air. But his eyes were never open, as though what he saw was not real, not of the world, but something inescapable, inside the ruin of his teeming brain.

Who would have believed that Spain's finest painter would die as a recluse in a farmhouse apart – and yet within sight of Madrid? That this mumbling semi-corpse was Goya, sweating in grimy sheets with the flies buzzing around the white spittle at the corners of his mouth? Goya, the man who had been the envy of Madrid, dying by a seeping river under a candle-coloured moon.

Unnerved, Arrieta glanced away. From the stable outside came the sound of a horse birthing a foal, its animal cries as wild and blinded as the crowding night.

12

Madrid

The following evening, a bushy-haired man with a freckled complexion and weak, pale blue eyes walked into the Golding house, Leon hanging back in the doorway of his study as Gina greeted Frederick Lincoln with a kiss to the cheek and ushered him into the small morning room. He moved slowly, wiping his forehead with his handkerchief, sweating in the Madrid heat although all the windows were open. His hands were long and very pale, freckles marking the skin like a sprinkling of dun-coloured paint.

'Leon,' Gina called out, turning as her lover walked in. 'Leon, this is Frederick Lincoln. He's agreed to hold a seance for us. We're very lucky – he doesn't visit many people any more. Do you, Frederick?'

He shrugged, but seemed fascinated by Leon as he walked into the room.

'Gina is an old friend of mine. My mother was Dutch and I was brought up in Amsterdam where we met.'

Nodding, Leon sat down at the small circular table and began to fitfully pick at the cloth which was covering it.

'Are you a believer in spiritualism?' Frederick asked, sitting down. 'Do you believe in life after death?'

Leon raised his eyebrows. 'How can I? I haven't died yet.'

'Not that you remember.'

'I don't think this is going to work,' Leon said suddenly. Gina gave him a pleading look and took his hand.

'I know all this seems strange to you, darling, but it might help your work. And nothing you tell Frederick will ever be repeated.' She turned to their guest. 'That's right, isn't it?'

'My business runs on trust,' the visitor replied. 'I don't break confidences. You have to believe in me, Leon. Trust that I can help you—'

'I don't need help!'

'Leon,' Gina said, intervening, 'you want Frederick to see if he can get in touch with Goya, don't you?'

He laughed. 'If he thinks he can.'

Unperturbed, Frederick studied him. 'Have you got the skull?'

'*What skull?*'

Gina took in a deep breath. 'No, he couldn't get it back in time—'

Enraged, Leon turned to her. '*I told you not to tell anyone!*'

'Frederick isn't "anyone"!'

Leon was close to panic. Jesus! Didn't Gina understand that she couldn't talk to anyone about the skull? What if

Gabino Ortega heard about it? And knew that he'd been lied to?

'You shouldn't have told anyone!'

'You can trust Frederick implicitly,' Gina reassured him. 'He only wants to help you.'

'Trying to make contact would be easier with the skull, but we'll go ahead anyway and see what we can get,' Frederick said evenly, glancing around the room. 'Perhaps we should try another seance when you get the skull back. I can't promise anything tonight.'

Leon's breathing was speeding up. If he'd been there, Ben would have been furious. *Keep quiet about the skull*, he had warned his brother. *Don't do anything until we have it authenticated* ... Yet now this bizarre man was in on the secret. And here he was, lying through his teeth, telling his girlfriend that he couldn't get hold of the skull, while all the time it was in his brother's possession in London.

Closing the door of the breakfast room, Gina smiled and regained her seat. The window was open to let in the cooling night air, a late bird making its last-ditch effort at a song. The main light had been turned off and only one small lamp was burning against the far wall so that the three figures sat in the semi-darkness. Uneasy, Leon thought of Detita and the stories she used to tell him, always in the half-light, when the furniture became islands of black rock and the shutters flapped like broken wings in the acid dark.

'We have to try and contact the other side ...'

Leon could hear Frederick's voice and found himself

shifting restlessly in his seat. Slowly the medium reached out and touched the tip of Leon's little finger with his own. On the other side Gina repeated the action, the three of them making a circle. Through his skin Leon felt the warmth of both of them, and a sensation of dread as Frederick continued to talk.

'We need to contact the spirit of this house, or any place nearby. We are trying to contact the painter Francisco Goya . . .'

Chewing his bottom lip, Leon stared at Frederick. Then suddenly, behind the medium, *a man stood motionless*, his face shadowed. Nervously, Leon giggled, Gina following his gaze but seeing nothing. Transfixed, Leon watched the vision move behind the medium's chair, then bend down and blow into Frederick's ear. But to Leon's astonishment, the Dutchman didn't seem to notice anything. Still staring at the apparition, Leon watched as the ghost hovered in the warm air, gliding about the stuffy semi-darkness of the room. Then, just as suddenly, it disappeared.

Confused, he giggled again, Gina and Frederick exchanging glances.

'This is no laughing matter, Mr Golding,' Frederick warned him. 'The word's out. You should be very careful who you trust.'

Leon's mind was swimming, just as it had done when he was a child. He was back, climbing the tree outside. High up, standing on the branch, another breath of wind telling him to let go, to fall flat into the terracotta earth. A daytime shadow chasing him in amongst the leaves.

'Leon, relax – stop fighting this,' Frederick went on, his tone kindly. 'There's nothing to fear. The spirits won't harm us . . .'

Oh, but they will, Leon thought.

'Is there anyone present?'

There was a sudden noise outside the door. Frederick carried on talking.

'Welcome, spirit. Come closer . . .'

No, *don't* come closer, Leon pleaded silently. Don't come out of my head or out of my madness. Don't come.

'We mean you no harm . . .'

But *I* mean you harm, Leon thought. I mean you to burn in hell. *I* mean you harm.

'I have a message for you,' Frederick said quietly to Leon. 'There is a woman here – an elderly woman. She was very close to you, to this house. She was born in this country. She comes to greet you. She used to look after you when you were young . . . She says she was right. She was right . . .'

Leon stared at him – was he talking about *Detita*?

'She knew you better than anyone. Even better than your brother. She says that you have to listen to her . . .'

'*I don't believe it!*' Leon snapped.

'She says I have to tell you that people passed by this house at night. Evil people. They meant harm. This is a long time ago. A long time ago . . .' Frederick's voice picked up speed, echoing in the confined space. 'They wanted to punish someone who lived nearby . . . She says she was right about the demons, only they were real.

93

Real people. They wanted to punish him . . . they stole his hearing . . .'

Unnerved, Leon took in a breath.

'She says you're searching for the answer. That you have to keep looking, searching. She is talking about the head . . .'

Irritated, Leon tried to pull away, but Frederick caught at his hand.

'Listen! She wants you to listen . . .'

'I don't believe in this! You're a fake. A bloody fake!' Leon snapped, trying to break the Dutchman's grip.

'She wants you to bring the skull back . . .'

'This is ridiculous! Bloody ridiculous!'

'She knows what happened up in that tree . . .'

At once Leon stopped, rigid in his seat.

'All those years ago, when you were only a boy . . . She says you heard a voice. Up in the tree, coming from in among the leaves. The voice told you to let go . . . She said "the tree made you do it" . . . She knows you better than you know yourself . . .'

'No . . .'

'She says she watches you . . .'

'Christ, no . . .'

'She watches you here, when you work. In your study . . . She watches you . . .'

'Let me go!' Leon hissed, finally pulling away and running to turn on the lights. His face was waxy as he challenged Frederick. 'It's a trick! You knew about Detita! Gina must have told you!'

'I didn't tell him anything,' Gina insisted, giving the Dutchman an unfathomable look. 'I didn't, did I?'

'No.'

Confused, Leon blustered. *'You're lying! You knew! You must have done!'*

He was reeling like a drunkard. Desperately he scratched around for a logical answer. It was a parlour trick, that was all. He tried to see it from his brother's point of view. Ben would have laughed – said it was a joke, a cheap con. Nothing else ... But Leon *had* seen something moving behind Frederick's chair.

Had he seen it?

What had he seen?

Madness?

His own?

Pushing Gina aside, Leon blundered out of the room and made for the garden. There he stood, panting dryly, in the night air. He could pretend that it had all been a sham, but he knew otherwise. Much as he loved Gina, he had never confided in her about his childhood accident. About his fall. About how the tree had told him to do it. So how had she known? Had he talked in his sleep? Jesus, *had he*?

And if he hadn't given himself away to Gina, the alternative was chilling. Because *someone* had *known*. It had either been Detita in that room or some other spirit, but they had known the secret Leon had hidden all his life. His first flirting with instability. His first plunge into the mind's labyrinth.

The tree told me to do it ...

13

Hand in hand with dusk, the restaurant lamps came on, lighting the water of the canal below. It was a mild, humid evening and people had taken the tables on the terrace, the soft lapping sound of the water and the muted breeze making a little city ripple of cool. In the distance, Paddington station huffed and shuffled its trains in the dusty night and the evening traffic slid under a shimmer of street lamps.

And in Little Venice – a knot of white stuccoed town houses bordering the canal in West London – the local high-grade supermarket closed for the night, the lights went out in the window of the French patisserie, and a middle-aged couple entered a nearby restaurant. Shown to their seats a moment later, the woman took off her jacket in the unseasonable warmth, the man beckoning to the wine waiter. On the table next to them, a younger couple were sitting in silence. The woman had taken a lot of care with her clothes, her dark hair glossy, make-up subtle. Beyond them, sitting alone, was a pale blond man reading the late copy of the *Evening Standard*.

Listlessly, the brunette scrutinised the menu, the waiter hovered, the blond man ordered paella and the middle-aged woman looked up to the night sky.

'Did you feel that?' she asked, surprised. 'Rain.'

Her husband scoffed. 'It can't be—'

His words were drowned out by a clap of thunder, violent electric lightning impaling the sky, its jagged white light reflected in the water below. At once the diners fled into the shelter of the restaurant. On the canopy outside the rain pelted down, splashing upwards as it landed, the thunder snapping overhead.

'Bloody weather,' the brunette's companion said, brushing the rain off his suit. 'You want a drink?'

She nodded. Beside her, the middle-aged couple squabbled and the blond man stood under the canopy by the door to watch the storm. The rain drummed incessantly on the metal tables outside, food washed off plates, some spilling on to the floor, the wine diluted, glasses overflowing as the waiters hurried to clear the tables. And then, just as suddenly as it had begun, the storm ended.

Apologising, the waiter showed his customers to other tables inside, only the blond man resisting.

'Just dry off my table and chair. It won't rain again tonight.'

Surprised, the waiter did as he was told.

Below, steam rose from the canal and spring trees shed

pendulous water droplets. Dividing his paper into two parts, the blond man sat on one half of the *Evening Standard* and then calmly began to read the remaining pages.

'Moron,' the middle-aged man snorted, moving to the bar.

His wife followed as the younger couple took a table by the window. Curious, the brunette watched the solitary diner on the balcony, his figure illuminated by the outside light.

'I thought you wanted to come out for a meal,' her companion said, irritated, 'but you look so bloody miserable ...'

She shrugged, staring ahead.

'You not feeling well?'

'I'm fine. Let it drop.'

A sudden movement on the balcony made her turn and look over to the blond man again. He was standing up and leaning on the stone balustrade, his eyes fixed on the water below. From where she sat, the woman could see nothing, only the restaurant's lights reflected in the still, unblinking, water.

'We could have a weekend away ...'

'Maybe.'

'Don't sound so bloody excited.'

The woman's whole attention was now centred on the blond man. He was standing, rigid, looking into the water below.

'Are you listening to me?'

The brunette no longer heard her lover. Watching the

fair-haired man, she again glanced out to the canal as he leaned further out, bending over the balustrade.

Christ! she thought suddenly. He's going to jump.

Leaping to her feet, the woman raced over and caught his arm, pulling him back. Surprised, the man turned and then quickly motioned for her to look down into the water.

'Look over there!' he said, pointing. 'There's something's over there.'

Hurriedly, she snatched a candle from an inside table and then leaned over the balustrade, holding the light as far as she could towards the water.

'No!' the man said urgently. 'Not there. Look over there!'

Leaning out even further, the woman shone the candle light over the flat, black water. The night was very dark, the moon obscured by cloud, the canal deep, its surface unbroken apart from a smattering of reeds and the dripping of water from underneath the balcony.

And then she saw it.

Floating on the water at the edge of the canal, hardly visible, was a bundle, wrapped tightly in a soiled white blanket. It was small, benign, but eerie. Gently, it glided away and began its grisly procession down the middle of the canal, on an almost imperceptible current. Transfixed, they watched its progress, the bundle finally passing under the full glare of one of the restaurant's outside lamps. The beam illuminated the blood-spattered wrapping – and the place where the parcel had come partially untied.

From which a disembodied hand, fingers outstretched, clawed its way to the light.

14

Madrid

Clasping his notepad, Leon walked towards the Museo del Prado, on the Paseo del Prado. The sight of the white ghost of a building, with its arches and columned entrance, never failed to move him, and this evening its ivory pallor seemed to shimmer against the purple evening like some vast, bottomless opal on a bishop's habit. Skirting the main entrance, Leon entered by the side door, reserved for staff and art historians working full time or on a consultancy basis for the Prado. Sliding his entrance key into the lock, he pushed open the heavy wooden door and passed into the web of back rooms and archives.

Originally built in the late sixteenth century as a science museum, the Prado was redesigned by Napoleon's brother, Joseph Bonaparte, and turned into an art gallery. But it was only when Ferdinand VII mounted the throne that it became the Royal Art collection, continuing the theme of royal and religious collecting begun by his ancestor, Queen Isabel La Catolica. Few visitors realise the massive scale of the Prado Museum, or know that it owns over nine thousand works of art: a collection so vast that despite the building's size, only fifteen hundred exhibits can ever be shown at any one time. Most of the most important works of Velasquez and El Greco are on permanent display, but many other paintings circle the gallery relentlessly in an ebb and flow of tidal genius.

Fittingly, Goya is triumphantly represented; and, equally fittingly, his work is housed separately from the main gallery in its own sumptuous architectural island. The visitor walks through the spectacular gallery rooms of the main part of the museum and then finally comes upon a small rotunda, swollen with Goya's paintings. But, interestingly, even here Goya could not be penned in; and gradually the accumulation of his works spread from the rotunda downstairs, to an anthill of darker rooms on lower floors.

Scurrying down the back stairs, Leon relished the quiet of the closed gallery, the crowds of tourists all tipped out into the street, the lights dimmed, only the necessary illumination marking out his pathway. Preoccupied, he hurried on, then paused in front of the painting of *The Family of Charles IV*. By the time Goya was painting the royal family he had become well known, respected and acid in his judgement. Yet although highly sexed himself, the artist was – like most of his contemporaries – outraged that the plain, vain and mendacious Queen Maria Luisa had given power over to her young bedfellow, the despised Manuel

Godoy. Duped, and glad to be relieved of the burden of kingship, Charles IV restricted his royal duties to asking Godoy nightly 'whether affairs were going well or badly'.

Leon studied the familiar figures, as always in awe of Goya's acerbic daring. The painter had held nothing in reserve. The Queen had been made plain and ridiculous, the King an idle buffoon. A noise from below jolted Leon out of his reverie. He had work to do, and he had to hurry. Admittedly the gallery was open to him at any time during the day, but at night he could only stay by special dispensation and had to leave by twelve.

Past the royal portraits Leon hurried, clutching his books, his shadow crossing the faces of *The Naked Maja* and *The Colossus*. He wasn't interested in the earlier images, just the ones which hobgoblined their way through his dreams and trick-or-treated into his studies. Leon knew that he was taking a chance, that by cutting down on his medication he wasn't just trying to please Gina or improve his condition. He knew exactly what his medicinal Russian roulette might mean, but cocked the gun anyway. By his reckoning he had a week, maybe two, before he would collapse and be forced back on to the drugs. He had to make sure that he found the answer in time.

Letting out a sigh of nervous excitement, Leon entered one of the rooms exhibiting Goya's Black Paintings and then paused. In front of him hung Deaf Man, originally painted on one of the walls of the Quinta del Sordo before being transferred to the Prado. He studied the work intently: the weird blacks, ochres and malevolent whites, the scurry of paint, hurried, as though the artist's hand was being guided. The left-hand figure in the picture was benign – an old man like a sage or a Biblical scholar – but leaning on his shoulder was a beast, half-man, half-skeleton, bald, blank-eyed, whispering into the old man's ear. But whispering what?

'Leon Golding?'

He spun round, almost losing his footing as a corpulent man called out from behind a pillar. Jimmy Shaw was limping slightly, his suit stained and crumpled, holding his hand across his chest, half-tucked into his jacket. His face was puffy, his eyes small in the swelling folds of flesh. He looked decayed, sick, like someone who had just stepped out of one of Goya's pictures.

'What . . .?' Leon stared at the vision, then realised it was only a man. A sick, fat man. 'What are you doing here? The gallery's closed to the public.'

'I had to talk to you,' Shaw said, keeping to the shadows and breathing heavily with the effort. 'I've been trying to talk to you for days. I called you on the phone, then lost my nerve.' He paused, running his tongue over his bulging lips. 'I thought I *should* talk to you in person about the skull . . .'

Immediately, Leon glanced around him.

'There are no guards here, Mr Golding. Only the ones on night duty at Reception. I hid here when the gallery closed—'

'What?'

'I hid here,' Shaw repeated. 'I stood over there, stock

still, for nearly a fucking hour. You're late tonight. I didn't think I could stand so still for so long.'

Nervous, Leon stepped back. 'I don't know what you want—'

'The skull. The Goya skull.'

'I don't have it!'

'Yes, you do.'

'I don't!' Leon replied, his tone shrill. 'I don't know what you're talking about.'

'I'm not going to hurt you,' Shaw went on, his speech muffled until he cleared his throat. He was dying – anyone could see that. He could see that. He just had to get the skull, get it to Dwappa, and he'd be all right. 'Give me the skull. I'll buy it from you.'

'I told you, I don't have it—'

'I'll give you a good price,' Shaw said, stepping out of the shadows into the full overhead light. His face was bloated, red weals under the eyes, his hand double-bandaged, although there was still a slight stench coming through the dressing.

Horrified, Leon stepped back again. 'You're ill—'

'Yeah, and I won't get better until I get the skull,' Shaw said earnestly. 'Listen to me, Mr Golding. You're going to get into deep trouble. Real trouble. There are people worse than me after that skull. One man in particular, he wants it. He's got a buyer for the skull. He hired me to get it for him and he won't rest until it's in his hands. You've got to listen to me—'

He reached out and Leon stepped further back.

'I'm trying to help you! Keep that fucking skull and you'll end up like me. Worse.' He sighed raggedly. 'What d'you want for it?'

Leon stood mute. He was terrified of the man in front of him, but he wasn't about to give up the skull. Around them the Black Paintings hummed under the lights and the fat man leaned against the pillar again.

'I could kill you—'

'What?'

'But what would be the point? You don't have the skull on you.' Shaw laughed shortly. 'So name your price.'

'The skull I had turned out to be a fake.'

'Oh, I heard you tell Gabino Ortega that. He didn't believe it either. I suppose Ortega wants it for his brother.' Shaw sighed again. 'Yes, I've been watching you, Mr Golding. I've seen who you've talked to. We're all watching each other.' He smiled, the oily skin of his cheeks creasing. 'Give up the skull, otherwise you'll regret it.'

'I tell you, I don't have it!'

Shaw bowed his head for a moment. 'I'm not used to all this, you know. Usually I have minions doing the dirty work . . . And that's what it is.'

Leon frowned. 'What?'

'Dirty work,' Shaw explained. 'It's very dirty work. And I'm stuck in it. Stuck tight. I can't get out of it, but you can. Just give up the skull and you'll be safe. I don't want it for the Ortega brothers. I've told you, I want it for someone else entirely. Someone much, much more dangerous. The Ortegas have money, but the African . . .' He

105

passed Leon a piece of paper. 'That's my number. Call me when you want to meet up. Bring the skull and I'll pay you what you want.'

'But—'

'I'm dying, Mr Golding,' Shaw said helplessly. 'If I don't get that skull I'll be dead soon. You want that on your conscience?' He stared at Leon. 'I don't think you could manage that – you're not that kind of man.' He tried to shrug, but winced. 'It's just a skull. It's just the head of a dead man ... I'm asking you, *begging you*. What's it worth? I want a dead man's head to save a life. *My life*. And I don't expect any favours, I'll pay you—'

'It's not the money.'

Shaw shook his head incredulously. 'It's *always* the money, Mr Golding.'

'You don't understand—'

'No, *you* don't understand. Because if you did – if you realised what that skull means – you'd have got rid of it already. And if you knew what's coming to you, you'd sell it to me now. You'd get the fucking thing off your hands and keep yourself safe.' He stared at Leon intently. 'Call me. I'll come and meet you whenever, wherever, you want. Just make it quick, for all our sakes. I'm trying to save you, Mr Golding. Please, *save me*.'

15

The Whitechapel Hospital, London

The following morning a good-looking mixed race woman of around thirty-five was waiting outside Ben Golding's office when he arrived at the hospital for his clinic. Seated beside her was her companion, a bored young man, staring at his text messages.

As the woman saw Ben approach she walked over to greet him. 'Mr Golding?'

'Yes,' he said warily, worried she might be an overanxious patient trying to jump the queue.

'I'm Roma Jaffe. My colleague and I would like to have a few words.' On cue, the bored young man got to his feet and stood beside her. Discreetly flashing her police identity badge she held Ben's gaze. 'Can we talk?'

A moment later she was seated opposite Ben Golding at his desk, a file in her hands, her expression professional. The dull navy suit she was wearing did not fully obliterate her figure and although her hair was pulled back from her face it didn't disguise the high cheekbones and strong jaw. Leaning against the wall behind her, Duncan Thorpe regarded his superior idly.

'I've been told that you're the leading reconstructive surgeon in London,' Roma began, 'and I need to ask your help with a case I'm working on. I'm investigating the murder of a man who was dismembered, and some of whose remains were found in the canal at Little Venice two days ago.'

Ben nodded. 'I read about it in the paper. Do they know who it was?'

'No, not yet.' She paused. 'We have the torso now, but no legs, and only a jacket. Which has no means of identification. But this morning a head turned up in the Thames. The pathologist believes that it belongs to the same man.' She pushed a photograph over the desk.

The decapitated head was all but destroyed, the skull partially exposed, the features battered. In order to be photographed it had been placed on a forensic examining table, a measuring rule beside it, a label with the time and date of its discovery lying beside the jawbone.

'How can I help?' Ben asked.

'I've got an X-ray too,' Roma replied, passing it over to him. 'And I wanted to ask you if there is anything unusual about the man's skull.'

Walking over to the window, Ben held the X-ray up to the light. For a long moment he studied it, then turned back to the policewoman.

'The skull's male, adult, around thirty-five, forty, I'd

say. And he's had some reconstructive surgery in the past. Broken cheekbone and jaw. Either an assault or a car accident—'

'Before death?'

'Long before,' Ben replied. 'It wasn't the cause of death, if that's what you're asking. But it's difficult to see any more with all the mutilation to the face.'

'Will you look at the remains?'

'Yes. But I'm not a pathologist – I can only tell you about any reconstructive surgery to the head.' He looked at her. 'Surely you have your own people?'

'Not as specialised as you, Mr Golding.'

Ben nodded. 'Do you have any idea who the victim was?'

'No. We're going to need some help in that area. Obviously no one could recognise him as he is.' She picked up the photograph and put it back in her bag. 'I believe you have a first-class reconstructor at the Whitechapel Hospital.'

'Francis Asturias,' Ben replied. 'He could recreate the victim's head for you. He's done it many times. For the police and for archaeologists. What else?'

She looked at him curiously. 'Should there be something else?'

'I had a feeling that there was more you were about to tell me.'

She smiled. 'The jacket we discovered with the torso had a card in the inside pocket.'

'And?'

'It was yours, Mr Golding.' She pulled out a small plastic bag and slid it across the table to him.

Glancing at it, Ben nodded. 'Yes, that's my card. So what? Maybe he was an ex-patient. Or someone who'd been given my details to contact me. Journalists, writers – all kinds of people have asked me for help over the years. There must be hundreds of my cards out there.'

'That's what I thought,' Roma replied, then flipped over the plastic bag and pointed to another number written on the back of the card. 'D'you know whose number that is?'

Jolted, Ben stared at the digits but kept his face impassive. He knew the number well, called it frequently – it was his brother's private mobile number. Found in the jacket of a dead man without a face.

16

When the police officers had left, Ben walked into the laboratory looking for Francis Asturias. He had tried to call Leon repeatedly, but his brother hadn't returned the messages and now Leon's mobile was turned off. Of course the matter of the card might not be important, Ben told himself, but it troubled him nevertheless. It wasn't so much that it was his business card, but the fact that it had been the only item found on a murder victim. Had he been a patient? If so, why did he have Leon's private number as well? And why had the man ended up – in pieces – scattered around London?

Troubled, Ben thought back to the X-ray he had seen. Nothing about the surgery seemed familiar, but then it hadn't been recent and certainly not undertaken by him. Which seemed to exclude the victim as an ex-patient. Jesus! Ben thought irritably. Why hadn't Leon called back? He had left enough messages, stressing that Leon mustn't use his mobile and should buy another one. But there had been no response.

'I've done it.'

At the sound of Francis Asturias's voice, Ben turned. The reconstructor was standing hands on hips, wearing a pair of old-fashioned motorcycle gauntlets.

Ben raised his eyebrows. 'Trying to stop biting your nails?'

'Very funny,' Francis replied, pulling off the gloves. 'I've been in the freezer. Got some nasty burns last time, so I thought I'd take precautions from now on.' He looked at the gauntlets admiringly. 'Got them at a car boot sale. Two quid.'

'You were robbed.'

Ignoring him, Francis moved over to a nearby work-bench, gesturing for Ben to look. The skull which he had brought over from Madrid was on a raised plinth, but it looked disappointingly dull, uninteresting. Beside it was a companion plinth, a damp cloth covering the rough out-line of a human head.

Curious, Ben glanced over at Francis. 'Is that the recon-struction?'

'Sure is.'

'Is it a secret?'

'Huh?'

'Can I see it?' Ben asked wryly.

Francis hesitated for a moment. 'In a minute. I wanted to ask you about something else first. A policewoman came to see me this morning – with a head they'd just fished out of the Thames. She said she'd already talked to you about it.'

'She had.'

'Is there something you want to tell me?'

Ben smiled. 'A unknown man was killed and dismembered. Various parts of him have turned up. Some in a canal in Little Venice—'

'But why involve you?'

'Roma Jaffe – the detective – wanted me to look at the mutilated head because it had undergone surgery in the past. She wanted my opinion.' He paused, wondering why he wasn't telling Francis about the card. 'Have you got it now?'

'Been a bit of a rush on heads lately. Up to my knees in them,' Francis replied. 'The police want a reconstruction.'

'How long will it take you?'

'Not long. I'm working with the pathologist.'

'I'd like to see the reconstruction when you're done,' Ben said evenly. He was more than a little curious to see what the head had looked like when it had been a breathing, living man. Curious to know if Francis Asturias's reconstruction would jolt his memory – and explain the victim's link to him and Leon.

'I knew you'd be aching to see it,' Francis replied, walking back to the Madrid skull and standing by the plinth. He had the air of a third-rate Las Vegas magician about to do a creaky trick. 'Ready?'

'I thought it was all done on computer now.'

Francis gave him a withering look. 'I don't work on computer – that's for amateurs. I work in the old-fashioned way, by hand . . . First you take the skull—'

'Hang on,' Ben interrupted him. 'So you don't make the reconstruction over the skull itself?'

'Never. You make a copy of the original skull, then use *the copy* for the reconstruction. That way you can poke about the replica without doing damage to the original.'

'Go on.'

'First you work out the landmark sights.'

'Which means?'

'The tissue and muscle depths,' Francis replied, shrugging, delighted to have an audience. 'Going on the shape of the skull, this man was a Caucasian, so from that I can work out the angle of the planes of the face.'

'Then what?'

'Then I gradually work out the outline of the bones, add muscle tissue, and try to reconstruct the forehead angle and the eyes. Of course the tip of the nose, the ears, eye and hair colour are always guesswork. We can only ever be sure of the bones we have, not the colouring or the skin texture of the subject.'

Patiently, Ben folded his arms. 'What about the Madrid skull?'

'Quite straightforward. Of course the age of the head had to be taken into consideration. And the fact that there were some parts of the skull missing.'

'I saw that,' Ben agreed. 'A few rough holes. You know what caused them?'

'Could be just wear and tear—'

'Were they peri- or post-mortem?'

'Post.'

'Could they be a result of violence?'

'Like what?'

'Blows to the head?'

'Doubt it. They were jagged. Uneven. Looks more like burial damage, animal attack.' Francis shrugged. 'I've done a lot of reconstructions for archaeologists and I've seen damage like this before on old skulls.'

'What about getting the pathologist to look at it?'

'I've already done that and he didn't know much more than I did. Although he *did* say that the marks could have been caused by rubbing or by persistent scuffing.' Francis paused. 'Which sounded macabre – until I remembered that case about the kids in Liverpool using a skull as a football. When they found it it was filthy and they couldn't make out what it was – just this grubby round object, so they kicked it around for a while. Boys will be boys!'

'Especially in Liverpool.'

Putting on his glasses, Francis picked up some papers next to him, reading aloud. 'The results have come through for the isotope and carbon dating. Having discovered what our man ate, it is consistent with Spanish grains from around the Madrid area, and the carbon dating puts him bang smack in the middle of your time period.'

'So?'

'Dates are accurate. Looks good so far.'

Unable to suppress his enthusiasm any longer, Francis snatched the cloth off the reconstructed Madrid head. Caught in full daylight, it seemed eerily realistic, the glass eyes gazing darkly into the laboratory, the chin flaccid, the outline of the cheeks slightly concave to represent the fact that they would have dropped a little with age. But the high forehead, the heavy mouth and the eye shape were disturbingly familiar.

A shiver of recognition, followed by unease, slid down Ben's spine. He knew this man almost as well as a member of his own family. A face which had gazed out of books and down from cheap calendars throughout his childhood. A face that belonged to the man Detita had talked of repeatedly, slipping him into the brothers' early life, into that hazy Spanish heat of their youth.

It was, without doubt, the face of the Goldings' long-dead neighbour in Spain. Francisco Goya.

'Jesus . . .'

'So,' Francis prompted him. 'What d'you think?'

Staring at the reconstruction, Ben hesitated. And felt – for an instant – not triumph for his brother, but fear.

'So,' Francis repeated. 'What d'you think?'

'I think we're looking at an old man. An old man who was arguably the greatest painter Spain ever produced.'

17

Madrid

The heatwave had finally broken, a storm marking the end of the freak weather, persistent rain making the weathercock rotate madly over the decrepit stables of the Madrid house. Inside, Leon drew the curtains and locked the windows, rechecking the back and front doors. He hadn't shaved and his clothes smelled of stale sweat as he moved back into his study. After his last visit to the Prado he had avoided the gallery, even been tempted to go back on his medication. But gradually his panic subsided. How *could* he stop when the answer was finally in his hands? All he had to do now was to write his theory up, put it down on paper, then – when it was completed – turn it over to the world.

He knew how the art world worked. How critics, writers and collectors all vied for the top slot. Men searched for decades to uncover something unknown, some detail previously unexplained, some nuance gone unnoticed. But the Black Paintings were in another league. No one had ever known their true meaning. Theories mushroomed but dwindled into supposition. A hundred explanations had been offered, but never proved, never fulfilling the hunger for the truth about the most macabre pictures ever painted.

So it followed that the man who solved the enigma would become famous. The man who cracked the cipher would be the envy of the art world. He would become an authority no one could question. Respected, revered, admired.

Locking the door of his study, Leon checked his mobile, hearing the messages from Ben. For a moment he was tempted to call his brother, but found himself uncertain, chewing at the side of his index fingernail. The piece of paper Jimmy Shaw had given him had no name written on it, just a mobile number. Tucking the edge of the note under his desk lamp so that he could read the digits without needing to touch it, Leon wiped his hands.

To his surprise he felt sympathy for the man. Obviously dying, Shaw had managed to elicit some compassion in Leon – and an unwelcome guilt. But it was *his* skull! Leon thought desperately. No one else's. And now everyone was after it. And after him. People had no right to be following him, questioning him. As for Gabino Ortega – what made him think he could demand details? He had been impertinently high-handed, almost imperious, although he was little more than a thug, challenging Leon outside the Prado. On his turf, talking to him as though he was a lackey!

Of course he had lied! What else could he do? Leon asked himself. He was hardly going to admit that he had Goya's skull . . . Slumping into his seat, Leon felt an overwhelming desire to kick out. All his life he had longed for an opportunity to dazzle everyone. To finally put to rest the rumours about his mental instability. No one could deny him respect when he had the Goya skull. That, together with his explanation of the Black Paintings, would silence everyone.

Calming himself, he reached for his papers and began to read. A buzzing sounded in his ears as he read about Goya's first major illness. About how the artist had been temporarily paralysed, his head full of noises. Normal speech and communication over . . . Sighing, Leon leaned back in his chair, placing the cut-outs he had made of each painting in the order in which they had been hung in the Quinta del Sordo. Soon he had the complete floor plans – upstairs and downstairs – in front of him, reading the paintings in the order they had been viewed.

Ground floor –
Deaf Man, with the
dead man talking to him:

The Pilgrimage:

Judith and Holofernes, the woman killing her rival:

Saturn eating one his children:

The Witches' Sabbath:

and lastly, Leocardia leaning on a burial mound:

Six of the fourteen Black Paintings which had been an enigma for centuries . . . Leon glanced at his notes, excitement rising. So it begins. The first painting, *Deaf Man*, was Goya himself. Goya had entered the Quinta del Sordo as an old, deaf man. The weird figure next to him, whispering into his deaf ear, was Death itself. He had come to the country house to die. But why? Leon looked at the next painting. Here began Goya's testimony of his country, *The Pilgrimage* – a series of deranged people walking blindly in the semi-darkness. The Spanish people, driven insane by war and brutality, no longer human, walking into the abyss.

Then he turned to the third painting – *Judith and Holofernes*. Throughout art history it had represented the story of the Jewish queen who had seduced and then decapitated her lover and conqueror. But Leon knew this was no historical reference – Goya had not been depicting Judith, but Leocardia, his lover at the Quinta del Sordo . . . Excitement building, he scribbled down his thoughts, his hands moving rapidly. It was as though something had unlocked his brain and body; as though he had an open channel through which the information was pouring.

God, if only he had the skull! Leon thought desperately. What wouldn't it tell him? What inspiration wouldn't it magic on to the page? He thought of Gina and the medium, then Detita – and smiled to himself. His triumph was close. Close, breathable, touchable. If he kept working . . . His eyes moved on to another painting – the same queasy colours, background darkness swampy with malevolence. This time it was *The Witchy Brew.*

But now there was no Biblical prophet, only an aged female, grinning maniacally, and next to her the same half-human, half-dead figure, leaning – always leaning – towards what still lived.

Leon blinked as a searing thought occurred to him, then moved forward to study the right-hand figure. He stared into blank eyes, his heart rate speeding up as an idea came to him. Was *that* what Goya was painting? Swallowing, he tried to control his emotions as he looked back at the picture. Had the artist made dangerous enemies? Had he risked his own safety? Was it true what Detita had said so many years earlier – that Goya had been cursed, made ill and deafened *deliberately*, not by witches but by someone altogether more human?

Goya had become Court Painter and won the admiration of Spain, but he hadn't kept it. What followed was his fall from grace, his questioning by the Inquisition, the Royals' favourite out of favour because of *their* fall . . . Leon stared at the paintings intently, thinking of Goya. Who knew more about the caprices of fate? Who else had painted so much depravity and madness? The pictures were hardly finished – rough works, painted hurriedly as though the artist was in a frenzy.

Avidly, his gaze moved from one painting to another. He saw the Jewish queen cutting off her seducer's head in *Judith and Holofernes*; he saw Saturn devouring the head of one of his own offspring, and the solitary, struggling dog, its head sticking above the quicksand, its body already sucked underneath into some gobbling, inescapable mass. So many decapitations, so many disembodied heads. Cut from their bodies. Stolen – just like Goya's own.

Jesus! Leon thought desperately. *Was the answer that obvious?* He looked around, afraid that someone could overhear his thoughts. Was that the truth? he asked himself, his heart rate increasing, blood fizzing in his ears. Saturn . . . *He knew!* Christ! Leon thought. Was it that? *Was this the evidence?*

Was Goya – in that remote, secluded house – leaving a testimony behind? He was ill, old, beaten down by tragedy and cynicism. Did he dream of the Inquisition coming back to his door? Asking questions about him and Leocardia? Reeling, Leon leaned back in his seat, putting some distance between himself and the illustrations. He could suddenly picture the deaf world Goya lived in. A candle-lit, silent place, hermetically closed, the old man casting his long shadow on the walls.

He rubbed his temples. He was too tired to work but too tired to stop. He *had* to write it down – and then hide it. Along with the skull he would secrete the riddle of the Black Paintings. He would write it down, spell it out. On paper it would serve as a testament. And perhaps, once written down, it would loosen its grip.

In his excitement a cry escaped his lips. Sweating, he found himself light-headed, a queasy giddiness about to overwhelm him. Bartolomé Ortega would be so jealous . . . Leon laughed to himself, wiping his mouth with the back of his hand. All the Ortega money wouldn't be enough. In the end it would come down to insight – Leon's insight. The solving of the Black Paintings was simple for him. After all, it was only one madman talking to another.

One madman talking to another . . . Leon repeated the words in his head, disturbed by the thought. Getting to his feet he felt the room shift around him and knew he had pushed himself too far and gambled with his stability. Staggering to the door, he clasped the handle. He would go for a walk – get out of the house, away from the reproductions which were calling out to him from the desk.

But no longer from the desk.

Now they were all around him. Panicked, Leon turned, staring frantically at the hallucinations which filled the room. Witches were turning into goats, men's faces were grinning without eyes and whispering without voices. He could hear the paintings talking, whispering, making catcalls in the dimness, as behind him the sound of unfolding wings beat like thunder against his skin.

His heart was pumping in his ears, his mouth open, gasping for air. The paintings vibrated in front of him, first becoming larger, swelling towards him, then retracting into murky black slivers of pure malice. And then he saw the painting of *La Leocadia*, Goya's mistress, dressed in widow's black, leaning on the huge dark mound of the artist's grave. But as Leon looked, the paint peeled away and under the earth was not Goya, *but himself.* Still alive but deaf, blind and mute, clawing under the weight of earth. And the mourner wasn't Leocadia but Detita, pressing Leon further and further into the suffocating earth.

In uncovering the secret of The Black Paintings Leon Golding had gone too far. Not only was he risking his sanity, but his life.

18

New York

Roberta Feldenchrist got out of the car, her chauffeur holding the door open for her. The warm air felt oily as she moved into the air-conditioned lobby of the apartment block. All her life Roberta – known to everyone as Bobbie – had lived on Park Avenue. All her life she had been surrounded by money, and when her parents divorced she stayed on with her father in the penthouse apartment, although the family actually owned three floors of the block. Her mother remarried but they had little in common and Bobbie rarely visited in France, even after Harwood Feldenchrist died.

Being an only child, it was not surprising that Bobbie inherited the Feldenchrist fortune and had full control. She left the property and banking interests to the board of directors her father had set up, but the running of the Feldenchrist art collection was entrusted to her. A life-long chauvinist, Harwood had made it clear that although

Bobbie wasn't a boy, she had been as near a son as he would ever get. She had often wondered if that was why her father shortened her name to Bobbie.

Walking into the apartment she paused, glanced at her mail and then moved into the drawing room overlooking the park and the view beyond. The view spoke of privilege. Here she was above the streets, up with the gods – spoiled, preserved, chosen. Just like the paintings on the walls which surrounded her. The picture closest to her was Fragonard. Her father had loved French art and so had she, only later being introduced to the Spaniards and finally revelling in Goya. Something about the darkness had appealed to her, the bullfights and carnivals showing a side of life that was cruel as well as celebratory.

Her gaze travelled across the wall, finally coming to rest on a small, dark-toned painting. Idly, Bobbie flicked on the overhead picture light to study the most controversial work in her late father's collection: a painting by Goya of two old men reading. There had been an argument over the piece for years, some experts denying it was by Goya, others pointing out that it was a perfect – if much smaller – facsimile of the *Old Men Reading* which had been at the Quinta del Sordo. No one could prove it was genuine, but then again, no one could prove it was a fake.

Bobbie studied the work thoughtfully. People might think she was a spoilt woman in her thirties with two failed marriages behind her and nothing between her ears, but they were wrong. Bobbie Feldenchrist had longed to settled down, have a family, and continue to build the collection in her spare time. She dreamed of a Ralph Lauren life – all fawn sofas and honey-haired children, all polished New York winters and summers in the Hamptons. She would be one of the old school *Swans*, the American ideal of the rich life ... Dully, she shook her head and turned away, walking back to the window to look at the familiar view and smiling bitterly to herself.

Half an hour earlier she had been told that the adoption had fallen through. Apparently the mother of the child Bobbie was about to adopt had changed her mind and no amount of money could change it back ... Bobbie stared ahead blindly, remembering another shock. In the very same room, two years previously, she had been told that she was sterile. Her breast cancer had been cured, the specialist reassured her, but the chemotherapy had made her barren. Bobbie had gone to the ladies' room and stared at her reflection in the mirror: a tall, slender, elegant woman dressed immaculately, her face made up skilfully. But inside the pristine form of honed skin and tailored muscle, the body had been corrupted by disease. Inside the perfection sickness had eaten into Bobbie Feldenchrist and the therapy had burned away the cancer. She might look perfect, but her womb wasn't going to carry a child and her breasts were never going to fill with milk. Bobbie had the Feldenchrist power and money, but she was the last of the Feldenchrists.

For a long time she had stood staring at her reflection, fighting a desire to smash the glass, to scream with frustration. But the Feldenchrists never behaved that way. It wasn't classy to be vulgar. If you could control your feelings, you could control your life ... Bobbie had smiled with bitterness. Her father had been wrong about that. Some things no one could control, not even a Feldenchrist. Not even with Feldenchrist money.

Taking in a slow, measured breath, Bobbie's thoughts came back to the present. *The baby wasn't coming.* She wasn't going to be a mother after all, even an adoptive one. As for the party, the celebration party she had planned for the weekend, she would have to cancel it. It was to have been her triumph – the moment when she introduced her one-month-old adopted son to the world. But now there was no baby. No triumph.

She could imagine how everyone would talk. How they would commiserate with her to her face but mock her behind her back. God, she couldn't even *buy* a baby – what kind of failure did that make her? Chilled, Bobbie moved around the apartment. She had been beaten by a slum girl – some Puerto Rican tart had cheated her. Tears stung her eyes, but she drove them back. She would put a brave face on it, would tell her friends that there had been a legal difficulty in the adoption. Better still, she would imply that the child had been ill in some way, perhaps mentally retarded ... Anything other than admit that the Feldenchrist finances had been of no to use to her at all. For a woman who had always taken money for granted, it came as a chilling realisation that its power was not absolute.

Her face expressionless, Bobbie controlled her anger and regained her poise. She would have to find something else to think about – to keep her occupied. Something to take her mind off her loss for a while. Turning, she moved back into the drawing room and began to flick through the Sotheby's catalogue. She would think about the Feldenchrist Collection for a while. Paintings wouldn't change, grow old, divorce her or die. They would endure, as would the Feldenchrist name. Not as a family, but as a collection.

It was something to hold on to, Bobbie told herself, then paused. Who was she kidding? Paintings were important, but they weren't going to fill the longing to be a mother. Her thoughts crystallised as she drew in another breath. Perhaps – if she found a child quickly – she wouldn't have to cancel the party and lose face. She could just postpone it.

She wanted a child. And, by God, she was going to get one.

19

'Leon, is that you?' Ben asked, startled by his brother's tone when he picked up the phone on his landline. 'Why haven't you returned my calls? Are you all right?'

'Fine.'

'You don't sound fine.'

'I'm busy.'

'Why didn't you call me back? I left messages all day.'

'I told you, I'm busy!' Leon snapped, his tone petulant. 'What's the fuss about?'

'Something odd's happened.'

'Same here,' Leon added wryly, thinking of how close he had come to collapse, and the run-in at the Prado with Jimmy Shaw. But he wasn't about to confide in Ben, to give his brother the satisfaction of being right.

'Why? What happened to you?'

'Nothing,' Leon said hurriedly. 'Go on with what you were saying.'

'The police came to see me today. They found a murder victim in London – a man with *your* mobile number in his pocket.'

'Who was it?'

'That's the point – they don't know yet. It just seems strange, that's all. I mean, that's your personal mobile number – you hardly ever give it out.' He paused, then carried on. 'Don't use that mobile again. Toss it. Get yourself another one.'

'Was my number written on a piece of paper?'

'No, it was on the back of one of my cards.'

'Oh . . . So, did *you* write the number on it?'

'No, it was written in your handwriting, Leon. I recognised it – the funny way you write the number four.'

There was a pause on the line before Leon spoke again. 'Who was the murdered man?'

'His face was virtually destroyed. I couldn't recognise him. But we're doing a reconstruction here—'

Stung into action, Leon was quick to react. '*What about Goya's skull?* I hope that's being worked on first—'

'Francis has already done it,' Ben said patiently. 'That's one of the reasons I was ringing you. The reconstruction looks good. I've seen it—'

'And?'

'It's Goya. What d'you want me to do with it?' He waited, expecting an answer. 'Leon, are you there?'

'*It really is Goya's skull* . . .' He was whispering, hardly audible. Unnerved, spooked.

'Are you OK?'

'I dreamt it would be Goya's and it really is . . .' Leon's exhilaration fluttered, then faltered as he remembered Jimmy Shaw. The enormity of the situation overweighed his excitement and he found himself – as always – turning to Ben for reassurance.

'Gabino Ortega was asking me about the skull—'

'How did he know about it?'

Leon stood up and closed the window. Even though it was hot and the room would be suffocating within minutes, he didn't want to risk being overheard.

'I don't know how he heard. No one was supposed to know apart from me, the Prado, and obviously the builder who found it.'

'D'you think he talked? Regretted giving the skull to you when he could have sold it to someone like Ortega?'

'No! Diego Martinez is a simple man, a good man. His father owed our parents a favour and it was his way of repaying them. By giving me the skull . . .' Leon trailed off, clinging to the phone. 'I told Gabino Ortega it was a fake, that I'd got rid of it. I said I'd given it to the church for burial.'

Knowing Gabino Ortega's reputation, Ben was wary. 'Did he believe you?'

'I think so . . . no, probably not.' Leon turned away from the window. 'Gabino's brother, Bartolomé, lives in Switzerland. He's the respectable face of the Ortega clan – and he's desperate to solve the riddle of the Black Paintings. We've talked about it on the few occasions we've run into each other at auctions – he's always asking me how my research is going. As though I'd tell him!' Leon's voice speeded up. 'He's obsessed by Goya. He'd do anything to get the skull off me.'

'But you said it was *Gabino* who approached you.'

'Yes, it was. But think about it! Gabino would want to get the skull for his brother. He's always sucking up to Bartolomé, because he funds his lifestyle. Gabino would see the skull as a way to ingratiate himself. Besides, he's here in Madrid. He probably thinks he has a better shot at getting it than Bartolomé in Switzerland—'

'Leon—'

He wasn't about to be interrupted.

'Gabino's a thug. Everyone knows that. Their grandfather killed his own wife, for Christ's sake! Of course they couldn't prove it and bought the police off. With that kind of blood in your veins, it's no surprise Gabino turned out the way he is. Always in fights. All kinds of rumours follow him around. I heard he'd—'

'Leon,' Ben said quietly, 'donate the skull to the Prado. That way it belongs to Spain and no individual can own it.'

'*Give it away?*' Leon shouted. 'Are you bloody crazy? Can't you see that all these people who want it only prove how important it is?'

'Who are "all these people"?'

'What?'

'You said "all these people", but you've only told me about the Ortega brothers. So who are they?' Ben was silent for a minute, then pushed his brother. 'Leon, tell me what's going on.'

'The other day . . . a man approached me in the Prado. A big fat Englishman. Sick, very sick.' Leon automatically wiped his hand down his trouser leg as though wiping off all traces of Jimmy Shaw. 'He said someone had hired him to get the Goya skull. Said that he had a buyer for it. He warned me that the man was very dangerous—'

'Christ!'

'He scared the hell out of me!' Leon admitted. 'He offered money, any amount I wanted – just said that if I had any sense I'd get rid of the skull. He said, "If you knew what's coming to you, you'd sell it to me now. You'd get the fucking thing off your hands and keep yourself safe."'

'Go to the police—'

'He said he was trying to save me. And that I could save him.' Leon thought back. *I'm trying to save you, Mr Golding. Please, save me.* Once he had started to confide, he couldn't stop, his panic rising. 'That was two days ago. I came back home and I haven't been out since. Just been working on my theory about the paintings. Just stayed home working . . . you know, working . . .'

Anxious, Ben tried to calm his brother down. 'How did you leave it with Gabino Ortega?'

'I said the skull was a fake.'

'And the Englishman? Did you get a name?'

'No.' Leon glanced at the paper half hidden under the desk lamp. 'Just a mobile number.'

'Give me the number.'

'I won't have time,' Leon said suddenly.

'Time for what?'

'*To finish! To finish!*' he cried, distraught. 'I nearly solved the last part this morning . . . I have to write it down, Ben.

If I don't get there first, I'll lose. Someone will get the answer before me; they'll get the glory—'

'*What answer?*'

'To what the Black Paintings mean!' Leon snapped. 'I've got it solved. I know what Goya did. Why he was ill. I know something that could have changed history. But I need the skull back now. *I have to get it back!*'

Ben could hear the staccato rhythm of his brother's voice, the threat of hysteria which always precipitated another attack.

'Leon, you are taking your medication, aren't you?'

'*I don't want the fucking medication!* It makes me slow; I can't think when I take it. I've found out so much – things you wouldn't believe—'

'I don't care about your work, I care about you. I'm worried about you.' Ben's voice was steady. 'Go to the police—'

'Fuck off!'

'OK, then give me the number of the man who approached you—'

'Why?'

'*I'll* give it to the police.'

'And then they'll know about the skull!' Leon shrieked. 'It would be all over the papers within hours. You're worried about me now – what about then? When it's public knowledge, how many more people will want to get hold of it?'

'Then do what I suggested, Leon. Get it off your hands. Donate the skull to the Prado. Make an announcement publicly so everyone knows you don't have it any more—'

'I can't give up on it! I'm inches away from telling the world what happened to Goya. *I can't just walk away now!*'

'You can't do this alone—'

'I'm not doing it alone! Gina's trying to help—'

It was the last thing Ben wanted to hear. '*Gina!*'

'She told me that we have to keep the skull safe. She wants to protect me and my work.'

'What the hell does she know about it?'

'We had a seance—'

'Oh, Christ, Leon!'

'The medium thought that if we had Goya's skull we much be able to reach him.'

Incredulous, Ben struggled to keep the irritation out of his voice. 'You really think you can get in contact with Goya?'

'Why not? The medium contacted Detita.'

The name swung into action and with it a malignancy which took Ben straight back to his childhood.

'Detita is dead. No one can bring back the dead. Detita is dead and Goya is dead, Leon ... Listen to me. This is bloody ridiculous. You can't let people fill your head with all this crap. As for Gina, I know you care about her, but she's not reliable—'

Leon dropped his voice, almost shamefaced. 'She's done some research on the internet for me—'

'Please, stop this.'

'I can't,' Leon replied, his tone distant, resigned.

Behind Ben, the door of his consulting room closed

suddenly, making him jump. Looking round, he checked that no was listening and then realised that he was clinging on to the phone so tightly the bones of his knuckles were straining against the skin. The hand found in the Little Venice canal came into his mind unbidden, followed by an image of the head the police had found later, the face mashed into nothingness.

'It's dangerous, Leon. I told you people would be after the skull – I knew this would happen. Didn't I say we had to keep it quiet?'

'I have to get on with my research—'

'You're endangering yourself.'

'I just have to write up my notes and it's finished. I'll stop then, I promise. I just have to get it down on paper ... Anyway, not everyone's against me. Some people are trying to help me. Some leave messages, others get in touch over the internet.'

Ben could feel his skin prickle. '*Do they know you have Goya's skull?*'

'But I don't, do I?' Leon replied. '*You* have it.' There was a note of malice in his voice, suspicion mixed with anger. 'Don't treat me like a child, Ben. I'm just as important in my field as you are in yours. This is my big chance and I'm not going to let anything stop me. Even you.'

'I'm not trying to stop you—'

'You're jealous, aren't you?'

'I'm just worried about you—'

'Stop worrying about me!'

'Leon—'

'Stop getting in my way!' he replied, his voice speeding up. '*I need that skull! I want it back!* It was given to me! I need it. It's mine!'

And then the line went dead.

BOOK TWO

What cruelty, for discovering the movement of the earth,
For marrying whom she wished,
For speaking a different language,
For being Jewish.

CAPTIONS GOYA WROTE UNDER
SOME OF HIS DRAWINGS

Quinta del Sordo
Madrid, 1821

*Impatiently, Arrieta flicked away the insects. Then, leaning back
in his seat, he looked slowly around the bedchamber. Below, the
doctor could hear the sound of a woman's footsteps, then her
voice as she called out to a little girl, Rosario. Was it true that
the child was Goya's? That he and his housekeeper, Leocardia
Zorrilla de Weiss, were lovers? His gaze moved back to Goya's
face, counting his pulse rate. It was too fast, but the artist was
unmoving, apparently asleep.*

*Almost choking in the heat, Arrieta opened the window fur-
ther and leaned out. In the distance, over the heat haze, he could
see the roofs of Madrid and knew that in the court the returned
King, Ferdinand VII, would be plotting further pogroms and
retaliations. No one was sure why Goya had moved to the farmhouse, but it was rumoured that it was to escape the restored
Inquisition. The ailing painter wouldn't have wanted to stay in
Madrid under the Inquisition's nose while they sniffed around*

his private life. After all, Leocardia was a relative by marriage of Goya's son, Xavier – a matter which could easily inflame the religious zealots. And besides, the Inquisition had been interested in Goya before, condemning his paintings of the Clothed and Naked Majas as obscene. The pictures had even been confiscated.

The model – believed to be the sensational Duchess of Alba – was dead . . . Arrieta sighed, remembering the woman who had been Goya's lover. Haughty, imperious, beautiful, she had intoxicated many men and inspired spite from the women of the court. Fearless, she cared little for convention, her reputation and beauty drawing Spaniards out on to their balconies to watch as she passed. Goya had painted her many times – as a duchess, a witch and a whore.

But the last time Arrieta had seen the Duchess of Alba she had been passing in her coach, unrecognisable, desperate as she had signalled for him to approach.

'Dr Arrieta,' she said, her face hidden behind a dense veil, 'I think you might find me much changed.' Carefully she lifted the net, exposing her features. The skin had peeled from her cheeks in weeping patches and the tip of her nose was eaten away. Around her lips blisters crowded the bare gums. And her hair, once waist-long and lustrous, had thinned, exposing the scalp beneath.

'What . . .?'

'. . . happened to me?' She held his gaze, still brave. 'I am poisoned, Dr Arrieta. And I will die . . . When you see Francisco tell him I loved him more than all the others. Tell him when you last saw me I was still beautiful. Lie for me.' She let the veil fall back to cover her face and tapped on the side of the coach. A moment later it moved off and she was gone. Two days afterwards news of the Duchess's death was gossip in Madrid. She was buried in haste. Whispers of poisoning and the involvement of Godoy, the Queen's lover, circulated the capital.

Francisco Goya never recovered from her loss.

And yet now he had another lover, Arrieta mused, thinking of Leocardia. But this woman was no duchess, no sumptuous aristocrat. This female was country-smart, ambitious, impatient and cold. Black hair, white skin, dark as a rook, and a listener at doors. No victim, this woman. Something else entirely. An odd companion for the painter's old age. A strange ally at the Quinta del Sordo.

But then the farmhouse had become a madhouse of its own . . . Dr Arrieta thought back to the night he had been called over the river, the water seeming to sweat with that molten boiling of earth into sky, the sun swelling like a pustule against the flank of blue. Moving into the cool interior of the farmhouse, Arrieta had waited for his eyes to adjust to the dimness as a lumbering figure approached him.

'Arrieta,' Goya said, staring into his doctor's face, 'I've been working.'

He had pulled at the younger man's sleeve, the smell of oil on his hands, a paint-spattered coat masking his naked upper body as Arrieta followed him into the dining room. A heavily carved dining table had been pushed up against one wall, the shutters half opened to allow some light, and much heat, to enter. In the middle of the wooden floor a bowl of luridly yellow lemons had given off an orchard scent.

As Goya had continued to tug at his arm, Arrieta had followed the painter's gesture towards the far wall. Nervously he had moved closer towards the huge image. Painted directly on to the plaster, the monstrous vision of Saturn shimmered in its meaty colours, the god maniacally tearing off the head of a nude.

'Remarkable,' Arrieta had said finally, as the artist drew his attention to the wall behind them.

This time the doctor had taken in a breath. The picture had also been painted directly on to the wall, but this time it was long and narrow, stretching almost the width of the dining room. Its meaning had been immediately apparent to Arrieta. It was a painting of a witches' Sabbath. But there was no gaiety in this depiction, no courtly titillation. The witches were gnarled, mad women, who in real life would smell and be scabby with lice. And the huge billy-goat shape of the Devil was no pictorial effect, just a blackened, inhuman misshape.

'What does it mean?' Arrieta asked, then repeated the words slowly so that Goya could lip-read.

He had taken a long moment to reply, then he had rubbed his temple, leaving a streak of paint at the corner of his eye.

'When I am are finished, then you will understand.'

A cat had leapt from the window sill on to the dining room floor. It had walked slowly towards the lemons then paused, a black shadow passing over the swollen fruit. And a memory came back to Arrieta in that moment; of a duchess rubbing lemon peel into her skin, trying, uselessly, to kill the smell of her dying.

20

Little Venice, London

'Nothing . . .'

Nodding, Roma Jaffe turned to see her second-in-command, Duncan Thorpe, walking over to join her on the restaurant balcony. He was thin, fair-haired, hardly out of his twenties, almost slow-looking, but clever.

'Nothing else on the canal, or the banks . . .'

'What about the card?'

'Just the two numbers on it,' Duncan replied, shrugging. 'Ben Golding's and another mobile number.'

'Not Golding's mobile?'

'I dunno. When I rang it was disconnected. We can't trace it.'

'And the laboratory couldn't get any prints on the card?'

'No prints either. It had been in the water so long there was nothing left.'

'The number must have been important, or it wouldn't have been left on the body.' Roma paused. 'After all, there was nothing else in the pockets. Someone wanted us to find those numbers.'

'We know one of them belongs to Dr Golding. That's a start.'

She nodded, thoughtful, as Duncan glanced behind him into the restaurant. 'I brought my girlfriend here once. Christ, they know how to charge.'

Roma let the comment pass. 'Nothing unusual about the blanket?'

'Cut from a piece of cloth which went out of production five years ago.'

'Naturally.' Roma checked her watch. 'They're doing the reconstruction at the Whitechapel now. Should be ready later today, or tomorrow. Then we do the usual: put up the posters and see who recognises him.'

'You want a coffee?'

She smiled wryly. 'Here? Can you afford it?'

'The manager said it was on the house,' Duncan replied, smiling as he walked off.

Her hair damped down from the rain, Roma Jaffe stood on the restaurant balcony overlooking the Little Venice canal. Behind her a group of waiters watched listlessly, as the manager tried to field off a reporter on the phone. His voice was raised, out of patience, the resounding bang of the receiver echoing out to the balcony where Roma was staring down into the water. A duck – that most innocuous of birds – paddled a comical pattern down the canal, disappearing under the stone archway, taking the same route as the mutilated body parts had done two days earlier.

Much as Roma had tried to prevent it, the press had got hold of the story and it had made headlines in the *Evening Standard* and in the dailies the following morning.

DISMEMBERED BODY
FOUND IN THAMES

The canal water was flicked with rain, drops making dwarf fountains on the surface. Perhaps it was because she was tired, but suddenly Roma wished that she had never taken on the task of heading up her own team of investigators. As Acting Head of the Murder Squad, her ambition had made her no friends. If anything, it had disturbed her previously smooth climb to the higher reaches of the London Metropolitan Police. After all the praise and promises of support, she had been left short-handed and short-funded, an opinionated harpy with something to prove.

'Coffee. Latte,' Duncan said, joining her. 'D'you think we'll ever find out who the victim was?'

'I hope so.' She changed the subject deftly. 'I didn't know you had a girlfriend.'

'Well, I see her now and again. Not really close.'

Roma sipped her coffee slowly, taking her time. She was hanging on to the priceless few minutes of quiet, watching the canal, relishing the escape from the phones. Her last case had been a murder in Holland Park. A drug addict had broken into an empty house to squat and found the remains of a woman who had been dead six months. Six whole months, Roma thought, in which no one had missed a visit or a phone call. Six months in which a young woman had mouldered in an expensive house. Eventually the victim had been named and her murderer caught. His explanation was simple: he picked her because he knew she wouldn't be missed.

He had been right.

'Well, here we go . . .' Roma said, staring at a text which had just appeared on her phone. 'Francis Asturias has come up trumps. Our faceless victim is no more. We've got a reconstruction.'

21

Humming to himself, Francis took off his gauntlets and looked at the reconstruction he had just completed. Not bad – not bad at all, he thought. All this practice was refining his art. He tilted his head to one side, scrutinising the very ordinary face he had just reconstructed. Caucasian male, around forty, with a slightly overshot jaw. Having toyed with the colour of the eyes, Francis had finally guessed grey; somehow it seemed to go with the man's face better than a darker shade. In fact, if he was honest, the victim's face was bland, his features veering on weakness. A man who would have passed unnoticed in a crowd.

Footsteps behind him made Francis turn as Ben walked up to the workbench and stared at the reconstructed head.

'You get the first look,' Francis told him. 'The police are on their way, but I promised you could have the first sneaky peek . . . So, do you recognise him?'

'No, I've never seen him before in my life.' He glanced over at Francis. 'How about you?'

'Means nothing to me.'

Ben watched as Francis turned away from the reconstruction, heading for the coffee machine. Careful not to be seen, he quickly took a photograph of the reconstruction, tucking his mobile back into his pocket as Francis returned.

Francis looked at his work thoughtfully. 'I'm fucking good at this, you know. I missed my calling – I should have been an artist. My old teacher said I had talent, but—'

Ben cut him off. 'Where's the Goya skull?'

Francis jerked his head towards a locked cupboard. 'In there. What's the problem?'

'And the reconstruction?'

'With it.'

'I have to ask you something, Francis. I need your help. I want you to make sure that the skull's safe. And that it stays here.'

Francis shrugged. 'It's going nowhere. No one even knows about it.'

'Good, because I'm going to Madrid tonight. Leon's sick. He wants the skull, but he mustn't have it. If he phones you, tell him I took it.'

'Anything else?'

'Don't tell him I'm on my way over to Spain,' Ben replied. 'I think he's in trouble.'

Francis sighed. 'I think you nursemaid your brother.'

'No, this is serious. Leon's off his medication, he's hyper, and I doubt he's had any sleep for days. Soon he'll have a collapse. Which could be dangerous, particularly now.'

'Why now?'

'Because he's in a mess.'

Francis laughed. 'Leon's *always* in a mess.'

'He's got obsessed with something he's working on. And it's unbalanced him . . . He was fifteen the first time he tried to kill himself. Of course, he might not be so bad this time. He might just start acting crazy. Like setting fire to his hair because he thinks it's full of spiders.'

'Shit . . .'

'It can get bad, and I don't want that.'

His mobile phone rang, interrupting them. Glancing at the unknown number, Ben picked up.

Leon's voice was shaking, panicked. '*You hung up on me!*'

'No, I didn't. The line failed. I'm glad you got another mobile.' Nodding to Francis, Ben walked out into the corridor to continue the conversation. 'Are you in your study?'

'Yes.'

'Good. Go on the internet and get into your emails.' He paused, waiting for Leon to do as he said. 'I sent you a photograph a little while ago. Is it there?'

'What photograph?'

'Just open the file, look at it, and tell me if you recognise the person.'

There was a short pause before Leon picked up the phone again. 'Where did you get this?'

'Just tell me if you recognise him.'

'It's the wrong hair colour, and his eyes were hazel. But yes, I know who it is. It's Diego Martinez. The builder who found Goya's skull and brought it to me.' Leon's voice wavered. 'Why have you got a photograph?'

'He was the man who was murdered in London. The man who had my card with your mobile number written on the back of it.'

Silence fell over the phone line. In Madrid Leon was staring at his computer screen, the face of the builder looking back at him. And as he looked at Diego Martinez he thought of Gabino Ortega and the fat man from England.

'Why would they kill Diego Martinez? Because of the skull . . .? Oh, Jesus, *because of the skull?*'

In London, Ben was trying to collect his thoughts.

'Leon, you have to stay calm. Take your tablets. Take them now while I'm on the phone. Can you hear me? Are you there? Hurriedly he moved into a vacant side ward, waiting for his brother's response. *'Are you there?'*

'Yes, yes,' Leon replied.

'Have you got your pills?'

He could hear banging on the other end of the phone, then Leon's bewildered voice. 'They aren't here!'

'They must be. Look again.'

'They're not bloody here!' he shouted. 'And Gina's not here either.'

Down the line, Ben could hear his brother's panic and the sound of running footsteps. Short of breath, Leon was panting down the phone.

'Her clothes are all gone! She's gone! Jesus, she's disappeared!'

'She might just have gone out—'

'*And leave the place messed up like this?*' Leon countered, his voice dropping, thick with unease. 'There's been a struggle here! There's been a fight. Someone must have taken her. Or they were looking for the skull. Or my papers. My papers! Jesus, where are my papers?' There was a flurry of activity over the line, then he spoke again. 'It's OK, I've got them! They're safe. I've got the papers. Jesus, it was that man at the Prado. It must be him. Or Gabino Ortega—'

'Leon, get out of the house.'

'They took her!'

Ben could feel his own heart speeding up. 'Do as I say, get out of there—'

'*Someone's taken Gina!*'

'Leon.' Ben fought to keep his voice steady. 'Listen to me—'

'*She's gone!*'

'Listen to me!' Ben shouted. 'Get a cab into Madrid.'

He could hear Leon's panic and the sound of him running from room to room in the old house. Then his brother's breathing, short and sharp, as though he was in shock.

'Leon, what is it? What is it?'

'I can hear footsteps upstairs.'

'Footsteps? Maybe it's Gina.'

Leon's voice was hardly audible. 'No, too heavy for her. It's a man's footsteps. *There's someone in the house* . . . Jesus! There's someone in the house.'

'Get out now!' Ben snapped. 'Go to the Melise hotel –

you know where that is. Get a room, and lock yourself in. Don't answer the phone or the door. I'll be there as soon as I can get to you. *Leon, are you listening?*'

'I should have rung that man back. I should have called him—'

'Get out of the house!'

'He said something would happen to me, and now he's taken Gina.' Suddenly Leon's voice stopped, silence over the line. Then he whispered. 'Someone's here. Someone's coming for me.'

'*Get out of there!*' Ben shouted.

An instant later he could hear the sound of his brother moving, running, taking the stairs hurriedly, the front door opening and then slamming closed. Clinging to the phone, Ben followed the rhythm of Leon's running feet: 'Are you out of the house?'

'I'm out,' Leon panted, 'I'm OK.'

'Make for the Hotel Melise. Stay there and wait for me.' He swallowed, fighting panic. 'Where are you now?'

'On the road. There's a car coming—'

'Make for the bridge, run over it, and keep running to the city. Don't get in any cars, unless a taxi comes along.'

'Jesus!' Leon panted, rapidly getting out of breath. 'I'm so scared.'

'Don't be scared. You're going to be OK. Where are you now?'

'There's a cab coming!'

'You're sure? It's got a light on it?'

'*Yes, yes! It's a cab!*' Leon shouted triumphantly.

Struggling to pick up the words, Ben could hear his brother talking to someone, then giving the address of the Hotel Melise. Finally he heard the sound of the car door slamming and the engine starting up.

'Are you OK?'

'I'm fine,' Leon answered. 'I'm on my way to the hotel.'

'Now, listen to me and do *exactly* what I say. Wait for me at the hotel. Don't go out, don't do anything. Don't trust anyone. Just wait for me. I'm coming, Leon. I'm on my way.'

22

Ten minutes later, Leon booked himself into the Hotel Melise, still clutching his notes and drawings. Hurriedly he flung them on to the hotel bed, locked the door and windows, then turned on the air conditioning. His head buzzed with the sonorous, mechanical sound, fear and fatigue dragging at him. Patting his pockets, he felt for his wallet and went over to the French windows that looked down into the street. There was no one around, certainly no one watching him.

He wondered if he could risk going out to see his doctor, but decided against it and instead lay down on the bed. The air conditioning murmured in the background, the fan whirling overhead as the sound of Madrid's night traffic mumbled behind the drawn blinds. Confused, Leon tried to reason with himself. *Had* he heard someone in the house or was he imagining it? But he hadn't imaged Gina's disappearance – she had gone. Or had she been taken? Where was she now? Was she alive or dead? He felt suddenly afraid, confused. Was it because he hadn't got in touch with the Englishman? Or because of Gabino

Ortega? Or was it because of what he'd found out? Was Goya's secret *that* important?

The fan coiled round and round overhead as Leon's eyes began to close. He should have taken his medication. Ben was right, he should have taken it. Not taking it meant he couldn't tell reality from fantasy. *Had* there been footsteps in the house? A burglary? *Had* Gina gone? His hands reached out across the bed to his briefcase, his fingers resting on the leather. Inside were his notes, his theory. Safe.

He would let himself sleep. The door was locked, the blinds drawn. He was safe. No one could see into the room, no one even knew he was there. And his brother was coming. Ben was on his way . . . Slicing the thick air, the fan blade spun, the sound mesmeric, hypnotic. Turning over on the bed, Leon closed his eyes. But the only images which came to him were of Goya and the Black Paintings, and the skull in the old cardboard box. Then Gina, leaning down to kiss him . . . Sweltering in the heat, he pulled off his shirt and trousers and walked into the bathroom. He would shower, wash the sweat off, make himself presentable for when his brother arrived. Prove that he wasn't a hysteric, out of control.

Turning on the taps, Leon stepped under the shower head. The water soaked his hair immediately, the perspiration and grime washing off his aching skin. His eyes closed and he fought a sudden desire to laugh. *He was safe; he was safe.* But the euphoria lasted only an instant, and in its place came pure, undiluted terror.

Someone was knocking on the door.

Pulling on a bathrobe, Leon moved into the bedroom and turned off the lamp and the fan. The place was suddenly silent, and clammy, the heat building up in seconds as he backed up against the wall. His head hummed, noises fluttering behind his eyes. He wasn't mad, he wasn't crazy, he told himself. He *had* heard footsteps at the house. And Gina *had* gone ... Under the door he could see the shadow of feet moving against the light, and held his breath. He wasn't mad. Someone was looking for him. He hadn't imagined it, after all. Someone was coming for him.

And he'd nowhere left to go.

23

Standing on the corner of the street, Jimmy Shaw watched the Hotel Melise. He had hardly slept the previous night, restless with pains in his back and legs, blood in his urine, his tongue darkening around the edges. Poisoned, alone and in a strange city, he had cried into his pillow like a child. His lumpen body hung on his bones heavily, his feet swelling painfully. His desire to live surprised him. He had no family and nothing to live for, but that didn't mean that he wanted to die.

For the first time Jimmy Shaw was experiencing the sordid lifestyle of his minions. People he had hired to do his dirty work in a dozen cities around the globe. Men he didn't care about or even think about. People paid, chivvied, threatened and cheated into line. Old lags, youngsters fresh off the streets, men who had fallen on hard times and into harder circles. People as remote from him as a maggot on the end of a fisherman's line. And now he was one of them. But not quite . . . Breathing heavily, air thick as soup in his lungs, Jimmy Shaw's voice was strained when he answered his mobile.

'Hello?'

'Shaw? It's Dwappa.' The African's voice was flat, without emotion. 'How are you feeling?'

'You're killing me.'

'Yes, I am,' Dwappa agreed. 'Which is why you have to get back to me soon. With the skull.'

'I'm on to it.'

'You know where it is?'

Shaw kept staring at the lighted hotel window, then wiped his forehead with a handkerchief. As he moved, he could smell the stench from his other hand and a burning sensation creeping up the veins of his arm. But his plan was still there, slipping through the miasma of his sickness.

'What if I die before I get the skull?'

'You won't.'

'What if I do?' Shaw persisted. 'You've poisoned me, you fucker, what if I don't get back to you in time?'

'You want to live, don't you?'

Shaw was sticky with sweat, matter collected at the corners of his eyes. 'What if you've tricked me?' he said, his voice harsh. 'What if you *can't* cure me? What if I get back to London, give you the skull – and I still die?' His cunning was automatic, vicious. 'I've been thinking about that. And wondering – what's to stop me getting the skull for myself and selling it to someone else?'

Dwappa kept the surprise out of his voice. 'By your reasoning, you'd still die.'

'But you wouldn't get the skull, would you?' Shaw

remarked, coughing and then spitting into the gutter. 'You see, I've been thinking about it, Dwappa, and I think that if I return with the skull you won't let me live anyway. Why should you? Why should you pay me when you can just wait for the poison to finish me off? No fee, no witness.' He was still watching the lighted hotel window, dangerous and desperate.

'I'm the only one who can save you, Shaw.'

'Well, be that as it may, I'm the only one who can get the skull. So, you see, I want a new arrangement.'

Wrong-footed, Dwappa hissed down the line: 'What new arrangement?'

'I want my fee now—'

'Hah!'

'I want the money now, Dwappa,' Shaw warned him, thinking of Gabino Ortega, 'or I sell the skull to someone else. You won't get it—'

'If I don't get it, you'll die.'

'My life for the skull.'

Dwappa took in a breath. 'It was *always* your life for the skull.'

'Pay me my fee in advance and I'll deliver,' Shaw replied steadily. 'I'll send details of the bank account to pay the money into, then wait till it's cleared. *Then* I'll come back with the skull.'

'What's to stop me killing you then and retrieving the money?'

'You think I'd leave it in an account you had details of?' Shaw countered. His brain was working fast although his breathing was becoming more laboured with every breath. 'Soon as I get it, I'll move the money on to somewhere you can't find it. Fuck, the Inland Revenue and the police can't find it, so you've no chance. That's what I'm good at – leaving no paper trail. You won't get the money back, Dwappa. And if you let me die, you lose the money *and* the skull. You pay me in advance, you cure me, and you get the skull. It's simple.'

He was gambling with his life and he knew it. Dwappa was the only person who could save him, but only if forced to do so. It was in Dwappa's interests to keep him alive, not kill him. Shaw knew how the African's mind worked and Dwappa certainly wouldn't let him die when he'd cheated him. He would come after Shaw instead. After Shaw *and* the money.

But he would worry about that later. From a distance.

24

When Ben finally arrived in Madrid it was late at night. And hot. Exhausted and unshaven, he caught a cab to the Hotel Melise, half running into the lobby towards the Reception area.

'I'm Ben Golding. My brother's staying here. Dr Leon Golding?'

The tired night porter looked at the reception book wearily. 'Oh yes,' he said in heavy accented English. 'In room 230. Second floor.'

Hurriedly, Ben walked to the lift, then decided against it and made for the stairs. Climbing as fast as he could, he came to the second floor and checked the room numbers, taking a right turn at the end of the corridor. Finally, he found room 230 and knocked.

'Leon, it's me, Ben. Let me in.'

There was no answer. He knocked again. 'Leon! Wake up! It's me. Open the door.'

Again, no answer. Uneasy, Ben tried the handle then turned it, the door unexpectedly opening. Slowly he walked in, flicking on the light and catching his breath. The bed was crumpled, sheets scattered, a chair overturned.

'Leon?' Ben called out, looking round the room. '*Leon?*'

Warily he pulled back the blind and glanced at the balcony. Unlocking the French windows, he walked out, then moved over to the edge and peered down, relieved to see nothing lying on the hotel forecourt below. His nerves on edge, he turned back into the room and relocked the windows, his body straining for any sound or movement.

'Leon?' he said again, jumping as the air conditioning kicked in, the fan overhead beginning its queasy swirl into the hot air.

Panicked, Ben looked around the room once more. Maybe Leon – despite all he had said – had just gone out? Maybe it had been his brother who had made the mess in the room. It wasn't beyond him, in his present mental state. Whatever had happened, there was nothing more he could do except wait. He wouldn't jump to any sinister conclusions, he would just wait until his brother got back . . .

Moving into the bathroom, Ben bent over the washbasin and ran some cold water, closing his eyes and splashing it over his face. Behind him, he could hear the fan whirling and the soft creak of the bathroom door swinging closed. Reaching for a towel, he dried his face and then opened his eyes.

In the mirror he could see the room reflected behind him – and the body of his brother, face bloated, tongue black and protruding, hanging suspended behind the door.

25

London

Moving down the backstairs of Mama Gala's shop, Emile Dwappa paused, listening. Beyond the curtain which separated the shop from the back rooms he could hear the fat woman laughing with a customer, his gaze flickering towards the tamarin monkey in the cage at the foot of the stairs. The animal stared at him, its pale eyes unblinking, as Dwappa reached for a piece of apple on the cage floor. At once the monkey scuttled to the back of the cage, hunched in the furthest corner, as Dwappa held out the fruit between his thumb and forefinger.

Immobile, the monkey regarded him. Only yards away the snakes uncurled themselves, one slinking towards the glass and raising its head. Dwappa kept holding out the fruit, and a moment later the monkey rushed towards him, grabbing for the slice of apple.

'What you doing?' Mama Gala said, walking through. 'I don't want the monkey feeding.'

Ignoring her, Dwappa let the animal take the apple, Mama Gala making a snorting sound as she glanced upwards.

'You haven't left that woman upstairs, have you?' she went on. 'I don't want her here. Always stoned, always stumbling round. She's no good to you – you should get rid of her.'

'Maybe I should get rid of you.'

Her fat hand went out and patted Dwappa's cheek in mock tenderness.

'You'll never get rid of me, baby boy. I'm your mama; you need me. And besides, I'm not afraid of you. I kept your father under control, and he was a mean son of a bitch. He learnt from me, you hear me? He learnt tricks from *me*. So don't get ideas, Emile. And if anyone should be afraid of anyone, you should be afraid of me.' She laughed, a booming from the guts.

He could feel the muscles at the back of his neck tighten, but kept his face expressionless. It irked him that his mother had such control. It plagued him that he did, indeed, stand in awe of her. That she terrified him. Her bulk had borne down on his whole life, her corruption fascinating and contagious. There was nothing he could think, or do, that would be new to her. Nothing that would shock her. She had the knowledge from the old country and used it with the swinging confidence of the totally corrupt.

He smiled at her with closely mimicked affection. From his earliest memories, Emile recalled how his father had told him about Mama Gala. Had spoken in revered tones about the stout woman who looked so benign and was so poisonously callous. Back in Nigeria she had been almost revered and when Dwappa Senior invited her London he had been half surprised, half proud, when she accepted his marriage proposal. There was no woman as casually cruel, as naturally unfeeling. Behind the round dark-skinned face which pretended kindness there was a terrible cunning. Mama Gala knew only too well how her appearance deceived people. No one would suspect her of anything sinister. By day she ran a health food shop – that was all. Talked to her neighbours, made jokes with the local police, waddled into the park with next door's toddlers. Known for her kindness, her advice.

But Emile Dwappa knew the other side. Knew that when the shop was closed at night, the lights turned off, that benign face dropped its pretence. Then Mama Gala moved upstairs to the flat above. She harried the old woman, who no one ever referred to by name, and ran her hands over the chopped herbs, making pouches of coarse leather and filling them with potions she knew the superstitious would buy. Mixing cereal with ground-up bone, animal urine and powdered herbs, she muttered incantations over the table top, her face sweating with the effort, her flabby arms wobbling in their short cotton sleeves. Once she had kept a turtle in a fish tank – the reptile huge, too big for the space, the water murky in days. Mama Gala had lifted the creature out with one jerk, slamming it on the table and driving a knife repeatedly into its soft underbelly.

Within seconds she had been covered in blood, smelling of it.

Gigantic and grotesque, she could have been amusing, but her expression, and the aura she gave off, was fetid. How many times had Dwappa seen her greet people who had hurried up the narrow stairs to the dim room above? How many gullible people had been sold potions and then threatened into silence, warned not to talk about her business outside? And God, no one ever did. Not more than once, anyway. There *had* been one young man, a year earlier, who Dwappa had hired to pimp for him. Bony and glib, he had hung around Mama Gala's shop doorway and smoked cannabis on the street outside, making obscene hand signals to the girls who walked past. Not overly bright, he had never believed in Mama Gala's covert reputation, and had made jokes about voodoo without realising that for her it was more than power, it was a religion.

Soon after the lanky pimp went missing. Three months later his remains were found in Shoreditch, a nail driven through his skull. No one talked about Mama Gala after that . . . Wary, Dwappa studied his mother. Wondered how it was that her weight obliterated her wrinkles, belying her age and making a malevolent child out of her.

'I want you to get that addict out from upstairs,' she said curtly. 'The bitch will bring the police round. We don't need that. I don't want anyone drawing attention to this place, you hear me?' She lost her patience fast.

'You said you were working on something. That you were going to make a fucking fortune—'

'I am. I've got a couple of things going.'

She put her head on one side and tapped his cheek. 'Pretty boy. Mummy's pretty boy. Like your daddy, hah?' Her hand moved away, her expression curdling. 'My queer little baby.'

He flinched, flushing, and she laughed, making a clumsy child out of him. Reminding him of when she had found him, years earlier, with his best friend. Didn't do to be gay in Brixton, she had told him. Didn't do to be homosexual when you were the son of Mama Gala ... She had wielded the information like a machete. Every argument ended in a sexual insult; every attempt to stand up to her was hobbled by a homophobic joke. Mama Gala didn't care if her son was gay or not, but she knew that *he* cared. And she knew that if people found out that Emile Dwappa was a fag, his reputation was over.

She never said that she would betray him. She didn't have to. Emile Dwappa knew his mother. He hated his mother. He feared his mother – and that kept him in line.

'You get enough money to get us out of here. You promised me that.' She narrowed her eyes. 'Or you think you make your fortune and up and leave your mama? That what you want, boy? To leave your mama?'

'I never said I'd leave you.'

'You'd die without me. Remember, I'm the only person

173

in the world who gives a shit about you. Without me, you're alone. Poor queer baby on your own. There's no one to look out for you but me. So you get us money, hey? You get that new house you promised.'

'I'm working on it.'

'Working on it?' Slowly she shook her head, her expression unflinching, feral. 'Well, work harder.'

26

'I'll come home,' Abigail said simply over the line from France. 'I'll get the first flight I can.'

Two days earlier she had hurried over to France to be with her father, who had had a stroke. They had never been particularly close, but she hadn't wanted him to be alone in hospital. And besides, arrangements had to be made for a nurse to stay with him when she returned to England. Her dutiful response had met with unexpected affection, the stroke releasing some of her father's usual reserve. Indeed – to Abigail's amazement – he had even talked about her mother, long since estranged from both of them.

But now Abigail's whole concern was centred on her lover. 'Darling, did you hear me?'

'Stay with your father,' Ben replied, his voice low as he sat, head bowed, in the laboratory of the Whitechapel Hospital. 'He needs you.'

'You need me too.'

'No, not like he does,' Ben replied, trying to get the image of his murdered brother out of his mind. The image which had haunted him all the time he was talking to the Spanish police. The image which had plagued him on the flight home to London. The image which he knew would never – however long he lived – lessen or diminish. It was burned into him. 'I should have got there earlier—'

'It wasn't your fault,' Abigail said softly. 'Leon was always struggling—'

'He was brilliant.'

'Yes,' she agreed. 'He was brilliant and you loved him and he loved you. He thought the world of you, Ben. But your brother was troubled.'

'You think he killed himself?'

She faltered on the line. 'You said that the police told you he'd killed himself.'

'Leon didn't commit suicide.'

'Ben,' she said gently, 'he'd tried it twice before.'

'It wasn't suicide.'

'All right, so what else could it be?'

He didn't answer her. Had already decided that Abigail was to be left in ignorance. The less he told her, the safer she would be. In fact, Ben was relieved that she had been called to France, away from London. Away from him and any connection to Leon Golding. Because his brother *hadn't* killed himself. He had been murdered. Just like Diego Martinez.

'Abi?'

'Yes?'

'I have to go now. I'll call you later.'

'Will you be all right?'

He nodded, then remembered that she couldn't see him. 'I'll be OK.'

'Make sure you eat something,' she said, clinging to the phone. 'I wish I was with you.'

'I know. I know.'

Silent, Francis Asturias watched Ben finish his phone call and then reached into his desk and pulled out a half bottle of brandy. 'You need a drink.' Pouring out two measures into glasses, he pushed one over towards Ben, who ignored it. Thoughtful, Francis downed his own drink and began to pick at the label on the bottle.

He had never known Leon Golding, but he had heard about him. About his ability and his instability. And on the occasions Ben had confided in him, Francis had learned about Leon's suicide attempts and the whole messy clotting of mental instability which had dogged his life. He had commiserated with Ben and never stated the obvious – that Leon Golding was profoundly, incurably unstable.

Again, Francis pushed the glass closer towards Ben, but there was no response. His face was expressionless, shock taking all colour from his skin. He seemed bloodless, as though his veins had been siphoned off as easily as a night thief would drain the tank of a deserted car. Outside, the lights went on in the Whitechapel streets, the glass dome of the lecture hall making a hot swelling into the London night.

Francis wasn't ready to risk words. He had listened instead when Ben returned to work, blank with disbelief and shock. In a flat voice he had told Francis how he had found his brother, then called the Spanish police. How the ambulance had taken Leon away in a body bag, the zipper closing over his distorted face.

After Leon had been moved to the mortuary Ben had insisted that the death was murder and demanded an autopsy. Something which would have happened automatically – if the police hadn't investigated Leon's life and uncovered his mental instability. From then on, they believed that Leon Golding had taken his own life. It had happened before, they told Ben. A depressed man hires a hotel room and then hangs himself . . .

'He wouldn't have done it,' Ben said suddenly, looking over at Francis. 'Leon was terrified that night. He was running for his life . . . I told the police about his phone call to me. And about Gina going missing.'

'What did they say about that?'

'That she was at the house when they went over later,' Ben replied, his expression challenging. 'But Leon told me she'd gone. He was insistent. He said that the bedroom had been wrecked, that her clothes had been taken. He thought they'd kidnapped her.'

'They?' Francis said softly.

'The same people who were after him.'

'And who were they?'

Slowly Ben turned to look his old friend straight in the face. 'Leon *was* running away from someone. He phoned me. I heard his panic. I heard his fear—'

'He wasn't taking his medicine.'

'He wasn't crazy!' Ben retorted sharply.

'He wasn't on his medication. You know how that affected your brother's judgement,' Francis went on, his tone calm. 'Leon had become obsessed with the Goya business. You told me that yourself, Ben. You said he was out of his depth—'

'That's right,' Ben agreed. 'Leon *was* out of his depth. And that's what killed him.'

Sighing, Francis pushed the glass again. Now it was pressing against Ben's forearm, but he still didn't pick it up.

'My brother didn't kill himself.'

'Have you spoken to Gina?'

Ben nodded. 'She's distracted. Crying. Saying that she shouldn't have gone to stay with her friend that night – that none of this would have happened if she'd stayed home ... Apparently Leon had shut himself off, and she thought he wanted to be alone. She said she'd told him where she was going, that he knew her girlfriend and had the phone number. She said that her clothes hadn't all gone – she'd just taken the ones she had with her that night.'

'So Leon was wrong about that?'

'I dunno,' Ben said, shaking his head. 'Their relationship was on and off. In the past Gina had left him for a while, then come back when Leon had calmed down. He loved her, but I don't know how much she loved him. She didn't take good enough care of him—'

Francis cut him off.

'But she wasn't kidnapped, was she? Leon was wrong.'

'Meaning that if he was wrong about that, he was wrong about the rest?' Ben asked, his tone challenging. 'That there was no one in the house? No one after him?'

Francis paused before answering. 'OK, if someone *was* after Leon, why?'

'For the skull.'

'*What?*'

'Goya's skull.'

'He didn't have it!'

'They thought he did,' Ben said. 'I told him to keep it quiet, but Leon couldn't. He said he hadn't told anyone, but Gabino Ortega knew about it and Leon said some Englishman had wanted to buy it from him.' Ben paused, about to confide about Diego Martinez, but changed his mind. Francis was a friend. He didn't need endangering.

'Who's Gabino . . .?'

'*Ortega*. He belongs to one of the richest and most infamous families in Spain. His grandfather was a murderer.'

'Shit . . . And who was the Englishman?'

'I don't know,' Ben said honestly.

Taking a long drink, Francis stared ahead for a while before continuing, 'You really think Leon was murdered?'

'God, how many times do I have to say it!' Ben snapped, finally taking the brandy and downing it in one shot.

'But how likely is it that someone killed your brother? And even if they did, why would they just to get a *skull*? I've got six in the fridge – they're welcome to them . . . Oh, come on, Ben, it doesn't make sense.'

'Where is it?'

'*What?*'

'Goya's skull.'

Rising to his feet, Francis moved over to the end of the laboratory and unlocked the fridge, calling over his shoulder, 'You want the original or the reconstructed head?'

'Both,' Ben replied, moving over to Francis's workbench and watching as he put down the skull. 'What's it worth?'

'Bugger all.'

'Unless it's famous,' Ben went on, staring at it curiously. 'Could it contain anything?'

Francis stuck his finger into the empty skull and wiggled it round. 'Nope.'

'What about inside the bone itself?'

'Nothing.'

'The teeth?'

'Nothing.'

'How d'you know?'

'Because it underwent scans when I was trying to authenticate it, that's how. Anyway, Goya hardly had any teeth left when he died.'

'What about the bone itself? Anything unusual?'

'There might have been. But after all these years most defects or diseases would be impossible to detect.'

Sighing, Ben reached for the powerful magnifying glass lying on the workbench beside him. Turning the skull around in his left hand, he peered at it from all angles.

'What *are* you looking for?'

'Anything.'

Disappointed, he put down the magnifying glass and then the skull. 'There are no markings, just age damage. Nothing clever, no words or symbols.'

'Not even a bar code.'

'It's valuable simply because it's Goya . . .' Ben went on, staring at the skull. 'I know how coveted these relics are. Museums would love it. The Prado would certainly want it, to exhibit next to Goya's paintings. I mean, no other museum has got anything like it. The best the Tate Gallery could come up with was Turner's death mask.'

'Did a museum or gallery approach Leon direct?'

'The Prado gave him free rein. It was Leon's find, it was his triumph.'

'Maybe there was something else which had caught people's interest, as well as the skull.'

'There was. Leon was working on a theory about the Black Paintings. He was researching Goya's life when he died.' Ben paused. 'Not that he needed to do a lot of that. We were brought up by a woman who was always talking about the painter, always filling Leon's head with stories. Spooking him.' He glanced over at Francis. 'This was my brother's big chance. Goya's skull would have made him famous and solving the riddle of the Black Paintings would have compounded his success.'

'How far had he got?'

'He said he was nearly finished.'

Francis raised his eyebrows. 'So what *do* the paintings mean?'

Ben shrugged.

'I didn't ask him. When he said he was talking to people involved with the occult I panicked. I warned him off because of what happened to . . .' He trailed off, censoring himself, unwilling to talk about Diego Martinez. 'I didn't want Leon being so reckless.'

'But he didn't listen?'

'No, he said people were approaching him via the internet. I know for a fact that he'd seen a medium—'

'Bloody hell.'

'He was grasping at straws. They had a seance, you know.'

'Don't tell me,' Francis said drily. 'They got through to Goya.'

'I think my brother actually believed that they could.' Ben sighed. 'The medium's a friend of Gina's, a man called Frederick Lincoln. She told me he was trustworthy. But even if no one gossiped outright, people knew that Leon was researching the Black Paintings and had found a skull which he thought was Goya's—'

'It was.'

They both looked at the skull, Ben the first to speak. 'Did *you* tell anyone?'

'No,' Francis replied, his tone injured.

'I had to ask.'

'No you fucking didn't.'

Carefully, Ben picked up the skull again. 'Can you put it into storage? Mark the box CAUTION – ANIMAL REMAINS so that no one will open it?'

Francis nodded. 'Easy. But what are you going to do now?'

'Clear my brother's name. I know what people are saying about Leon – that he was unstable, that he killed himself. Why not? He'd tried before, it's an obvious conclusion to jump to. If he hadn't been my brother, maybe I would have said the same. But he *was* my brother, Francis, and I loved him and knew him better than anyone on earth. *And I know he was murdered.*'

'If you're right,' Francis said quietly, 'then you might be in danger too.'

'I know . . . But someone killed my brother and they're not getting away with it.' He gestured to the skull. 'Hide it, Francis, and then forget about it. Forget everything I've told you. Everything.'

27

Madrid, Spain

The following day dawned thick with the threat of a storm. Sapping heat clung heavy on the air, the breeze swamped, hardly able to move the dust. Composed, Gina walked into Leon's study and sat at his desk, fingering the pen he had last used. In front of her some papers were torn, others piled high in no particular order, a few rough drawings tossed into the waste-paper basket. Idly, she reached into the bin and smoothed out a piece of paper, an amateur drawing of a bull staring inanely at her. Leon had never been a gifted artist. He had wanted – longed – to be able to paint, but it wasn't his forte.

Holding the paper to her lips momentarily Gina turned as she heard footsteps behind her. 'Are you all right?'

Nodding, Ben moved over to the desk, avoiding her eyes. 'They've finally agreed to do an autopsy on Leon.'

Her voice was dull. 'Why did they change their minds?'

'I insisted – called on some of my medical contacts.'

'Why an autopsy?'

He paused, staring past her into the hall beyond. Childhood memories came swinging back – Leon running down from the hot summer playroom into the hallway and slipping on the floor which Detita kept as shiny as a plate of black glass. Leon as a child, struggling like a netted fish against the suffocation of his instability. Leon as a young man, passionate but muted with medication. Happy at times ... Ben kept staring, almost seeing his brother coming from the back garden with a handful of soil.

We have to keep this, Ben.

What for?

If you keep the soil from the place you love most, you'll never leave.

And now Leon as Ben had last heard him on the phone, panicked, his voice urgent. Running down the same stairs, skidding on the same black-ice floor, racing for safety. And not finding it.

'Ben?' Timidly Gina reached out her hand and brushed his. 'Ben, I'm sorry ...'

He looked down at her, his voice puzzled. 'What for?'

'For not being here. For leaving Leon,' she answered, tears beginning hot and slow like the Manzanares river beyond. 'I should have stayed that night.'

'So why *did* you go, Gina?'

'He was angry with me for disturbing him. He wanted to be left alone to work.'

'But he'd stopped taking his medication. Why didn't you make him take it?'

'You couldn't make Leon do anything he didn't want to!' she snapped back. 'You know that as well as I do.'

Her hand reached for his again, but again he didn't take it. He couldn't offer comfort because he wanted to blame her, punish her, even though it wasn't her fault. And he knew that. Had always known that one day Leon would go too far, drop too fast, before any of them – parent, brother, lover – could catch him. His decline had been inevitable, as much a part of him as his expressions and habits. The rapid reflexes, the way he put his feet up on his desk and clasped his hands behind his head. The way he gobbled up information and then passed it on, his hands working with the words as though – if either paused – the whole conversation would evaporate.

'I loved him, you know.'

Ben nodded but didn't reply immediately, and when he did, his tone was incisive.

'You should never have put him in danger—'

'I didn't hurt him! How did I endanger him?' she hurled back.

'You encouraged him with his book about the Black Paintings. You let him get involved in the occult, when you knew it would be bad for anyone as fragile as my brother. You shouldn't have introduced him to people like Frederick Lincoln. You knew how vulnerable he was. Didn't you realise he might be in danger?'

'From whom? Frederick is a friend. I told you, I've known him since I was a kid. His family lived in America for a while, near us. We used to play together, then they went back to Holland when Frederick was in his early teens.' She took in a ragged breath. 'I would trust him with my life—'

'You certainly trusted him with Leon's.'

Stunned, she leaned forward in her seat, her eyes hostile. 'I would never have done anything to hurt your brother! If you were so worried about Leon, why didn't you come over to Spain more often? I was always there for him—'

'Except when you walked out.'

'We had a fight! Couples do. We were no different.' She was openly hostile. 'You were certainly relieved when we got back together. It took some of the pressure off you, didn't it, Ben?' She kicked out at the chair in front of her. 'Don't try to attack me to cover up your own feelings of guilt!'

Shaken, Ben struggled to breathe, Gina's words resonating in his head, their accuracy damning. It was true, he *had* been glad that Gina was back in his brother's life. He *had* wanted a breathing space, time to work on his own relationship with Abigail. Time to catch up on his own life.

'I'm sorry for what I just said,' Gina murmured, shamefaced. 'I shouldn't have been so hard on you.'

'Maybe we should both have looked after him better.'

She took a breath, choosing her next words carefully. 'I have to know something . . . Will you tell me the truth?'

'If I can.'

'Why was Leon in danger?'

'There was someone in the house. Leon heard them. He thought he was going to be killed.'

Incredulous, she shook her head. '*Killed? Why?*'

'You know why.'

'No, I don't!'

'Didn't Leon tell you what had been happening lately?'

'Like what?'

He couldn't tell if she was lying and continued warily. 'D'you know someone called Diego Martinez?'

She shook her head.

'Gabino Ortega?'

'I've read about the Ortega family.' She paused, staring at Ben. 'What have they got to do with any of this?'

'Leon didn't kill himself. There was more to it than that.'

She shook her head impatiently. 'You *can't* make a conspiracy out of this, Ben. You have to admit the truth. Your brother was only ever a danger to himself. We both know he'd been suicidal before—'

'Leon *didn't* kill himself.'

She stiffened in her seat, her eyes suspicious. 'How can you be so sure?'

'Because my brother was on to something. He had the one thing he'd been searching for all his life. A way to make the big time. He would never have killed himself.'

'He was hyper, manic,' she blundered on. 'I kept telling him to go back on his medication. I begged him, but he refused. And then he told me was taking it again. I didn't believe him, but I didn't want to argue with him in case he did something stupid.'

'Like what?'

'Like go away. Cut me out entirely.'

'Leon would never have gone away,' Ben replied dismissively. 'He was committed to what he was working on. He was excited about it—'

'He was sick!'

'*He was winning*,' Ben insisted. 'You knew him, Gina, but I knew him better. When he attempted suicide before, it was because he was lost, drifting. But when he got that skull, Leon knew he was on the edge of a triumph. That's why I *know* he didn't kill himself.'

'But if he didn't commit suicide, that means someone killed him.' She shuddered. 'Who?'

'I don't know.'

Unnerved, she struggled with the idea. 'But why would anyone kill Leon?'

'I don't know that either.'

He wasn't sure of anything any more – whether Gina was in some way culpable, or whether she was also in danger. He couldn't read her.

'Leon told me that he was talking to people on the phone and over the internet.'

'He was,' she agreed. 'And a man came to talk to him last week . . . What's all this about? The skull?' She turned to Ben, her face as white as a dying moon. '*Does someone want that skull?*'

'Gina—'

'*But he didn't have it!*' she shouted, suddenly panicking.

'He was having it authenticated in Madrid. You know that. He didn't have it.'

'Gina, try and calm down—'

But she was scared, getting to her feet and moving around restlessly. 'I don't know where it is now. God, what if someone thinks it's here? They could come here . . . *Could they hurt me?*'

'No one's going to harm you—'

'How d'you know that?' she countered. 'You're talking about Leon being murdered, and going on about that bloody skull. Well, I was involved. Jesus, *I was involved.*'

Levelly, he held her gaze.

'It might be safer if you left here. Go home to the USA, Gina. Let me sort this out.'

'I can't go away! I can't just up and leave. This was *my* home too. Leon was my partner – how can you expect me to walk away?'

'It would be safer for you—'

'Why don't you just find the skull?' she asked, impatient and rattled. 'Don't *you* know where it is?' Suspicious, she stared at him. 'You do, don't you?'

A beat passed between them. Ben saw the hesitation and noted it. Did she think he was lying to her? And if so, why? Did she think he suspected her of something?

'Well, *do* you know where the skull is?'

'No,' he lied.

'But surely you could find out? You could ask around, track down Leon's contacts. They would talk to you . . . Find it, Ben. Please. I'll help you.'

Her voice dropped suddenly, as though she had lost power. Moving to the window, she closed the shutters, the house stifling and silent around them.

'You don't trust me, do you?'

He ignored the question and returned to something she had said earlier. 'What did the man look like? The man who called here?'

She closed her eyes to help herself remember. 'He was dark-skinned, maybe African, tall, about thirty-five.'

'What was his name?'

She shrugged. 'I dunno.'

'Did he come by car?'

'Yes, a cab.'

'And he was on his own?'

'Yeah . . . I showed him into the library and called for Leon.'

'How did he react when he saw him?'

'Fine. Said hello and offered him a seat. They seemed to get on.'

'As though they already knew each other?'

She thought for a moment. 'No, not like that. But the man was very charming, easy to like. In fact I could hear them laughing when I went to make some coffee. When I took it in to them the man was saying that he would contact Leon by email.'

'Then what?'

'A little while later Leon came to bed and fell asleep.'

'He didn't seem upset? Afraid?'

'No. He fell asleep almost at once,' she replied. 'Is the visit important?'

'I don't know. But I want to see Leon's emails.'

Surprised, Gina stared at him. 'He never mentioned any emails from this man—'

'You said he was being secretive.'

'About some things!' she snapped. 'But not everything. Your brother always told me if he was worried. There was nothing he was scared of, nothing that spooked him. He would have told me.'

'I still want to see the emails,' Ben repeated. 'Please.'

A low, dark headache beginning, he followed Gina as she moved into Leon's study and flicked on the light. The memory was almost unbearable . . . Leon passing the skull to Ben that first day; Leon standing in the doorway, listening and watching, as astute and nervous as a child . . . Turning on the computer, Gina accessed the emails and then drew up the list of incoming messages, some with names as a heading, others completely anonymous. Unknown people from anonymous places, Ben thought uneasily. But they had all known where Leon Golding had been and where to find him.

Carefully Ben read every email. Some were in answer to Leon's enquiries, others obvious cons.

I agree that the painter was not in his right mind. That is why the paintings are not to be trusted, or believed. However, if you send me $400 I can forward some original, and insightful, information.

'Crazy.'

Over his shoulder, Gina was also reading the emails, her finger suddenly jabbing at the screen as an address came up: Gortho@3000.com.

'That rings a bell.'

The message read:

I could call by on Thursday. The gallery would be most interested and would give you full credit.

'No name on it,' Ben said. 'Anything kosher would have a proper name.'

'Unless they were trying to make sure no one else could contact them.'

Ben glanced over his shoulder. 'I thought you didn't believe in a conspiracy?'

'I don't know what to believe any more,' she replied crisply, turning her gaze back to the screen. 'What was it referring to?'

'The skull, I suppose.'

She chewed the side of her fingernail thoughtfully, watching as Ben typed a note in reply to the email and pressed the SEND button. A moment later a reply came back stating that the message could not be received as the address no longer existed.

'Dead end,' he said bitterly.

'Damn it! Do we *have* to wait until the authenticator of the skull gets in touch with us?' Gina asked, her tone wary. 'I mean, can't we approach them?'

Inwardly, Ben flinched, thinking of the skull he had left at Francis's laboratory in London. The skull Gina thought was still in Spain.

'They *would* come back to us with the results, wouldn't they? Or would they contact the Prado direct, now that Leon's . . .?' She stopped, fighting emotion. 'You have to talk to them.'

'I've been in touch already.'

'Oh,' she said listlessly. The computer screen threw a greenish cast on her face as she stared at the list of emails. 'What did you say?'

'That Leon didn't commit suicide.'

'Did you tell them that you thought he'd been murdered?'

'Yes.'

'Was that wise?' she asked, turning to him, the green light playing on her profile.

'We're talking about the Prado, Gina. Not a bunch of gangsters.'

'I don't know what to think about anyone any more,' she replied, her tone lost. 'Did they ask you *who* killed Leon?'

'No. I don't think they believed me. After all, it was no secret that Leon had tried to commit suicide before.'

'Was he . . . was he . . . dead when you found him?' Gina asked, her voice breaking.

Ben closed his eyes for a moment before replying. 'Yes, he was dead.'

'I just wondered if he said anything . . . you know . . .'

'He was dead when I got there,' Ben repeated, touching the back of her hand briefly. 'And no, he didn't say anything. He didn't leave a note either. No explanation. And if Leon *had* committed suicide, he would have left a note. He did before.'

Her head bowed, Gina dropped her voice even further.

'Ben?'

'Yes?'

'Did Leon tell you about the baby?'

28

'You must keep it a secret. You can't tell anyone what I'm about to tell you,' Ellen Armstrong said, her voice lowered as she leaned across the table towards Bobbie Feldenchrist. 'I would be in such trouble. But I'm telling you because you confided in me the other day and because it might be a way out of your . . . problem.'

Sipping a glass of Chablis, Bobbie raised her eyebrows. She was dressed in a cream Chanel suit with a brown silk blouse, her amber hair drawn back into a chignon. Immaculately distant, she observed the rotund woman in the seat next to hers. Bobbie knew only too well that Ellen needed her as a friend, just as she knew that Marty Armstrong was a brilliant man. His capacity for invention was impressive, but he had little business sense, and that was where Bobbie came in. On a number of occasions she had offered advice to Ellen, advice she knew would be passed on and acted on. Which it always was. In return,

Bobbie had Ellen's devotion. The only caring, maternal influence in her life. Because Ellen Armstrong was that rarity in New York – a kind woman who could keep her mouth shut.

'What "problem", Ellen?'

Her voice lowered. 'About your adoption.'

'It's delayed.'

'Oh, Bobbie,' she said, pulling at the cuff of one of her sleeves. 'We know that's not true, honey. I heard it fell through.'

'How did you hear that?'

'Marty heard, and he told me.'

Taking another sip of Chablis, Bobbie stared across the restaurant, her face impassive. How Marty Armstrong knew so many intimate details, about so many important lives, was a mystery to everyone. But somehow he always knew the gossip, somehow he always sussed out a person's secret or weakness. Luckily for Bobbie, the Armstrongs were on her side.

'Ellen,' she said quietly, 'if you've something to say, say it. I hate mysteries.'

'I know of someone who could get you a baby,' Ellen replied. 'Quickly. No questions asked. It would cost you, but that's not a problem, is it? This man could be the answer to your prayers.'

'Who is he?'

Ellen leaned back in her seat. 'Are you interested?'

'I might be,' Bobbie admitted, a vein in her neck beginning to throb. 'How quickly could he get me a child?'

'Within days.'

Bobbie's eyebrows rose. 'Is it legal?'

'Does that matter?' Ellen countered, leaning back over the table. 'You want a baby, Bobbie, and I don't believe that postponement story of yours. No one does really. We all think you were let down.' She paused, her tone sympathetic. 'Everyone knows how difficult the adoption services are. All that paperwork, even for someone like you. And there's a shortage of American babies. Children that would be more likely to go to a proper family. Or at least a couple.' The words hit deep and Bobbie pushed her glass away from her.

'I know all this.'

'So let me help you to cut through all the red tape.'

'I don't want to get involved in anything illegal, Ellen. It wouldn't do for the Feldenchrist name.'

'How badly do you want a baby?'

'You know how badly.'

'Then take this help.' Ellen smiled, hurrying on. 'Oh, Bobbie, you have a score of lawyers on your side. If anything went wrong you could bury this man without breaking into a sweat. You've got a name that no one would go up against.'

Pausing, Bobbie allowed the waiter to lay down her meal in front of her. The steam rose up from the poached salmon, the scent of the fresh fish suddenly intoxicating. As she stared at the plate, every portion seemed brighter, the colours psychedelic, vegetables humming with vibrancy, white sauce ethereal, pale as a goose feather.

Excitement made her hand shake as she reached for her fork. 'Does this man work on his own?'

'Of course.'

'Where does he come from?'

'Africa.'

'Oh . . . Would the baby be African?'

'I believe so.'

Pausing, Bobbie was about to refuse the offer and then considered the idea further. A black child was not something she had imagined for herself, but then again, why not? How magnanimous would she appear adopting not some healthy WASP child but a baby from an impoverished country? Mentally Bobbie rewrote her previous scenario, tried it on to see if she could accommodate it, and decided that she could. An African child, a black baby – how radical, how modern, how like Madonna. How freethinking of her.

'You said this man could get me a baby within days?'

'By the weekend.'

So the party could still go ahead, Bobbie thought, her spirits lifting. She would have her baby, just as she had said. And more than that, she would make a real statement about adoption. Stop her detractors short and prove herself again . . . *No one* denied Bobbie Feldenchrist what she wanted. Not some Puerto Rican slut or some by-the-book adoption society.

'I would want the child to be healthy. And it would have to be a boy.'

'I know that.'

'Who is this African man? What do you know about him?'

'Not much.'

'You're making me nervous now.' Her tone hardened 'Is he a criminal?'

'I don't know much about him. It was Marty who suggested him. Apparently he's helped a couple of other women who wanted to adopt. I suppose Africa's no different to here. Girls get in trouble and need a way out, so they give their babies up.'

'They have a choice?'

'Oh, Bobbie,' Ellen said, chiding her gently. 'You *do* worry about things so much. The girls get their lives back so they can move on – and they get paid well.'

'I suppose this man takes a commission?'

'It *is* a business, honey.'

'So how do I do business with him?'

Ellen dropped her voice to a whisper. 'He'll call and see you about the money.'

'Then what?'

'He'll have the baby brought to you. After that, you won't ever have to see him again.'

Bobbie's tongue ran over her dry bottom lip. She was suddenly nervous, terrified about her decision. But she wouldn't go back on it. She wanted a child, and now she was going to get one.

'Just one thing,' Ellen said suddenly. 'You can't mention where or how you got the baby. Or tell anyone about this man.'

'Is he ...' Bobbie paused, wanting to ask the question and at the same time not wanting to hear the answer. '... is he dangerous?'

'You want a baby, don't you?' Ellen asked steadily. 'Well, sometimes we have to go about things in ways we wouldn't usually choose.' She patted Bobbie's hand maternally and changed the subject. 'Now, eat up. A new mother needs all her strength.'

29

The next day it rained. And it kept raining, right through the afternoon and into the turn of dusk. It rained so hard that the traffic slowed down on the New York streets, the headlights bouncing off the slick roads. The clouds rained down like they hadn't rained for years, as if they wanted to get rid of all the collected water which was making their white froth heavy. Downspouts overflowed, drains choked and were smothered under the onslaught, and a million American pigeons hunched up against the windows of a thousand office blocks. Along the sidewalk, people hurried under awnings and into doorways, a sulky moon dozing in a gap between the clouds. At the Guggenheim Museum they were having a Roy Lichtenstein show, and in Central Park the drivers with their pony traps waited for customers under the dripping trees.

Emile Dwappa watched the rain with indifference. Standing across the street from Roberta Feldenchrist's apartment block, he watched the comings and goings of the wealthy and their cars. He wondered, fleetingly, which car he would buy when he was rich, and decided that he would go for an English Jaguar. Class, he thought solemnly, was everything. Who wanted a BMW – the Brixton drug-runners' car? Or some flashy pimp Cadillac? He didn't want to be noticed, he wanted to be rich. And if nobody else noticed how rich he was, that was fine by him.

Glancing at his watch, he looked up at the penthouse apartment, its lights shining out into the driving rain. Even from street level, the place looked big. He wondered what it would be like to have so much space for yourself. Space up above the masses, away from the dog shit on the streets and the drains which crept down into the sewers below. He wondered then if he would like to live in New York and realised instantly how much he disliked the place. There was no sun, for one thing. Oh, it was raining at the moment, but the previous day it had been fine. And still no sun had got down into the crazy paving of the streets. And all the shadows, he thought, shaking his head. What was the point of walking among buildings so tall that you were always in half-darkness?

Turning his face upwards, he let the rain fall on his skin for a moment and moved into the shelter of a doorway. Roberta Feldenchrist was expecting him . . . the thought was amusing. One of the richest women on earth needed *him*. She wanted what he could give her. Only him . . . He had already worked out what he would charge her. She would baulk at the sum, of course, but she would pay. She had no choice. He thought of the cuttings he had read in the society pages, about how Ms Feldenchrist was giving a baby shower at the weekend for her adopted son

. . . It amused him to think of the expression 'baby shower'. Sounded like they were going to drown the poor bastard.

Dwappa had done his research meticulously after his brother had tipped him the wink about Bobbie Feldenchrist. And now he had a very clear picture of a rich cow who had always got her own way – until Mother Nature had slowed up her progress. No amount of money could make a barren woman fertile again. The chemotherapy, he thought idly, had stopped the Feldenchrist line short. But Ms Feldenchrist wasn't going to let fate, or nature, stand in her way. Even when her first attempt at adoption failed.

But that, he decided, was what you got for doing things the right way. Bureaucracy could topple the mightiest plans. Exhaling, Dwappa ducked out from the doorway and walked across the road, dodging a yellow cab and making for the entrance to the apartment block.

Immediately he was stopped by Reception.

'Can I help you?'

'I have an appointment with Ms Feldenchrist,' he replied, his expression unperturbed.

'Your name, sir?'

'She's expecting me. I'm her seven o'clock appointment.'

The porter hesitated, noting the man's expensive suit and watch, then asked again. 'Your name, sir?'

'Please call the penthouse and tell Ms Feldenchrist her guest is here,' he replied, holding the man's stare. 'I'll take full responsibility.'

Moments later Emile Dwappa, with his expensive watch and $200 haircut, arrived at the penthouse, ringing the buzzer to be admitted from the escalator reception area into the apartment proper. Above his head a security camera trained its beady eye on him, the blinking of an alarm sensor flickering in a corner. He knew then that his image had been taken and that he would probably also be monitored inside the apartment. Obviously security for Ms Feldenchrist should anything go wrong. But then again, he reasoned, perhaps it would be turned off. After all, she wouldn't want their meeting to become common knowledge.

Suddenly the door buzzed and he walked in.

'You're very punctual,' a voice said behind him, and he turned to see Bobbie Feldenchrist walking towards him. She had that look only rich women have – an expression of languid arrogance. 'Please, sit down.'

He did so, facing the windows and looking at the lights on the Chrysler building, thinking about how the remake of *King Kong* wasn't as good as the original.

'I suppose you don't use your curtains?' he said, disarming her with a smile.

'No,' Bobbie agreed, surprised at his elegant English accent and his expensive clothes. This was no thug off the streets. 'It's very good of you to come and talk to me, Mr . . .'

He had expected her to try and get his name and ignored the hint, moving on to the business in hand. 'I believe I can help you. I hear you want to adopt a baby.'

She took a long breath, as though putting the reality into words was somehow intensely exhausting.

'I do.'

'I can make that happen for you, Ms Feldenchrist.'

Her hands wound around themselves tightly. 'You know of a child?'

'A baby boy, yes.'

A cry sounded in her throat and Bobbie glanced away for an instant. 'Can you bring this child to me?'

'Of course. In two days.'

Again she made a low sound in her throat, as though she could hardly hold on to her emotions. 'Where is the child coming from?'

'Africa.'

'Where in Africa?'

'That's not important.'

She turned back to him to pursue the matter, then winced. His expression had closed off, his charm suspended. In his coldness he was warning her, more effectively than words, that he was in charge.

'I would like to know something about the baby.'

'I don't think,' he said, getting to his feet, 'that we can do business after all.'

Gasping, she stood up, following him. He was making for the door and then paused, knowing her hopes would be raised when he didn't leave at once. Slowly he began to walk around the room. One by one he stopped in front of the paintings, his face unreadable, his eyes curious. These were some of the famous Feldenchrist paintings. His research had told him about the Spanish masters in the Feldenchrist Collection and he remembered reading about the painting he was now looking at.

'Is this a Goya?'

She nodded stiffly.

'Creepy.'

'My father liked it.'

'Do you?' he asked, smiling.

'Yes, I do. I like most of the Spanish masters.'

'Expensive taste,' he replied, charming her again. 'I didn't think there were many of the Old Masters in private collections any more.'

'Some.'

'Like in the Feldenchrist Collection?'

She was trying to cover her impatience. After all, he wasn't here to talk about art. 'We have a good selection of works. My father collected all his life, and I carried on where he left off.'

'You enjoy it?'

'Yes, I do.'

'But it's not the same as being a mother?' He paused, staring at a Murillo drawing. 'How much is this worth?'

'I don't think that's any of your business—' At once Bobbie checked her temper, horrified to see that he had taken offence and had moved to the door. 'Please don't leave! I'm sorry if I asked too many questions.'

'You shouldn't ask *any*,' he replied, turning to her and noticing the fine lines around her eyes and the first slackening around the jaw. Time, he thought suddenly, was not on her side. 'If we do business together, we have to trust each other. I have to trust you and you have to trust me.'

She nodded eagerly. She would have agreed to anything just to prevent him from walking out.

'Yes, yes.'

'I can have the baby here on Saturday.'

'*Saturday* . . .' she repeated, frowning as he handed her a piece of paper.

'That's a precaution. Just in case you're recording my visit . . .' Dwappa explained, pointing to one of the cameras. '. . . I thought you might prefer to have the finances remain a private matter.'

She read the amount of money written and laughed. 'This is absurd!'

'How much is a baby worth? You have to ask yourself that question, Ms Feldenchrist. Ask yourself how much you want a baby for your "baby shower". How much you want a little Feldenchrist heir. You don't want to look like a failure, do you? I mean, you can't have children naturally, can you? So how embarrassing would it be if you failed to *adopt* one?'

She took a step back. 'How dare you!'

'Dare what?' he responded. 'You wanted to meet me. You wanted me to get you a child. I'm offering you that – for a fee.'

'It's a massive sum!'

'Like you haven't got it.'

Her composure was disintegrating fast. Threatened, she knew she had no choice but to agree. She would pay up and then she would have her child. After that, she could forgot the whole sordid affair. Uncharacteristically, she ducked the reality of her situation. That this man would have something on her for life. That he would have control and the means to exploit her if he chose.

She knew, but she still agreed. 'All right.'

'I want the money in cash.'

'Of course,' Bobbie replied, hardly able to keep the bitterness out of her tone. 'Is the baby a healthy boy?'

'One hundred per cent. I'd like the money when I bring the child here on Saturday.'

She nodded, her voice low. 'What time?'

'I'll call and tell you exactly,' he replied, 'and when we've concluded our business deal, Ms Feldenchrist, I want you to promise that you won't say anything to anyone about me. Instead you'll say that your original adoption went through. It was postponed, that was all. You let everyone think this was the only baby you were ever going to adopt.' He turned to go, then turned back. 'It's very *aware* of you to adopt a coloured baby. I'm sure you'll be admired by all of your friends. The Third World needs more people like you.'

She caught the sarcasm in his tone and flushed. 'I just want a child—'

'And I just want to fulfil your wish. But remember, never mention me. If you do, neither your name nor your money will save you.'

'Is that a threat?'

'Yes,' he replied, taking one last look at the paintings

which surrounded him. 'You have a good life. You don't want to risk that, Ms Feldenchrist . . .'

She was rigid with shock, all colour going from her lips.

'So remember this. If you mention me to anyone – if you even drop a hint that I exist – I'll personally make you sorry you were ever born.'

Frightened, she stepped back, bumping into the settee behind her. In that instant she realised exactly what she had done – that the pact she had made was for life. And she also knew that if she broke it, he would kill her.

30

'I got a call from Ben Golding,' Duncan said, glancing over at Roma. 'He's viewed the remains of the Little Venice murder victim and faxed his report through to your office. Professional, huh?'

'Usual practice.'

'He could have cried off.'

She glanced at him, puzzled. 'Why?'

'His brother's just died.'

'*What?*' she exclaimed. 'What happened?'

'He committed suicide, in Spain.'

'Why would he do that?'

'Oddly enough, Ben Golding's insisting that his brother *didn't* kill himself. He says he's been murdered.'

Surprised, she took a breath. 'What makes him think that?'

'Didn't say, but he was emphatic about it. Mind you, he was in shock, I could tell that. He was talking too much over the phone. Not like himself at all. You know, talking like he couldn't stop. He said that everyone was putting his brother's death down to a suicide, but he had found the body and he reckoned he'd been killed. Then he just shut up, like he'd said too much.'

Roma frowned. 'Imagine finding your own brother dead . . . What else did he say?'

'He said he was still in Madrid—'

'Madrid?'

'That's where his brother lived.'

'What else?'

'Nothing else. Not about his brother anyway. Started talking about the Little Venice case instead.'

Her eyebrows rose. 'That's odd.'

'Why? You asked Golding for a professional opinion. He was working on the case.'

'Did he mention anything about us finding his card on the body?'

'No.'

'Obviously he's seen the reconstruction?'

'Yeah.'

'But he didn't recognise the victim?'

'Said not.'

Frowning, Roma pushed a stack of papers to one side of her desk and leaned forward. The chair creaked morosely as Duncan took a seat opposite his boss. Placing her hands over the Little Venice file, she stared at him. 'Have we any leads on this?'

'No,' he said, trying to read her thoughts. 'What is it?'

'Huh?'

'You look thoughtful. What about?'

She shrugged.

'It just seems odd, that's all. That business of Ben Golding's card on the murder victim. And now his brother's been killed.'

'You think the cases are related?'

'I don't know. But it's a hell of coincidence, isn't it?' She doodled on the pad in front of her, making looping spirals on the page. 'Did Golding say *why* he thought his brother had been killed?' She looked up. 'No? Then we need to ask him.'

31

In the glossy centre of Madrid, a solitary man was seated at a table, a half-empty coffee cup in front of him. Overhead the slow curl of a fan chugged into the afternoon warmth, the arched windows opening out on to a wrought iron terrace, rusted in places. Only minutes earlier a woman had come in and watered the plants outside, taking care not to splash the leaves or the flowers. A careless drop of water, magnified by Spanish sun, could work like a lens, scorching the fragile, pulpy greenness underneath.

From the open window came the sound of the city: car horns, shouts, the occasional punctuation of laughter. But inside the room was quiet, interrupted only by the noise of the lift shuddering to an impatient halt on the landing outside. Sighing, the man looked upwards into an inverted, painted well. Figures from pastoral mythology cavorted in fleshy groups, a painted sky the colour of a Russian sapphire. A froth of clouds drew the eye downwards to the tops of carved pelmets and gilded pictures frames, standing cheek by jowl with ceremonial documents and antique weaponry.

The palatial office of Gabino Ortega told everyone immediately how wealthy he was. The fact that he did very little work in it did not matter. It was a front for him – a stage set for an actor playing a tycoon. But now Gabino was finding himself at a loss, his mobile still in his hand, his mind seething. Leon Golding was dead.

So where was the fucking skull?

His irritation accelerated into anger as he pushed back his chair and stood up. He had been too slow. He should have got the skull off Leon Golding as soon as he had heard that it was in his possession – either bought it or stolen it, but got hold of it nonetheless. The lame lie about the skull being a fake and buried in a churchyard had been almost laughable. Surely Golding had realised that he hadn't believed him – that he had, instead, had him watched?

Thank God he hadn't told Bartolomé about it, Gabino thought suddenly. He would have looked like a fool. Glancing up, he watched the man who had just entered the room, a scrawny picture restorer in his seventies, who nodded as he took the seat offered to him.

'So, where is it?'

'The chambermaid said she never saw any skull,' Lopez replied. 'She said she would have remembered something like that.'

'Did she go through Leon Golding's things?'

Lopez nodded, shifting in his seat. 'You can't let anyone know about this—'

'About what? That you've got people working in the hotel, ready to thieve anything important they come across?' Gabino pulled a face. 'I'm not interested in what you do in your own time, only what you do for me. And now I want to know about Golding. Did the maid go through his things?'

'She didn't have time. The hotel room was never empty. Leon Golding checked in and stayed in. After he'd topped himself, his brother arrived and found the body—'

'*His brother found him?*'

'Yeah. And when the maid finally had the chance to get into the room, all Leon Golding's stuff had gone.'

'Ben Golding took it?'

'Yeah.' Lopez sucked at a hole in one of his back teeth. 'But I know where he went – to the family house. His brother lived there with his girlfriend. She's still there.'

'And Golding's there too?'

'Yeah.'

Gabino paused, trying to think, trying to cover his annoyance at the fact that something which should have been so simple had turned out to be so complicated. Only an hour earlier he had received confirmation of his court hearing – the date set in a couple of weeks' time. Even the Ortega money and lawyers had failed to get the assault charge dropped. There was a rumour that Gabino would be made an example of, his violence curtailed by a long overdue jail sentence.

He realised that in Switzerland his brother would have heard the news by now. He also knew that, having endured many years of Gabino's excessive behaviour, this might well turn out to be the act which finally broke Bartolomé patience and terminated the gravy train. And now Gabino had lost sight of the one thing which could have placated his brother: the skull of Goya.

'There's one other thing . . .' the old man said carefully. 'Leon Golding's brother is challenging the fact that it was suicide.'

'Of course he killed himself!' Gabino said impatiently. 'Leon Golding was unstable. Everyone knew that.'

'Did you know he was having tests done on the skull when he was killed?'

Gabino's head jerked up. 'Who was doing them?'

'Dunno. But they were done in London.'

'*London?*' Gabino took in an irritable breath. 'How d'you know?'

'I have my methods,' Lopez replied enigmatically. 'The skull is Goya's. Proven.'

'I knew it! He knew that bastard was lying when he said it was a fake . . . D'you know who found it and gave it to Leon Golding?'

'Diego Martinez. A builder. Who's since gone missing.'

'Missing . . .' Gabino replied thoughtfully, pulling at his shirt cuffs, the crescent-moon cufflinks catching the hot Madrid light.

'I spoke to someone at the Prado,' Lopez went on. 'Since my restoring days I've had contacts—'

'Get on with it!'

'Apparently the Museum felt comfortable that Leon Golding should have carte blanche. He was one of their staff, after all. But he *could* have tricked the Prado. Gone somewhere else with the skull.'

Gabino could sense that the old man was working up to something. 'Did he?'

'I don't know,' Lopez replied. 'But I saw him talking to an Englishman called Jimmy Shaw a few days ago. I also saw the same Jimmy Shaw outside the Hotel Melise on the night Leon Golding committed suicide. Or did he? If his brother's right, maybe Leon *was* killed. By Jimmy Shaw.'

'And?'

'Jimmy Shaw might have the skull now.'

Thoughtful, Gabino took a long breath. 'Find out who Jimmy Shaw's working for.'

The old man nodded, but didn't get up to leave. Instead he kept talking. 'It seems to me that you've got a real problem. You've only got a short time to find that skull for your brother.' Lopez had already worked out the connection between the court case and Gabino's allowance. 'The skull could be with Jimmy Shaw *or* Ben Golding.'

'Start with Shaw.'

'I would – but I can't find him,' Lopez replied, leaning forward in his seat. 'I found out where he'd been staying, but no one's seen him for twenty-four hours, since Leon Golding was killed. He's gone missing.'

'So the builder who gave the skull to Leon Golding is missing, Leon Golding is dead, and now this Jimmy Shaw has disappeared.' Gabino took in a slow breath, trying to fight his impatience. 'Talk to Ben Golding. Make him an offer.'

'He might want to keep the skull, out of respect for his brother.'

'It was Goya's fucking skull, not Leon's!'

'Still,' Lopez persisted, 'Golding might want to keep it. Might want the kudos for himself. Goya's head would be very welcome in London – build up their tourist trade nicely.'

Gabino's face was tight. 'Ben Golding's a doctor. What would Goya's skull mean to him?'

'More than you might think. The Golding brothers grew up close to where the Quinta del Sordo used to stand. Leon was an art historian. They probably know as much about Goya as any Spaniard. Ben Golding might believe that he has a right to the skull.'

'Then disabuse him of the notion,' Gabino said sharply. 'And do it soon.'

32

Switzerland

All morning Bartolomé had waited for a phone call from his brother. He had expected Gabino to apologise, to try to explain as he usually did. Try to shrug off the charge of assault as something unimportant, a light-hearted misunderstanding that would be sure to be thrown out of court. Bartolomé knew otherwise. Gabino wasn't walking away from having smashed a glass into a banker's face. No one walked away from that. Not even one of the richest families in Spain could smother that.

The victim's photographs had underlined the casual violence. His check had been slashed to the bone, his trigeminal nerve severed, leaving his face with a slack, left-sided droop. Bartolomé knew that a jury would look at that face and Gabino would be damned . . . But why should he care any longer? Bartolomé thought. He had made too many allowances for a brother who was corrupt. Had tried to ameliorate too many unpleasant and sordid situations.

Strangely it wasn't the assault which had finally turned Bartolomé against his brother. It was the fact that Gabino hadn't told him about the Goya skull.

'Are you working?' Celina asked, walking over to her husband's chair.

'No . . . not really.'

'But you were thinking,' she prompted him. 'About what?'

'Gabino.'

Sighing, she leaned against the desk and looked at Bartolomé intently. 'The case?'

'No . . . something else,' Bartolomé admitted. 'Something I haven't told you about.' She was surprised, but said nothing, just let him continue. 'The skull of Goya has been found . . .'

Her hand covered her mouth automatically, smothering her response.

'And Gabino heard about it.'

'. . . and he's got it for you?'

Smiling bitterly, Bartolomé shook his head. 'No, he never even told me about it.'

Her expression hardened. 'How long has he known?'

'A week. I kept expecting a call from him. I even thought he might visit, surprise me with the news. They found the skull in Madrid. Gabino *must* have heard about it.'

Celina sighed, finding herself in the position she had occupied, on and off, for many years – between the two Ortega brothers; between two totally dissimilar men who had only a fortune in common.

'But Gabino had no reason *not* to tell you—'

'Malice,' Bartolomé said flatly. 'He knew how much it would mean to me and so he didn't want me to have it.'

'No,' Celina said, shaking her head. 'No, I don't believe it. Talk to him. Ask him about it.'

'Never.'

Turning away, Bartolomé stared at the blank wall facing him. Nothing would induce him to talk to his brother about the Goya skull. Nothing. Gabino had been too secretive this time, too clever by half. And he would return his brother's cunning in full measure.

'I'm disinheriting him.'

'What!'

'I'm cutting him off from the family,' Bartolomé replied, his tone fixed. 'He's done nothing for years except spend money and disgrace the Ortega name. I've talked to him about it over and over again, but he never listens. He runs with the wrong crowd, the wrong women; he plays at working, wastes money on the useless projects of his cronies and invests in the schemes of men eager – and clever enough – to dupe him.' Straightening his tie, Bartolomé put up his hands to prevent his wife's protestations. 'I've tried for years to love him. Even like him. But when I look at Gabino I see only a liar and a fool—'

'Bartolomé, he's not like you. He's reckless, but he has good qualities.'

'He has no goodness in him. While I've spent years behind that desk working, he's been undermining me.

223

Hard work is a joke to him, my pride in the family name regarded as comical. He pities me!' Bartolomé said fiercely. 'You think I don't know it? You think I don't look into Gabino's eyes and see it? He wants to fuck and spend money, but nothing else. Nothing else is sacred to him.'

Her voice was soothing.

'Darling, think about what you're saying. Gabino is your brother—'

'I have a son. I have Juan.'

'*We* have a son,' she corrected him, walking over to her husband and touching his shoulder.

Feeling the muscle tense under her fingers, Celina moved away. When Bartolomé was in one of his rare tempers, nothing could comfort him. Of course she realised the real reason for her husband's decision. It wasn't just that Gabino had been mean-minded, petty-spirited, withholding from his brother – who had given him so much, so willingly – something he would have treasured. It wasn't the deception that hurt, it was the contempt. Despite decades of being indulged, Gabino was indifferent to his brother's one passion.

'Think about it—'

'I *have* thought about it.'

'He's your brother,' Celina said again, coolly controlled. 'A member of the Ortega family.'

'But is he a *worthy* one?' Bartolomé asked. 'Our name's been corrupted in the past. I've spent my life trying to undo the damage my ancestors – especially my grandfather – inflicted on it.'

'And what price a name?' she asked, standing up to him. 'You put a name above a brother?'

'*This* brother, yes.'

'But not another brother?' she queried. 'What kind of brother would you approve of? Someone hard-working, loyal? Trustworthy? Dull? What brother would suit you and the Ortega name?'

'I hate him!' Bartolomé spat out. 'God forgive me, but I do. I hate his face, his mannerisms, his lies. And now he's gone too far—'

'Gabino's no different to how he always was.'

'And you always make excuses for him!'

'Yes, I do,' Celina replied, her tone icy. 'Because I try and make you see that this is more than just an argument between the two of you. You are more than siblings – you are part of a family, a business, a heritage. Your arguments can't be petty – your lives are on a grander scale.' Composed, she leaned against the desk again and folded her arms. 'You're right, we have a son. And because of Juan – because *he* will carry on the Ortega name – we can afford to be more lenient with Gabino.'

'My grandfather would have cut my brother off—'

'Your grandfather was a killer,' she replied, without a flicker of emotion. 'You know it, Madrid knows it, I know it. Where do you think Gabino's aggression comes from? It's in his blood. It's in yours too, Bartolomé. It's only your responses which differ. You control it, he does not. You fight it, he surrenders to it. You are afraid of it, Gabino revels in it.'

Slowly Bartolomé turned to look at his wife. He was, as ever, impressed by her.

'It would have been such a small thing to tell me about Goya, but it was such a *massive* thing to hide. It required such spite.'

'I agree.'

'And yet you ask me to forgive him?'

'No, not forgive, accept.'

'I accept, he rejects.'

Nodding, Celina studied her husband. 'If you throw Gabino out, if you cut him off from the family, think about what will happen. You think it will be the last you hear of him? Gabino is not your grandmother, Bartolomé. Not some woman without power. He's got friends and cronies. He could gossip, talk about your business, betray you.'

'He might be doing that now.'

'No,' she said briskly, shaking her head. 'There would be no profit in it now. No sport either. But if you disinherited him, Gabino would expose every detail of your life and work. You treasure your privacy, Bartolomé; think what it would be like to have your life trawled across the papers. How would you cope with that? Everything about you would be public gossip. Everything about *us*, our son, our home. By the time Gabino had finished we wouldn't have an inch of earth to ourselves that hadn't been tainted.'

Bartolomé could picture the life she was describing and paused. He wanted desperately to be rid of the brother he disliked and reviled; had hoped that the affair with the skull of Goya had presented him with an opportunity to finally cut off the restless scion of the Ortega family. But once again his wife had stayed his hand.

'Why didn't he tell me?'

'About Goya?'

'Yes.'

'Why does the tide come in and out?' Celina asked, walking over to Bartolomé and cupping his face in her hands. This time there was no resistance. 'I know how hard this is for you. Remember, I know Gabino too . . . But listen to me, and think about this carefully – you can hate him, mistrust him, even banish him, but you'll never be rid of him. Instead accept him *and watch him*. Something that is easier to do close by than from a distance.' Unflinching, she held her husband's gaze. 'Gabino was born an Ortega and he will die one.'

33

Madrid

Sitting in the kitchen of the old house, Ben listened as Gina walked about the rooms upstairs. Noises from the past shuffled around the old table, Ben's initials driven deep into one corner and beside them, lighter scratches – LG. Staring at the initials, Ben reached out his hand, his fingers covering the marks, Detita's voice coming back to him.

Can't you hear it, Ben? Leon can hear it. Leon can hear the dead talk.

And just as easily he could hear his own reply:
The dead don't talk. The dead are dead . . .

His hand pressed down on the wood, on his brother's initials, the wind muffled against the window, the creak of the weathervane making little rusty sighs. Hardly breathing, Ben thought of his brother as a boy, saw him turn on the drive and wave. Saw him older, wearing glasses to read, picking at some bread Detita had made. Saw him crying, trying to speak, but shaking instead because he could hear noises.

The tree told me to do it . . .

And then he remembered Leon at the head of the stairs on the day their parents died . . . Other sounds came back, unwelcomed. The noise of a lost bird cawing from across the river, the smell of the Manzanares in a swampy summer, flies droning against the catch of tide. Throughout how many queasy summers had they lived here? Ben thought, glancing around him. Perhaps he should never have left Spain – should have stayed with his brother, worked in Madrid.

I should have saved him. I should have saved him . . .

Turning, he jumped, startled, at the sight of Detita standing in the kitchen door, Tall, her expression impassive, her white nightdress fluttering in the draught from the window.

'Ben?'

He blinked and the image had gone. Instead it was Gina watching him.

'My God,' she said, walking over. 'Are you all right?'

He nodded abruptly, but he could feel the heat coming from her and when she sat down at the table next to him he could see the outline of her breasts against the thin fabric.

Fanning herself with her hand, she shrugged. 'I couldn't sleep.'

'Thinking of Leon?'

'Can't stop thinking about him. I miss him so much,'

she said simply, pushing her hair back from her face with an impatient gesture.

As she reached up, her breasts pressed against her nightdress. Ben glanced away. He felt hazy, oddly light-headed. Not because he wanted her, but because he was uncomfortable. Surely this woman – Leon's woman – wasn't flirting with him? His gaze moved to the wall over the old grate, where a mirror suspended from a brass hook reflected the back door. Sometimes – when he had been a boy – he had crept out at night, running to the bridge. And there he'd stood and clapped his hands, as Detita had taught him.

. . . When you need me, come at midnight to the Bridge of the Manzanares, clap your hands three times and you will see black horses appear . . .

And he had clapped his hands, but had seen no horses. Except once. Only once did he see the black horses and, panicked, he had run back to the farmhouse. Run in at the back door which he could see reflected now in the mirror, and stood in the kitchen, waiting for the thudding of the hooves to pass . . . I never told you I saw them. Ben thought blindly. I should have told you, Leon.

His gaze moved upwards into the knotting of pipes above his head, almost as though, illogically, he believed he would see his brother there.

'You don't have to leave straight away, do you?' Gina said softly. 'This is your home . . . I'd like you to stay. I'd like the company.'

'I have to sort out Leon's things . . .'

'We can do that tomorrow. I can help.'

Ben wasn't listening. '. . . I was brought up here . . .'

'I know.'

'. . . with Leon.' He paused, looking around, painfully lost. 'I should have visited him more often – you were right.'

'You came when you could.'

'I should have come more often. He must have been lonely.'

If she took the words as an insult, she didn't show it. 'He was a lonely man, but you couldn't have done anything about that, Ben. I couldn't. No one could.'

'He had no one.'

'He had me.'

He turned to her. 'Sometimes.'

She blinked. Once.

'Why are you still here, Gina? You were scared before, asking me if you were in danger.' He was baffled, and showed it. 'Why would you *want* to stay here?'

'I wouldn't – unless you wanted me to.'

His confusion was so absolute he couldn't answer and the silence yawned between them.

Then suddenly the mood broke, Gina drawing back, and shifting tactics. 'I asked you before, *did* Leon tell you about the baby?'

'No.'

She shrugged in reply, turning away so that he had to fight to hear her.

'I miscarried, Ben. I lost your brother's baby.'

'I'm sorry.'

'Leon was too. It mattered to him so much. He wanted that baby . . .' She looked at him desperately. 'I keep wondering if the miscarriage didn't play on his mind. He was already overworked, under terrible stress – then that happened.'

'You think it unbalanced him?'

'I think it made him worse,' she said quietly. 'I think having a child would have helped him. Stabilised him.'

'You think so?'

'Don't you?'

'Maybe,' Ben conceded. 'We'll never know now.'

Her eyes filled and she looked away quickly. 'I suppose you want me to leave? It's your home, after all.'

'Leon's dead, Gina. There's no reason for you to stay.'

'Isn't there?' she asked. 'I could cook for you – while you're here, anyway. You *are* going to stay in Spain for a while, aren't you?'

He shook his head.

'No, not long—'

'But—'

'I've told you. I just want to sort out Leon's things and then go back to London. I think you should go home too, Gina. Go back to your family.' He turned to her and held her gaze. 'It would be better – and safer – for all of us.'

Without answering she walked off, the door closing softly behind her. He couldn't tell if she was angry or upset, but he waited until he heard her move back into the bedroom she had shared with Leon. For nearly twenty minutes he sat in the semi-dark, wondering if she would come downstairs again. Finally, believing she was asleep, he moved into Leon's study.

The smell of dust and books was overpowering and he was initially tempted to open a window, but resisted. Instead he flicked on the desk lamp and riffled through his dead brother's papers. There were many volumes on Goya, many reproductions, but finally Ben found what he had been looking for – Leon's notebooks. Tucking them under his arm, he picked up his brother's laptop and walked to the door. The house was completely silent. It could have been empty, without any imprint of Gina. Without any imprint of the adult Leon.

Instead the place was full of boys' murmured voices, Detita's footsteps making their solemn way down the main stairs . . . Spooked, Ben glanced up, but the staircase was empty. Without making a sound, he hurried to the bedroom he had been using and packed the few belongings he had brought with him. Pushing Leon's computer and notebooks in with his clothes, he added the papers he had found at the Hotel Melise and walked out to the car.

Day had yet to dawn, a little morbid light smearing the horizon, water sounds coming, muffled, from the river. The breeze had dropped and the weathervane was silent, but as Ben turned back to the house he caught sight of a figure watching him from an upstairs window. The outline was vague, the only distinct portion of the figure being the hand pressed against the glass, the palm white as the flesh of a lily.

34

New York

The baby shower had been a success and attended by
assorted society mothers and matrons, Bobbie Feldenchrist
had introduced her adopted son, Joseph, to New York. As
was befitting a woman who had everything she needed,
Bobbie and her child were indulged with gifts, each more
inventive than the last. Invitations to beach houses and
foreign homes were extended to the new family, people
remarking in whispers that old man Feldenchrist would
never have expected his fortune to be passed on to a black
upstart from Africa.

To her face, people complimented Bobbie on her liberal choice. True to his threatening word, Emile Dwappa
had delivered the baby that previous Saturday, taking the
cash from Bobbie and dropping his voice to remind her
of their agreement. He chucked the baby under the chin,
declared him a fine child, and then spent several minutes admiring Bobbie's art collection again. She was too

preoccupied to take offence. Soon he would be gone, she told herself – and she had what she wanted from him. With no real conditions except one – silence. She had merely to stay quiet.

And why, in God's name, would she do otherwise? What benefit could possibly be had from telling anyone the real circumstances of the child's adoption? As for Ellen and Marty Armstrong, they weren't going to break her confidence. They relied too much on the Feldenchrist handouts to betray her.

So Bobbie had let Dwappa look at her paintings and had waited patiently for him to leave.

'What would be the greatest addition to your collection, Ms Feldenchrist?' he had asked finally.

'I don't know.'

'An unknown Velasquez?'

'There *are* no unknown Velasquez works.'

'What about an unknown Goya?'

Her smile had warmed, almost amused. 'I doubt it.'

'That it exists?' he countered. 'Or that it would be the greatest addition to your collection?'

'I don't understand.'

'I was just asking about your collection . . .' Dwappa had continued, making for the door and then turning. '. . . in case I hear of anything you might be interested in purchasing.'

She had missed the trap and suddenly found herself teetering on its slimy brink. But Bobbie wasn't a Feldenchrist for nothing, and she knew that one of the first rules of combat was to appear uninterested. All she had to do was to get the African out of her home. He had delivered everything she wanted from him, and she desired no more communication. If he persisted, Bobbie reassured herself blithely, she would call on her considerable money and legal power to make sure he backed off.

'The Feldenchrist Collection is complete. I don't think we need any more purchases.'

'Don't be too sure,' Dwappa had replied, making for the door.

Through the glass panels Bobbie had seen him press the elevator button and wait for the light to go on above the floor guide overhead. Slowly, she had counted the elevator up, floor by floor, then exhaled when it had finally arrived at the penthouse and Dwappa got in. But at the last moment he had looked up, catching her eye through the glass panel separating them. And then he had pointed his finger straight at her, like a rapier, as the elevator door had closed on him.

That night sleep had been difficult to find.

'Bobbie?'

She jumped as Ellen Armstrong came out of the penthouse elevator and walked towards her. 'How's the baby?'

Bobbie smiled warmly. 'He's good. The nanny's taken him out for a walk.'

'You're a natural mother, Bobbie. We all commented on that at the baby shower.' Ellen took a seat and crossed her plump legs. On her lap she clung to her Chloé bag, her fingers clawing into the pliable leather.

'What's the matter?'

'Nothing,' Ellen replied, but she was jumpy.

'What is it? Are you in trouble? Need some funding?'

'No! No!'

Surprised, Bobbie felt momentarily lost for words. Ellen shifted in her seat uneasily and then dropped her voice. 'I know we aren't supposed to talk about him—'

'Who?' Bobbie said, knowing already who she meant.

'The African.'

'What about him?' Bobbie asked, but there was a catch in her voice and she felt her palms moisten.

'We found out something. It's not to be repeated. I mean, I didn't know about it when I put him your way. How could I have done? I just heard that he could get a child for you. I didn't know anything else—'

'*Know what?*'

Ellen paused, biting her lip for a moment before pressing on. 'He's involved in some sordid things, Bobbie. Got a reputation for all sorts. He trades in a lot of things, and other stuff . . .'

'*What* other stuff?'

'Marty said he traffics children from Africa.' Ellen smiled. A stupid woman out of her depth and trying to make the deadly sound trivial. 'For people to adopt.'

Quickly, Bobbie rose to her feet and walked to the window, as though she could – even from penthouse height – see down into the streets to the nanny pushing her child below.

'Hell, Ellen, how stupid d'you think I am? If this is some kind of trick to get money out of me—'

'No, no!' Ellen insisted. 'I didn't know about the man before. I just wanted to help you. You wanted a baby so much and I just wanted to help—'

Shaken, Bobbie sat down, thinking. The bond between herself and her adopted son had been immediate, her thoughts engrossed by the newcomer. The family name meant that Joseph would have the finest schooling and the family money would ensure a platinum life. But what really struck Bobbie was how, within days, he had consumed her whole life. No man, no husband, had inspired such love in her. Nothing on earth had ever meant as much as this child.

She had carried him round the drawing room, pointing out the pictures. Didn't some specialist believe that a baby could absorb information from its first months? He would learn about the Feldenchrist artworks, about the importance of maintaining the Collection, and the name itself. Pride had flushed through every pore as Bobbie had talked to her baby, her own passion finding outlet. In time Joseph would run the collection, own it; in time he would inherit every drawing, sculpture and painting. He would go to the auctions, bid the other dealers down, wield the Feldenchrist money as all fortunes *should* be wielded – with unquestionable confidence.

Bobbie had learned that lesson a decade earlier, when her ruthless instinct made her tackle an important dealer from France. Later she bid against, and won against,

Bartolomé Ortega. Their association then developed into an unlikely affair, their mutual interests and ambitions making them into a power couple. But the allegiance hadn't lasted, Bartolomé ending the relationship when he met Celina. Within the year Bobbie was married too, but her ruthlessness had increased as she sought to make the Feldenchrist Collection ever more prestigious – some said in an attempt to show Bartolomé Ortega what he had lost.

Bobbie's marriage hadn't lasted, but her ambition had grown. And now she had a son she would be even more ruthless.

'Ellen, we have to keep this little secret to ourselves, you understand?' she said, with an edge to her voice. The African had threatened her – he could do the same to her son. And worse, he could tarnish the Feldenchrist name irrevocably.

'I won't tell anyone!'

'Good ... I've been thinking about that project Marty was interested in.' She threw out the words like a fishing net. 'I think I might invest, after all.'

Ellen caught the drift in a millisecond. 'That would be marvellous. I wouldn't know how to thank you.'

'I just want your silence. You understand, Ellen? No gossip, no innuendoes, nothing. You can do that, can't you?'

Ellen was all hurried agreement. 'Oh, of course, of course—'

'Not a word, Ellen. Not a single word.'

*

It was very late that night, just edging into morning, when Bobbie woke and flicked on the lamp by her bed. Half asleep, half awake, she glanced at the clock. Three thirty. Her first instinct was to go back to sleep, but she knew she wouldn't rest and instead made her way to her study. In the apartment there was absolute silence, the nanny asleep, Joseph in his room beside hers.

Only Bobbie awake, only Bobbie pacing and thinking. Her gaze moved to the computer screen, fighting the impulse to turn it on. To trawl the internet for information, to investigate the man who had sold her a child . . . A moment lunged at her. Her hand moved over the keyboard. She hesitated, then turned the computer on.

Automatically Bobbie glanced behind her, but there was no one in the room, no one watching, and the blinds were drawn at the windows. No one would know she had been on the computer, that she had been looking. No one would know . . . Warily she typed the words into the search box, then pressed ENTER, and a whole listing of information came on to the screen. All about child trafficking.

Again Bobbie looked round, then turned back to the screen. Information came up – along with the remembered words:

Keep quiet, tell no one . . .

Her hands shook.

She had to know.

She had to look.

Or did she?

Flicking the OFF switch, Bobbie stumbled to her feet.

Her legs unsteady, she walked down the corridor. Dear God! she thought. If anyone found out about her son, Joseph would be taken away from her. If the police discovered that she had had anything to do with the African they would take away her child.

She would have to keep quiet – and not just because she had been threatened. She would keep quiet to protect herself and her child. No one would know about the African from her. No one would know the truth of where her adopted son had come from. If anyone asked, she knew nothing.

Nothing, nothing, nothing.

35

London, Whitechapel Hospital

Tie unfastened, Ben Golding walked into the children's ward, making for his patient's bedside. The long, delayed flight from Madrid had caught him unawares, his eyes puffy, his breath smelling of fresh toothpaste from a quick clean-up in the doctors' restroom. Pushing all thoughts of the farmhouse, his brother and Gina out of his mind, he smiled at his patient, a boy of six who was sitting on his bed with his arms wrapped tightly around his knees. Picking up the notes from the bottom of the bed, Ben read down the page and checked the blood results, finally smiling at the child and moving on to his next patient.

'I thought you were still in Madrid.'

Ben looked up to see Megan Griffiths walking over to him, her smile sympathetic but forced. 'Sorry to hear about your brother's suicide.'

'It wasn't.'

'What?'

'Suicide.'

'But I heard—'

'It wasn't suicide,' Ben repeated, gesturing to the patient nearest to them. His eyebrows raised, he glanced back at Megan. 'What's happening here?'

Clearing her throat, Megan began. 'Sean's stable, even put on a little weight. Do you want to operate tomorrow? You've got a space in the afternoon.'

He hesitated. 'No, leave him for another couple of days.'

'But I thought—'

'I'm the consultant in charge.'

'But I was standing in for you while you were away, Mr Golding.'

'Then it's a good thing I'm back, isn't it?' he replied, walking off.

Thirty-five minutes later Ben had finished his ward round, making for his consulting room with Sean's file under his arm. Away from his patients he felt tiredness sidle up to him like an unwelcome mongrel rubbing at his calves and he paused, taking in a breath and leaning against an old wrought iron radiator. Behind him, the water pipes banged morosely to the timing of the corridor clock. His gaze moved over to the blank gold face, painted images marking out the corners of the clock's surround: spring, summer, autumn and winter. His eyes fixed on the images, then on the clock again, on the large black hands and the ponderous swinging pendulum.

Suddenly a gowned figure passed in the loggia, nodding to Ben, unrecognisable in his surgery greens. He nodded back, trying to straighten his tie along with his thoughts. But his mind buzzed with unease – with the image of his dead brother, and Gina, and the skull. Without telling Francis, Ben had removed the skull from the hospital storage and taken it home. Agitated, he had paced the house, going from room to room, thinking of his study and dismissing it as being too obvious a hiding place. Finally he had walked into the kitchen and stood for a long moment staring at the washing machine.

He had taken his laundry out of his overnight bag and wrapped the skull in a shirt, together with the authentication papers and Francis Asturias's report, pushing the bundle to the back of the drum. Slamming the door shut, he had then turned the dial to a full programme and heard the comforting click of the lock. Of course he hadn't pressed the START button, but it would look more convincing if anyone broke in.

He had had no idea who – if, anyone – would break in.

All the way to the Whitechapel Hospital Ben had kept wondering if he was right about Leon. Just how well had he known his brother? Maybe Leon *had* committed suicide. Maybe his instability had made him hear voices in the house. Maybe, in his madness, he had taken his life, after all.

But he didn't believe it.

Reaching the consulting rooms, Ben paused when he saw two decorators setting up ladders. One of the men setting about scraping down a door surround – apparently the area was about to be repainted. Momentarily catching his foot in a dustsheet, Ben turned to the nearest man. 'How long will this take?'

'Depends,' the man replied sullenly. 'Three days, at most.'

'Three days?'

'Or so.'

Ben took in a breath. 'It's just that my consulting room is over there and I need to use it for my patients.'

'Didn't you get the memo about the redecorating? It went all over the hospital yesterday.'

'I was in Spain yesterday.'

'Can't blame me then if you didn't see the memo, can you?' the man replied sourly, then relented. 'We knock off at five thirty. Then we'll be out of your way till morning.'

Nodding, Ben ducked under the ladder and walked into his consulting room. The smell of paint was not overly strong, the repetitive scraping on the woodwork outside soon dropping into the mixed clutter of background noise. A stack of mail was waiting for him together with some reports, typed and ready for signing. Turning up the gas fire, Ben heard the comforting hiss enter the room and sat down, picking up the first of the reports and beginning to read. A few minutes passed, the gas hissing, the rain beating against the window and the desk lamp making a yellow island of illumination on the papers as the daylight failed.

Making a correction on one of the reports, he then signed another, leaning back to read a third. In the distance he heard the sound of the church clock chiming and realised that an hour had passed and that the decorators would soon be leaving. Pausing, he then heard the noises of the men packing up in the corridor outside, followed by the smack of the ladder hitting the side of the wall as they left it for the night.

Concentrating, he steeled himself to think of work and not Spain, not the skull, or the lost baby. Not Leon or the man Gina had told him about. The stranger who had come visiting Leon during the last week of his life ... Weary, Ben's head nodded and he snapped himself awake impatiently. He would finish his reports and then go home, retire early and maybe find a few hours' grace in sleep.

Coughing, he turned on his recording machine. There was silence outside, and slowly he began to enter his report:

'Case notes on Sean McGee, aged six years and three months. Admitted to the Whitechapel Hospital four months ago, to have a malignant tumour removed. Operation performed by Ben Golding. Operation successful, no recurrence of tumour at the site or elsewhere.'

Pausing, Ben glanced at the child's notes, then at the X-rays, holding then up to the lamplight to look more closely. The gas fire kept hissing, the corridor outside silent, the rain stilled. Satisfied, he laid the X-rays down on the desk and began to dictate.

'The child's overall condition is good, and he has lately regained some of his lost weight. Blood pressure and pulse normal, reflexes—'

Suddenly there was a noise outside and Ben glanced towards the door. It began as a soft banging and then altered, becoming eerie, like someone scraping their fingernails along the wall.

And then he heard footsteps, quiet but unmistakable. Bugger it, he thought. The decorators were back.

'Who's there?'

Silence from outside the door.

Walking into the corridor, Ben glanced around. The place was deserted. No patients, staff or decorators. No lights on anywhere, except his room – and a soft glow coming from the loggia in the distance.

'Is there anyone there?'

Silence again.

Impatiently he walked back into his room, then sat down and started to dictate again.

'The patient presented with—'

The sound came back. Only this time there was an accompanying noise, like two men walking and whispering. Frowning, Ben looked at his watch. It was later than he had thought, seven o'clock. No one would be in the consulting rooms now, and the nurses would be busy changing shifts. Unless ... He wandered over to his secretary's office and opened the door.

'Sylvia, are you there?'

No answer.

Turning, Ben walked the length of the consulting room corridor, stopping at every door, opening it and looking inside. Every one was empty. No lights burning, no evidence of anyone working late. His thoughts shifted tack. Maybe the consulting rooms had been broken into?

Addicts looking for drugs. It happened quite often. Curious, he moved down to the last room, opening the door and looking into the darkness.

'Anyone there?'

No response.

But he felt something. A creeping sensation that he *was being watched*. Unnerved, Ben paused, his hand gripping the door handle. His breathing speeded up, sweat sheening his skin as he heard a movement behind him.

'Who is it?' he snapped, his voice loud to cover his anxiety. 'Come on, who is it?'

Silence. Slowly he looked around, then pulled the door closed and began to walk back down the corridor. He longed for the familiar sounds of the hospital – a stretcher clattering along the lino, a phone ringing, the siren as an ambulance arrived at A & E. But the consulting rooms of the Whitechapel Hospital were eerily silent, locked off from the main body of activity, not even a cleaner, bucket in hand, to break the quiet.

He wondered suddenly if he should run, and then dismissed the idea, embarrassed by his own nerves. He was tired, that was all. Tired and spooked – which was hardly surprising considering what had happened in the last few days. His imagination was playing mental hopscotch with him, Ben told himself – that was all ... Out of patience, he turned and made for his consulting room again, slamming the door behind him and sitting down at his desk.

He would finish his work, and go home. Have a drink and get some sleep. Everything would be clearer in the morning. He couldn't afford to let *his* imagination get out of control. Taking in a breath, once more he began to dictate:

'. . . Sean will undergo a further operation shortly, undertaken by myself. Megan Griffiths will be in attendance, and George Turner the anaesthetist.'

He paused, adding an afterthought for his secretary:

'This is a message for you, Sylvia. Just in case I'm in theatre when—'

Suddenly Ben stopped talking. There *were* footsteps outside the consulting room door. No mistake. No imagination this time. They were real. Automatically he looked behind him, then turned back to the door, staring at it. The whispering began again, together with a muffled shuffling, the handle of the door beginning to turn.

In that instant the gas fire hissed, the noise spurting around the room as someone began to rattle the door handle. Mesmerised, Ben kept to his seat, a pulse throbbing in his neck, a feeling of dread overwhelming him. And as the door finally opened, he saw a rush of darkness and nothing more.

36

It was the aggressive, unending ringing of the telephone that finally jerked Ben out of his sleep. Leaping up, he knocked over some papers and for an instant couldn't recall whether he was in Spain or London. Then he remembered the noises he had heard and realised he had simply fallen asleep at his desk and dreamt them.

Feeling foolish, he snatched up the phone. '*What?*'

'Ben?'

He relaxed when he heard Abigail's voice. 'Where are you?' he asked.

'In London. My father's better and I wanted to come home to see you. I'm going back in a few days, but at the moment I've got a nurse to cover for me . . . Are you OK?' she went on.

She didn't mention the problem she was having with her face, the swelling under her skin on the left side. A swelling no one knew about but her. Too small to be seen, but not too small for her to feel.

'I'm fine, darling. Tired—'

'You sound it. You didn't stay at the hospital last night, did you?'

He rubbed the sleep out of his eyes.

'I came back for my clinic, but I must have been more tired than I thought and dropped off.' Outside, the hospital clock chimed ten – and he suddenly remembered the skull. 'Are you at my house?'

'No,' she said, surprised. 'I'm at my place.'

'Don't go to the house!'

'But—'

'I'll explain later, but don't go near my place.'

'Is this anything to do with Leon?' she asked, disturbed. 'Ben, what's going on?'

'I can't explain over the phone. I'll tell you more when I see you.' He paused, then confided something which had been bothering him. 'I spoke to Gina. She was still at the farmhouse. She told me she'd lost Leon's baby.'

'Oh, God, I'm sorry—'

'I left Madrid without telling her. Just took Leon's notes and his laptop—'

'*You didn't tell her?*' Abigail said, surprised. 'You just upped and left? That's not like you, Ben.'

'I don't trust her.'

'Why not?'

'Because she lied to me. And if she lied to me once, she could lie to me about everything else. She was very interested in the skull – too interested. Gina doesn't know I have it – she thinks it's still in Madrid – but she seemed very keen to get hold of it.' He thought back. 'And she was reluctant to let me look at what Leon was working on—'

'So you stole it?'

'He was my brother!'

'She was his lover,' Abigail said softly. 'And she was once carrying his child.'

'No, she wasn't.'

'You just said—'

'I know what I said – Gina told me that she had lost Leon's baby. Well, she might have been pregnant, but not with his child. Leon had mumps when he was eighteen. *My brother was sterile . . .*'

Abigail took in a breath.

'The baby wasn't his. Of course she could have made the whole story up just to get sympathy, get me on her side. She's very manipulative and she had a big influence on Leon, always so keen on him writing that book about the Black Paintings. Even when I didn't want him to do it, even when I warned him off, she kept pushing the idea.' He thought of her behaviour the last time he saw her. 'I don't know if Gina was doing it deliberately, but I think she was screwing my brother's head up. Leon wouldn't have stood a chance with a woman like that.'

A moment passed before Abigail spoke again. 'You don't think she had anything to do with his death, do you?'

'I don't know,' Ben said honestly. 'But I wonder what it would have been like living with her, in that house. What Leon's last weeks and days were like . . . The whole atmosphere was eerie there. Not just because Leon was dead – there was more to it than that.'

'You're tired, darling. Get some rest.'

'I will, and I'll see you tomorrow,' he said, hurrying on. 'But don't come round to the house—'

'I won't, I promise. But you're scaring me, Ben. If you're in trouble, call the police.'

'No, not yet,' he replied. 'I will if I have to. But not yet.'

He was lying to her and his conscience needled him. But what was the alternative? To tell her he had the skull at his home? The skull which had already cost two lives? And how could he risk telling her about Diego Martinez, the builder whose find had set the whole series of events into motion. Had he been killed because of the skull? And if so, why had he been murdered in London, not Madrid? Did the same person who had killed Martinez also kill Leon? Abigail was right about one thing, Ben thought. He would go to the police when he had proof, but not before. It was *his* brother who had been murdered and it was up to him to prove it.

Reaching for his coat, Ben walked out, locking the door of his consulting room behind him. Skirting the decorators' ladders, he hurried towards the loggia, the glass windows and ceiling full of London greyness. In the distance he could hear a phone ringing, and as he approached the back entrance he saw an ambulance pull up, its light flashing.

Preoccupied, Ben walked to his car and got in, turning on the wipers to clear the rain off the windows. In the rear-view mirror he watched a stretcher being taken out of the ambulance and hurried into the A & E department, the ambulance men returning a moment later with the stretcher empty and folded. Sighing, Ben started the car and pulled out on to the Whitechapel Road, waiting at the first set of traffic lights and drumming his fingers on the steering wheel. Still weary, he rubbed his eyes and then moved on when the lights changed, making for home.

It was nearly half an hour later that Ben finally arrived back, finding a parking space opposite his house. Hurrying up the front steps, he fumbled with the lock, pushing open the door and walking in. The place seemed unwelcoming as he put down his overnight bag and flicked on the hall light. Picking up his post from the floor, he moved into his study, spotting a fax and scanning it.

FOR THE ATTENTION OF DR BEN GOLDING

He read on, skipping the formalities:

The autopsy findings on Mr Leon Golding are as follows . . .

Automatically Ben held his breath.

Conclusion: suicide.

Conclusion: suicide . . . Ben read the two words again, the image of his brother's body flickering behind his eyes. Leon hanged. Leon dead. Leon killing himself . . . Exhaling, he put down the fax, not bothering to read any more of the report. He already knew that the Spanish coroner would have backed up his findings with the bald facts – that Leon Golding had tried to commit suicide twice before. That he had been unstable. That his life had always been only an inch away from death.

Pouring a drink, Ben sat down with his legs stretched out in front of him, promising himself that he would get drunk. And then, remembering that he was operating later, he put down the glass. Idly, he riffled through his post, and found to his surprise that his hands were shaking and he was fighting tears. Embarrassed, he walked into the kitchen and began to make himself something to eat. His actions were automatic, unconsidered: the cutting of the bread, the buttering, the slicing of the tomato and some cheese. He made the sandwich because he needed to eat, not because he cared what it would taste like, filling the kettle and setting it to boil.

His mind kept replaying images, like scenes viewed through a train window, passing fast and unfocused. Leon, Gina, Abigail, Francis, the hospital . . . His eyes aching from exhaustion, he began to eat. Slowly he chewed the food, making little saliva, forcing himself because he hadn't eaten for hours. When he had finished the sandwich, he would sleep. But it was unappetising and Ben could only eat a little. Turning, he was about to put the plate on the draining board and paused.

Something was different, he could sense it. Slowly, he looked around the kitchen – and then realised that the door of the washing machine was ajar. Bending down, he felt around inside the machine frantically, then dragged out his clothes, his hands rummaging, panicked, around the back of the empty steel drum.

The skull was gone.

BOOK THREE

... I should like to know if you are elegant, distinguished or dishevelled, if you have grown a beard, if you have all your own teeth, if your nose has grown, if you wear glasses, walk with a stoop, if you have gone grey anywhere and if time has gone by for you as quickly as it has for me ...

LETTER FROM GOYA TO MARTIN ZAPATER

Spain, 1821

Shuffling across the dry stretch of grass outside the Quinta del Sordo, the old man paused beside the fountain, plunging his face under the fall of water. The coolness shimmered against his skin, pumping the aged blood into the pores, making his pulse thump to the liquid sensation of cold. His mind wandered from the hot day back to the court, to the past. When he had dabbled with colour and women, mocking the majas while he slept with them. Taking a salary from the king while the ruler slept and hunted his days away, and his Minister in Chief, Godoy, ruled over Spain and the bed of the Queen Maria Luisa. Godoy, a suspected murderer. The man rumoured to have had the Duchess of Alba killed.

Goya lifted his head out of the water, letting the heat dry the flutter of hair. Not bald, even past eighty, but deaf as a stone tomb. Inside his head the dull humming of blood beat in rhythm to the vibration of his footsteps as he made his way into the largest room of the house, on the left of the ground floor. Insects, plump with feeding, made trapeze movements over his head, a

259

lizard basking on the window ledge outside. Once, many years before, he had lain on a bed with the Duchess of Alba, both of them watching a lime green lizard making its showy way across the bedroom floor ...

She had been poisoned, taken from him, the motive unclear. Jealousy, greed, her fortune up for the taking after her death. Or maybe she had been killed because she was, in truth, most frightening. Too wild, too reckless, her reputation tainted by rumours of her dabbling in the occult.

Soon it would be dark ... Sighing, Goya picked up a paintbrush. The handle was worn, smeared with grease and an echo of old paint. No one was paying him for his work. There was no sponsor, no collector, to please. The house and the walls were his, to do with as he chose.

Like the bulls he had admired so often in the ring, Goya sighted his target and moved towards it. The wall fell to the onslaught of darkness, figures emerging half-completed, half human, winding in a mad procession. Mouths gaped, eyes extended, insanity in the turn of bodies, a demented congregation smearing their ghoulish progress across the wall.

'... I have painted these pictures to occupy my imagination, which is tormented by all the ills that afflict me ...'

He had sent the confession to a friend, but knew he could not risk confiding the whole truth in words. Anything written could be retained and used as a weapon against him.

The written word had held danger before. Earlier in his life he had scrawled captions under his works, the most damning reserved for The Disasters of War, the eighty aquatints which he had never published. Under the drawings he had made comments like a war correspondent writing from the front:

One cannot look at this.
This is bad.
This is how it happened.
I saw it.
And this too.
Why?

He had charted the war atrocities and recorded them, but kept them secret. The reason was obvious. A famed liberal, Goya could not risk retaliation from the vicious Ferdinand VII. He was too old and too weak for political grandstanding. Too frightened to rebel publicly.

Staring at his work, Goya moved up to the belly of the wall, his breath warm against the paint and plaster underneath. He knew the pictures wouldn't survive in the Spanish climate. Oils mixed with white preparation of calcium sulphate, together with the adhesion of glue, would fade quickly in the heat and the damp from the nearby river. But that wasn't important. He wasn't creating the paintings to be admired, but to leave behind a testimony of what was happening to him.

His mind slipped backwards, losing its hold on the ratchet of memory. He was back in the summer of 1796, in Andalusia, at the country estate of the widowed Duchess of Alba. They were lovers, of course, and Goya ran the gauntlet of the Inquisition in return for her soft mouth and violence of nature. Resting his face

261

against the wall, the old man felt the wetness of the paint and remembered leaning his head against his lover's moist thigh. So extraordinary had she been, the Duchess's image had repeated itself constantly in his work. Chief sorceress, witch of the heart.

Witches in the Spanish court, witchcraft in the Spanish court. Satanism a sop against the grinding control of Catholicism and the Inquisition. Where there was ignorance there was superstition, and he had painted it . . . Pushing back from the wall, Goya turned, facing another mural, startled by his own vision.

Slowly the day began to shift, dusk at the windows and the open door. Lighting the oil lamps, he turned back to his work. Blisters on his palms made his actions intermittently clumsy, the straining of weak eyes made his head throb, and the swelling of worn muscles ached in the heat.

But still he carried on.

37

The first soft rains of April had given way to a truculent temper of wind and early dark afternoons, spring taking her time. The previous night Ben had slept intermittently, troubled by noises and the image of his dead brother. When he woke he remembered that the skull had been stolen and sat on the side of the bed, his head in his hands. Who had broken into his house? And, more importantly, *how had they known the skull was there?*

The answer unnerved him.

They knew because they had been watching him.

They had followed the skull from Madrid to London. From Leon to Ben. From the hospital to the house. Someone out there wanted the skull badly – and they were determined to get it. Leon had not taken his own life. The skull was important enough for someone to kill for it. Leon hadn't just been hearing noises and voices – he had been followed, robbed, hanged. And meanwhile, what had Gina been doing? Hadn't she encouraged Leon to write about Goya? Brought Frederick Lincoln into his life? Confused Leon's thoughts with mediums and the raising of the dead?

It would have been amusing to some, Ben thought. But not to Leon. Not to a man who had heard voices all his life. And then there were the Black Paintings. Pictures so disturbed they had confounded generations. Paintings which had spooked – and, some said, cursed – anyone who had tried to decipher them.

Getting to his feet, Ben moved into his study and reached behind the largest bookcase, his fingers scrabbling to catch hold of the edge of an over-stuffed envelope. Finally he pulled out Leon's hidden testimony. To his relief all of his brother's paperwork was intact, which meant that who-ever wanted the skull either didn't want the theory or didn't know of its existence.

The phone rang suddenly, interrupting Ben's thoughts. Roma Jaffe's steady voice came down the line.

'How are you? I was told you were back in London.'

How did she know that? Ben wondered.

'I'm coping. How's the Little Venice investigation going?'

'Slowly.'

'No leads?'

'Nothing concrete,' Roma replied. 'We did a recon-struction, but no one recognised the victim.'

'No one?'

'No . . . Did you?'

Surprised, Ben took a moment to answer. 'Why should I?'

'He had your card in his pocket.'

'That doesn't mean I knew him. As I said before, there could have been a dozen reasons why he had my card.'

'But why was there nothing on his body apart from your card?'

'I don't know.'

'It's a mystery,' she said slowly. 'You couldn't identify the facial surgery either, could you?'

'No. I just know I didn't do it.'

There was a stilted pause before she spoke again.

'I'm very sorry about your brother. It must have been a terrible shock. Duncan said that you didn't think he'd killed himself, and that you wanted to prove it.'

Closing his eyes momentarily, Ben regretted his uncharacteristic outburst and tried to mend the damage.

'I was very upset when I spoke to your colleague. I'd just found Leon's body.'

There was another swinging pause.

'What were the findings of your brother's autopsy?'

'They said it was suicide.'

'But you don't think so ... So that means you must think that someone murdered him? Who?'

'I don't know.'

Even over the phone Roma could sense that he was holding back. 'Do you know *why* your brother was killed?'

Detita was standing by the stove, stirring something in a pot. Behind her, at the kitchen table, sat the young Ben and Leon arguing good-naturedly over a book. Finally, Ben let go of the book and Leon leant back in his chair, holding the volume tri-

265

umphantly to his chest. In the distance came the angry sound of a dog barking, the wind clapping in the trees outside. The atmosphere changed in an instant, from homely to threatening.

'You hear that noise?' Detita asked, turning to the brothers. 'That's Goya. The old man's come back. He's looking for his head . . .'

Snorting, Ben laughed, but Leon glanced over to the window, unnerved.

'Someone came to see the old painter at the Quinta del Sordo. Goya knew them, knew what they wanted to do . . .' She paused, making sure the words were leaving an imprint on the cloying air as she pointed beyond the window, the outside lamp shuddering in a late summer wind, Leon transfixed. 'He heard devils passing his house at night, on horseback—'

The firelight caught in her eyes for a heartbeat, yellow darts of flame in the blackness of her pupils. And behind that, somewhere Ben had never gone, was the place where she had taken Leon a long, long time before.

'Mr Golding?' Roma said, raising her voice slightly over the phone. '*Do* you know why your brother was killed?'

'No.'

He was lying, she could sense it, and she fired a volley into the dark.

'Why were you asking about the Little Venice murder?'

He fielded the shot. 'Why wouldn't I be interested, since I'm involved in the case?'

'But Duncan said you were talking about your brother being killed, and *then* you asked about the murder. And you've just asked me about it too.' She pressed him. 'I wondered if you thought there was a connection between this killing and your brother's death?'

'How could there be?'

'I don't know. You tell me.'

There was a temptation for him to confide, to tell her that someone had broken into his house. But then she would ask what they had stolen and somehow Ben wasn't ready to talk about the skull, or his suspicions. Because they would sound absurd, and because she might write him off as a hysteric. Certainly she would exclude him from being involved in the Little Venice murder investigation – and he couldn't have that. He needed to know as much as he could about Diego Martinez. In case his death held a clue to Leon's.

So he didn't confide. He lied. 'I'm sorry I can't help you.'

'Really? You don't know anything?'

'No,' he said, his tone final. 'Nothing at all.'

38

Fiddling restlessly with his house keys, Carlos Martinez sat outside Roma's office, waiting to be seen. He had been at the police station for half an hour, his gaze constantly moving over to the wall where there was poster of the reconstruction. Underneath were the words:

DO YOU KNOW THIS MAN?

He had seen it for the first time coming out of the Underground. Had stopped, taken aback, trying to work out if the face was who he thought it was. The eye colour was wrong, so was the styling of the hair, but he knew who it was. When he saw the second poster he found himself shaking, the eyes of the reconstruction looking blankly at him, not as they had done in life. But then again, this wasn't life, was it?

He hadn't gone home. Instead he had walked to the police station and told the desk sergeant that he wanted to see a detective. After showing them the photograph of Diego that he carried in his wallet it was clear that his son was indeed the face in the poster.

Leading the shaken man into her office, Roma closed the door behind them and showed him to a seat.

'I'm Inspector Roma Jaffe. I'll be handling your son's case, Mr Martinez. I'm very sorry for your loss ...'

He nodded, started fiddling with his keys again, his head down.

'Can I ask you when you last saw your son?'

'A week ago,' the old man said, lifting his gaze, his eyes blurry with cataracts. 'He'd come to London to visit me. He did twice a year, and we'd promised to meet up again last night. But Diego didn't call or come to my place, and I was worried. It wasn't like him.'

'You said he was visiting London?' Roma prompted him. 'Where did he live?'

'Madrid.'

The word took a swing at her. 'Madrid ... Did he work in Madrid?'

'He took over my business there.' The old man went on, his voice dropping then hurrying on, the accent obvious. 'He wasn't making a lot of money, but he'd kept it ticking over. You know, times are hard everywhere ...'

She nodded.

'Diego was my only child. He grew up with me, but when he was in his twenties I met someone and I moved over to London to be with her.'

'And your son stayed in Madrid?'

'He had friends there.'

'Family?'

'No, Diego was divorced.'

Roma nodded, her voice gentle. 'Do you know if your son had any enemies?'

'Because he was killed? He was, wasn't he? He was killed.'

'Yes, I'm afraid he was.'

'Who did it?'

'I don't know,' she replied honestly. 'But now we know who he was, we can move the case forward. *Did* your son have any enemies?'

He shrugged. 'No, he wasn't a man like that. No one envied Diego.' There was a long pause. 'I don't think he knew a lot of people in London, apart from me.'

'What was the business?'

'Builder.'

'Had he had any arguments with clients lately?'

'Who would kill him? No!' Carlos Martinez replied shortly. 'Diego kept himself to himself. He was quiet. He would do anything for anyone. He was kind, almost too kind.'

Pausing, Roma remembered the card found on the body and fired a volley into the air. 'Did your son know a Doctor Ben Golding?'

'We all did,' Carlos said, smiling. 'A long time ago, Dr Golding's parents gave me a loan which saved my business. I never forgot it. We owed them a lot.'

'So you knew the family?'

'Dr and Mrs Golding were killed when the boys were in their early teens.' Carlos paused, rubbing his right eye. 'I'd known Miriam – Mrs Golding – when she worked at the Prado. I'd done some building repairs there and she hired me to work on their family house.' He was looking back, remembering. 'It needed work. Big old house, with bad plumbing. Rundown, always something needing repair. I had to replace the guttering too ...' He trailed off, then rallied. 'There were two boys – Ben and Leon. Ben came to London—'

'Did you know him here?'

He shook his head. 'Nah, we weren't in touch. I haven't seen him since he was a teenager.'

'What about Leon?'

'Oh, I knew Leon. And Diego knows – *knew* – Leon quite well.'

Roma leaned forward in her seat, intrigued. 'Did your son work for Leon Golding?'

'On and off,' Carlos replied. 'Leon's a bit ... troubled, but pleasant enough. Diego did some repairs for him quite recently. I know because he told me all about it on his visit and about Leon's girlfriend. He said she was beautiful, but he didn't trust her.'

'Why not?'

'He knew her already,' Carlos continued. 'Diego said that she didn't remember him, but he'd done some urgent repair work for Gabino Ortega in Madrid – and she'd been Gabino's girlfriend at the time. He remembered her because they'd argued and Gabino had ended the affair and she'd taken it badly. Threatened him, said she'd pay him back.'

'What's her name?'

'Gina . . . I don't know her surname. Diego would know . . .' He trailed off, biting his lip to stop himself crying. It took him several seconds before he could speak again. 'On his last visit, my son seemed different. He said he'd just seen Leon Golding and that he'd done him a favour.'

'A favour? What kind of favour?'

'Diego found something in the cellar of an old house in the centre of Madrid. They had been digging up the floor, which hadn't been touched for centuries, and he found this skull. It was interesting because Diego knew the history of the house, knew that Goya had stayed there.'

She was baffled. '*Goya?*'

'The painter, Goya. He'd lived there for a little while,' Carlos went on. 'The skull had been hidden for a long time and when Diego found it he thought it might be the painter's . . . Leon had talked to Diego about Goya for years, so he gave it to him. Our whole family owed them a debt. I mean, I paid back the money a long time ago, but there was more to it than that. Leon was the right person to give the skull to. And besides, Diego knew how much it would mean to him.'

Roma studied the old man. 'I don't understand. Why would it mean so much?'

'Leon Golding's an art historian, very well known. An expert on Goya.' He took in a breath, tugging at his keys, making them jingle erratically. 'Diego said he was over the moon with it. Thought it would make his name. Leon took Diego out for dinner as a thank you.'

Was this the time to tell him that Leon Golding was

dead? Roma wondered. He had just found out his son had been murdered – did he need to know about Leon? Thoughtful, she glanced away, making some notes. So there *was* a link between Ben Golding and the victim. More than a link – a bond. And he'd denied it. Why?

'I was going to come and talk to the police anyway,' Carlos said quietly, lifting his head and fixing his eyes on Roma. 'Diego wouldn't say anything, but he was being followed.'

'Did he know who was following him?'

'No. It was in Madrid.' Carlos sighed. 'He came to London to see me, but also to get away from Spain. He said his house and his business had been watched. He was scared. Really scared. I told him to go to the police, but he wouldn't.'

'Did he say why he thought he was being watched?'

'The skull,' Carlos said flatly. 'It's worth a fortune. The art world would want it, and private collectors. I know because of the conversations I used to have with Miriam Golding. She said that one day the skull would turn up—'

'Why isn't it with the body?'

'It was stolen,' Carlos said. 'A long time ago. The story's well known in Spain. Not over here, but at home, yes. Goya's our most famous painter and the tale of the skull's a legend. You know, folklore. People have been looking for it for a long time. They say it's cursed, but who knows . . .' Again he trailed off, remembering his son. 'Maybe they were right.'

'Did your son say anything about the people he thought were following him? Any descriptions?'

'No, nothing like that.'

'Did he receive any phone calls? Messages?'

'Not that I know of.'

'Did you know that Diego had Ben Golding's card in his pocket?'

He didn't react as Roma reached into her desk drawer and pushed the evidence across to him. After another moment, she flipped the card over to reveal the mobile number on the other side.

'D'you know this number?'

'Of course I do. It's Leon's number. Leon Golding's.'

She sighed deeply, the old man watching her. 'I'm very sorry to have to tell you this, Mr Martinez, but Leon Golding is dead.'

39

In the Whitechapel Hospital Ben was walking down the Loggia with Sean McGee's file under his arm, Megan Griffiths running behind to keep up. The boy's operation had been a success, but Ben was late for his afternoon clinic and had missed lunch. Having stood in for Ben when he was in Madrid, Megan was surprised to see a file she didn't recognise – the notes on the Little Venice murder.

'Can I look at it?' she asked.

Ben shook his head. 'No, it's confidential.'

'It's all over the newspapers. It can't be that confidential.'

'My part in it is,' he replied, putting the file into his briefcase.

Expecting his registrar to leave, Ben was surprised to find Megan hovering as they reached his consulting rooms.

'You were asked for your medical opinion, weren't you? Can I help?'

'I've already done the examination,' Ben replied, curious. 'Why do you want to be involved?'

'It's not the kind of thing that happens every day. Murder, involving a patient who had had facio-maxillary surgery—'

'Which is something you couldn't have known unless you had already looked at the file,' Ben replied, infuriated. 'I'll have to put that in your assessment, Dr Griffiths—'

'Don't tell me you wouldn't have done the same!'

'I probably would have, yes,' he admitted, 'but not for the same reasons. I suppose you want to write up the case?'

She nodded, holding his gaze defiantly. 'It would be the chance of a lifetime. You know how difficult it is to get a posting at a good hospital. A doctor needs every bit of help they can find. And an innovative paper, with a well-known case, would help me a lot.'

Sighing, Ben moved behind his desk and sat down. He knew that if he tried to stop her, Megan Griffiths would do the paper anyway. She would gamble on the notoriety of her work outweighing her mentor's disapproval. He was tired and under stress, and her interference rankled.

'You realise that it would be unethical for you to publish anything until the murder becomes public knowledge? Or until it has been solved?'

'What if it *isn't* solved?'

'There's nothing to stop you from writing it up anonymously,' Ben replied, 'but that would defeat the point, wouldn't it?'

Defiant, she went on the attack. 'You don't like me, do you?'

'You're right, I don't.'

Without saying another word, she turned on her heel and left.

For the remainder of the day Ben regretted the altercation and he knew he had made an enemy out of a colleague – something he would normally have avoided at all costs. But life wasn't normal at the moment. Leon was dead and the police were asking him questions, and instead of seeking their help, Ben was lying to them.

Returning home later that evening Ben paused at the doorway, almost reluctant to enter. When he did walk in and turn on the light, he half expected his house to be broken into again. But the furniture was in the same place as it always was, the post on the mat at his feet. As he bent to retrieve it, he could hear the answerphone clicking off in the study.

By the time he got to it, the caller had rung off, the red light flashing three times. Three messages. Checking the room, he pulled the curtains closed, then flicked the PLAY button.

'*Ben, hi, it's me . . .*'

He relaxed at the sound of Abigail's voice.

'*. . . I just wanted to say hello. I wondered when you were coming round. Anyway, phone me when you get in.*'

A pause followed, then her voice again, gentle.

'*I miss you. Bye.*'

Saving the message, Ben played the next, smiling when he heard Francis Asturias's booming voice. His tone was pretend outrage, mock angry.

'*Bloody Golding! Call me back, you prick. I've got some news.*'

Replaying both messages, Ben realised that Abigail would be safer if she returned to France and stayed with her father. In France she would be away from him. In France, she would be safe . . . An unexpected noise behind him made him turn, but it was only a pigeon on to the window ledge outside. Rolling his head to loosen his neck muscles, he clicked on the answerphone to access his last message.

The voice was a man's. Disguised and ominous.

'*I've got the skull, Mr Golding . . .*'

Ben stared at the phone as the muffled voice continued.

'*If you're tempted to talk to the police, remember Leon. Remember your brother and what happened to him.*

'*I'm watching you.*'

40

There are fifty-nine steps leading from the back exit of the Whitechapel Hospital to the laboratory. There is a lift but it's seldom used, too erratic to be trusted. Staff climb the stairs or take a short cut through the main body of the hospital, via Reception. The fifty-nine steps at the back are divided into dozens, a landing after every twelve except for the last flight. No one knows why there are only eleven steps here, but the last leads to a landing, the laboratory and, off that, storage.

Baffled, Francis Asturias stood in the storage room of the Whitechapel Hospital. He thought at first that he was imagining things, but then opened the box marked CAUTION – ANIMAL REMAINS again and felt inside. It was empty. The skull was gone. Tipping up the box, he rummaged through the shredded paper, but he could see at once that there was nothing there and glanced back to the shelf. It was definitely the right box. It was the *only* box marked CAUTION – ANIMAL REMAINS.

Reaching for a cigar stub in his pocket, Francis remembered that he couldn't light up inside the hospital and chewed the end of the smoke instead. The skull had been there the previous day – he had checked – but now the box was empty. Preoccupied, he moved over to the door, fingering the key. Perhaps he had left the storage room open? He dismissed the idea immediately. For over thirty years Francis Asturias had locked up at night. The laboratory *and* the storage room. He'd never missed once.

So maybe there was another key. But who would have access to another key? And even if they did, why would they bother to go into a storage room which was just a repository for old files and junk? How would they know what to look for? Deep in thought, he walked downstairs to the back of the hospital and then moved behind a row of waste bins. Lighting up, he inhaled morosely on his cigar and nodded to a colleague who passed on his way to the car park. The evening was unseasonably cold and Francis shivered and pulled his white coat around him.

Inhaling again, he felt the bite of the tobacco on his tongue and glanced towards the main body of the hospital, lit up against the wintry dark. Half hidden in the shadow of the bins, he finished his smoke and moved back up to the laboratory. It was empty, no one due until the morning, but he had one more thing to do before he went home.

Flicking on a desk light over the workbench, Francis took out his mobile and dialled a number.

Ben picked up on the third ring, having obviously read the caller ID. 'Francis, how goes it?'

'Well . . .' He shuffled his badly scuffed shoes. 'I've got a bit of a problem. The skull's gone.'

'Shit! I forgot to tell you.'

'Tell me what?'

'I took it from the hospital.'

'*You* took it?'

'When I came back from Madrid.' He paused. 'I'm really sorry – I forgot. I should have told you.'

'Arsehole,' Francis said distantly. 'I was dreading telling you, thought you'd go mad—'

'The whole thing's academic anyway. I've been burgled. Whoever broke in took the skull.'

He could hear a low whistle coming down the line, Francis obviously gathering his thoughts. 'So you took the skull from the hospital? But now someone's taken the skull off you?'

'That's about the measure of it.'

'I see . . .'

Curious, Ben prompted him. 'What is it?'

'It's funny, I kept thinking about our conversation the other day and what you'd said,' Francis went on. 'About the skull being dangerous, and how you didn't want anyone to know about it. Or even where it was. And then a thought came to me. I mean, *I'd* handled the Goya skull, and the pathologist had seen it. Of course I'd told him to keep it a secret, but he might have told his secretary, might have left a note hanging about. People in hospitals gossip all the time . . .'

'So?'

'. . . And then Leon died, and you started talking about how you thought someone had killed him. That was scary,

Ben, fucking scary. And now you're saying that you've been burgled.'

'What is it, Francis?'

'You went off to Spain in such a hurry I didn't have time to tell you before you went. And you never return your bloody messages—'

'*Tell me!*'

'I swapped skulls. *I* have the Goya. Whoever robbed you got a fake.'

At the other end of the line, Ben flinched. 'So where's the real skull?'

Francis was about to tell him. He was forming the words. But although his lips moved, no sound came from them. Instead a sudden and tearing pain made him drop the mobile, his left hand going to his throat, arterial spray drenching his fingers as he tried to breathe. As his knees gave way, Francis made one desperate last effort to hold together the gaping wound. But bubbles of bloodied foam came from his mouth and he slumped to the ground, the knife coming down again and severing his spinal cord.

The last thing Francis Asturias saw before he died was his mobile being turned off, and then dropped into the pool of his own blood.

41

Passing the monkey's cage at the back of the health shop, Emile Dwappa paused, glancing through to where Mama Gala was sitting, picking her nose. Her bulk, hot in all its fleshy weight, sagged in the chair, her feet in wide sandals, the toenails long and ridged. Around her head she had, as always, a tightly woven turban. Dwappa knew why. It wasn't some cultural fashion – it was to cover the fact that she was virtually bald. Only once had he caught her without the turban and stared, fascinated, for a long time, watching through the door of her bedroom. Her head had been covered with the scars of old sores, the back of her neck criss-crossed with lesions.

Outside, the rain had emptied the street, only a few school kids hurrying home, Mama Gala watching them. Under her arms the sweat patches swelled into dark half-moons, and her black eyes, with their yellowing whites, were alert. Shifting her position in the chair, she picked some matter from the corner of her left eye and stared at her son, her expression full of malice. He knew she was angry, looking for a reason to be provoked to violence. So strong was the sense of imminent menace around her, it leached from the floorboards of the shop, over the dried herbs and the packets of health foods, staining the labels and smearing the cheerful red lettering outside.

'So?' she said slowly.

'What?'

'You said you were going to get us out of here.' She picked her nose again listlessly. 'What happened to the big idea? I don't see no big money coming in.'

He smiled, thinking of Bobbie Feldenchrist. 'It's working out – have a little more patience.'

She was surprised, and showed it. 'How much patience I need?'

'How much money you want?'

Her gaze moved over to him again, fixed him, made him remember the times he had wet himself when he was a child, so terrified of her he could hardly breathe.

'You said we were moving,' Mama Gala went on. 'We should move on, get out of here soon. I don't like being poor. I don't like living like this.' She studied him. 'Don't you hold out on me, boy. Don't you think you can make money and run off and leave me here.'

'I won't leave you—'

'No, you fucking won't!' she snarled. 'I want a big house. A *really* big house.'

And he wanted to put her in a big house – a huge place with enough room for him to breathe. With air that wasn't already tainted with her. He wanted to load his mother with money and buy himself some life. And he would, soon. Very soon.

'I had to set it all up. It took time. The first part's working out just perfect.' He thought of the baby being cosseted in New York. 'Any time now I'm on to the second part. Then I can move in for the kill.'

'Fuck time!' she snapped, heaving herself to her feet. 'I've heard too much about time. I want to get out of here, you hear me?'

'I hear you.'

'So, now you hear me – you do it!' she snapped, moving behind the counter and beginning to chop some dried herbs.

Her skin gave off an acrid smell, her hands greasy with sweat. And for an instant he couldn't relate what he was seeing to the genial woman who babysat for the neighbours' children. All the time she rocked them and sang songs, her feet tapped on the rug. And under the same rug were loose floorboards, and under the loose floorboards pornographic tapes, tapes crackling with malice.

Sing me a lullaby, they asked her, and she sang, tapping her feet on the corruption below. Rocking the children over the discs of the bad, the mad and the dead.

Hearing the shop door open, Mama Gala looked over at the visitor, her expression challenging as she stared at the fat man.

'You again?'

'I want to see Emile Dwappa.'

Shaw was sweating, leaning against the door jamb, his

face bloated, shiny. Although freshly bandaged, his hand was swollen to twice its size, the stink of decay unmissable. Trying to work up enough saliva to speak, he pushed himself upright.

'I want to see him. He's expecting me.'

Slowly Mama Gala turned her head and beckoned to her son. Gesturing for Shaw to follow him, Dwappa moved to the stairs. Hiding his triumph, he watched as Shaw grunted his way up the narrow staircase.

When he came within a yard of Dwappa, the African waved his hand in front of his face. 'You stink.'

'You did this to me!' Shaw gasped, breathing raggedly. 'You cure me now.'

'All in good time,' Dwappa replied, glancing at the package under Shaw's arm. 'That it?'

'Yes.'

'Did you get your money?'

Shaw nodded. But the action hurt him, tore into his neck muscles, every inch of his body sweating and blistering. 'I got the money. And I got the skull.'

He could hear his own breathing, his lungs gluey, exhausted. On the flight from Madrid he had been isolated, the other passengers moving away from him, the stewardess asking if he was fit to fly. He had lied, said he had suffered an allergic reaction, that he would recover within twenty-four hours. And all the time he had been following Ben Golding, knowing *he* had the skull. After all, if Leon no longer had it, his brother must have.

Back in London, it had been easy to track Golding and

later break into his home. It hadn't even taken long to find the skull. But what had been *really* interesting was the phone message Shaw had heard while he was in the house. A message from Francis Asturias about the skull – a message he had not completed.

Although the message had said nothing specific, Shaw's instincts had been roused. He didn't know what Francis was alluding to, only that his antennae for deception were tipping him off. So he had shifted his watch from Golding to Asturias. Had tracked the reconstructor to the Whitechapel Hospital and watched him. Shaw knew he looked sick enough to be a patient and no one would ask him why he was there. And before long Shaw discovered that Francis Asturias was a close friend of Ben Golding, and that he had reconstructed the Little Venice murder head. Which meant that he would know about the card Shaw had planted on the victim – the card which pointed to Ben Golding's involvement.

The rest was easy to guess. Who else would Golding allow access to the skull but Francis Asturias? Who else would Golding confide in after his brother's death? Who else would be privy to the whereabouts of Goya's head? All roads led back to one person and one person only – Francis Asturias.

Not that Shaw had meant to kill him. He had meant to scare him off, to warn him to keep his mouth shut. Time had been getting so short, he had known he was dying, but at least he had the skull. At least he could give Dwappa what he wanted in return for his life . . . But when Shaw had got to the laboratory the reconstructor had been talking on the phone. And Shaw had heard his words.

. . . I swapped skulls. I have the Goya. Whoever robbed you got a fake.

The misery of the words had slammed into Jimmy Shaw like a demolition ball. After all his striving, after all the tracking, the travelling, the threat of his own death creeping up closer – ever closer – behind him, he had ended up with the *wrong* skull.

In his rage he had struck out. And in killing Asturias he had not only expunged his own fury, but had made sure there was no one living who could question the validity of the skull. Because when Shaw had stolen it, he had taken Asturias's authentication papers too. No one would challenge its authenticity, least of all Dwappa.

Jimmy Shaw had had no choice. He had been too sick to start looking for the real skull. Time had bested him, and he knew he would be lucky to make it to Dwappa before he passed out. There was to be no more running after skulls, from London to Madrid. It was over. Jimmy Shaw had got a skull.

Only he would know that it was the wrong one.

'So, this is it?' Dwappa said, taking the skull and weighing it in his hands. 'Not as heavy as I thought.' Slowly he unwrapped the package, staring at the head.

'I kept my word,' Shaw said thickly. 'Now you keep yours. Cure me.'

Ignoring him, Dwappa kept his eyes on the skull, imagining how proud his mother would be. Soon she could have the house she wanted, the clothes she wanted, the power she wanted. And get off his back. Stick to her potions and her lies, keep to her secrets – but keep away from him. And after he had done the final deal, he would have money enough to travel. He could go anywhere. No more Brixton, no more Mama Gala breathing her fetid breath down his neck.

Composed, Dwappa turned back to Jimmy Shaw. Surely he didn't believe he could be cured? He couldn't be that stupid! Although, Dwappa had to admit, the trick with the money had been an inspiration. Of course, he had had no real intention of giving Shaw cash in advance. It simply went into Jimmy Shaw's bank – and was never transferred. Shaw received confirmation of the deposit, but by then Dwappa had moved the money on again. Back to his own account.

Tilting his head to one side, he stared at the sick man. 'How many?'

'What?'

'How many people died to get hold of the skull?'

'Three,' Shaw lied.

He reasoned that the higher the body count, the more impressive it sounded, even though he had only been responsible for the deaths of Diego Martinez and Francis Asturias. Let Dwappa think he had killed Leon Golding too. No point disabusing him.

Panting, the fat man leaned against the wall, his left hand leaving a sweat mark on the paint. 'Here are the authentication papers,' he said, passing Dwappa the reconstructor's notes. 'It's Goya's head. Proven.'

'You did well.'

'Now you return the favour,' Shaw said, swallowing with effort. 'Get this fucking poison out of me.'

He was trying to bargain with a young, fit man who had no pity and no intention of saving him. Jimmy Shaw had served his purpose. His slow poisoning had kept him alive just long enough to find the skull. His belief in a cure had kept him going while his body grew steadily more toxic.

Shaw's eyesight was beginning to blur and panic was only moments away.

'You have to help me.'

He watched as Dwappa's gaze moved to his bandaged hand.

'Does it hurt?'

'What the fuck d'you think?' Shaw replied. 'Give me something.'

'Like what?'

'Cure me!'

'But I can't do that.'

Shaw had suspected it all along. Although the medication he had been given in Spain had affected a temporary recovery, new symptoms had begun and his fingers were turning black. Blinking, he stared at Dwappa and then slid down the wall, ending up sitting on the floor. His throbbing hand lay against his bloated stomach, his fat thighs sweaty, greasy with the matter which was seeping out of his body. Across the room he could see the old woman watching, his eyes blurring as Dwappa stood over him.

'What ... what about the money?'

'No money. No one gets one over on me ...' Dwappa replied, crouching down on his haunches and jabbing at the pus-filled wound on the back of the fat man's hand.

Shaw winced, felt fresh blood soak the dressing, his heart thumping sluggishly, its action slow.

'You'll be dead in a few minutes.'

His eyelids were closing and his face muscles slackening, losing all expression. Emile Dwappa never saw Jimmy Shaw laughing at him, smirking, and thinking that it was almost worth dying to know that he had crossed the African.

All Dwappa saw was a gasping, bloated man. A fat, beaten, stupid man. A man who had been hired, used and disposed of. Emile Dwappa had never taken Jimmy Shaw seriously.

And never once suspected that he would – in the end – destroy him.

42

In the morgue, Ben was looking at his old friend's body in the minutes before the autopsy began. The injuries were savage, the wound in Francis Asturias's throat inflicted with force, his spinal cord severed by the plunging down of the knife blade. Shaken, Ben stared into the reconstructor's face, knowing that he was responsible for his death. Just as he was responsible for Leon's. The guilt was crippling.

'I'm so sorry,' Roma said, coming up behind him, 'but we need to talk.'

The morgue was uninviting, the tiles glistening as though snow-covered, Francis's body on the table, ash-white, darkening underneath where the blood had settled after death.

'Mr Golding, can we talk in your office, please?'

Turning, he nodded, Roma following him as they made their way back to Ben's consulting room. Gesturing for her to take a seat, he took his and stared at her. There was no animosity in the look, only a blind incredulity.

'Do you know any reason why Francis Asturias was murdered?'

'No.'

She changed tack abruptly, hoping to catch him out. 'What about Diego Martinez?'

The name reverberated in Ben's head. 'Who?'

'Oh, I think you know,' Roma replied. 'Mr Martinez's father recognised his son from the reconstruction. He came in and told us about Diego. About how he had known your parents in Madrid. About how they had given him a loan when he was in difficulties. A loan which meant a lot to him.'

Ben considered before answering. 'Now you mention it, I do remember Mr Martinez—'

'What about his son? Remember him now? He knew you and your brother.' She checked her notes. 'When his father moved to London to marry an Englishwoman, Diego stayed on in Madrid to run the business. He did work for your brother recently. And his father said that he did Leon a favour.'

Ben said nothing, couldn't control his thoughts. Leon dead, Francis dead, and now the police had found out about Diego Martinez. How long before they knew about the skull? Or did they already know? He slumped back in his chair, rubbing his forehead, hearing Francis's voice on the phone and the last words he had said to him.

It's a fake.

And then he thought of the message on his answerphone.

Don't talk to the police . . . I'm watching you.

Confused, he looked at Roma Jaffe. He wasn't supposed to talk to the police. He had been warned . . .

'Do you know what the favour was?'

'What?'

'I know this is very difficult for you, Mr Golding,' she said sympathetically, 'but I have to ask these questions. They could be important. Do you know what favour Diego Martinez did for your brother?'

'No.'

She sighed, leaning forward. 'He gave him a skull . . .'

Mute, Ben stared at her.

'It's Goya's skull. Apparently worth a fortune. Mr Martinez knew your brother would want it.' She hurried on. 'He found it and gave it to Leon, and now both of them are dead. Murdered.' She went on. 'Mr Martinez's father said that Diego had been threatened. Was your brother threatened?'

Again he said nothing.

'I can help you—'

'Help me?' Ben replied curtly. 'How can you help me? Leon's dead, Francis is dead, this Diego Martinez is dead—'

'Because of something they all had in common. Leon was given the skull in Madrid. Did he ask you to have it authenticated?'

Silence.

'What about Francis Asturias? He was a reconstructor – he did the Martinez skull for us. Did he reconstruct the Goya head for you?'

'I don't know.'

'I don't believe you,' she said flatly. 'He was a friend of

yours, the person you would be likely to go to first. Especially if you wanted to keep it quiet.' Sighing, she leaned back. 'If these three men were killed because of that skull, you're involved. Which means that you might be in danger too . . . Where's the skull now?'

Ben shook his head. 'I don't know anything about it.'

'You must do! Leon was your brother. You were very close. He would have come to you—'

'He had his own life!'

'He relied on you. I've been told that. You were his elder brother, you were successful and stable.'

Flinching, Ben turned on her. 'Meaning that he wasn't?'

'He committed suicide, Mr Golding.' She paused. 'But then again, you don't believe that, do you? You've told everyone that you think Leon was murdered. So why deny it now?'

'Did I deny it?'

Impatient, Roma changed tack. 'Your card was found on Diego Martinez's body. You were the last person to talk to your brother before his death. And oddly – going from his mobile phone records – you were talking to Francis Asturias around the time of his murder. You have to talk to me, Mr Golding, because this is beginning to look very suspicious.'

Incredulous, he stared at her.

'You think I had something to do with Leon's death? You think I killed these men?'

'No,' she replied, tempering her tone, 'but it looks very odd that you won't talk to me. Just answer my questions, please.'

His gaze moved away from her towards the door as she continued.

'I've heard some things about your brother's girlfriend, Gina Austin.'

He looked back at her. 'What things?'

'Did you know she was involved with Gabino Ortega? And that he dumped her?'

'No,' Ben said honestly, remembering how Gina had lied to him, pretending that she had only known the Ortegas by reputation.

'How did Gina Austin get on with your brother?'

'Why don't you ask her?'

'We've tried. She's not at the farmhouse any longer,' Roma replied. 'Do you know where she is now?'

He had the impression that he was drowning, pulled under dirty water and a slow choking of mud.

'No.'

'You're not being very helpful—'

'Well, neither are you!' Ben hurled back. 'You come here asking me questions. Why aren't you trying to find out who killed Leon? And Diego Martinez? And Francis Asturias? Find out, because I'd like to know. Francis was a nice guy, eccentric, funny. I liked him. Perhaps I was even fond of him. All the time I've been at the Whitechapel I've known him. And he would do anything for anyone. And now someone's stuck a knife in him and you – *you* – have the nerve to suggest that I did it!' He got to his feet. 'I'm not answering any more of your questions. If you want to talk to me again, we'll talk in front of my lawyer.'

Surprised, Roma stood up. 'There's a connection between these deaths and I'll find it.'

'Good. Well, let me know when you do.'

43

New York

He was the last person she wanted to see. But when the intercom buzzer sounded from below, Bobbie allowed Emile Dwappa to come up. She had made sure that her son and the nanny were out of the apartment and had dressed herself as though she was going to a business meeting. Which, in a way, she was. The African had to be made to realise that his usefulness to her was over. He had brought Joseph into her life and for that, she had paid him amply. There was nothing more she wanted from him. If he was difficult, she would have to put pressure on him.

Turning to the mirror in the entrance hall, Bobbie studied her reflection as though examining a painting. The Issy Miyake suit was flattering but dark. As for her make-up, there was nothing soft about it – nothing welcoming. Only she would know that behind the image she was moist with anxiety. She didn't know the full extent of the African's dealings – she didn't want to. She just wanted to make sure that when he left her apartment he would never return.

Expressionless, Bobbie watched the elevator come to a halt at the penthouse, saw the doors open and the African walk out with a small briefcase. He did not seem surprised to find her waiting for him. Instead he moved past her into the drawing room and sat down.

Infuriated by his familiarity, Bobbie's tone was curt.

'I thought our business was concluded. In fact, that was why I agreed to see you today, to impress upon you that there is no reason for us to meet again.'

He glanced round, unconcerned, Bobbie nonplussed.

'Mr . . .' She paused, realising that she had never known the man's name and now certainly did not wish to learn it. 'Do you understand what I'm saying?'

His narrow face was as impassive as hers. Only he realised that she was affecting her stance, whereas he was fully in control.

'What would you say would be the most important find in art?'

Her eyebrows rose, irritation barely concealed. 'I don't think—'

'How's your son?'

Again, she was taken unawares. 'Joseph's very well.'

'Can I see him?'

A moment of unease threatened to capsize her.

'He's out with his nanny.'

'He has a nanny?' The African's pale eyes seemed amused. 'I bet you got him the best nanny in the world.

Who *are* the best nannies?' he asked, then pretended to think. 'Oh, yes, Norland nannies. English.' He could see Bobbie flinch and carried on. 'Do you really think I don't know *everything* about your child?'

She swallowed, but kept her voice steady. 'Why did you want to see me?'

'You didn't answer me.'

'About what?'

'About what would be the most important find in art.'

'I don't know,' she replied shortly, 'That would depend on what people were looking for. One person might want a piece of sculpture, another a Rembrandt.'

'What if the piece wasn't art, but something personal to the painter?'

Despite herself, Bobbie's attention was caught. 'What kind of personal thing?'

'Like Leonardo's hand.'

She laughed, surprising herself. 'If you think someone has the hand of Leonardo you've been duped. People often try and pass off fakes as artistic relics.'

'But what if this was *proven* to be authentic?'

For an instant she forgot her fear and felt only the thrill of the collector scenting a find. 'You have proof?'

'Yes. From a leading art historian and a top forensic reconstructor.'

She laughed nervously. 'Indeed.'

'I've become aware that many private collectors would be desperate to own this object. Bartolomé Ortega for one—'

'*Bartolomé Ortega?*' Bobbie repeated, startled by the name coming from such a source. 'He's involved?'

'He wants to be.'

Her voice steadied. 'What *is* the object?'

'It's very rare. Very rare indeed.'

'Are you going to tell me what it is?'

'A skull.'

Her eyes flickered. 'Whose?'

'Goya's.'

To his surprise, she laughed. 'Oh, not again! Poor Goya. To my reckoning his skull has been "found" three times. Each time it was a hoax.'

'The Prado don't think it's a hoax.'

She stopped laughing. '*They have it?*'

'No.'

'But they've seen it?'

'They know all about it. They allowed one of their leading historians to have it examined.'

Sitting down, Bobbie could feel her legs shake. So one of the great mysteries of art history had finally been solved. The missing head of Francisco Goya had been found after being stolen nearly two hundred years earlier. The head of the greatest Spanish master who had ever lived . . . She could imagine what her father's reaction would have been – astonishment, followed by an overwhelming desire to own it. But how could an individual, even a Feldenchrist, add such a treasure to their private collection?

But then again, what was the African doing in her

apartment *unless* he was coming to sell? Jesus! Bobbie thought, her heart drumming. Did he have it?

'Why did the Prado allow this historian free rein?'

'Because he found it. Or rather, it was found and passed to him.'

She leaned forward slightly in her seat. 'Who is he?'

'Who *was* he,' the African corrected her. 'Leon Golding. He committed suicide only the other week and the skull left his hands.'

Bobbie had heard of Leon Golding, but she hadn't known about his death. And she didn't want to know because knowing might be dangerous for her. She was tempted to ask the African to leave, but instead her gaze moved to the small briefcase beside his feet, her breath quickening.

'I hadn't heard about Mr Golding's death. He was a gifted historian.' Her gaze fixed on the case, hardly daring to believe what she was thinking. 'Was the skull found with Mr Golding?'

'No, there was no sign of it in the hotel room.'

'Was it at his house?'

'No.'

'So what happened to it?'

'Apparently it was stolen.'

'*Stolen?*' she echoed, her eyes flicking from his face back to the bag at his feet. 'Do the Prado know?'

'Oh yes.'

'And Bartolomé Ortega?'

'He knows it's missing.'

'But he hasn't found it?'

'No.'

'He has a lot of contacts and money. I would have thought Mr Ortega would have been able to get hold of the skull—'

'His contacts must have failed him.'

'But he would want it badly.'

'He must have had the wrong contacts.'

'Do I have the right one?' she asked, staring at the dark leather of the case and imagining what was inside.

The skull of Francisco Goya – and she, Bobbie Feldenchrist, would own it. It wasn't difficult to picture her coup, or the animosity which would follow from the likes of Bartolomé Ortega and the Prado. That an *American* would end up possessing a priceless Spanish treasure ... The thought made her covet the skull even more. What a triumph for her and the Feldenchrist Collection. It would make the cover of *TIME* magazine, would be talked about in every artistic circle around the globe.

Bobbie tried to keep her thoughts composed, but longing overtook her. She sighed, taking in a breath. The skull wasn't hers yet. Not yet.

'Well,' she repeated calmly, '*do* I have the right contact?'

In reply Dwappa bent down and lifted the case on to the table between them. Slowly he opened it. Bobbie leaned forward, her hands extended, but he brushed them away. Instead he lifted out the skull himself, passing it to her in silence.

She could feel her hands shake as they cupped the discoloured bone, her gaze travelling across the empty eye sockets and the jawline, her memory fleshing out the bareness until she could imagine the artist restored. The man who had pictured the Spanish court, the *majas*, the Disasters of War ... Swallowing became difficult, emotion so intense it was almost erotic. To own *this*, to own the head of one of the greatest painters who had ever lived! She could see it in a display cabinet, behind unbreakable, bulletproof glass, with one of Goya's pictures on display beside it. People would come from all over the world to visit the skull, to pay homage to the artist and, in doing so, to the Feldenchrist name. She would be recognised as the greatest collector alive, because she would own the greatest artistic relic in existence.

Her voice was husky when she spoke again. 'Are you sure it's genuine?'

He nodded. 'I told you, I have authentication.'

Then he put out his hands.

Bobbie immediately leaned back, out of his reach. It did not matter that she was holding the head of a dead man, a skull which had been wrenched from a corpse. To her it possessed no spirituality, but was merely an emblem of triumph.

'Give it back to me, Ms Feldenchrist.'

She was curt with desire. 'How much do you want for it?'

'Five million dollars.'

She made a short, snorting sound. 'Five million!'

'You have it.'

'You're mad.'

'So give the skull back to me,' he replied implacably.

'Three million.'

'I won't bargain,' the African said, staring coldly at her. 'It's a lot less than you paid for your son.'

She winced, remembering Joseph – then put all thoughts of him aside. 'Five million is too much.'

'The Prado would want this skull. No doubt they could raise the money.'

'Five million? I don't think so. Besides, they wouldn't pay *you* for it. They wouldn't do anything illegal.'

'But Bartolomé Ortega might. And he's a rival of yours, isn't he? And I believe he was more to you in the past . . .'

Bobbie shrugged, trying to bluff. 'So why don't you go to him?'

'Maybe I already have. Maybe I'm just waiting for the highest bidder.'

Bobbie stared at the African, her confidence fading. 'Has he put in an offer?'

'He might have done. What's your offer?'

'I'll match his.'

'No,' the African replied, suddenly changing tack. 'I think I might ask something else from you. What if I asked you to exchange your son for the skull . . . ?'

The words made a hissing sound in her ears.

'What would you say, Ms Feldenchrist? Give me your son and I'll give you the skull.'

'You're not serious?' she croaked, still holding the skull to her, the hard bone pressing into her chest.

'What if I am? Your son for the skull.'

Incredulous, she stared at him – at the narrow head, the smooth, dark features, the seeming absence of malice in this most malicious of men. The skull seemed to rest against her, warming, soothing. No one else possessed such an object. No one. A woman could adopt a child any day. Hadn't she proved that? But there was only one Goya skull – and she was holding it.

'So, Ms Feldenchrist, what's it to be? Your son or the skull?'

Her fingers were holding the head so tightly she could hear her nails scratch against the bone.

'Just give me back your baby and you'll beat Bartolomé Ortega. It's not a hard choice for you to make, is it?'

'I ... I ...' she stammered.

'Come on, make the choice!'

Letting out an odd mewling noise, Bobbie stared at him. 'I ...'

The African laughed suddenly, taking the skull from her hands. 'Relax. I wouldn't be so cruel,' he said, his taunting over. 'What would I want with that kid of yours? No, Ms Feldenchrist, I want money. I want five million dollars for this skull.'

She was beaten and she knew it.

'All right. I can get it for you.'

'I know that,' he replied, tucking the skull back into the packing and closing the case. 'I'll come back tomorrow at four. You give me the money then, in cash, and I'll give you the skull.'

Quickly he moved to the door, pausing by the elevator. Behind him, Bobbie leant against a pillar, her face ash white, her body drained. Finally the elevator came to a halt at the penthouse and Dwappa turned back to her.

'Aren't you lucky, Ms Feldenchrist?'

'Why?'

'That I didn't make you choose,' he replied, walking into the elevator and turning back to her. 'When you think about our meeting later you'll remember the choice you were ready to make.' He smiled as the doors began to close. 'What *would* it have been, Ms Feldenchrist? The baby or the skull?'

44

London

'I had to come,' Abigail said, walking past Ben into the hallway. Once inside, she kissed him, then pulled back and looked into his face. 'You look terrible. Handsome, but terrible—'

'You shouldn't have come here. I told you not to.'

She ignored him. 'I heard about Francis. I rang your rooms. Your secretary told me.'

She could see that Ben was shaken, Francis's death coming so soon after Leon's. Concerned, she touched his cheek, trying to soothe him. His composure was weakening. Other people might not notice it, but Abigail could see the difference. His appearance was altering, his outer, physical size somehow overwhelming the inner man.

'What's going on?'

'You know what's going on—'

She shook her head. 'No, I know *some* of it, but not all. Talk to me.'

'I can't. *I daren't*,' he said, turning away from her and walking into his study. Alarmed, she followed him. 'I want you to go back to France, Abi. Go back there until all this is sorted out.'

'*All what?*' she queried. 'I've only got half the story, Ben. You have to talk to me. Don't cut me out.'

'*Talk to you?*' he said simply. 'Jesus! That's the last thing I'd do. Francis is dead because I involved him. I can't risk you. You have to go back to France—'

'And if I refuse?'

'Don't do that,' he said anxiously, touching her face. 'Please, don't do that.'

Pulling her to him, he rested his lips against her hair, breathing in the scent of her. He knew that in rejecting her he was exiling his last ally, but he had no choice. From the moment Leon had been given the Goya skull all their lives had changed. A malignancy had begun which was now spreading hourly. Knowing that his own safety was in question, Ben was aware that he might not be able to stop its progress, but he wasn't going to sacrifice anyone else.

'Go back to France,' he repeated, kissing her cheek. Then he drew back, touching her skin and feeling the slight swelling underneath. 'Abi, what's this?'

She smiled lightly. 'Nothing. I'm having it checked out.'

'Let me look,' he replied, turning her to the light and staring at her face. The doctor again. 'You've got to have that seen to. It might be nothing, but—'

'Stop worrying,' she said, hurrying to reassure him. 'It's

all organised. I'm having a biopsy. I'm going into the Whitechapel tomorrow.'

'Without telling me?'

'Ben, stop it! I was going to tell you, but other things have happened before I could. Don't look at me like that – it's nothing to worry about. You're not my doctor any more – Mr North is doing it. He was going to talk to you about it this afternoon.' Her voice softened. 'Relax, darling. This is me, Abigail. I'll be fine and everything will work out in the end.' She led him to the sofa, sitting down beside him and resting her head on his shoulder. 'You have to get some rest.'

'Malcolm North's a good doctor,' Ben said, preoccupied. 'He knows his stuff. You'll be in safe hands.'

'And what about you? Whose safe hands are you in?'

'Not yours, Abi.'

She smiled, almost regretfully. 'I know you're trying to protect me – and I love you for it – but you have to trust someone.'

'Not you. I won't put you in danger.'

'What danger?' she pressed him, sitting up and looking into his drawn face. 'Is there a connection between the deaths of Leon and Francis Asturias?'

'Let it rest—'

'I'm not a fool, Ben!' she snapped. 'I know about Leon and the skull. And I know you gave it to Francis to authenticate—'

He gripped her hands so tightly she winced. 'You're hurting me!'

'Forget everything I told you, Abi. Please, leave it alone.'

'Why? What are you going to do?'

'I don't know who killed Leon or Francis, so how can I *do* anything?'

'You need to sleep—'

'I can't sleep!' he snapped back. 'I have to go to Madrid tomorrow, to Leon's funeral—'

'Then let me come with you.'

'No!' Turning away, he shook his head. 'I wish my brother had never got hold of that bloody skull. I wish he'd never seen it. The moment Leon touched it, his life fell apart. It tipped him over the edge.'

'He was always near the edge—'

'And they pushed him over.'

'*For a skull?*' Abigail asked incredulously.

'We're talking about *Goya's* skull – what wouldn't a collector do to own that? Dreams are made on lesser stuff. Leon used to talk about the competitiveness of the business. How a dealer or historian was desperate to find something valuable, or prove a theory. Poor bastard,' Ben said gently. 'Poor, sorry bastard . . .'

She took his hands in her own.

'. . . Leon thought that the skull would make his name. And if he solved the Black Paintings, he'd be set for life. But he was competing with the likes of Bartolomé Ortega, and God knows who else.'

'You don't have the skull any more, do you?'

He was desperate to confide – to tell her about Francis's

confession and about being threatened – but he held back, giving her the partial truth.

'I don't have the skull.'

'Thank God,' she said with feeling. 'But surely whoever has it will have to explain how they came by it?'

He smiled bitterly. 'No one will ever know that it was stolen from me. People would deny knowing how it came into their hands. The provenance would be blurred. Leon used to tell me all about it – the fudged backgrounds, the made-up histories. There would just be vague stories of the skull being found—'

'That was Leon's story.'

'That wasn't his *story*, it was the truth. The skull *was* found and passed over to my brother—'

'But now it could be anywhere,' Abi said, her head on one side. 'Why don't you let it be?'

'*What?*'

'What can you do, Ben? Leave it to the police. Let them handle it. If there's anything to find, let *them* find it.'

She was afraid for him, and for herself. Afraid of losing the man who had given her back her life. Afraid to lose the protector she had fallen in love with. To her shame Abigail realised that despite her sympathy for Ben, she was angry with Leon. Angry with the dead man who was threatening her security and the life she prized.

'Just back off—'

'*My brother was murdered!*'

'You've no proof of that. The Spanish coroner ruled it suicide. You've no evidence, and with Leon's background of mental instability no one would believe you.' She leaned towards Ben, her mouth dry. 'Leave it alone. Whoever wanted the skull has got it back. Forget about it, then you'll be safe. They have no reason to come after you unless you give them a reason.'

Incredulous, Ben stared at her. 'So I let my brother's killer get away with it?'

'What else can you do?'

'Jesus! You just don't get it, do you? I can't walk away,' Ben replied. To her amazement he seemed close to tears. 'I was supposed to look after Leon. Everyone knew he was unstable, that he needed protection. I had a duty of care to him—'

'He was *not* your patient.'

'*No, he was my brother!*' Ben snapped back. 'He was my home, my family. He was my sibling. For years there were only the two of us – the Golding brothers. I was meant to look out for him. *He needed me.*'

'You did what you could—'

'I wasn't there!' Ben shouted, almost beside himself. 'I didn't save him. I failed him . . . And I can't live with that.'

Desperate, she pleaded with him. 'Leave it alone, Ben, please. I love you—'

'I know. And I love you.'

'I don't want to lose you—'

'And I don't want to lose you.' And then he lied. 'It'll be all right, Abi. It's just all been such a shock. It'll take some time to come to terms with.'

His thoughts were running on and he realised that

having Abigail admitted into the Whitechapel Hospital was the perfect solution. At the Whitechapel, he could keep an eye on her. As a patient, she would be surrounded day and night, with nurses to keep watch over her when he wasn't there. What better place to be protected than a hospital? It was, he thought with relief, even better than her returning to France.

Then he remembered what else Abi had said: *They have no reason to come after you unless you give them a reason.*

And that was *exactly* what he was going to do. He wasn't going to be warned off. He wasn't going to give in to threats. He was going to do the opposite and draw attention to himself. Ben Golding might not know who had killed his brother and his friend, but he knew how to find out.

He wasn't going to run or hide. Instead he was going to make himself visible. And then they would come after *him*.

BOOK FOUR

... I have painted these pictures to occupy my imagination, which is tormented by all the ills that afflict me ...

GOYA ON THE BLACK PAINTINGS

Quinta del Sordo, Spain, 1822

Her shadow fell across the whitewashed wall of the house as she carried the washing indoors. The heat had been so intense that the clothes were still hot under her fingers as she folded them. Leocardia had no interest in local gossip. She had no reason to explain why her marriage had failed, or why she had chosen to live with Francisco Goya.

She leaned against the door jamb, full-hipped against the hard stone. The old man's deafness was no impediment to her. He did not hear her frequent outbursts, her temper hot as dry sand. He remained painting while she cleaned the house; he remained painting while she cooked, eating everything she gave him grate-fully. And he remained painting while she bathed and then stood, half-naked, in the doorway, letting the night air dry her.

The bawdy libertine, the late Duchess of Alba's lover, the painter kings had bowed to, was now a willing captive in the enclosed world of the Quinta del Sordo . . . Languorously, Leocardia moved upstairs, the heat rising with her. The old man was painting a fresco in their bedroom, another of the garble of murals with which he was mapping the interior. She moved towards him, knowing he would sense her coming, and rested her chin on his shoulder, looking at the painted figures of the Ministration: *one grimacing man in the foreground, one to the left, and a woman laughing behind. Not as disturbing as some of the images, Leocardia thought, then realised that the foremost figure was masturbating.*

Amused, she stretched her arms above her head, then walked over to the window and relit a batch of candles. Sometimes, when she had the patience, she talked to Goya slowly so that he could read her lips; chastised him for working too long, in too poor a light. He would listen and shrug, grabbing at her backside in a memory of earlier desires.

And, as always, Goya's demon figures flickered in the lamplight, Leocardia's own image in the room below them. Her image, huge as an icon, leaning on a mound of earth.

'What's under the ground?' she had asked.

Again a shrug, a word scored impatiently into the wet paint underneath.

'Me.'

Leocardia was no stranger to superstition. To her, dark forces were as much a part of life as sunlight. But in the few years since they had moved to the Quinta del Sordo she had seen Goya's original paintings of the dancing figures obliterated under the Pilgrimage of St Isidore, *the meadow turned to a rocky outcrop, as barren as the madmen who walked there.*

Still watching him, Leocardia thought of Dr Arrieta. He believed Goya was suffering from a breakdown and that his last illness had taken a mental toll. He was afraid, Arrieta said sadly, that the old man might never recover . . . Leocardia's eyes fixed on the painter, unblinking, her expression unfathomable. Knowing he was watching her, Goya turned and tilted his head to one side, regarding her.

Many times he had thought of sending Leocardia away, but he knew he would not. He would let her stay. He needed her. He was afraid of her. He was afraid without her. The summer would capsize itself and the autumn would slip out of her greenery, but she would stay.

Outside, Goya could sense a late wind picking up. It swung through the trees, taking the steamy heat from the river and creeping into the Quinta del Sordo unseen. Behind him stood a massive painted image of despair: a solitary dog in a desolate landscape, only its head showing as the quicksand dragged it under to something no one could see.

For an instant Goya stared at the image and the dog's head turned. It barked once, the sound unheard, its eyes full of terror and the fear of coming death.

45

Richmond

Walking up the driveway to a secluded eighteenth-century house outside London, Ben ducked under some overgrown hydrangea bushes as he reached the front door. Wisteria, grown reckless, knotted about the windows and the porch, and a rose – long in the tooth – raked its thorny teeth against the brickwork.

Finding the bell, Ben rang it several times before footsteps approached the door, a young woman opening it and smiling.

'Can I help you?'

'I've come to see Mrs Asturias. My name's Ben Golding. She's expecting me.'

Elizabeth Asturias was sitting in the breakfast room, nursing a copy of the *Telegraph* and a cup of tea. As Ben walked in, she took off her reading glasses and jerked her head towards the dining chair next to her.

'Nice obituary for Francis in the *Telegraph*,' she said, tapping the paper with her index finger. 'Bastards didn't have the same kind words for him in life.'

The comment, delivered in razor-sharp English, came as a shock. Over the years Francis had mentioned his wife in passing, but always with dry humour, suggesting that the classy Elizabeth had had little time for him and less affection. But the ageing woman Ben was now looking at had the telltale puffy eyes of grieving and an unexpectedly short temper.

'I told him to retire – would have liked him home.' She stopped, shouting at the young cleaner. 'Careful! I can hear you clattering those dishes about. They chip, you know.' She glanced back at Ben. 'He liked you.'

'I liked him.'

'Hmm,' she said simply, tossing the paper to one side. It landed on the floor like a shot bird. 'They killed my poor lad. Francis . . . Of all people. It's so . . . unnecessary.' Her eyes filled and she wiped them briskly with the back of her hand. 'Killed him. Who would do that? *Why* would anyone do that?'

'I don't know—'

'Oh, don't lie to me!' she snapped fiercely. 'I was married to him. I knew what was going on. Francis used to tell me everything. Of course I pretended that it bored me, but he knew I loved the gossip.' She sighed, staring at her fingernails and wincing as the cleaner made another noise. 'Go for the post, dear!' she snapped. 'Oh, and get some bread from the shop while you're at it.'

They waited for the young woman to leave, Elizabeth

watching her pass the window and go down the drive before turning back to Ben.

'Now we can talk properly. Francis told me about that bloody skull of yours. Or should I say, your brother's?' She raised one eyebrow. 'He's dead too, isn't he?'

Her directness caught Ben off guard. 'Yes, he is.'

'Killed, I believe?'

'Who told you that?'

'Francis did! Don't be bloody coy,' she said shortly. 'I've told you, he told me everything. He said you were insisting that your brother was murdered.'

Ben paused, surprised by how much she knew.

'I came to pay my respects—'

'Bullshit! You came for something else,' she said perceptively. 'I know you were in Madrid and couldn't make the funeral, but you sent me a letter and a wreath – you had no need to come and pay your respects in person. *Unless* you wanted to ask me something.'

'You're smart.'

'I know,' she said bluntly. 'Retired university lecturer in Classics. I was a psychotherapist too. Francis won't have told you that; he hates – *hated* – shrinks.' She glanced over to the window and the view of the drive. 'I'm sorry I never met your brother – he sounded interesting.'

'He was.'

'Why do we always lose the good ones, hey?' she queried, tapping the teapot with the arm of her glasses. 'You want a cup?'

'No.'

'I don't blame you. The cleaner makes bloody awful tea.'

Smiling, he thought for a moment then glanced back at her.

'You're right, I did come to ask you something. Francis reconstructed a skull for me—'

'The Goya skull?'

'Yes, the Goya skull,' Ben replied, 'but you don't know that.'

'I've just told you.'

'But now you have to forget that you know about it, Mrs Asturias. It's not safe for you to know about it.' He paused, trying not to alarm her. 'Francis rang me just before he was killed ...'

'And?'

'He told me that someone had stolen the skull.'

She was genuinely shaken.

'He didn't tell me. Poor sod didn't have time, I suppose.' Her bravado was her way of coping, keeping back the grief. 'You know who took it?'

'No,' Ben admitted. 'But there's more. The skull that was stolen wasn't the real one. Francis had swapped them. Whoever has the skull now, has a fake.'

Caught off guard, she laughed, shaking her head.

'How like him! Francis loved to make everything complicated. Couldn't let anything be simple ...' Pausing, she caught Ben's eye, her intelligence obvious. 'So where's Goya's skull?'

'I don't know. Francis was going to tell me, but he didn't

have a chance. That's why I'm here – to ask you if you know.'

'No, I don't.' She was genuinely regretful. 'If I did, I'd tell you.'

He had expected as much, but the disappointment still stung. 'Did Francis have a workshop here? Or a study?'

Rising to her feet, Elizabeth moved over to the door. She was unexpectedly tall. Beckoning impatiently for Ben to follow her they moved through the hall and down a narrow passageway into the kitchen, then walked across a courtyard into an outbuilding. The property was decrepit and neglected, but obviously of considerable value. And Francis's retreat was just as impressive.

'He used to sulk in here,' Elizabeth said fondly, holding back the door. 'We had a wonderful sex life, you know. Even up until his death. Wonderful lover.' She glanced over at Ben. 'You're shocked, of course. The ageing population isn't supposed to have desires, is it?'

'Why not?'

She winked, amused. 'Good answer!' Sweeping her arm across the room, she went on. 'Help yourself. Have a rummage – I don't mind. This is all of it. Francis loved machinery, computers, all kinds of technology – you name it. The dotty professor act was just that – an act. He could tackle anything.'

Walking around, Ben opened cupboards and searched them, bending down to look at the neatly stacked shelves. They were filled with paint tins, machinery, and hundreds of tools of all shapes and sizes. But no hidden boxes, no crumpled bags, no concealed skull.

Still searching, he asked, 'Did he spend a lot of time surfing the net?'

'The only net Francis surfed was the one he used when he went fishing.' She pointed to his fishing tackle. 'Have a look in the basket – it might be there.'

Ben did as he was told.

'No, nothing.' He glanced back at her. 'Where would he hide something? You knew him, you knew how he thought. What would Francis use as a hiding place?'

'He used to hide his cigars behind the bath panel, but I found them and he never did it again.' She paused, thinking. 'If he brought the skull home, he would have hidden it here for safety. Kept it away from me and the house. He knew what a bloody nosy old bat I am ... But we don't know for certain if he brought it home.'

'No, we don't.' Hurriedly, Ben continued his search, then glanced over at the row of blank computers.

'Did Francis use the internet for work?'

'Oh no! He just liked to fix computers. Take them apart and then put them back together again. Or buy old ones' – she gestured to one of the first Amstrad machines – 'and repair them. I suppose it wasn't so different from what he did at the hospital, putting people's faces back together again.'

Ben pointed to a door. 'May I go in here?'

'If you want to have a pee, go ahead.'

Amused, Ben walked into the lavatory and checked the cistern. Empty.

'Did Francis talk about all his reconstructions?'

'What?'

He moved back into the main room so that she could hear him. 'Did he talk about the reconstructions?'

'Only the interesting ones.'

'What about Diego Martinez?'

'The man who was chopped up and left all over London?' Elizabeth nodded. 'He liked that case, although he did say that when he'd reconstructed the head he was disappointed. Thought the man looked dull. He said that his death was probably the most dramatic thing that had ever happened to him. Francis felt sad about that one.' Her expression veered between affection for his memory and the remembrance of his loss. 'He had such respect for people. Such fondness . . .'

Still walking around, Ben opened the worktable drawers. 'May I?'

'Help yourself.'

'What did he say about the Goya skull?'

'He was proud to have reconstructed that head,' she said simply. 'I've always loved Goya's work, but Francis wasn't interested in art. Having said that, he was touched by what he did. I even found him looking at some of Goya's work afterwards. That was a bloody surprise.'

He glanced over at her. 'The skull's not here, is it?'

'I think you'd have found it if it was,' Elizabeth replied, sighing. 'D'you want to search the house?'

'Can I?'

She shrugged.

'I don't mind, Mr Golding. The skull means nothing to me. And if it helps you to find out who killed your brother and my husband, I'll give you all the help you need.' She held his gaze. 'Yes, I've worked it out. Diego Martinez, Francis – they're connected by the skull, aren't they, Mr Golding? I think they must be, because otherwise you would never have warned me to forget everything I knew about it.' She turned to the door, flicking off the light but inadvertently turning on another switch.

Surprising both of them, the computer next to Ben came on.

'Is this one fixed?'

'The only one that is,' Elizabeth replied. 'The rest were work in progress.'

Connecting up to the internet, Ben ran down the Received and Sent emails. Elizabeth had been right: her late husband hadn't spent much time using the computer, and less sending messages. There was nothing of interest, mostly spam. Then, for some reason Ben could never explain, he checked the Delete file.

And there, in among emails from seed catalogues and Amazon was the address Gortho@3000.com.

46

Prosperous in a dark silk suit, Bartolomé Ortega walked towards the graveside. The heatwave had not returned; the weather had cooled its heels and the late sun was now limp, leaden with cloud. Outside the city, across the river, the old cemetery gates creaked solemnly in the dry, brisk breeze. Occasionally they shuddered against their rusty hinges, the lichen-coated stone eagles portentously silent on the gateposts above.

Also silent, Bartolomé Ortega glanced ahead. There was a reasonable turnout for Leon Golding's funeral, and even though the coroner had ruled it a suicide he was pleased to see that the body would be laid in consecrated ground. Punishment after death was for God, not man. But although Bartolomé was feeling generous towards Leon Golding, his anger with his brother had not lessened. Every day he waited for Gabino to come to him with the news of the skull, and every day he stayed away deepened their rift.

Behind his sunglasses, Bartolomé looked around, his gaze fixing on the figure of Ben Golding standing as though immobilised beside his brother's grave. His presence was as impressive as always, but there was a poignancy, a kind of desperation about the man which caught, and held, Bartolomé Ortega's attention. Ben Golding's grief was absolute, his silent guard as eloquent as a thousand pious words.

Slowly, Bartolomé's gaze moved across the other mourners, nodding to several people he knew. Then he spotted a woman standing slightly to one side, a good-looking redhead who seemed familiar.

'That's Leon Golding's girlfriend. Well, she *was* . . .' he heard someone whisper behind him.

So this was Gina Austin, was it?

Bartolomé studied the woman who had once been Gabino's mistress, her honed, athletic body evident even under the mourning black. She was trying to be inconspicuous, but her movements were too extravagant for a funeral and he found himself automatically disliking her. There was no doubt she had beauty, but she seemed to be more interested in the living Golding than the dead one.

Solemnly, they all watched Leon Golding's coffin being lowered into the ground, Bartolomé wondering momentarily why he had lost out on the greatest find in art history. If Gabino had told him about the Goya skull he would have got it away from the historian, would have made certain that an unbalanced man wasn't left in charge of a priceless artefact. He had admired Leon Golding's brain – and had always feared that the Englishman would solve the mystery of the Black Paintings before he did – but to be bested by him was unbearable. And it was all Gabino's fault.

Disappointment left Bartolomé limp. If only he had got the skull away from Golding, taken the object under his own weighty and wealthy wing. He would have offered his services to the Prado immediately, impressing upon them the importance of the find and the equal importance of preserving it, and how *he* was the best person to undertake the mission. But his brother had kept quiet and Bartolomé had missed his chance. And now where was the skull? London, probably, with Ben Golding, Bartolomé thought bitterly. It *could* have been his. It *should* have been his – if his idle brother had secured it for him.

His face expressionless, his eyes narrowed behind his dark glasses, Bartolomé kept watching Ben, thinking of the Golding brothers. Thinking enviously of their bond – a closeness he had never experienced with Gabino. He could see the loss in Ben Golding's face and thought of the skull again and of the old rumour which had surrounded it. Some had sworn that it was cursed. That anyone who touched it was tainted. The same people spoke of the Black Paintings in hushed tones. There *was* a meaning to them, they said, but it was fatal to the person who uncovered it.

Such superstition used to amuse Bartolomé, but he was no longer quite so sure that mockery was justified. And, as a cloud shifted over the cemetery, he felt a distinct unease. A hoarse wind blew up, throwing dust about the mourning stone angels and the dilapidated urns. Holding her hand to her face, Gina turned away, but Ben Golding stood motionless as though he hadn't noticed the turn in the weather, the sun whey-faced behind a darkening cloud.

Glancing at the grave, Bartolomé stared at the coffin of Leon Golding, the varnished wood already spotted with the first bold shots of rain. Soon there would be a downpour, he thought. Water would fill the grave. Over time a little would leach into the coffin, the Spanish earth holding fast to its adopted son.

But it wasn't Leon he pitied. Instead, Bartolomé looked back at Ben Golding and realised that if there was a curse, it had already found its next victim.

47

'What do you want?' Gabino asked, walking past Gina in his office and moving out on to the balcony.

The heat was stifling, the earlier storm having passed, the sound of traffic rising from the street below. He looked down, Gina moving over to him and standing only an inch away, their shoulders almost touching. She was banking on his previous desire for her, hoping it could help to reinstate her into the powerful Ortegas. But Gina was no fool. Gabino had rejected her once and she needed more than the lure of sex to reel him in.

'I've missed you—'

'Especially since Leon Golding killed himself,' Gabino replied, bad-tempered with the heat, a sore throat making him irritable.

'I loved you,' she said, touching his arm. But the action only annoyed him and he shrugged her off.

'It's over. It was over a long time ago. Don't come back here now you need another meal ticket.' He leaned towards her, his face pushed close to hers. 'You had your turn.'

Stung, she kept her temper. This was no time to lose control. Gina knew that her looks were at their height, but within a couple of years they would wane, their rangy athleticism lunging fast to wiriness. If truth be known she had latched on to Leon at a party, hoping that by being with him she might move on to his more illustrious brother. But Ben had never shown the least interest in her, and Gina had found herself in the tiresome position of being the girlfriend of a brilliant, but hysterical, man. Determined to make the most of her situation, she had given herself another year to entrap Leon and had been sure of success – until events had altered everything.

'Don't you feel anything for me?' she asked, still standing beside him, as though she could force some intimacy.

He shrugged. 'You were a good lay.'

The words punched the air out of her and cemented her plan.

'I see . . . So you're not interested in the Goya skull any more?'

He turned so quickly it was as though he had been spun round. 'You've got it?'

'What if I have?'

Suddenly he was all attention. *The skull* – the way back into his brother's wallet.

'Gina, you sly one,' he teased. 'What *are* you playing at? I mean, I knew Leon had the skull, but I didn't imagine that he gave it to you . . . Or did you take it?'

Pausing, she juggled her words.

'You want it?'

'You know I do.'

'For Bartolomé?'

He shrugged again, but this time Gina laughed.

'Don't try and fool me! I heard about the court case. Well, everyone in Madrid's heard about it. I suppose your luck would run out eventually – everyone's does.' She was baiting him, back in control and repaying him fully for insulting her. 'I imagine that if you could give Bartolomé the one thing he wants above anything else he would do you a favour in return. Perhaps see to it that you don't go to jail.' She sat down, crossing her legs, mean-spirited. 'Your brother could do that, couldn't he? I mean, he has the money to organise something like that.'

Silent, Gabino watched her as she continued.

'But the question is, *would he*? Bartolomé's really pissed off with you, Gabino. You always tried his patience. I remember when we were together you mocked him so much, and always expected him to take it. But no one takes it forever, do they? You've disgraced the Ortega name and he could make you pay for it. I mean, your own father was disinherited, wasn't he? I suppose Bartolomé could do the same to you.' She looked round. 'All this money, power . . . all your toys – it would be hard to lose all that, Gabino. Not many women would be interested in visiting you in jail if you had nothing.'

His expression was hostile. 'So what are you offering?' he asked. 'You *are* offering something, aren't you?'

'I can get the skull for you.'

'Really? Who's got it?'

'Leon's brother.' She was intent, watching Gabino's face, watching him trying to disguise his interest.

'Are you sure?'

'No, not sure,' she admitted. 'But Leon didn't have it with him when he killed himself and it's not in the house. I know – I've searched. So I reckon he must have given it to his brother.'

'And you think Ben Golding will give it to you?'

'No,' she admitted. 'I think I'll have to get close to him, find out where it is, and then tell you.' She paused, letting the implication work on him.

'You're such a whore.'

'And you're different?' she countered. 'You'd sell yourself for money any day, Gabino. You need this skull – really need it. And I'm the only person who can get it for you.'

'And how much is this going to cost me?'

She moved over to him, her hand resting against his flies, her fingers moving rhythmically.

'I liked being your woman, Gabino. Liked the lifestyle.' Her lips moved against his neck, her breath hot. 'You missed me – you know you did.'

He kissed her eagerly, then drew back, looking into her upturned face. 'How long will it take you to get the skull?'

'Not long,' she said confidently. 'Ben Golding's a man, isn't he?'

48

After his brother's funeral, Ben returned to the empty farmhouse and walked the rooms like a stranger. His thoughts drifted between Leon and Francis Asturias, wondering why the dead reconstructor had had an email from the same source as Leon. Gortho@3000.com. Had he talked to someone? Had Francis found himself incapable of keeping the skull a secret? Or had the draw of big money proved too much for him?

No, Ben thought, it wouldn't have been that. Francis had been born into money, had no need to make more. So was it a need for excitement? Or danger? Francis was getting old. Did he crave some spark of a thrill? Did he fancy himself part of a scenario which spoke of the past, a dying painter, and a relic which would be lusted after? Perhaps he didn't realise at first what it would lead to, and when he did it was too late ... Above all, Ben wanted to believe that his old friend had not betrayed him. That it had been folly on the part of Francis, not malice. Not treachery.

Moving into the bedroom Leon had shared with Gina,

Ben looked around. One wardrobe was crammed with Leon's clothes, some arranged in perfect order, others haphazard on hangers. Next to it was another wardrobe. But this was empty and the adjoining bathroom that Gina had used was cleaned out too. All that remained was a deodorant and a lipstick in the medicine cupboard.

Thoughtful, Ben moved over to the bedside cabinet and opened the top drawer, surprised to find Leon's medication and remembering his brother's panic.

. . . Have you got your pills?

They aren't here!

They must be. Look again.

They're not bloody here! And Gina's not here either.

But the pills had been there all along. And the police had said that when they checked the house Gina had been there too. So had Leon been mistaken? Walking out of the bedroom, Ben paused on the corridor outside, looking towards the window at the end of the landing. Long ago Detita had arranged to have bars fitted. She told Leon that it was to stop anyone breaking in, but to Ben she had said it was to stop his brother jumping out.

Breaking in, jumping out . . . Flicking on the lights to brighten the sombre hallway, Ben moved downstairs. He tried to convince himself that the funeral proved Leon's death, but his brother was still everywhere – a garden hat on a hook by the back door, a glass with his fingerprints, and the desk chair with a worn cushion which Leon had always tucked into the small of his back. Memories choked the farmhouse, they hovered in the garden and called from the cupboard under the stairs. Every little terror Leon had ever felt crowded into the house; every broken night and hazy day stood in testament to him until Ben could bear it no longer and made for his brother's study, slamming the door behind him.

He had checked on Abigail earlier. When he phoned the Whitechapel he had been told she was sleeping. Telling the sister not to wake her, Ben passed on a message. Then he asked to speak to Dr North. To his intense relief, Ben was told that the biopsy was benign.

'. . . but there's some muscle degeneration in her cheek, due to scarring from previous surgeries. It will need an operation, Ben. I can do it, if you want me to.'

'No one better. Have you told Abigail?'

'Yes, she was fine about it. She's had enough operations to know the drill. She did say she wanted to talk to you though.'

'I rang earlier, but she was asleep. I'll talk to her in the morning,' Ben had replied, pausing. 'Is it complicated?'

'No,' Dr North had replied calmly. 'And I mean no. I realise Abigail's your partner, but I'm not lying to you. It's a simple operation—'

'So how soon can you do it?'

'Tomorrow afternoon. She should stay in for a couple of days—'

'Keep her in longer, will you?' Ben had asked. 'I'm not in the country and she needs looking after.'

It would be ideal knowing Abigail was safe in hospital. Dr North would undertake the operation and she would be looked after as she convalesced.

'Abigail needs to stay in for a week, in case there are any complications. Her skin's fragile after all the previous operations, so her recovery needs to be watched carefully.' He had paused, no longer the doctor, now the lover. 'Take care of her, will you? She matters a great deal to me.'

Remembering the conversation, Ben sat down behind Leon's desk, fingering a millefiori paperweight. On one side there was a small chip from where his brother had thrown it in a fit of anger many years ago. It had been Christmas and Leon had been slighted by a colleague who had questioned his work, intimating plagiarism. Always an original thinker, Leon had reacted badly and had hardly spoken for the remainder of the holiday. It had been Detita who had finally drawn him out. And within half an hour Ben had heard them laughing in the kitchen and felt the sharp anguish of the sudden outsider.

Dismissing the memory, Ben opened his case and took out all of his brother's notes, finally preparing to read Leon's theory on the Black Paintings. Noticing the fading light, he pulled the desk light closer to illuminate the notebook.

To Whom it May Concern

This is my full and studied theory of Francisco Goya's Black Paintings. I told no one that I had finally completed the solution, possibly in a mistaken attempt to protect myself and my brother. The finding of Goya's skull has caused much grief and confusion. Anxious to avoid further problems I did not want it to become known that I had solved the Black Paintings. Whether my secrecy was necessary or just an absurd overreaction, only time will tell.

Here follows what I believe to be the meaning of The Black Paintings.

Pausing, Ben stared at his brother's words. So Leon had finished his theory, and had lived long enough to set it down. Slowly, he turned over the first page and began to read the solution to pictures which had haunted generations.

Goya, being a liberal, was hated by Ferdinand VII and when the King regained the throne he was terrified. It was common knowledge that in the past the Inquisition had investigated his affairs. His lover, the Duchess of Alba, had been poisoned. And now here he was, deaf and old, at the mercy of a vengeful king.

Looking at the painting of The Dog I believe that Goya was making a metaphor for Ferdinand - the Dog of Spain.

Leaning back, Ben stared at the accompanying paintings, matching Leon's notes against the relevant work.

I believe that Goya - always a liberal, always an ally of the liberals - became directly involved with the liberals who made up a substitute government in Spain, in 1822. Unfortunately, their attempt failed in 1823, and the reinstated King was brought back to Madrid. Back on the throne, his power absolute, Ferdinand VII went after his perceived enemies in order to exact a terrible revenge.

At the time Gentz wrote:

'The King himself enters the houses of his first ministers, arrests them, and hands them over to their cruel enemies . . . the king has so debased himself that he

has become no more than the leading police agent and jailer of his country.'

The painting which hung next to The Dog is entitled Asmodeus. The title was not chosen by Goya, so - if it is <u>not</u> viewed as some mystical allegory - the image becomes more immediate, its message lucid.

This picture has puzzled art historians for many years. But perhaps its meaning is not as profound as previously believed? It depicts men floating on air, at the mercy of the elements. Unable to reach the safety of the high mountain, or the firm ground beneath them, they are buffeted by fate, dreading the future ahead of them and looking back fearfully at their past. This scene depicts the fate of Everyman. And also Spain, uncertain, cut off from her roots.

As we read the paintings, we next come to The Holy Office . . .

Ben turned to the reproduction, then back to Leon's notes.

In among the crowd of hags and the feared and vicious clergy is a man dressed in courtly robes. Elegant and groomed, he stands out from the procession of grotesques, his head bent towards the swollen form beside him. The gold of his chain is luminous, drawing the viewer towards him. He seems to be an Inquisitor, and I believe this man was sent from the court to deal with Goya on the instructions of a King who believed himself betrayed ... He is carrying a glass of water, which signifies life, and beside him is a monk. Monks and nuns were the very people Ferdinand VII hired to spy on his captives and report back to him. They were his own black army of quislings.

Underneath, Leon had jotted down some short, scribbled notes, almost as though he was thinking too quickly to put them into proper sentences.

(Goya was watched while he was at the Quinta del Sordo. Was Detita right? What of the mountain in the backgrounds of the paintings? The same shape, over and over again. The shape of some terrifying, ever-present threat? Or the place of safety, always out of reach?)

Ben read the passage again, then turned the page. This time Leon had organised his thoughts into a lucid continuation of his essay.

Deaf and old, Goya had exiled himself at the Quinta del Sordo. Away from court and ridicule of his infirmity, he was confronted by the silence of his own thoughts and memories. Guilt, remorse and fear colluded to force him into a malaise which would kill him unless he conquered it or escaped it. From what we know, his illness was not a recurrence of his old sickness, but on closer examination there is a pattern - a very clear intimation of the slow death of Francisco Goya.

Whistling through his teeth, Ben read on.

The Black Paintings are a ruse, a way for the artist to chart out a map of the history of Spain. And of himself. And of his life. Ultimately his death.

A creak on the floorboards made Ben tense. The threat on the phone had unsettled him, and here he was – alone in a remote house, in his dead brother's study. He thought of the skull and cursed Francis for hiding it, for leaving him guessing. And worse, for leaving him doubting a man he had long taken for a friend.

Every memory seemed a gargoyle hunched over the past. Lack of sleep, his grief over Leon and Francis and the threat left on his answerphone were finally undermining him. His thoughts, usually incisive, were becoming mushy. He wanted to confide in someone, but didn't dare. He wanted to get help, but couldn't.

Dry-eyed, Ben turned back to his brother's notes.

... the next painting, entitled The Ministration, depicts a man masturbating,

*something which would have been distasteful and cer-
tainly not commissioned by a patron. But we look at
the act with judging eyes, without considering another
viewpoint - that the man is not relieving himself, but
is caught forever <u>without</u> relief. Sexually impotent, like
Goya, not just from age, but from disease.*

Disease ...

Ben's gaze fell on the small pile of books in front of
him. All Leon's books, all well-used, thumb-marked and
dog-eared with reading. Slowly he ran his hands over the
covers and spines. *Goya's Life, Goya's Court Paintings, Goya's
Caprichos, Goya's Disasters of War* ... every book was so
familiar to him. As familiar as if they had been his own.
But in a way they *had* belonged to both brothers. Passed
down from their parents, read from by Detita.

Goya's life had been a parallel existence to theirs. So
close, it could have been the memoir of a family member.
So well known; their own lives lived within memory of
the Quinta del Sordo and the Spaniard's reach. Every
etching, drawing and painting had been looked at by the
brothers, every anecdote Detita told them repeated, until
Leon's uneasiness had censored Ben's teasing. How fitting it had been that the old man's skull should come
into Leon's hands, because no man would have valued it
more.

So much that it had cost him his life.

Deep in thought, Ben flicked through the preparatory
tapestry drawings and the paintings which followed on.

This was the youthful Goya, seducing women and climbing the precipice to the top of the Spanish court. This was the dark man who had made love to a nun, and had painted nudes so daring the Inquisition had come after him. This was the young, lusty Francisco, with his dowdy wife and his bed full of *majas*. This was the court painter who, although not well born, could insult the royals obliquely with his satire, could flatter a doomed duchess, and who was wily enough to keep his balance on the political tightrope of Spain.

Closing the book, Ben opened another, feeling a closeness to his brother, almost hearing Leon talking behind him.

Look at this, Ben – just look at this. No one could paint fabrics like Goya ...

His hands moved over the colour prints, over the painting of Mariano, the son of Goya's only surviving child, Javier. There had been rumours that Javier had created the Black Paintings, but it was unsubstantiated. Thoughtful, Ben opened one of Leon's last notepads. His words were written loosely, some in shorthand, others down the margin, vertically, as the ideas hit him. Just looking at his handwriting brought back the clever flightiness of Leon's brain, coupled with his intense – and haunting – perception.

Pausing, Ben looked up, the rain blowing softly against the windows outside. Thinking of what he had read so far, he reached for the book on Goya's Black Paintings and began to look at the illustrations. The images were familiar to him. He had grown up with them, seen them in the Prado, on mugs, on tea towels and on the sides of buses.

Turning to the frontispiece, Ben read the words written by Goya's son, Javier.

... his own predilection was for the paintings he kept in his house, since he was free to paint them as he pleased ... they were always his special favourites and he looked at them every day ...

Ben wondered about that. Wondered how a man could take pleasure from such bleakness. Then he glanced back at the painting of *The Dog*. Suddenly a dull, far-off thunderclap echoed outside, rain striking the window sill.

'He never let me read them ...'

Startled, Ben looked up to find Gina standing in the doorway.

Calmly, she pointed to the notebooks. 'I saw you'd taken them the other morning. You didn't have to do that – I wouldn't have stopped you. You were Leon's brother, you were entitled to have them. All this is yours now. The house, everything.' She leaned against the door frame, her silhouette outlined against the hall light.

'How did you get in?'

'You left the front door open,' she replied coolly, moving towards the desk. 'I can't bear this room. Too sad ...'

Leaning back in the chair, Ben watched her. 'Why did you come back, Gina?'

'I was driving past and I saw your car. I wanted to talk about Leon and you're the only person I can talk to.' She sat down, her knees pressed together like a child's. 'I miss him. He was good to me. Temperamental, yes, but kind. Always kind.' She thought of Gabino, still stinging from his treatment, her calculating mind weighing the odds. 'I know you don't trust me.'

'You lied to me.'

Her lips parted, then closed in a thin line. 'About what?'

'Losing Leon's child.'

'I did lose a baby—'

'I don't doubt that, but it wasn't Leon's. He was sterile,' Ben replied, trying to work out what she wanted and wondering if he *had* left the front door unlocked, or if Gina had kept a key to the farmhouse.

'It was a stupid lie . . . but I wanted to get you on my side.'

'I was already on your side. Leon was dead. I could imagine how that would hurt you. But lying to me? You lost my sympathy then, Gina. And my trust . . .'

She clenched her hands together, her face drawn.

'I asked you why you came back. It wasn't to talk about Leon,' Ben went on. 'So what was it?'

Her indecision confounded her. She hadn't expected Ben to discover her lie about the baby and her confidence wavered. Any attempt at a hurried seduction of Ben Golding would only damn her further in his eyes.

The plan fluttered like a torn banner . . . Silent, she stared at the floor under her feet. There were indentations in the dark wood, deep and polished shiny over the decades. She had asked Leon about them once and he had told her the story Detita had told him: that the indentations were the Devil's footprints. Lucifer had come to look over the writer's shoulder, dictating madness. And then he'd laughed and told her he was joking.

Her eyes remained fixed on the indentations as she thought of Gabino Ortega. How he had used her. How she had used him. How she had used Leon. How, throughout her life, Gina had manipulated men and been manipulated in return. She felt a sudden weariness at the thought of Gabino and wondered if his lifestyle, five years on, would prove as satisfying as it had once done. If the sex and duplicity would be bearable. If even his towering wealth would compensate for the dry ache of a woman who would soon be aged out of the market.

'Gina . . .?'

Realising that Ben was talking to her, she blinked slowly.

'Sorry, I was thinking about – Jesus, I don't know what I was thinking about. It's getting late. I should drive back to Madrid.' She stood up, then paused. 'Can I stay the night?' her voice was businesslike, almost cold. 'I can use the room Leon and I used to have. I'll leave you alone to work.'

He could hardly refuse. 'OK.'

Her gaze moved back to the notepads in front of Ben.

'Did he do it? Oh, come on, you can tell me that! Did Leon solve the Black Paintings?'

Remembering what he had heard about Gina's previous relationship with Gabino Ortega, he lied.

'No.'

'He told me he was close.'

'Not close enough.'

'Like the skull. Not close enough . . .' Her tone was expressionless. 'He gave it to you, didn't he? I know Leon must have, otherwise he would have got it back from Madrid and the phantom specialist. Thinking back, I never saw the skull after you came to the house – which means that you took it to London. You did, didn't you?'

He shook his head.

'Leon had the skull. I don't know what he did with it.'

'He didn't have it when we did the seance.'

Leaning forward, Ben held her gaze. 'Why do you care about it so much?'

'It mattered to Leon.'

'And you're going to fulfil his legacy, are you? Save his reputation?' Ben asked, bitterness obvious. 'If anyone should do that, it should be me. But the funny thing is, I don't care about his work. I miss Leon. I'm only reading his notes on the Black Paintings now because he was my brother and it's a way to feel close to him. No other reason. I don't have the skull. Truly, I don't.'

She wasn't sure if he was lying or bluffing. 'So where is it?'

'God knows. It was lost for centuries, it's lost again.'

For a long moment she was silent, then smiled faintly. 'I'm glad.'

It was the answer Ben had least expected.

49

The following morning he woke and lay in bed, listening and wondering if Gina was still in the house. But all he could hear was the sound of the ancient plumbing and the cawing of rooks outside the bedroom window. Having taken all Leon's papers upstairs with him Ben had still slept half-heartedly, wondering what Gina was doing in the house. Was she there for sentimental reasons or still trying to find out the whereabouts of the skull?

He found her too transparent to be clever, too clumsy to make a good liar. Obviously Gina didn't know that he was privy to information about her past. That he had already guessed her tactics – that she was trying to obtain the skull for her ex-lover. Whether to effect a reconciliation or secure a big payoff was the only thing Ben wasn't sure about ... Pulling on his clothes, he moved out into the corridor, looking towards the bedroom where Gina had slept. The door was closed and as he walked downstairs he was surprised to see the door of Leon's study open.

As he went in, Ben heard the muted tones of a news

broadcaster and walked round the desk to find his brother's old computer turned on. He looked at the headlines – a riot in India, the USA President taking a break at Camp David. Puzzled, he sat down, watching the tickertape strip of running news across the bottom of the screen.

. . . The skull of Francisco Goya has been found, and is now in the possession of the Feldenchrist collection in New York. This is the greatest art find for centuries . . .

A breath caught in his throat, his gaze moving towards a Post It note stuck on the nearby phone.

You were right – you didn't have it.
Gina

Jumping up from his seat, Ben moved to the bottom of the stairs and called out for her.

'Gina! Gina!'

But there was no answer, just the soft swell of dust and silence, and memory.

50

New York

Standing beside one of the newspaper booths, Ben gripped the magazine in his hand. The few people who passed him would never have believed who this anxious-looking man was. The composed surgeon Mr Benjamin Golding, FRCS, had been left behind in Madrid. Left at the farmhouse, written away in the letter to Abigail which said he was going away for a few days. That he would keep in touch. That she mustn't worry.

That was the man he had left in Madrid.

This man was different. This man was obsessed, driven. For the first time Ben understood something of his brother's sickness. Or maybe it wasn't *just* Leon's illness. After all, hadn't Detita seen it in him too once, many years before? But Ben had cheated her out of her hopes of manipulation. Turning weakness into order and protecting his brother, he had swerved around his own mental potholes. But now his whole focus – and his hold on sanity

– was fixed on finding his brother's killer. The person who had stolen the Goya skull.

He stared at the magazine again, then smoothed it out on top of the paper booth. In all her callous triumph, Bobbie Feldenchrist stared out at him, the caption underneath reading:

GREATEST FIND IN ART HISTORY
GOYA'S SKULL IN
FELDENCHRIST COLLECTION

Ben didn't know how it had arrived in the Feldenchrist Collection, and he knew that no one ever would. Its provenance would be sanitised, its sojourn in a London washing machine overlooked, its resurrection in Francis Asturias's hands denied. It had come to rest in one of the wealthiest and most powerful collections in the world. In New York. The Spaniard's head, so used to *majas* and hunting, would be gawped at by gum-chewing crowds and camera-punching tourists.

It was, Ben thought, so shabby. So out of place among the car horns and police sirens. It should have rested with the painter's corpse, or within sound of the Manzanares and the river birds. Within sight of Madrid, not in New York. And if there had been any justice in the world, Leon should have been on the cover of the magazine, his alert, slightly nervous face stamped with his achievement.

'Give it to me,' Leon had said imperiously when they were boys. 'I want it!'

It had been a summer, but overcast, the Spanish sun taking a day-long siesta. In the garden, an emerald lizard had shuffled its cool way across the lawn and from the kitchen had come the smell of herbs, cooking slowly in an earthenware pot.

'Ben, give me the bat,' Leon had said, the nervous tapping of his foot giving away his impatience. 'I want to play cricket.'

'You're such a liar! You know damn well you just want to give it to that girl. And girls aren't even interested in cricket. Dad gave you that bat—'

'And Dad's dead,' Leon had replied. But the steam had gone out of him and, shrugging, he had glanced down, trailing his kid's foot along the dry earth. 'One day I'm going to be someone. I'm going to be famous. Marry the best-looking girl in Spain. One day people will know my name. You'll see, Ben – one day everyone will know my name.'

The memory vanished as a car horn blasted alongside Ben, making him jump back from the kerb, the magazine dropping to his feet. Putting up his hand to stop the oncoming cars, he bent down to retrieve it, ignoring the impatient tooting as he moved back on to the sidewalk. Still immersed in his own thoughts, he walked into a cafe and ordered an espresso and Danish, opening the magazine and spreading it out on the table in front of him.

The piece described the impressive Feldenchrist Collection, their particular interest in Spanish art, and Harwood Feldenchrist's ruthless acquisition techniques – techniques he had passed down to his daughter. As he sipped his coffee Ben read on about Bobbie Feldenchrist, her two failed marriages, her brush with cancer, and her recent adoption of an African baby.

An African baby . . .

Throwing some coins on to the table, Ben left the cafe, the magazine pushed deep into his pocket. Walking quickly, he hailed a cab and asked to be taken to the Feldenchrist Collection, off Park Avenue.

The cabbie looked at him through the rear-view mirror.

'You English?'

'Yes.'

'This your first trip?'

'No.'

'You here on business?'

'In a way.'

'So, what you do for a living?'

'I'm a surgeon.'

'You're kidding me!' the cabbie replied, obviously shocked as he took another look at the big, crumpled man in the back seat. 'I mean, don't get me wrong, but you don't look like no doctor to me.'

'I had a bad flight,' Ben said simply, lapsing into silence.

When the cab finally dropped him off at the main entrance to the Feldenchrist Collection Ben paused, catching a reflection of his image in a glass door. Taking off his coat and trying to smooth down his hair, he moved from the warmth of the city into the crisp, air-conditioned cool of the gallery building. Obviously the Goya skull was big news, posters already advertising Bobbie Feldenchrist's coup, a massive image of the skull itself erected over the Reception desk.

Ben stared at it as though mesmerised. He thought of Detita and her stories, of his childhood growing up near the old site of the Quinta del Sordo, and of Leon showing him the skull that first time. On that hot afternoon, in his study . . . But what he also noticed was the *absence* of something. Goya's skull had had three holes in it. This had only two.

It was definitely the fake.

A moment later a small group of people entered, walking in a huddle, a manicured woman in their midst. Her face was impassive, the same as it was on the magazine cover. Stepping back, Ben watched her progress as a photographers took a series of pictures, Bobbie Feldenchrist pausing momentarily under the vast poster of the skull.

'Ms Feldenchrist,' someone called out. 'When is the skull going on display?'

'We have to make sure that it's completely protected before we can risk showing it to the public,' she replied, sleek with success.

'Will it be displayed behind bulletproof glass?' another journalist asked.

'My security advisors are looking into that at the moment.'

'What about theft?'

'The Feldenchrist Collection has never been burgled—'

'But surely the skull of Goya would be a real target,'

the woman persisted. Bobbie turned to her.

'The skull will be exhibited only when we are convinced that it's completely safe from harm.'

'So where is it now?' Ben asked suddenly. The group turned to look at him, Bobbie glancing over their heads to catch sight of the questioner.

'Who are you?'

'An art lover,' Ben replied, walking closer, '. . . who would like to know where the skull's being kept.'

'I hardly think I could tell you that. It would be a breach of security.'

'Are you sure it's authentic?' Ben continued, the journalists glancing from him to Bobbie and sensing that there was something more to his questioning than idle curiosity.

'The skull *is* Francisco Goya's,' Bobbie replied. She was about to walk away when Ben called after her.

'Who authenticated it?'

She stopped in her tracks, turning back to him. 'When the skull is exhibited, its history will be published along with the authentication papers.'

Francis Asturias's papers, stolen with the real skull. The same papers which had been stolen with the fake. Real papers, wrong skull.

'Why can't you tell me who authenticated it?'

'Who are you?' Bobbie asked curtly.

'Someone who has a long-held interest in the skull.'

He could see her react. The momentary shimmer of unease.

'Well, I'm sure if you leave your name and address my

colleagues will be pleased to invite you to the opening night, where all your questions will be answered in full—'

'I'd like to talk to you now,' he retorted, moving to her side and edging one of the security guards out of the way. Dropping his voice, he said quietly, 'My brother was Leon Golding. Talk to me – or I'll talk to these journalists instead.'

Putting up her hand to keep the guards back, Bobbie forced herself to smile as she shook hands with Ben, throwing the journalists off balance and giving the photographers a posed shot. Then she guided him into the back of the gallery. When they were out of sight her smile faded and she ushered her unwelcome visitor into her office.

'What the hell is all this about?'

'The Goya skull was stolen. From me—'

'Hah!' she said shortly, 'You can't imagine how many lunatics have been writing to me saying the same.'

'Their brothers weren't murdered.'

She flinched. 'I thought your brother committed suicide?'

'Leon was killed. For the Goya skull.'

Laughing, she tried to appear nonchalant. 'I don't think so.'

It wasn't entirely unexpected that someone would challenge her right to the skull, but she hadn't expected the challenge to come from this quarter. Taking a deep breath, Bobbie looked at the man in front of her, wondering how to play him.

'The Feldenchrist Collection bought the Goya skull for an undisclosed sum of money, in order that it be preserved and exhibited worldwide. We have been in touch with the Prado, Madrid, and are already in talks about allowing them to exhibit it on loan.'

'Who did you buy it from?'

'You don't need to know that, Mr Golding,' she replied. 'It was purchased from a respectable source.'

'Who?'

'You don't need to know that—'

'But I do,' Ben replied, leaning forward in his seat. He was cold with tiredness and exasperation, crumpled from a hurried flight, with nothing for company but the memory of his dead brother. 'I think someone came to you with the skull – someone not in the least respectable. And I think you wanted that skull so much you didn't ask too many questions, just forked out what they asked. It would be worth it to you – to get one over on all the other collectors and even the Prado. I can see how that would be difficult to resist. But still, dealing with the wrong type – weren't you worried that it would get out? Tarnish the Feldenchrist name?'

She flinched and he caught the reaction.

'Or maybe,' – he paused, his thoughts clicking, ratchet by ratchet, into place – 'maybe he had something on you? Did he blackmail you?'

God, Bobbie thought angrily. She had been so stupid to allow this man into her office. But then again, she had had no choice. She could hardly have walked off and left him to talk to the journalists. Not Leon Golding's brother . . .

'*Blackmail me?*' she replied, amused. But her glance automatically went to the photograph of Joseph on her desk.

And Ben noticed.

'Is this your adopted son?'

She nodded, not trusting her voice.

'Where did he come from?'

'That's none of your business!' she retorted, calming herself. 'I can assure you that the Feldenchrist Collection purchased the skull through the correct channels. And my son was legally adopted.'

'Did I suggest anything else?'

'You said—'

'What? Did I say anything about him *not* being legally adopted?'

She faltered and changed the subject. 'I understand that you must be very upset about your brother's death, Mr Golding. I knew of his reputation. Because of that, we can forget that this unpleasant conversation ever took place. If you leave my office now there'll be no need to call the police—'

Instantly Ben was on his feet, leaning over the desk towards Bobbie Feldenchrist.

'*It's a fake!* Your skull is a fake. I saw the real skull, the one my brother was given. *And it's not this one—*'

'Don't be ridiculous!'

'I had the Goya skull in my possession and it was stolen from my house,' Ben snapped, staring into her upturned face. 'My brother died for that skull. My brother was murdered for it – you think I wouldn't remember it? You think I wouldn't know the real one? Who sold this skull to you?'

'That's not—'

'*Who?*' Ben pointed to the photograph of Joseph on her desk. 'You reacted when I asked about the baby. Did the same person who sold you the skull get you the child?'

She paled. 'No!'

Ben knew he was on the right track and pushed her. 'You don't know where that child came from, do you? You wanted to have an heir, and you didn't ask questions. Is that why he brought you the skull, Ms Feldenchrist? To make sure you never asked questions?'

'I want you to leave!'

'*You don't know what you're dealing with!* This man's responsible for the deaths of three men. Think about it. Three men directly involved with the skull are now dead.' He paused, his voice warning. 'But it's the wrong skull. He fooled you. Or he was fooled. Either way, this is just the beginning—'

'I want you to go!'

'You think he won't want more? Jesus! You can't *imagine* what he could want. He'll come back and you won't be able to do anything about it – because you can't even admit you know him.'

Shaken, she flinched, trying to regulate her breathing. Bobbie had always been afraid of the African but now she could see the hopeless situation she was in. She wasn't in control, *he* was. He had sold her a fake. And there was nothing she could do about it, because he could black-mail her into silence.

'You have to tell me the truth,' Ben said quietly. 'That skull cost my brother his life.'

'You don't know that,' Bobbie replied, her confidence returning as her thoughts cleared. If Ben Golding had any real proof, he would have gone to the police already. 'How can you make a connection between your brother's death and the skull? Everyone knows Leon Golding was unstable—'

To her surprise, Ben nodded. 'Yes, he was. And demanding – irritating at times. But he was my brother, and when I found him hanging behind the bathroom door in some bloody Spanish hotel room, it wasn't right. *And it still isn't*—'

'None of this has anything to do with me!'

Wearily, Ben stood up.

'All right, have it your own way. But when you look at that skull, Ms Feldenchrist, I want you to remember that it's a fake. It was never Goya's skull. The real one was swapped at the last moment—'

'This is ridiculous!'

'It's true.' His voice fell. 'I'm not lying to you. Aren't you going to admit it's a fake?'

'Can you prove it is?' she countered. 'Remember, I have the authentication papers that were drawn up at the Whitechapel Hospital, London.'

'They refer to the real skull—'

'Oh dear, Mr Golding,' she said with mock pity. 'As I

have *those* papers, which came with *this* skull, your theory won't hold water, will it?'

'It will if we compare Francis Asturias's findings against your fake.'

She took in her breath, outmanoeuvred, then rallied. 'I'll look into the matter—'

'You won't admit it, will you? You can't – you'd look a fool. And I can't prove it either, because you've got the only copy of the notes.' Walking to the door, he paused, then turned back to her. 'But when you look at that skull – *that fake* – I want you to see *my brother's face*. When you pose for your photographs, I want you to know that it should have been *him*. He should have got his day in the sun – not rotting in a graveyard. And one day – God help you – you'll regret this. You'll wish that you weren't so grasping and greedy that human lives counted less than your own bloody triumph.'

51

In the basement of the Feldenchrist Collection a morose-looking French forensic pathologist named Maurice de la Valle was pulling on his laboratory coat. Preoccupied, he washed his hands and then carefully stretched on a pair of rubber surgical gloves. With considerable caution, he made sure that the gloves fitted his fingers and allowed complete freedom of movement. Finally he walked towards a sealed storage vault and entered a fourteen-digit number, unfastening the lock and taking out a small box. He then placed the box on his worktable and, after wiping down the metal surface, spread out a piece of black plastic sheeting. Finally he took the lid off the box and lifted the skull out, placing it in the centre of the sheeting.

He turned as Bobbie Feldenchrist came in. She seemed agitated. 'I want to see the authentication papers again . . .'

He shrugged, passing them over to her.

'You checked these?'

'Of course I did. Twice.' He glanced at her, surprised that she should query his actions but not daring to show his annoyance.

Ignoring him, Bobbie stared at the skull. Her head reverberated with Ben Golding's words. Was the skull a fake? Had the African duped her? Had she really paid out a fortune for a worthless lump of bone? Christ! she thought desperately. If anyone found out, her reputation was bankrupt. She would be a laughing stock, the supposed crowning achievement of her collection not the skull of a genius but a nobody.

She could hardly question the African. He would deny his deception, and even if he didn't he could blackmail her into silence by threatening to expose Joseph's adoption.

Trapped, Bobbie felt the dry taste of failure. 'This is the head of Goya . . .'

'Yes, the head of Francisco Goya,' de la Valle replied with solemnity. 'One of the most important art finds in history.' Lovingly he let his forefinger trace the cranial markings on the skull, then move around the orbit of the eye sockets. 'I've waited all my life for something like this.'

Close to retirement age, he had felt nothing but disappointment with his career – until the skull had been handed over to his care. From being a respected, if undistinguished specialist, he was suddenly promoted, even being photographed with Roberta Feldenchrist for a piece in *Vanity Fair*. Maurice felt a swelling of professional pleasure. His retirement – when it came – would be pedestrian no longer. Thanks to Francisco Goya he would be able to travel, giving lectures about the skull, explaining his pivotal role in the phenomenal find. The long dry years which had stretched before him, heading inexorably towards a lonely death, were now bulging with promise.

Bobbie was still reading Francis Asturias's report, her gaze moving back to the skull.

'How many holes in the skull?'

'Three. Animal damage, or wear and tear,' he said eagerly, pointing them out one by one.

'But two of them aren't really holes, are they, Maurice?' Bobbie said firmly, looking at the skull. 'Those two, they're more like splits, breaks in the bone.'

His eyes flicked back to the skull and he took the notes out of her hands. Reading the report, he said:

' "Three holes, two smaller than the third . . ." Yes, Ms Feldenchrist, but I'm sure they meant a hole.' He looked at her questioningly. 'A split, a hole – what difference? Only language.'

Oh, but was it? Bobbie thought. Perhaps, again, she had been too quick to see what she wanted to see.

'What if this turned out *not* to be Goya's skull?'

He felt a shifting sensation under his feet as his future shuddered in front of him.

'You doubt its authenticity?'

'What if I did?'

He was close to tears, disappointment making him emotional. 'It *is* the skull, Ms Feldenchrist,' he insisted desperately. 'It's Goya's skull.'

'Well, make sure you tell everyone that, Maurice,' she said coolly. 'You're right. A split, a hole – what's the difference?'

Leaving the laboratory, Bobbie walked back to her office and slammed the door closed. She had seen the evidence with her own eyes. Maurice de la Valle might fool himself, deny the obvious, but Ben Golding had been telling the truth. It wasn't Goya's skull.

Numbed, Bobbie stared at the desk, the intercom interrupting her thoughts, her secretary announcing that she had a visitor who refused to give his name.

'Then tell him I can't see him,'

'He says you'll want to see him. It's about Joseph.'

Bobbie's head shot up.

'Show him in,' she said, watching as Emile Dwappa entered. He was dressed in an exquisite suit, his hair newly cut. Her money was being put to good use, Bobbie thought bitterly.

'I wasn't expecting you today,' she said.

He was momentarily taken aback. 'You look angry.'

'*You bastard!*' she snorted, fighting to control her rage. 'You robbed me—'

'What?'

'The skull's not genuine,' Bobbie went on, beside herself with anger and momentarily forgetting her fear of the African. 'What did you come back for? To gloat? I mean, you've got me over a barrel, haven't you? I can hardly expose you without exposing myself, can I? Jesus! I can't believe how stupid I've been. All that money . . .' She paused, grabbed at a breath. 'You can whistle for the other half of your payment!'

Dwappa blinked, the motion slowed down, oddly feline.

'I want my money!'

'We agreed that you'd get the rest when the skull was delivered. *Well, it's not the real skull!*'

Dwappa was finding words difficult. 'Who told you it wasn't the real skull?'

'Ben Golding. He came over to New York to tell me. And let's face it, if anyone should know, he should.'

'So he has the real skull?'

'How the fuck would I know? I just know that *I* haven't got it.' She thought aloud. 'But then again, if Golding knew about the swap, he *must* have the real one.'

'*Golding . . .*' Dwappa said simply, his body rigid.

And Bobbie Feldenchrist could see in that instant that the African hadn't cheated her. He had believed the skull was Goya's too. In fact, both of them had been cheated . . . Dwappa's hands moved to his face, his eyes widening for an instant before he turned his gaze back to her. She could see his thoughts shifting, unnerved by her news, as his whole carefully constructed plot vaporised. His skin became ash coloured, shock-dry – and without thinking, she laughed at him.

She laughed because the man of whom she had been so afraid had turned out to be a fool.

52

Whitechapel Hospital, London

Struggling to open the door while carrying several patients' file notes and a packet of biscuits, the ward sister finally pushed it open with her hip. Clicking her tongue, she then turned on the electric fire, her hand resting for an instant on the old radiator. Cold again. Bugger it! She would have to phone down to the caretaker and get him to drain the air out of the system. It always took hours. Hours in which the temperature could drop impressively.

She thought longingly of her sister, working in a private clinic off Wimpole Street. Now that was more like it – better wages and pleasant working conditions. Not like the Whitechapel Hospital – repaired, patched up, modernised in places like a transplant experiment.

Nibbling at a biscuit as she put the kettle on to boil, the sister glanced at the clock. Nine fifteen. She would be on shift until seven in the morning, but that was all right with her. The nights were usually quieter, although sometimes there were emergencies. A patient might start bleeding from an operation incision, or rupture internally. And if the operation site was infected, that was dangerous. Every nurse was trained to know that the facial/cranial area bled the most.

Luckily, such scares were rare. Both Ben Golding and the pompous Dr North were skilled surgeons. North might not empathise with his patients in the way Golding did, but he was steady as a judge in an emergency.

She looked up as a nurse walked in. 'How goes it?'

'Quiet,' Kim Morley said, taking an offered biscuit. 'Everyone's settled. I've just checked on Abigail Harrop, and she's comfortable. I was wondering why she's no longer Dr Golding's patient.'

'Because now she's his girlfriend.'

She raised one eyebrow. 'That's romantic. I used to dream about marrying a doctor, but now I'm not so sure. I fancy an IT engineer – someone who works regular hours.'

Smiling, the sister reached out for a stack of patients' files and shivered.

'I'm going to the storeroom to read these. Phone that bloody caretaker, will you, and get the radiator fixed.'

It took Kim Morley three calls before she finally managed to get hold of the caretaker. When he did answer his pager, he said he was stuck in the Intensive Care Unit.

'We need the radiator fixing—'

'I can't be in two places at once,' he replied. 'There used to be three caretakers here. Now there's only two. One man per shift. And every night I have to do everything –

and all the time my pager going off like the bell on a bleeding ice-cream van.'

'So come when you're ready—'

'Well, it'll be when I'm ready, won't it?' he countered. 'I'll try and be up there in a hour or so.'

Irritated, Kim clicked the pager off and looked out of the nurses station window on to the ward. Everyone was quiet, only one female patient reading a book, her light making a moody puddle in the semi-dark. It was getting colder and – despite the administration memo warning against spiralling electricity costs – she turned on the second bar of the electric fire. All was silent and calm, she thought with relief. Eleven p.m.

Turning back to her notes, Kim was surprised when the caretaker suddenly walked in, tossing his bag down on to the floor.

'Be quiet! You'll wake the patients.'

Ignoring her, he walked over to the radiator and felt round the back. In silence, he took a key from his bag and stuck it into the release knob and a hissing sound emerged.

'Oh, Christ! You've got a bleeding leak, as well,' he said, his hand reaching under the radiator. 'You never said anything about a leak.'

'I didn't know there was one,' Karen replied. 'The radiator wasn't working—'

'Well, it's working now. And it's leaking now,' he replied, exasperated, as he knelt down. 'Look at this,' he told her, jerking his head towards the bottom of the radiator. 'Look, see that? That's water, that's what that is. Pass me my bag.' Impatiently, he rummaged through the contents, then took out a monkey wrench and handed the nurse a torch. 'Hold that, will you? This shouldn't take a minute.'

And as she did so a man passed, unseen, by the double doors of ward. Tentatively he paused, looking towards the nurses' station and seeing that the nurse and caretaker were occupied, their stooped figures clearly visible in the bright office light. Beyond the station the rest of the ward was in darkness, even the reading light now turned off. Checking that no one was watching him, the man moved to the side rooms, checking the names on the three doors.

She had been sleeping, but Abigail's eyes opened in panic as a hand suddenly covered her mouth, and a man – hardly discernible in the darkness – leant down over her.

'*Shut up!*'

Terrified, she struggled, her screams muffled as he picked her up, finally losing consciousness as the chloroform took effect.

In silence, Emile Dwappa checked that the corridor was empty, then lifted her on to his shoulder and made for the back stairs only feet away. An instant later the exit door closed behind them, the nurse still talking in the room beyond.

53

After cleaning her teeth, Roma tucked her shirt into her skirt and brushed her hair, fixing it tightly into a ponytail at the back of her neck. Checking her reflection one last time, she left the Ladies and walked out into the corridor, heading towards the squad room.

As she entered, one of the older detectives, Jimmy Preston, stood up.

'There's been a woman snatched over at the Whitechapel Hospital. The officer in charge thought we should know.'

Roma frowned. 'Why?'

'The ward sister said that the woman's called Abigail Harrop. She's Ben Golding's girlfriend.'

Behind them, Duncan rolled his eyes. 'Bloody hell—'

Roma cut him off. 'Does Golding know?'

Jimmy shrugged. 'Dunno.'

'Find out,' she said, beckoning for Duncan to follow her into her office. Once there, she launched into him. 'This feels wrong.'

'What does?'

'All of it! Everything to do with Ben Golding. His brother's death – which he insists was murder – and Diego Martinez and Francis Asturias being killed. *All* of them involved with that skull. And now his partner's been abducted. Come on, Duncan – it's all related. It has to be.' She paused, thinking aloud. 'Martinez was murdered in London. Ben Golding found his brother's body in Madrid, and Francis Asturias was killed at the Whitechapel Hospital. All places Golding could have been.'

'You think he killed his own brother?'

'I honestly don't know,' she said, shrugging. 'Leon Golding was unbalanced – everyone said that, even Carlos Martinez. He told us that Diego found the Goya skull and gave it to Leon. An incredibly valuable artefact that everyone wanted. Then Leon was found dead—'

'*Because his brother killed him?*'

'He could have done. He knew Leon would trust him. He was the only person Leon *would* trust. He could have killed him.'

Duncan shook his head. 'For what?'

'The skull!' she retorted. 'Remember what we were told – it's worth a fortune.'

'But Golding's a doctor. What would he want with it?'

'Money?'

Duncan pulled a face. 'Nah, I don't believe it.'

'All right, let's take it step by step. Ben Golding was called in on the Diego Martinez murder to give his opinion on the surgery the head had undergone. What if he *knew* we would call him in? He's the leading expert in London, so it would be natural to involve him. And, being involved, he would know everything that was going on with the case from the start.'

'But we found his card in the victim's pocket,' Duncan said, 'with Leon Golding's mobile number on the back.'

Twisting her pen in her hands, Roma continued. 'Ben Golding knew we would become involved after Leon's death, because we'd eventually tie him to Diego Martinez and the skull. Remember how he denied knowing whose mobile number it was on the back of the card?'

'But someone else could have planted that card to put suspicion on Ben Golding—'

'Just go along with me for a minute, Duncan. Golding saw Francis Asturias's reconstruction of Diego Martinez, but he said that he didn't know the victim. Surely, if he was innocent, he would have admitted he knew him?'

'But it was *Leon* who knew Diego Martinez, remember? Ben Golding hadn't seen him for a long time.'

'He's not a stupid man, he would have remembered . . . And then there's the Goya skull. Francis Asturias must have reconstructed it. He was the obvious choice. And then what happened? He was killed. And the last number listed on his phone records? Ben Golding.'

'You really think a respected surgeon would kill for a skull?'

'I don't know,' Roma admitted. 'But I've been thinking about it for a while and wondering about the Golding brothers. We know Leon was unstable, but what about

Ben? In comparison to his nervy brother he might seem very stable, but perhaps he's not quite what we think he is.'

Duncan took in a slow breath. 'All right, I hear what you're saying . . . But now his girlfriend's been abducted, and Golding's out of the country. So it can't be him.'

'But *is* he out of the country?' Roma queried, standing up. 'I want you to get a file on Leon Golding. His life, how he died. I want to know everything about the man.'

'We'll have to go through the Spanish police—'

'So do it!' she snapped. 'Leon Golding was an art historian. What was he working on? Find out. I want his notes, his computer documents—'

'From Spain?'

'Don't argue with me, Duncan,' she said wearily. 'Just get the information. But keep it quiet. Jimmy can know, but no one outside the department, you hear me? *No one is to know about this.*' She glanced at her watch hurriedly. 'And find out about Ben Golding too. I want to know all there is to know about those two brothers. *Everything.*'

Duncan had been trying for nearly fifteen minutes to make himself understood by the Spanish police when Jimmy Preston came into the squad room and rescued him, gesturing to Duncan repeatedly until finally he covered the mouthpiece.

'*What!*'

'You talking to Spain?'

'What the fuck d'you think I'm doing?'

'I think you can't speak fucking Spanish,' Jimmy said evenly, 'and I can. Pass me the phone.'

Impressed, Duncan watched as his colleague launched into perfect and fluent Spanish, making notes as he chatted, even laughing down the line. Finally, Jimmy passed the phone back.

'They said they'd like to say goodbye to you. And that your accent was the worst they'd heard in a decade. Thanks for the laugh you gave them.'

'Very funny,' Duncan replied, slamming down the phone. 'Did you ask them for the information?'

'Yeah. They're sending copies of what they have on Leon Golding's death by fax. But apparently his computer's gone missing, so they don't know what he was working on.'

'They agreed to help? Just like that?'

Jimmy shrugged. 'Well, they moaned about it. I promised to send authorisation from this end. They said they would have to have it rubber-stamped, et cetera, et cetera.'

'Which means?'

'We should have it this afternoon.' He leaned across the table towards Duncan. 'Apparently when Ben Golding insisted on his brother's autopsy, someone in the police force decided that they'd have another look at the file. You know, just in case they were wrong and it wasn't suicide. After all, Ben Golding's a respected surgeon and his brother was important in Madrid—'

'So what *did* they find?'

'Nothing,' Jimmy replied. 'But they knew he was working on Goya,' he went on, reading his notes. 'Francisco Goya the painter. He's a national treasure in Spain—'

'The bloke who did that picture of the naked woman?'

Jimmy sighed. 'And to think that I thought you were ignorant . . . Only Goya didn't just paint naked women, apparently he painted some weird stuff too. He did a series of works called the' – Jimmy glanced at his notes again – 'the Black Paintings. They were dark and Leon Golding was studying them.' Duncan eyes widened. 'The police also said that there was a rumour going round that Leon Golding had found Goya's skull. And . . .' again checking his notes, 'there's a record of their interview with his girl-friend. She said that Leon had been in the middle of a nervous breakdown. That he'd been working too hard. Got obsessed. She even said that they'd had a seance—'

'You *are* joking?'

'Hear me out. Leon Golding's girlfriend was worried about him because he had mental health problems, but nothing life-threatening. But then suddenly he *dies*.' Jimmy looked at Duncan and held his gaze. 'Sounds convenient, doesn't it? Dying just after finding a priceless artefact.'

Duncan made a low whistling sound. 'You're thinking along the same lines as Roma. Who knew about all of this?'

'The same person who knew about everything else.' Jimmy countered. 'Who knew all the people involved, and how to play them. A man at home in Madrid as much as London. Perhaps a man clever enough to make himself look sane. The only person who *could* know everything – Ben Golding.'

54

New York

Scrutinising the Englishman, the concierge of the hotel watched as Ben walked into the reception area. There was something unsettling about Mr *Harris*, he thought, checking the information on his reservation card. Idly his gaze moved down the London address, the occupation – salesman, indeed – and then the card details. Everything in order. But the concierge hadn't been in the hotel business for fifteen years without having a sixth sense for trouble and he knew when a guest was running away from something. They always came with little luggage and didn't tell anyone where they were staying. No next of kin. No trace. As for the address, obviously false.

Turning to the receptionist, he asked, 'Has Mr Harris had any phone calls?'

'No, sir.'

'Visitors?'

'No, sir.'

'Any messages?'

She shook her head and the concierge glanced back to where Ben stood waiting for the lift. Just as he thought – no one knew that he was staying at the hotel.

Ben's clothes, noted the concierge, were fresh, and he was wearing a clean shirt, but his walk was slow and he seemed anxious, turning around repeatedly. The concierge had seen the same look before. It usually meant a marital fight, a bad business trip or a planned suicide.

There had been two suicides in his hotel career, and he had tried to anticipate the warning signs. There was nothing more complicated than trying to move a corpse out of a room without any other guests seeing it. In fact, on the previous two occasions the bodies had been moved late, taken down the industrial back lift to an ambulance waiting in the alleyway outside ... The concierge was still thinking about the suicides when his attention was called away by the receptionist. When he looked back, Ben had entered the lift and was already making his way to the fourth floor.

He was wondering why no one had approached him, or even followed him. He had expected to be watched, even attacked. But nothing had happened, which was somehow more disturbing. Was he the only person who knew the skull was a fake? Surely he was, or he would have been approached by now. And although he had made himself into an obvious target, no one had made a move.

Walking into his hotel room, Ben locked the door and took off his coat. His shirt was sticking to his back even though the weather was cool, the collar of his open-necked shirt rubbing against his neck and leaving a red welt. Emptying his pockets, he hung his jacket in the wardrobe and moved out on to the balcony. Glancing up, he saw nothing sinister, only the base of the upper balcony. Moving back into his room, he checked under the bed and then walked to the door, looking out. The corridor was empty, but at the end of the passageway a fire door was just swinging closed. Unsettled, he returned to his room and relocked the door.

His reflection in the bathroom mirror seemed odd, as though he was looking at himself from a distance. Muzzy from lack of sleep and anxiety, he did another check. The room was secure, he was safe. *He was safe.* All that mattered now was sleep. That was imperative, or he wouldn't be able to go on. He would sleep for just a couple of hours. He would be all right, Ben told himself. The door was locked, the windows closed and bolted. He would lie down, get some rest, and then he would be able to think more clearly and decide what to do next. Prepare himself for what was coming.

Because he knew something was coming. He knew it deep inside himself. He knew it without being told. His visit to Bobbie Feldenchrist had not gone unnoticed. His plan, however naive, had worked. *He had been seen.* So how long would it be before Bobbie Feldenchrist admitted that she had a fake? How long before she challenged the person who had brought it to her? And how long before he suspected Ben Golding? The man already responsible for three deaths wouldn't hesitate to kill again . . . Hardly able to keep his eyes open, Ben took off his shoes, walked to the bathroom and moved over to the toilet, lifting the lid.

Inside the bowl, a pig's bloated, severed head stared up at him.

55

Reeling back, Ben steadied himself by grasping the edge of the washbasin. He knew then what his brother had felt; knew the same terror Leon experienced while he waited in another hotel room. Shaking, Ben backed out of the bathroom, turning quickly to check that there was no one behind him. He knew he had to leave the hotel before anyone discovered what had happened.

Wiping the sweat from his hands, Ben threw his few clothes into a bag and pulled on his coat. Then he moved to the door and walked out, putting the DO NOT DISTURB notice on the handle. With luck no one would enter for a while. Taking the back stairs, he moved out into the alleyway behind the hotel, looking round to check that no one was following him. And as he hurried on, the memory of his brother's last conversation came back.

Someone's watching me. Oh God, someone's here . . . Jesus, I'm so scared . . .

And then he heard his answer:

You're going to be OK. Just wait for me. I'm coming. I'm on my way.

But he had been too late.

Moving out on to the street, Ben looked around then hailed a cab.

'Airport.'

As the cabbie nodded and pulled out into the traffic, Ben stared out of the car window. He would get back to London, to safety. Maybe he would even go and see Roma Jaffe and ask her for help. His hands shaking, he tried to fasten his jacket, but gave up, flinching at the memory of the pig's bloodied head, his mind blurring with unease as the cab dropped him at the airport and he headed for the Departure Lounge.

It was the last – under-booked – flight to London and there were only a few passengers waiting. Ben's gaze moved around hurriedly, glossy, pristine images drenching his consciousness. Models promoting perfumes and handbags blurred with the background noise, a crying child forcing him to change seats.

Finally, an announcement sounded overhead.

'Flight BA 7756 for London is now ready for boarding at Gate 14. Would passengers please keep their boarding passes and passports to hand.'

Hanging back, Ben let the other passengers board the plane first, then took his seat at the back. Across the aisle, a businesswoman took out an iPod and began to listen to music with her eyes closed. Looking down, Ben composed himself and then glanced out of the window into the darkness, his reflection looking back at him momentarily before he turned away.

The weight of fear hung over him, exhaustion pressing down on his body. Closing his eyes as the plane crawled up to the clouds, Ben finally slept. As the engines hummed and the businesswoman's iPod whispered its tunes, he began to dream. Sweating, he shuffled in his seat, his breathing quickening as he remembered Diego Martinez, the dead body of Francis Asturias, and his brother's terrified words.

Someone's watching me. Oh God, someone's here—

Terrified, he jerked awake. 'God Almighty!'

Concerned, the stewardess came over to him. 'Is there something the matter, sir?'

He was befuddled, her face coming in and out of focus. He couldn't remember where he was and mistook her for a maid coming into his New York hotel room. *She would find the pig's head . . . she would find the head.*

'I don't know anything about it!' Ben snapped, beside himself with tiredness and confusion.

The stewardess looked puzzled, the other passengers curious. Ben had a sudden, crazed impulse to cry. A madman in polite society.

'You don't understand!' he said, 'I don't know anything!'

'Calm down, sir,' the stewardess said kindly. 'We can sort this out when we get to London.'

And then Ben realised that she was humouring him, and thought of all the times he had humoured his brother. When he was irritated by him, or didn't believe him, or was trying to protect him. And he suddenly knew how it felt to have the whole world staring in at your own personal insanity.

56

London

The young man off the 16.35 flight from Berlin to London was washing his hands in the men's room at Heathrow airport. Idly, he checked his reflection in the mirror, then leaned forward to squeeze a blackhead on his nose. Deep in concentration, he jumped as he heard an odd sound behind him.

'Hello?'

No answer.

'Hello?' he asked again, surprised as he had thought himself alone.

Warily he moved over to the cubicles. All the doors were open, apart from two. Curious, he pushed the first door. It swung open. The cubicle was empty. Then he pushed the second door.

'Fucking hell!' he said, rushing in. 'Hang on, mate, just hang on!'

He thought the man was dead at first, jammed between

the side of the cubicle and the toilet, tied to the cistern pipe by a rope around his neck. If he had lost consciousness he would have fallen forward and choked to death. His attacker had drawn his knees under his chin, tied his arms behind his back and taped over his mouth. Blood was coming from a cut over his eye and from a deep incision on the back of his head.

Hurriedly the young man untied him, unknotting the rope around his neck. Once released, he slumped forward on to the floor.

'Hang on! I'll get an ambulance.'

Gasping, Ben took in a breath and struggled to get up, the young man helping him on to the toilet seat. He was reeling in shock, trying to get his bearings.

'I'm OK. I'm OK.'

'What happened to you?'

'I'm OK—'

'You need a doctor—'

'I *am* a doctor.'

Trying to get some feeling back into his arms, Ben rubbed at the aching muscles. He hadn't anticipated the attack. He should have done, but he had let down his guard momentarily and been jumped. The blow to the back of his head had knocked him unconscious, only regaining his senses when his attacker had gone.

'You've been robbed,' the young man said, pointing to Ben's bag, its contents scattered around the toilet. Leon's notes and laptop had been taken out and discarded. Obviously the skull was all that had mattered to his attacker. The theory was unimportant.

Struggling to his feet, Ben stuffed the contents back into his bag. So Bobbie Feldenchrist had talked. She must have challenged the man who had sold her the fake, and he had come after Ben to get hold of the real skull. Which he didn't have ... The killer must be panicking now, Ben thought, desperate that the Goya had eluded him. After so much bloodshed, so many deaths, how pointless to know that it had all come down the wrong piece of bone!

The young man was still hovering over Ben, concerned. 'I should get help.'

'I'll be fine.'

'But why would anyone hurt a doctor?'

'Mistaken identity. Forget it, please. Don't tell anyone.'

His rescuer was suddenly suspicious. 'And why didn't they take the laptop? I mean, if you were mugged—'

Ben put up his hands.

'Ok, I'll tell you the truth. It was someone's husband ...' He paused, wanting to throw the young man off track and to elicit some male sympathy. 'I was fooling around with his wife.'

The young man grinned. 'Got caught out, did you?'

'Yeah.'

'Was she worth it?'

Slowly Ben dabbed at the wound on his head. 'Yes,' he said wryly. 'She was worth it.'

57

'How long is she staying here?' Mama Gala shouted at her son as he came into the shop, slamming the door behind him. 'I've got some white bitch upstairs and you go off and leave me to it!'

Rain had seeped into the shoulders of Dwappa's jacket, his expression strained as he turned to his mother.

'I had to make a trip—'

She slammed her meaty hands down on the counter and walked over to her son, looking him up and down like a side of bad meat. Above their heads was a locked room, the old woman outside guarding the entrance, and inside was an unconscious Englishwoman, Abigail Harrop. A couple of times Mama Gala had gone into the room and stared down at the mattress on the floor on which Abigail lay drugged. She had wondered about the bandage around her head, the blond hair matted with blood and sweat, but had not interfered. Instead she had made sure that the drugged woman stayed drugged. And silent.

'Is she' – Mama Gala jerked her head upwards – 'part of your plan?'

She is now, Dwappa wanted to retort. She wasn't originally, but now she certainly is.

He had left New York before Golding, numbed by the news of the skull being a fake. And on the flight over he had decided to raise the stakes and abduct Ben Golding's partner. Dwappa knew the woman was in the Whitechapel Hospital because, having been watching Golding for days, he had discovered her identity. At first Abigail Harrop had seemed unimportant, but suddenly her role had turned out to be pivotal. Because as soon as Golding heard about her abduction he would give up the skull.

'You don't answer your phone no more?' Mama Gala snapped, catching hold of her son's arm, her grip ferocious as she pulled him round to face her. 'You look sick, boy. Your plan not working?' Her turbaned head leaned to one side, her tongue jutting out momentarily like a snake tasting the air. 'You failing me? Is that it – you failing me?'

His confidence collapsed, his longed-for escape from his mother derailed. He had money, yes, but not all of it – not enough. He had been cheated. Ben Golding had cheated him. He had upturned his plans and made a fool out of him. And Emile Dwappa couldn't bear it. This was to have been his chance, his triumph. And Golding had beaten him.

But he would suffer for it. For every day Emile Dwappa had to stay with his mother, Golding would suffer. For every indignity, every torture she inflicted on him, Golding would suffer. For the postponement of his new life, Golding would suffer.

Shocked by what Bobbie Feldenchrist had told him, Dwappa had moved fast, organising his cousins in New York to pile on the pressure. After his meeting at the museum he had arranged to have the pig's head left as a warning in Golding's hotel room. Then he had gone back to London. On his return he had personally abducted Abigail and now he was waiting for Ben Golding to come back, but not before arranging his attack at Heathrow only minutes after he had landed.

Dwappa was piling shock on shock, throwing Golding into confusion, cranking up the fear so that in the end he would give up the skull without a fight. He wasn't sure if Golding already knew of Abigail's abduction – he was simply increasing the pressure so that he would realise just how much danger he was in. Dwappa knew that he would already be running scared. It didn't even matter that Golding hadn't had the skull in his luggage – Dwappa hadn't expected him to be travelling with it. What he *did* expect was panic. And that would come soon, Dwappa told himself, just as soon as he knew that Abigail Harrop had been taken.

He could feel his hatred intensify. Other acts of aggression, even the killing of Jimmy Shaw, were bland by comparison. He would do to Ben Golding what had been done to him. He would buckle him, take everything from him, make him beg for his woman. Make him plead for Dwappa to take the skull. And then he would kill him.

'Look at me, boy,' Mama Gala said, her grip tightening on his arm.

Instantly Dwappa's viciousness faltered, his aggression diluted in her presence. To her he was a gay boy, a queer, the son she had ridiculed and baited constantly, goading him and forcing him to please her, always please her. *It should have worked out*, Dwappa thought, panicked. He should be giving her the money now – money to keep her quiet. To get her a new house. To give him space. To buy his freedom from this terrifying maternal tyrant.

He remembered what had happened to his father and felt his bladder loosen.

'You failed, boy?'

'No,' he said, repeating the word more loudly as he thought of Golding. 'No. There's just a delay.'

She touched his face, ran her heavy hand down his throat and then pressed against his windpipe, choking him. For a moment her eyes widened with pleasure, then she moved away.

He could hear the rain outside and see the street lights coming on as he watched her turn the sign on the door to CLOSED.

58

Certain that he was being watched, Ben let himself into his house just after dusk had fallen. Just as he did so, Roma Jaffe came running up the front steps and confronted him.

'I need to talk to you.'

Surprised, he opened the door and stood back as she entered, followed by Duncan. Showing them into his sitting room, Ben turned on the lamps and took off his coat. He was trying to compose himself and clear his thoughts, wondering if they had already heard about the incident in New York. But how could they? He had used a false name and address. They couldn't know about it.

More confident then he felt, Ben challenged Roma. 'What d'you want?'

'Where have you been?'

'Why d'you want to know?'

Roma shook her head impatiently. 'You should talk to us.'

'Not without a lawyer present,' Ben replied, on his guard.

'Do you *need* a lawyer?'

'I don't know. But I've just been doorstepped by the police and they won't tell me why—'

'Your partner's been abducted.'

He sat down, wondering for an instant if he had heard her correctly, his reaction muted with shock. '*Abigail? When?*'

'In the early hours of this morning.'

'This morning . . .'

'Where were you?'

'Where's Abigail, more like!' Ben snapped. 'She was having an operation at the Whitechapel. She was in hospital.' He was blustering, white-faced. 'How was she taken from a hospital?' He rubbed his forehead with his fingers, distracted. 'Christ Almighty! Who took her?'

'Mr Golding, we need—'

He cut her off. 'What are you doing here? You should be looking for Abigail—'

'Where should we look?'

'*Where should you look?*' he hurled back. 'You're the fucking police – you should know.' Pausing, he stared at Roma, his expression incredulous. 'You think I had something to do with this?'

'Did you?'

'I was in New York!' he replied, pouring himself a scotch without offering one to Roma or Duncan. Downing it in one, he turned back to her.

'You've got blood on your shirt, Mr Golding.'

The room fell silent as Ben turned away to look out of

the window. He was trying to plan, but all he could think of was Abigail. He could see that the police had changed their attitude towards him. They were talking to him like a suspect. God, Ben thought, he had to get their attention off him! And fast, because he knew his girlfriend was going to be used as a bargaining tool. Abigail in return for the skull. If Ben antagonised the police – or worse, if he was taken into custody – he might never see her again.

The police would never find her. Or the abductor. No one knew who he was, or what he looked like. No one knew his name, not even Bobbie Feldenchrist . . . Ben kept staring out of the window, his face averted. It was obvious what would happen next. He would be approached, asked for Goya's skull in return for Abigail. *But he no longer had the skull*. And without it he had nothing to bargain with.

'Why is there blood on your shirt?' Roma repeated.

'I had a fall at the airport.'

'Any witnesses?'

'I was in the gents,' Ben said curtly. 'I slipped, hit the back of my head on the basin.'

Roma and Duncan exchanged a glance. 'Do you know why anyone would abduct your partner?'

'No. And shouldn't you be looking for her instead of interrogating me?' He relented. 'I'm sorry, I'm just worried about her . . . You asked me where I was. I went to New York on a short trip to attend a conference and I've only just come back.'

'You didn't call the hospital while you were away?'

'Of course I did! I called three times, last time yesterday morning. Abi was fine, making progress. She knew I was coming to see her tonight . . .' he trailed off.

'Has she any enemies?'

'No.'

'What about you?'

He lied without hesitation. 'None that I know of.'

'Really?' Roma said. 'But you're having a hard time of it lately, Mr Golding, aren't you?'

His expression fluttered, tiredness making his thoughts unsteady. *Jesus! She thinks I'm involved. She thinks I'm after the skull for myself.* He wanted to laugh, but couldn't. Could only see images of Leon, Abigail, and the pig's head jammed in the toilet bowl. Shaking, Ben struggled to control himself. *You were in Madrid. You were the last person to talk to your brother . . . Your number was the last one called on Francis Asturias's phone . . .* He thought of Diego Martinez, had a sudden memory of a thin boy at the farmhouse many years earlier, followed by an image of the decapitated head. A murdered man, with Ben's business card in his pocket . . . Unsteady, he reached for a chair and sat down.

Had he been in New York?

He couldn't remember.

He was tired.

He'd been travelling.

He was back home.

No, he was in London.

Home in London.

Home in Madrid.

His eyes closed then reopened. Was he crazy? *Christ, was he going crazy?*

Roma was watching him, seeing what she thought was an imminent collapse. 'First there was your brother's *suicide* ...' She paused, waiting for Ben to correct her. But he didn't, so she continued. 'Then the murder of Francis Asturias. And before that, the death of Diego Martinez.' She was certain of her theory, spelling it out for him. 'All these incidents happening one after the other. It must be very hard to cope with. Confusing, even.'

He turned, stared at her, his expression bewildered.

'But then again, they all have a common denominator, don't they?'

Silent, Ben continued to look at her.

'The skull. It all seems to have started with that Goya skull, and gone on from there.' She was sure she had him. 'Wouldn't you agree, Mr Golding, that since it was found a lot of odd things have happened? You told me yourself that it's very valuable. That some people would go to extremes to get it. I'm afraid to say that I'm not happy with what you've told me, Mr Golding. Don't leave London again without telling me—'

'What the hell!'

Poised, she went in for the kill. 'I don't have enough evidence to charge you. *Yet.* But I've got my suspicions and I'll prove them—'

'Based on *what* exactly?'

'As I said before, the skull,' Roma replied, her confidence rising. 'You see, I've been thinking about this whole business, mulling it over, and I've come to a decision. *Perhaps the person with the skull is the one we should be looking for?* Perhaps *he's* responsible for everything?'

Ben saw his chance and grabbed it.

'But the skull's in the Feldenchrist Collection, New York,' he replied, holding her stunned gaze. 'And the exhibition opened yesterday.'

59

Madrid

'You stupid bitch,' Gabino said sourly, looking over at Gina as she walked in. 'They've got the skull in the Feldenchrist Collection.'

She had heard the news in Madrid, at the farmhouse. Had seen it reported on the internet and then left the house without talking to Ben. So the skull was found, she thought bleakly. Any chance of her securing it for Gabino was over. Any chance of winning him back was over too.

Unusually quiet, Gina looked around the familiar sitting room in Gabino's flat. She had never anticipated being in such a precarious situation. Leon's death had left her destabilised. After having him devoted to her, being able to control and manipulate him, it came as a shock to Gina to realise that her lover was gone, and with him, her power. She had not been Leon's wife so she had no entitlement to his house or his money, and her attempt to gain the interest of Ben Golding had been a failure.

She was now looking at an uncertain future without male protection. Propelled from the safety of the farmhouse and the reclusive life she had led with Leon, Gina realised that going back to her old party girl existence wasn't an option. She had been off the circuit too long and had become the ex-lover too many times to excite fresh interest.

For a while she might have fooled herself into thinking that she still had a chance with Gabino, but her promise to secure the skull for him had failed miserably, and now Gina found herself homeless and alone.

'I thought I could get the skull for you,' she said imploringly. 'If Ben Golding still had it, I could have done—'

'But he didn't, did he?' Gabino replied, his tone dismissive. 'If I'd known you were going to waste my fucking time, I'd never have listened to you.'

Her temper flared.

'You couldn't get the skull either! If you were so smart, how come you didn't get it?' She moved towards him. 'I'd have thought the Ortega money would have counted for something—'

'I wasn't on the doorstep, was I?'

'What's that supposed to mean?'

'You were sleeping with Leon Golding. You were by his bloody side all day. If anyone could have got hold of the skull, it should have been you.' He was snappy with anger. 'You're losing your touch, Gina – you must be. After all, Leon Golding was a walkover. Poor bastard, everyone knew he was crazy—'

'He was twice the man you are!'

'But with a fraction of the income,' Gabino replied unpleasantly. 'Which, let's face it, is all that matters to you.'

'It's not all about money!' she hissed. 'I care about you!'

'You care about yourself.'

'There was more to it than that—'

'Not for me,' he said indifferently. 'It was an affair, Gina, that was all. You're not the kind of woman a man marries.' She flinched at the words. 'You're one of a hundred other women on the make. We had a good time, but that was all it was.' He stared at her, eager to vent his frustration on someone. 'You didn't think I was ever serious about you, did you?' he smirked. '*You did?* God, Gina, women like you are just good for fucking—'

She slapped him hard, Gabino reacting immediately. Drawing back his fist he pounded it into her face, her nose bleeding with the impact as he grabbed her hair and pulled her on to the sofa.

'You stupid bitch!' he said, his mouth inches from her ear. 'You could have saved me. You could have done something useful for once!' Enraged, he slapped her hard across the face, Gina whimpering as she put up her hands to protect herself. 'But you're worthless.' He punched her in the stomach. 'Hopeless.' Again he punched her, catching her forearm as she tried to fend him off. 'Slut!' Turning, he moved away, then ran back, kicking her in the stomach. '*How dare you think I could love you!* You're a fucking whore!' After one final kick, he bent down and picked up her handbag, tossing it on to her lap. 'Get the fuck out of here!'

Moaning, Gina clutched her stomach and staggered to her feet. 'You shouldn't have done that.'

He moved over to her, jutting his face into hers aggressively. 'Why? What are you going to do about it?' he sneered. 'You're nothing, Gina. Just a sad bitch with nowhere left to go.'

60

For once, Bartolomé had travelled without his wife. Celina was suffering from food poisoning and unable to leave Switzerland, even in a private jet. So he arrived alone at head office to meet up with his lawyer. Every month he came to the Spanish capital, leaving his reclusive bolt-hole in Switzerland and braving the heat and press of Madrid. He disliked the few days he spent in the city, and was particularly irked to find himself visiting not once, but three times within the space of a few weeks.

And all because of Gabino. All because his younger brother was due to attend court for a hearing regarding the charge of grievous bodily harm to a notable banker. At any other time Bartolomé would have suppressed the charges. He still could, if he chose to. But Gabino had committed an unforgivable sin in his brother's eyes and had neither apologised nor explained why. The news that Bobbie Feldenchrist now owned the Goya skull had added further friction. To Bartolomé, it was inconceivable that an American could possess the skull of the greatest Spanish painter who had ever lived. It should have stayed in Spain, he thought bitterly, in the Ortega collection.

But although Gabino had known about it and had been on the spot in Madrid, although he had known of his brother's passion for the painter, he had let the opportunity slip. It was something Bartolomé would never forgive him for. And because of Gabino's casual neglect, all his other foibles seemed magnified. His recklessness and violence were suddenly no longer excusable; his boorish behaviour was repulsive. Bartolomé knew that if his wife had been with him she would have calmed him down, made the inevitable excuses for his brother. But Celina wasn't with him and, freed from her judicious advice, he was looking for a way not to help Gabino, but to punish him.

So for a prolonged, overheated hour, Bartolomé had listened to his lawyer and heard all the details about Gabino's attack on the hospitalised victim. He had also seen the photographs of the damage inflicted and felt a repulsion which was hard to shake. The photograph of Gabino at the police station was also shown to him, his brother's drunken expression belligerent and threatening.

'We could have a word with someone,' his lawyer began. 'Get the charges dropped.'

Shaking his handsome head, Bartolomé swallowed the fury which was curdling inside his stomach.

'Why should we?'

'The Ortega name, the publicity—'

'Why should we always clean up after my brother?' Bartolomé remarked.

'Because if we don't the damage will be much worse.'

'We should get him into line—'

'We can't,' the lawyer replied patiently. 'You know that, Bartolomé. We've tried for years. Gabino's out of control.'

'So maybe this time we let him suffer the consequences.'

Folding his arms, the lawyer raised his eyebrows. He could feel Bartolomé's frustration and shared it, but his advice would remain what it always had been – pay up and keep Gabino's transgressions quiet. Not that they were *that* quiet. All Madrid knew about Gabino's excesses, but the alternative was worse – having an Ortega in court. The press would relish such an opportunity; a scrum would ensue which would result in every uncomfortable detail being exposed. And with Gabino's sins would be resurrected the murder of their grandmother, Fidelia.

How long, thought the lawyer, before a business enemy would seize their chance to undermine the whole Ortega fortune? They could prove nothing, but digging up the murder of Fidelia would remind everyone of the family's cursed past.

'You couldn't handle the fallout—'

Bartolomé turned to him, his expression intense. 'So I'm going to be tied to this madman all my life?'

'You have a son,' the lawyer said hurriedly. 'Think of Juan.'

'Think of my son? Excuse and protect my brother because of my son?' Bartolomé snapped. 'What has my son to do with this?'

'His future—'

'Is what he makes it!' Bartolomé roared, then quickly dropped his voice, controlling himself. 'My son is not

Gabino. Juan's growing up in Switzerland, away from Madrid, away from any reckless influences—'

'Which is all the more reason to suppress Gabino's assault charge,' the lawyer interrupted him.

He had known the family and worked for them for over thirty years. There was nothing he wasn't privy to, nothing he didn't know or hadn't concealed. And, as always, his sympathy lay with Bartolomé. He could see a respectable man struggling against his family's reputation and knew that if Bartolomé had been an only child, the Ortega name would have flourished. Refined and cultured, Bartolomé was the perfect ambassador for a family who had a sordid past. As an only child, in time he could have buried all the old scandals.

But he *wasn't* an only child.

'Bartolomé, we have to suppress this charge.'

To the lawyer's surprise, his client waved him away with his hand. 'I have to think. I can't make a decision now.'

'You should—'

'Give me time,' Bartolomé replied, smiling fleetingly. 'I know you're trying to help me. I understand, but I have to think about this a little longer.'

The lawyer didn't know about the Goya skull, didn't know that Gabino's failure to secure it for his brother had resulted in a cataclysmic emotional shift. But as he left the room and walked out into the over-heated sunshine he felt suddenly, overshadowed by the expectation of tragedy.

61

London

Having found the address among Leon's possessions, Ben walked towards a row of old-fashioned red-brick terraced houses, the newer high-rise flats behind glowering over them. Between green wheelie bins was a discarded pram, a cat curled up in the seat, and beside it an overstuffed carrier bag reeking of sour food. Checking the house numbers, Ben knocked on the door of 289 and waited for a response.

'What d'you want? Get off the doorstep!'

Surprised, Ben bent down, lifted the flap of the letterbox, and called out: 'It's me, Mr Martinez. Ben Golding.'

He could hear the opening of several locks, and finally Carlos Martinez opened the door and stepped back to let his visitor enter. They shook hands awkwardly, Carlos showing Ben into the front room, the street outside obliterated by net curtains stained with mould. Taking a seat in front of an old 1950s tiled fireplace, Ben watched as Carlos reached for roll-up and lit it.

He seemed sad, shrivelled. 'I never thought I'd get to see you again,' he said.

'It's been a long time.'

'Yes, a long time.'

'I wanted to talk to you about Diego. I'm very sorry about what happened.'

'Yes . . .'

'Your son knew my brother—'

'And we've lost them both.' His Spanish accent had softened, only the sibilant S's making his origin obvious. 'It was a bad way to die, Mr Golding. My son didn't deserve that.'

'Leon didn't deserve to be killed either—'

Carlos's head jerked up. *'He was killed?'*

'Yes.'

'I heard he committed suicide,' the old man replied, his expression suspicious. 'Why are you here? I mean, you're welcome – my son thought the world of your brother – but I'd like to know why you're here.'

It was a reasonable request.

'I think that the deaths of your son and my brother are connected.' Ben paused, noticing that Carlos's hands had begun to shake. 'Have you been threatened?'

'No. But Diego was.'

'By whom?'

Silence: Carlos was torn between confiding and lying.

'Please, Mr Martinez,' Ben urged him. 'I wouldn't be here unless it was very important. Someone I love is in trouble, and I think the man who has her was responsible for Diego and Leon's deaths.' He could see Carlos inhaling on his smoke, his glance moving to the telephone. 'What is it?'

'Diego had a call the night he went missing.'

'Who called him?'

'I dunno. But they invited him out for a pint at the Fox and Hounds, London Road. It's a rough place, but Diego liked the barmaid.' Carlos paused, as though the memory of his son's love life was unbearably futile. 'I went with him once – she was nothing. He could have done better, much better.' He ground out his smoke and immediately began to roll another, Ben letting him take his time. 'Diego always went to that pub when he was in London. The place has a bad reputation, but he said it was exaggerated.'

'What kind of reputation?'

'Petty criminals, old lags,' he sighed, glancing over at a faded wedding photograph, a striking woman standing beside a younger version of himself. 'That was his mother. She died over twenty years ago. I'm glad. Glad she didn't have to live through this.' He bowed his head, a perfect parting on the right-hand side of his scalp. 'It's a meeting place, the pub, where all the runners for the bosses hang out.'

'Who're the bosses?'

'There's a few, but two big names. It wasn't always like this, but now the place has gone to seed, these are the last terraces to come down. To be honest, I don't go out much any more. Don't dare to. Larry Morgan runs half of

Brixton, Emile Dwappa the other half. They split it between them. Morgan handles drugs and Dwappa handles all sorts . . .' He stared hard at Ben. 'Have you spoken to the police?'

'I can't.'

'Could I get into trouble talking to you?'

'You might, but not with the police,' Ben admitted, hurrying on. 'I didn't want to come to you, but I had no choice. I think your son's at the heart of all this—'

'How could he be?'

'Because Diego found the skull.'

Nodding, Carlos glanced around the dismal room. Old-fashioned wallpaper, a 1970s gas fire and a mock leather sofa all pointed to poverty. To making do. The man in the wedding photograph had been handsome, almost cocky, but now Carlos Martinez was smoking too much and talking as though he couldn't stop.

'That skull . . . it started it all, didn't it? I told Diego when he found it to leave it alone. In Spain we think such things are dangerous. And Goya – well he was a madman at the end, wasn't he?'

'Where did Diego find the skull?'

'Under a concrete basement in an old house, in the centre of Madrid. He was called in to do some work, and had to get the floor up. It hadn't been touched for years. About eighty-odd years ago someone had poured concrete over it to make it level. Diego said it took nearly a week to break the floor up and get to the tiles underneath.' Carlos took a drag of his cigarette. The first two fingers of his right hand were yellow, nicotine-stained. 'A few of the tiles got broken, and that was when he found the skull . . . Jesus! I wish he'd never touched it.'

'Why did he think it was Goya's skull?'

Carlos glanced away, remembering. 'The painter had stayed in the house—'

'But he didn't die there?'

'No, he died a long time afterwards, in France.'

'So why would the skull have come back to Spain?'

'Who knows? The owner of the house might have been responsible for the skull being stolen. They might have felt guilty and buried what they'd done, thinking it would never be found. How do I know?' Carlos replied shortly. 'I only know this much because I admired your mother and she used to tell me about her work and about Goya.' He smiled to himself. 'I was a builder, just a builder, but I liked her stories. And then later she used to talk to Diego and he used to come over when I was working at your house and play with Leon. And you . . . You don't remember him?'

'I remember him very well,' Ben replied. 'He used to get sunburned.'

'Yes, yes, he did.' Carlos frowned. 'The day Diego found the skull, he rang and told me about it—'

'Did he tell anyone else?'

'I don't know. I doubt it. He wasn't the type to go around bragging . . .' Carlos trailed off.

'What is it?'

'He couldn't hold his drink. Two beers and he'd talk.

He could have told the barmaid at the pub when he came to London. Boasting a bit, trying to impress her.'

'So anyone could have overheard?'

'I suppose.'

'And passed on the information to Dwappa?'

Distressed, Carlos shook his head. 'I told him to get rid of the skull! Give it to a priest and have it buried. It's bad luck to handle the dead. It was bad luck for my son. Bad luck for your brother. Bad luck for you.' He stared at Ben. 'Is your friend in danger?'

He nodded.

'Yes, she's in real trouble and I have to find her. Like I said, the man responsible for the deaths of Diego and Leon now has Abigail.'

'He was after the skull?'

'And he got it.'

Deliberately lying, Ben tried to protect Carlos Martinez from the whole truth, but the Spaniard was no fool.

'But if he has the skull, why is he still after you?'

Ben let the question pass.

'And why would he take your friend?' Carlos sat upright, his back pressed against the chair as though he was bracing himself. '*Have you got the skull?*'

'Don't ask.'

'Oh, God Almighty—'

'Just help me,' Ben pleaded. 'Tell me what I need to know to find Abigail. I have to know who this man is. So far he's had the upper hand. He watches me, follows me, threatens me – but I can't see who I'm up against. And I have to, or he'll win. D'you understand? *I'm going to lose her.*' He was almost pleading. 'I'm fighting a phantom, Mr Martinez, and I need your help.'

'I don't know what I can tell you.'

'You said your son was being watched?'

'He thought he was being followed in Madrid. And he *knew* he was being watched in London.'

'Did he see who was watching him?'

'He said it was a white man ...' Carlos concentrated. 'Very fat.'

Tensing, Ben remembered what Leon had told him about being approached outside the Prado. By a sick, obese man. 'Did he have a name for him?'

'No.'

'What about the two men you mentioned before? Larry Morgan and ...'

'Emile Dwappa.'

'What can you tell me about them?'

'Morgan went to jail last month—'

'What about Dwappa?'

'That bastard's always around. Got his fingers in everything. Comes from a Nigerian family. There are dozens of them, all over the place. Some in the USA, some in Europe, a few in London. He's always got people working for him – you can never get to him direct. Cruel bastard, they say.' He hesitated, spooked. 'I don't want to get on the wrong side of him, Mr Golding. I want to help you, but—'

'Don't you want to know who killed your son?'

'He's dead. Knowing who killed him won't bring him

415

back,' Carlos replied. 'Knowing who murdered your brother won't bring Leon back either—'

'It might save the woman I love,' Ben replied, knowing how much he was asking but unable to hold back. 'If you want me to go, tell me now. I'll go, I'll understand. Just tell me to go and I will.'

Outside, a car horn sounded in the street, followed by the faint jingle of a mobile. Lighting up another smoke, Carlos stared blankly at the fireplace, trying to decide what to do. He was wondering how much he wanted to live, having lost his wife and son. Wondering how much he wanted a life away from the terrace he knew, transported into a high-rise ghetto. He was wondering what his wife would say – and then, finally, he leaned forward in his seat.

'Dwappa's into gambling and trafficking—'

'*Trafficking?*'

'Rumours, yes. They say he traffics kids for adoption by rich white people.' Carlos could see he had said something important and hurried on. 'They said he can get anything for a price. He's very clever, never been jailed, never been charged with anything. Probably because everyone's so scared of him.'

'And he's scared of nothing?'

'His mother,' Carlos replied, glancing around as though he expected her to be in the room, listening. 'If Emile Dwappa's dangerous, his mother is ten times more so. If I remember rightly, I think she's got a shop—'

'Where?'

'I don't know. And I don't want to know. Because if I do, I might recognise it. I might have bought something in it. Might have given money to the mother of man who killed my son.' He bit down on his lip to calm himself. 'She deals in animals ...'

Ben thought of the pig's head which had been stuffed into the hotel lavatory.

'Imports them from all over. Monkeys, reptiles, rare animals. And she deals in black magic, they say. Maybe that's what some of the animals are for. Voodoo.' He smiled hopelessly. 'I've never seen her, but people talk about her like you'd talk about the Devil. I've never known anyone inspire such fear. Someone said she's responsible for eleven deaths over the last twenty years.'

'And you believed them?'

He shrugged. 'I don't know. But it's a reputation which would put the fear of God into anyone, isn't it?'

Of everything he had heard, it had been the trafficking which had caught Ben's attention most. It couldn't be a coincidence that Bobbie Feldenchrist had just got a child from the same man who had sold her the skull. It *had* to be Dwappa ... Slowly he ran the name over in his mind, learning to hate it. Emile Dwappa. Emile. Dwappa.

'Are you going to try and find him?' Carlos asked quietly.

'Yes.'

'Don't mess with people like him. Look what happened to your brother, to my son—'

'How can I *not* mess with him?' Ben countered. 'I have to get Abigail back—'

'And the skull?'

'What about it?'

'I'm guessing he wants the skull in return for her.' When Ben didn't answer, Carlos continued. 'So give it to him, Mr Golding!' He paused, seeing the empty look on Ben's face, a shudder going through him. 'Oh, Christ, you haven't got it, have you?'

Without answering, Ben rose to his feet and walked out.

62

As he walked back along the street, Ben could sense that he was being watched and felt in his pocket for the Stanley knife he had bought. If anyone attacked him again, he would have something to fight with. He could at least leave a mark on his assailant. Hurriedly, he crossed at the lights, making for his car and getting into the front seat. Locking the doors, he thought over what Carlos Martinez had told him.

Now he had a name: Emile Dwappa. Finally he knew his adversary, knew the man who had abducted Abigail. The man who would ask for the skull in return for her safety. *The skull he didn't have*, Ben thought hopelessly. If Francis had lived only moments longer he would know where it was, but Francis had died with the secret. And now he had nothing to bargain with. Empty-handed, impotent ... Ben thought of the contact he had found on Francis's computer, the email Gortho@3000.com – the same contact that had been in touch with Leon. The address that must belong to Emile Dwappa.

And yet Francis had never mentioned receiving that

email. Had he hidden the fact deliberately? Was he – God forbid – *involved* with Dwappa in some way? Ben wanted to reject the idea, but forced himself to consider it. Had Francis Asturias betrayed him and tried to do business with Dwappa directly? Or had he overplayed his hand and swapped the skulls, believing that he could sell the original without anyone knowing? Was his supposed confusion during their last telephone conversation a double bluff? A way of pretending that he had been helping Ben, while instead he had secreted the skull away for his own later advantage?

Certainly Francis Asturias was clever enough to pull off a deception, but *would* he? Had boredom made him reckless? Or greedy? Turning on the engine, Ben suddenly noticed a piece of paper stuck under his windscreen wiper. Getting out of the car, he looked round the deserted street, then read the words.

THE SKULL FOR THE GIRL.
YOUR CHOICE.

He scanned the street again, but saw no one. Parked cars, a pub at the end of the road, but no people. No one suspicious. No one passing. No one watching. But he knew that in one of the houses, behind a door or at a boarded-up window, he was being scrutinised. Tense, he got back into the car and drove off, checking his rear-view mirror every few seconds on the uneventful ride home.

When he got back to his house Ben hurried in, locking the door behind him. Drawing the curtains and flicking on a lamp, he then glanced at his answering machine, but there were no messages. Surprised, he flipped on the computer. Among several emails – one from the principal of the hospital asking why he had temporarily passed over his patients to Megan Griffiths – there was an address Ben recognised: Gortho@3000.com.

Taking in a slow breath, Ben opened the message.

Come to Lincoln's Inn. Wait outside the Hunterian Museum at 10 p.m.
Bring the skull.

Sitting down, Ben typed a reply.

How will I know you?

He waited several minutes for an answer. It was short and clear.

I know you, that's enough.

He could feel his heartbeat increase and glanced at the clock – four ten p.m. He had just under six hours to find Emile Dwappa.

Carlos's words came back to him – *Dwappa's mother had a shop . . . She dealt in animals . . . voodoo . . .* Animals. Ben paused, reaching for the phone book and looking under the heading Pet Stores. He knew that it had to be either in, or close by, Brixton, but other than that he had nothing to go on. Running down the list, he stopped as he saw Mama Gala's Supplies. Something about the African name in among all the Indian and English names jumped out at him.

Reaching for the phone, he punched out a number. The handset picked up on the third ring.

'I'm sorry to trouble you again. I just have to ask you one more thing,' Ben said hurriedly. 'Does the name Mama Gala's mean anything?'

There was a tense silence.

'Mr Martinez?'

Whoever was on the other end of the line said nothing, just replaced the receiver with a resounding click.

Unnerved, Ben stared at the phone. Had Carlos cut him off? Or was there a more sinister explanation? Ben knew he was being watched. Had someone followed him to Carlos Martinez's house? Was someone there now, threatening the old man?

As if in answer the phone rang out beside him and Ben snatching it up.

'Mr Martinez?'

'No, it's Mark Steinman,' the principal of the Whitechapel Hospital replied shortly. 'What the hell are you playing at?' he snapped. 'You've left your patients—'

'In the care of my registrar.'

'You think she's capable?' Steinman retorted.

'It's only temporary.'

'I don't care. You don't just go off like that without getting authorisation.'

'I had good bloody reason. Abigail Harrop was abducted from your hospital. Francis Asturias was murdered there. You think I'm upset? You're fucking right I am!'

There was a pause before Steinman spoke again.

'Face it, Ben, you've not been yourself since your brother died. I understand, but it was hardly a shock to anyone, was it? Your brother had always been unstable – his suicide was only a matter of time.' His tone was midway between irritation and commiseration. 'You have to see it from my point of view—'

'*Your point of view?*'

'As you've just pointed out, Francis Asturias was murdered here and your partner was abducted from one of our side wards. We've had the police around asking questions. It's causing all kinds of disturbance, and frankly, your behaviour hasn't helped matters.' He paused, forming the next insult. 'I thought you were a steady pair of hands, but I was mistaken. Megan Griffiths told me that you'd been preoccupied, jumpy, and that you'd been taking a lot of time off, getting her to fill in for you.'

And there it was – hospital politics. Ben's personality clash with his registrar had finally given her an opportunity to undermine him – to make her first play for the top job. Megan Griffiths might want Harley Street, but she was savvy enough to know that being consultant, then senior consultant at the NHS Whitechapel, would shoo her in nicely for private practice.

To his chagrin, Ben realised he had played into her hands. At any other time he would have been more astute, but events had hobbled him and she had taken advantage.

'I've worked at the Whitechapel for twenty years,' he said slowly. 'My work has been exemplary—'

'I don't argue with that,' Steinman replied, 'but what's been happening lately would affect any man. No one blames you for being preoccupied, but your registrar isn't the only person to notice the . . . change in you.'

What the hell was he intimating? Ben wondered. That he was losing his mind?

'Change?'

'Perhaps you're tired. You should take some time off until everything's sorted out. No one wants to see you having a breakdown.'

'With due respect, Mr Steinman, I doubt you would have said that to any other consultant. Just because my brother was unstable doesn't mean I am.' He could feel his throat taut with anger. At the time he most needed support, there was none. Instead he was being threatened from every quarter, each part of his life capsized: his partner, his work, his life, even his sanity.

'Ben, take a week off. Keep away from the hospital—'

'Keep away?'

'You need a change of environment.'

Furious, Ben snapped back. 'Have you been talking to the police?'

'Not about you. I just think you should take a week off.'

'Are you sure a week's enough for a breakdown?'

'Well,' Steinman replied damningly, 'that depends on you, doesn't it?'

Slamming down the phone, Ben ran his hands through his hair, struggling to contain his anger. He had been sucker-punched by Megan Griffiths and resented it. Resented being excluded from the Whitechapel. Resented being edged out by the police and his colleagues. He was, he realised, completely on his own. He had no allies. All he loved most had been destroyed or taken from him.

His gaze fixed on the clock. He had just under six hours to trace the man who had killed his brother and abducted his partner.

Six hours to find a way to bargain. And nothing to bargain with.

63

Madrid

Her face swollen and bloodied, Gina pushed her way into Bartolomé's office, his secretary trying to stop her but failing as Gina stood defiantly in front of Bartolomé's desk, holding a blood-soaked cloth to her cheek.

'Gabino did this.'

Waving away his secretary, Bartolomé offered Gina a seat. She was a different woman from the one he had seen at Leon Golding's funeral, her eyes brilliant with malice, her sexuality suspended.

'Look at what he did.' Slowly she took away the cloth to reveal a deep knife cut three inches long running across her jaw line. She could see Bartolomé's eyes widen as he stared at the injury and felt a moment of triumph. It would be worth it, after all.

Determined to have her revenge on Gabino, Gina had done something that would have seemed unbelievable only days before. Rocked from the beating he had given her, she had formed a plan so ruthless it took all her courage to set it in motion. Throughout her life beauty had been her calling card, her entrée to money and influential beds, but her allure was waning. She could no longer rely on looks and sex alone – that currency was devalued. The inflation of age had hobbled her.

Staring at herself in the mirror, Gina had felt the knife in her hand. It was light, but the blade was razor-sharp. For several moments she scrutinised herself, her heart thumping as she prepared to make the leap from using beauty to using cunning. Then finally she had lifted her hand and – in one movement – attacked her face.

At first the blade had sliced through the flesh easily, but then it had snagged on the bone, blood coming fast and warm as she clasped a cloth to the wound. Momentarily faint, it had taken her a moment to work up enough courage to look in the mirror. When she did, another Gina had confronted her.

Her face was ashen, but her eyes triumphant.

Of course Bartolomé didn't know that Gina had injured herself, cutting her own face for a future she was determined to secure at any means.

'You need a doctor.'

'Yes,' she said, nodding. 'But I had to come here and talk to you. Your brother did this.' She showed him the bruises on her arms and forehead. 'And these. He beat me. He kicked me. In the stomach, as if I was an animal. As if I was inhuman.'

Mute, Bartolomé leaned against the desk, staring at his

brother's ex-lover. To attack a man was one thing, to assault a woman quite another. But he was clever enough to realise that Gina hadn't come to see him just to show him Gabino's handiwork. There was a frigid determination about her, a calm infinitely more threatening than hysterics.

'Why did he do it?'

'We argued.'

'About what?'

'You.'

'*Me?*' Bartolomé repeated, surprised. 'What about me?'

'You know I was living with Leon Golding. He was working on Goya's Black Paintings – he had a theory about them.'

'Many people have theories,' Bartolomé said warily, knowing that of the two of them, Leon Golding had always been more likely to solve the enigma first.

Gina nodded, then took a large crumpled envelope out of her bag and slammed it down on the desk. She could see Bartolomé's eager glance and nodded.

'Yes, that's it. I took a copy. Leon never knew, no one knows. I don't know why I did it, I just did.'

His hands ached to touch it, but he resisted, wanting to hear everything she had to say.

'He had the Goya skull too.' Gina could see she had his full attention and carried on. 'Of course you know about that now – it's in the USA – but when Leon first had it he was willing to sell it.'

The lie was perfectly formed, and did its damage.

'*Sell it?*'

She nodded. 'I told Gabino, because I knew how much you would want it. I begged him to tell you – but he wouldn't. He refused, said *why should he*? He enjoyed denying you the thing you most wanted.' Her voice was neutral, without malice, the words ripping into Bartolomé. 'He laughed at you – always has done. Thinks he can do anything and you'll never let him be punished. Thinks that the charge of assault will be crushed. That you'll see to it that it never comes to court.' Pausing, she touched the wound on her face. It was worth it – worth disfiguring herself to get revenge. 'But he won't get away with this. I'm going to the police. I'm going to make sure Gabino pays for this.'

Stunned, Bartolomé stared at her. But he wasn't listening any more, just thinking about the Goya skull, and how his brother had made certain he wouldn't get it.

'*You offered the skull to Gabino?*'

'Yes.'

'Why not come to me direct?'

'I know Gabino, and he lives in Madrid. You're usually in Switzerland,' she replied evenly. 'Naturally I thought he'd pass on the news to you.'

'He never did.'

'No, I know that now. Bobbie Feldenchrist has the skull, doesn't she?'

The words slashed into him. 'What d'you want?'

'For Leon's theory?' she asked, glancing at the envelope. 'Nothing. I knew how distraught you'd be about the skull. I thought that maybe the theory would help make up for it.'

He shook his head.

'No . . . that's not all of it. Why are you really here?'

'Your brother beat me up,' Gina replied. 'I want him put away. Jailed. I want to see him behind bars – and he will be, if I give evidence. If I go on the stand and tell the world about his excesses. People might forget him attacking men but they won't forget him beating up a woman.' She touched her face. It barely hurt with all the adrenalin rushing through her. 'Of course a lot of other things will come out too. Gabino will retaliate. He plays dirty – he'll want to drag you down with him.'

Bartolomé was breathing heavily. 'Are you trying to blackmail me?'

'No.'

'Then what?'

'I want you to tell your brother to marry me.'

His astonishment was obvious. '*I beg your pardon?*'

'You heard me. I want to be Gabino Ortega's wife.'

'You still love him?'

'No, I loathe him. I don't want to love him, I want to punish him. For everything he said to me. For every bruise, for every sneer, I want to make his life a living hell. And in return I want to have the Ortega name and some of the Ortega money. I want security, a home, status.' She paused, breathing in to steady herself. 'Think about what he did to you – denying you your dream when it was offered to him on a plate. Gabino could have got you Goya's skull. You could have had it in the Ortega collection, in Spain. You could have triumphed over everyone else in the art world. But he stopped it. *He stopped you.*' Her eyes flickered with spite. 'Give me my revenge and you'll have your own. Being married to a woman he hates will burn into Gabino. Being shackled to someone he said was only worth fucking, will turn his brain.' She laughed drily. 'I don't care which option you chose. I'll go to court and ruin him, or you'll see to it that I keep quiet, marry him and destroy his life. Either way, he'll get what coming to him.'

'And you?'

'I had my chance of happiness, but I chose not to see it or take it,' she replied, shrugging. 'That's my hell.'

'It's blackmail.'

'I'm blackmailing Gabino, not you.'

'What if he won't agree to it?'

'He will, if the alternative is having his allowance cut off and being thrown into jail.'

'What if *I* don't agree to it?'

'Then I'll go to the police and press charges.'

Gina raised the cloth to her face again, her eyes dead. Was he going to agree or not? She couldn't tell, but she was determined to have the Ortega name and promote herself from penury to prosperity overnight. Lying had been no problem, but perhaps her manipulation had only got her so far. Perhaps Bartolomé needed one last little push.

'You have a son. I don't think you'll want to endanger Juan's future.'

'What?'

'Scandal and bad publicity can wreck lives,' she went on, Bartolomé's full attention caught. 'It's not a risk you should take.'

'*Risk?*' he echoed. 'What risk?'

'You don't know?' She affected surprise. 'I'm sorry, I thought . . . Your brother said you knew . . .'

He was dry-mouthed, staring at her as though he realised that whatever she said would destroy him.

'Knew *what*?'

'Gabino . . .' she paused, focused and pitiless, '. . . is the father of your son.'

BOOK FIVE

Quinta del Sordo, Madrid, 1824

From across the river came the chiming of the night clock. Ten minutes fast, already ten minutes into a future hour. Surrounded by flickering candles, on the table, the worktop, the window ledges, even the floor, Goya painted in the tremulous light. Raw from lack of sleep, his body aching, his legs swollen and dry with the heat, he worked on. He was completing the last of his Black Paintings – an eerie, morose image of a decrepit woman hunched over a bowl of gruel, a skull-headed creature seated beside her. Both of them were looking to their left, gazing out of the window of the bedchamber.

Gazing out of the bedchamber, over the river, towards Madrid. Gazing out to the Court in the distance. Look where I look. Look . . .

Pausing, he felt a vibration under his feet and moved to the window. Outside a man was approaching on a horse, his presence unexpected at so late an hour. Although Goya couldn't hear it, he could imagine the whinnying of the horse, pressed into nocturnal service, its hooves throwing dust patterns on the scorched earth. But why would someone be out so late? Come to the Quinta del Sordo on what night purpose?

Still watching, Goya saw the man pause, staring at the farmhouse. He was wearing dusty black clothes, a white ruff marking him out as a fellow of the court, a gold cross swinging round his neck as he stared at the shape in the window. Goya knew that Leocardia was asleep in a chair downstairs, her daughter on her lap, but still he waited for the front door to be unfastened, for her to hurry over to the stranger and greet him.

Seen before, noted before. Coming over the fetid river to the Quinta del Sordo – the Deaf Man's House.

Turning away, Goya glanced over at the painting of the Holy Office, recognising the man outside as the man in the picture holding the drinking glass. His offering, his gesture from the court, his salutation.

This from the King, from Ferdinand. This from the Royal hand . . .

When Goya returned to the window, the man on horseback had gone. Suppressing fear and exhaustion, the old painter resumed his work. It would not be long now. Soon he would be finished. Soon the evidence would be complete.

His lifted his right arm, stiff in the joint, his full brush smearing the paint on the wall. He could sense the other paintings around him, sense them watching. Every figure playing a function in the grim commedia he had created. He had spent his life describing the indescribable – the cruelties and viciousness of his age, the tyranny of the Court and the ruthless hectoring of the Inquisition. Paintings, drawings, etchings had all presented the truth in vivid, brutal detail, but this time Goya was leaving behind a covert truth – an enigma, a riddle which depicted the unthinkable.

A secret too dangerous to be committed to paper or spoken out loud.

Let the court view him as a dangerous, treacherous madman. Let the world believe the same.

Goya knew that eventually fate would intervene. The Black Paintings might remain a mystery for a little time or for centuries, but one day someone would come looking ... He leaned against the wall, smearing the paint with his bare arm. Terror, age and exhaustion hung over him. He had lived through wars, survived the Inquisition, grown old amid plots, treachery and carnage, but now he wondered if – finally – death was imminent.

A little longer, he pleaded. A little longer ... It was almost finished, he reassured himself. When this last image was completed, he would leave the Quinta del Sordo.

Or be buried there.

64

For more than an hour after Gina had left, Bartolomé sat motionless at his desk. His thoughts came adrift, untied themselves, then knotted back together into one twisted coil of rope. Dismissing his secretary, he thought about his wife. Wondered how a woman he had loved so much had cuckolded him with his own brother and managed to fool him for so long.

Because much as Bartolomé wanted to laugh off Gina's claim, he knew in his heart it was true. He knew it because – now he let himself admit it – he had always had his suspicions, never spoken aloud, but there nonetheless. How convenient it had been that Celina had finally conceived after so many failures to get pregnant – just in time to prevent the Ortegas from adopting a child! By giving birth to Juan, Celina had cemented her position in the family, securing her future and her son's.

There had been other pointers too, now blindingly obvious. Juan was a handsome child, not tall like his father but stocky – like Gabino. And his temperament had little of Bartolomé's patience; Juan was mercurial, reckless, capricious. Even his interests told of his true parentage. Juan loved toy guns, cars, weapons. He had no time for books or music . . . It was so obvious, Bartolomé thought helplessly, but he hadn't wanted to see it. And for four long years Celina had hidden the truth.

For four years she had made love to Bartolomé and been privy to every aspect of his life and work. And for four years she had raised Gabino's child as his.

Shaking, Bartolomé clenched his hands together, pressing the palms into each other, heart line to heart line, lifeline to lifeline, crushing the blood out of the flesh. But it didn't help. He realised that her betrayal was the reason why she had always defended Gabino. Had always stayed his hand when he had wanted to punish his brother.

He was born an Ortega, and he will die an Ortega . . .

She had said that about Gabino, but she was also saying it about their son. Saying that blood was everything. Even crossed blood, treacherous blood – even that was to be accorded respect.

But to choose Gabino!

The lusty, violent, coarse Gabino. To choose the brother he hated, despised, to bring *his* cuckoo into their sweet nest . . . Bartolomé struggled to contain his anger, remembering Celina's old jealousy of Bobbie Feldenchrist, the pressure she had put on him to end the relationship. No other person had ever fazed Celina like Bobbie. No other woman had ever caused her a moment's concern. Jesus! Bartolomé thought. Why hadn't he married the American?

They were alike in so many ways, they were both collectors, and even if the relationship had faltered they would always have been bound by their common passion.

Bartolomé's face was expressionless as he tried to decide what he should do. Divorce his wife? Disinherit his brother? But if he did, he knew only too well what the outcome would be – the whole sordid story would be exposed, his business colleagues in Madrid and Switzerland mocking him. Celina was right about one thing – if you came from a powerful family body you could never risk cutting off any limb, however septic. You had to treat it, cure it, but never amputate and risk a corpse.

Slumping back into his seat, Bartolomé felt ashamed and foolish the same time. Then his gaze fell on the envelope Gina had left on the desk and he reached out for it, his mind clearing. Carefully he drew out the papers, Leon Golding's handwriting indecipherable in a few places but otherwise readable. A slow excitement shifted over his despair as he began to read. Leon's theory was strange, oddly convoluted. He leaned back, reading on ... Was it true? Bartolomé wondered. Could Leon Golding *really* have solved the enigma of the Black Paintings?

A solution to his problems came to Bartolomé in that instant. He might not have the skull of Goya, but he had the theory of the Black Paintings. True or not, it was artistic Semtex, enough to cause an explosion of interest in his own collection overnight. If he said the theory was his, who would challenge him? And if anyone did, he had been working on the paintings' meanings for years so it was quite plausible that he might have come to the same conclusions as Leon Golding . . .

Bartolomé's usual integrity deserted him, bitterness taking precedence. Honour was for fools. His grandfather had known that. Gabino knew that. So why should he behave differently? he asked himself. What reward was there in being noble? What recompense for industry and integrity? What was the prize awarded him for a blameless life? A cheating wife. A treacherous brother. Another man's child foisted upon him.

His thoughts slid onwards. No, he couldn't punish his wife or his brother publicly, but he could torture them privately. Clutching the papers, Bartolomé thought of Gina and how she would make Gabino jump. How every day of their marriage she would torment and hound him, curtailing his activities, and if he resisted she had only to come to Bartolomé and he would reduce his brother's allowance to a pittance.

As for his wife . . . Bartolomé's hands rested on the papers, then he reached for the phone and tapped out a number he hadn't used for over a decade.

And in New York, Bobbie Feldenchrist answered and began to listen.

65

London

Anxious for the safety of Carlos Martinez, Ben drove over to the old man's house and knocked. Then he knocked again. Impatiently, he waited, looking around, but the place was in darkness and when he peered through the letter box, the hall was cool and empty.

'What you doing?'

Ben turned to find a sullen girl watching him. She had a baby balanced on her hip and was wearing a plastic bomber jacket, with three rows of silver rings in her ears.

'I was looking for Carlos—'

'He's not in.'

'D'you know where he is?'

She shook her head, shifting her baby from one hip to another. 'I dunno. Why d'you want him?'

'I was just coming to see him—'

'I never seen you round her before,' she said, her plucked

eyebrows raised. 'You don't look like anyone I've *ever* seen round here. You police?'

'No.'

She thought for a moment. 'He went out – Mr Martinez. He went out a bit back. Rushed off, in a hell of a hurry.'

'Did he say where?'

'Nah, I just saw him. I didn't talk to him.'

'Was he on his own?'

'Relative?'

Ben frowned. 'What?'

'Are you a relative? I mean, coming here, asking all these questions. You must be family.'

'No, I'm a friend.' Ben paused, then corrected himself. 'I *was* a friend, a long time ago ... Mr Martinez's son—'

'He was killed, wasn't he?' she said, putting a dummy in her baby's mouth and jiggling him on her hip. 'Shame that. People round here talked about it a lot—'

'Did you know Diego?'

'Nah.' She studied Ben, curious and wanting to talk to ease her boredom. 'Never met him.'

'Does anyone know why he was killed?'

She cocked her head over to one side. 'You ask a lot of questions.'

'I'm worried about Mr Martinez,' Ben said in reply. 'You said he left in a hurry.'

'That don't mean nothing.'

Glancing about him, Ben hesitated before asking the next question. 'Look I need some information and I'm wondering if you can you help me. I'm looking for a shop.'

'You do a lot of looking too.'

He smiled, the girl smiling back in return. 'What kind of shop?'

'Mama Gala's.'

Her friendliness closed off as she turned and began to walk away, Ben following. 'I'm sorry, I didn't mean to scare you ...'

She was walking fast, the baby mewling and mouthing at its dummy.

'Just tell me where the shop is.'

She stopped and turned to him. 'Three streets from here. Turn left, right, walk to the end of Lamb Lane, cut through the alley into Gardenia Street. It's the shop in the middle of the row – you can't miss it. Although, frankly, I would.'

'Has it any connection to Emile Dwappa?'

'It's his mother's place,' she replied, turning then turning back. 'It's not for the likes of you—'

'How d'you know that?'

'You'll see,' she said, moving off. 'You'll see.'

Mama Gala was sitting in the semi-dark. She had closed the shop and finished cashing up, and was now listening to the soft moaning coming from the room above. The bloody Englishwoman had woken up. Fuck her. Heaving herself to her feet, Mama Gala walked to the bottom of

444

the stairs, calling for the old woman above. A moment later, her wizened head appeared over the banister.

'Shut her up,' Mama Gala said simply. 'Shut her the fuck up.'

The old woman said nothing, just moved off. Mama Gala waited – two seconds, three seconds, four, and then silence. The moaning had stopped. Her slow gaze moved to the front door of the shop and then out into the street beyond as she scratched the back of her head.

She had given her son one last chance to prove himself. She hadn't asked what the drugged woman was for; she wasn't interested what Emile did with her. All that concerned her was money and the getting of it. She had guessed that the woman was to be bartered – for what, she didn't know and wouldn't ask. All Mama Gala had done was to elicit a promise – under threat – that her son would make a deal to transport them from Gardenia Street to Money Land and remain firmly, irrevocably, under her greasy thumb.

Sitting down again, she stared at the locked door of the shop. Something told her that tonight would bring changes, that by morning the life she knew would be over. Slowly and deliberately Mama Gala hummed under her breath, her breathing rank and quick with excitement.

Checking his watch, Ben frowned. Time was slipping away from him and before long he would face Emile Dwappa and be forced to admit that he didn't have the skull. That he had nothing to offer in return for Abigail. And then what?

Ben knew that if he had any chance of saving his lover he had to find the real skull before ten p.m. Getting back into the car, he reached for his mobile and put in a call.

Mrs Asturias answered immediately, her tone imperious. 'Who's this?'

'Ben Golding. I came to see you the other day—'

'I remember, I'm not senile!' she snapped. 'What is it now? Did you find the skull?'

'No,' Ben replied, 'and I have to. You've no idea how important it is that I do.'

'My husband died because of that bloody skull, so I can guess.' Her tone was sharp, businesslike. 'You rushed off very quickly the other day after you'd read something on Francis's computer. I have to admit I couldn't help looking at it afterwards. Meant nothing to me. What was it?'

'I'm not sure,' Ben said honestly, 'but—'

'Go ahead.'

'Have you *any* idea where Francis could have hidden that skull?'

'I've thought about that ever since you came to see me, but I've no more idea than I had then.'

'He had a strange sense of humour. Maybe he put it somewhere only you could guess? Or maybe the hiding place is a play on words?' He was scrabbling for inspiration. 'Francis liked reading, liked crosswords and jokes. He always had a clever turn of phrase. He was good with words—'

'Especially four-letter ones.'

'Perhaps he put it somewhere funny.'

'*Funny?*'

'Humorous. Somewhere that would be a joke.' Ben faltered. 'I don't know what the hell I'm talking about.'

'Believe me, Mr Golding, if there was anything obvious – or even peculiar to us, to Francis and me – I would have told you.' She sighed expansively. 'I went through all his things, like people do when someone dies. I thought I'd find something which might help you, or maybe even a love letter he had never sent. To me, of course. I find I'm rather sentimental all of a sudden.' Her voice teetered, then righted itself. 'In some ways, Francis was a bloody fool of a man. I used to tell him that I'd leave him and find myself someone better, but he knew I never would . . . God loves drunks and fools – and I find I agree with Him on the latter.'

'Are you all right?'

'Of course! I shall snap my way through old age like a cornered crocodile.' She paused. 'And you? How are you?'

'Under pressure.'

'Because of the missing skull?'

'And other things.'

'You sound exhausted. Shouldn't you get some rest?'

'I haven't got time.'

Highly intelligent, she picked up on an undercurrent. 'Are you in trouble?'

'Yes, serious trouble. And it's not just me.'

'Are you afraid?'

'Yes.'

'It's good to be afraid sometimes, Mr Golding. It makes

us fight for what we care about . . . Will you let me know what happens to you?'

'If I can.'

They both knew what he meant.

'Diego Martinez, your brother, Francis – they weren't enough?' she carried on hurriedly, without giving him time to reply. 'Of course they weren't. And now it's your turn, is it?'

Ben avoided the question. 'No one's been bothering you, have they?'

'No, Mr Golding! No one bothers old women. I dare say I shall have to live out the rest of my life *un*bothered.'

'Promise me, Mrs Asturias, that you'll never talk to anyone about any of this. Never mention our conversations or the skull—'

'You told me once, you don't need to repeat it!' she snapped. Then her tone softened. 'Make it worth it.'

'What?'

'My husband's death. Make it matter. Or what's the bloody point?'

66

It was just after eight p.m. when Ben reached the Whitechapel Hospital and parked around the back of the cardiac unit, avoiding the consultants' spaces where someone would be sure to recognise his car. His trip across London had been delayed and he was almost running when he entered the back entrance of the hospital, taking the narrow stairs up to the laboratory two at a time.

Across the door was blue and white tape, **POLICE – DO NOT ENTER**, which fluttered as he opened the door and walked in. The darkness surprised him and for an instant he was tempted to turn on the light, but he waited until his eyes had adjusted to the gloom. Outside rain had begun to fall; it drummed on the glass roof of the hospital dome and rattled the metal sign which hung at the entrance to the Radiology department below. Six lengthy workbenches stretched out in front of Ben as he moved towards the first one, which Francis had always used. Moonlight, at once brilliant and sombre, lit the wooden surface and the chalk outline of the last of Francis Asturias.

It required no effort to conjure up the memory of Francis

with his stringy grey hair, shabby suede shoes and gauntlets – madly, weirdly practical. Above Ben's head he could see the punishingly bright lights Francis used when he was working, and on a plinth to his left a reconstructed head sat waiting for a master who would never return. In the sink lay an old mug and a glob of clay, their shabby poignancy surmounted by the silver shapers Francis used to smooth his sculptures. And more stirring than this, than any of his belongings, was the smell of chemicals and the soft, dry scent of discarded clay.

Could this man really have betrayed him? Ben thought, looking around and then moving over to the large walk-in fridge at the other end of the laboratory. Could Francis Asturias have cheated him? A noise overhead made him pause, but a few moments later the footsteps moved off and faded on the twisting stairs beyond.

Dry-mouthed, Ben ran his tongue over his lips and opened the fridge door. It swung towards him, heavy on its hinges and smelling of dead water. Inside, jars of specimens and dissected organs grinned from the shelves of their cold tomb. For over fifty years the laboratory had shared a fridge with the overspill from the clinical laboratory downstairs, Francis complaining monthly about the lack of space.

Curious, Ben walked further into the fridge, his body illuminated in the glare of the inside light, a warm dark outline against the white ice. Pulling back the cover from a partially dissected heart, he threw it back over then bent down and peered under the shelves, finding nothing. Still crouched down on his haunches, he tried to shape-shift himself into Francis Asturias's thoughts. He had had the skull and then it had been stolen, but only after he had taken the original and replaced it with a fake. So where would he put the real skull? Where would a man like Francis Asturias hide such a prize?

Another sound made Ben jump to his feet. This time the footsteps had come to a halt. They had paused outside the laboratory door and torchlight shone into the room. Slowly and deliberately the light arced round. It hit the workbenches and the lamps overhead, darting across the windows and finally coming to rest on the table where Francis had been killed.

Then the light went out.

But a shadow remained on the other side of the door.

Immobile, watching, Ben hung back in the cold confines of the fridge. Anxious, he looked around for a way to escape, but he couldn't move without being seen and realised that his only chance was to remain silent and unmoving. The cold leeched into his feet as the seconds passed, his breath white feathers tugged out of his lungs. And *still* the figure didn't move.

Then, very slowly, the door of the laboratory opened. As it did so, the light from the corridor followed behind the outline of a figure. A figure which suddenly moved, lunging forward and slamming the fridge door shut.

It was eight fifteen p.m.

67

Knocking on Roma's door, Duncan entered with the air of someone who has to report bad news and is trying desperately not to run away from it.

Sensing his anxiety, Roma raised her eyebrows. 'All right, what is it?'

'We lost Golding.'

'*You lost him?*' She was so angry she was hardly audible. 'I thought you told me that since he came back to London we had him under surveillance.'

'We did.' Duncan hurried on. 'Golding returned to his home, then went to see Carlos Martinez—'

'Martinez?' Roma queried.

'Yeah, that was when we lost him. After he left. He took a cab and there was a diversion and we lost him in traffic on the Edgware Road.' Duncan shrugged, trying to make the best of the complicated breakdown in communications. 'It wasn't my watch—'

'So whose was it?'

'Peter's—'

'Peter's usually good . . .'

'Yeah,' Duncan said reluctantly, 'but he's getting slower. Look, it could have happened to me, Peter or Jimmy. It could have happened to anyone.'

'Don't bother with the excuses, just get on with it. What did Martinez say?'

'No one's spoken to him. No one said for us to watch Martinez—'

'No, I said to watch Golding! And that means to watch anyone he sees!' Maddened, Roma slammed her hands down on the desk. 'Why d'you think he went to see Martinez when his partner's just been abducted?' Her eyes bored into Duncan. 'They had a connection from the start, with that bloody skull. And I thought Golding was involved with its theft, but I was wrong—'

'He *was* acting oddly—'

'You don't need to try to make me feel better, Duncan,' she retorted, hurrying on. 'Like I said, I was wrong about Golding's motives, but I think I know what he's up to now.'

'You do?'

She leaned back in her seat, staring at Duncan. 'What would you do if you were Ben Golding? I know what I'd do. I'd try to find Abigail Harrop. And get my back on my brother's murderer at the same time.'

'But if we don't know who the killer is, how can Golding have found out?'

'I don't know,' Roma admitted. 'He's played a very close game since the start. Everything he's ever said has been half truth, half lie. He's always kept more from us than he's confided. We've been jerked around from Spain to London, New York to Spain, London to Spain, hearing bits of everything and the whole of nothing. Golding's clever.' She paused, holding Duncan's gaze. 'And he's willing to take a risk because he's lost a brother, a friend – and now perhaps his partner.'

'He's out of his depth—'

'He doesn't care. He's blinded to logic – he just wants to save Abigail Harrop. Probably to make up for the fact that he couldn't save the others. And *that*,' she said curtly, 'is why Golding's doing our job.'

She rose to her feet, indicating that their conversation was over. The closeness between them was suspended, her irritation absolute.

'Find Golding.'

'Where?'

'*I don't know, just find him!*' she shouted. 'Start with his home, his work, every place he's been lately. I won't have another death on my conscience. Talk to his neighbours, his colleagues – do whatever you have to do but find him. And *quick*.'

68

Incredulous, the principal stared at Megan Griffiths, then hurriedly unlocked the door of the walk-in fridge.

'What the hell—' Ben snapped, moving out into the laboratory and looking from Megan to Mark Steinman.

Steinman was the first to talk. 'Dr Griffiths saw you break in—'

'I didn't break in! I work at this bloody hospital!' he roared, rubbing some feeling back into his hands and stamping his feet as he stared at his registrar. 'Have you lost your mind?'

Shame-faced, Megan Griffiths blustered. 'Everyone knows you've been behaving oddly—'

'*Oh, for Christ's sake!*'

'I saw you come in. You didn't turn on the light,' Megan blundered on. 'It seemed odd.'

'And locking someone in a fridge doesn't?'

'You've been under a lot of pressure—'

'Don't try to psychoanalyse me! I'm not the crazy one here. I'm sorry to disappoint you, but you'll have to wait a bit longer for your promotion, Dr Griffiths.'

Enraged, he brushed past both of them, Steinman moving with him towards the door.

'What *were* you doing here?'

'Looking for a specimen I was having examined—'

'In the dark?'

'There's a light inside the fridge. I can vouch for that,' Ben retorted, glancing at his watch and quickening his steps as he headed for the stairs. It was eight twenty-five p.m.

'You've been put on leave—'

'But not suspended!'

'Where are you going?' Steinman demanded as Ben moved off.

'What's it to you? I'm on holiday, remember?' he countered, running down the steps. At the bottom he glanced up and saw two tiny figures peering down at him from the top floor. 'Dr Griffiths?' he called.

She leaned over the banister to hear him.

'Yes?'

'Don't take me on again.' His tone was warning. 'You'll lose.'

Running to his car, Ben followed the directions he had been given, driving towards Gardenia Street and parking. On the corner several youths were lounged against some steps, smoking, and an older man turned to watch Ben as he passed. There were no smiles, no welcomes of any sort, only a sullen menace as Ben walked over to the shop in the middle of the row. On the door hung the notice CLOSED. Ben glanced at his watch – eight forty-five p.m.

Putting up one hand to shield his eyes from the street lamp, he looked in at the window. Rows of herbs and dried concoctions swung from meat hooks and wooden racks. Underneath packets of teas and bags of maize a row of fruit came into view, and then suddenly he heard the unmistakable sound of a monkey screeching.

The hairs on the back of his neck rose. Looking up, his eyes searched the darkness. The lettering was hardly discernible in the dim light. But then he saw, red as blood, the words – MAMA GALA's.

Flicking on his mobile, Ben heard it ring out.

'Come on, Roma, pick up. *Pick up!*' he whispered urgently, but as it clicked over to answerphone he rang off without leaving a message.

Looking down Gardenia Street to make sure that no one was watching him, Ben moved round to the side of the shop. As he peered through a window, a parrot cawed, alarmed, and Ben spotted the outlines of several other cages in the gloom. As quietly as he could, he moved down the narrow alleyway, making for the back yard, and in that instant a light came on in a window overhead.

Startled, he stepped back as two figures appeared on the street beyond, blocking his way, another driving up in a car and pausing by the kerb side. Standing his ground, Ben watched as a tall black man got out of the driver's seat and came over to him. He knew without being told that this was Emile Dwappa. Without hearing a voice or being given any hint of his identity, Ben knew that this was the man who had caused his brother's death.

457

He had a patina of menace, well-honed, experienced. It spoke of a multitude of cruelties and a complete indifference. Even in his walk there was an impression of savagery. He engaged no one's notice, returned no one's eye contact, and when he came up to Ben his body jutted forward like the blade of a knife.

He was, in that instant of recognition, truly terrifying.

'You couldn't wait for our appointment?'

Ben shook his head. 'No, I couldn't wait.'

'You should have,' Dwappa replied, beckoning for Ben to follow him.

Unlocking a side door, Dwappa pushed it open, the odour of herbs and sage taking a swing at both of them as Ben entered first. He was anticipating an attack, his hand automatically going into his pocket to check that the Stanley knife was still there. In the dimness he could just make out the cages, and the rows of meat hung up on butcher's hooks. The smell of sawdust and animal urine caught at his throat as Dwappa showed him into the shop, gesturing for him to take a seat at a round table in the office behind.

'You found me. That was smart,' Dwappa said, sliding into his chair, his eyes on Ben. 'How?'

'Mostly luck,' Ben replied, sitting down opposite the African, his eyes moving towards the street outside. God! he thought helplessly. Why hadn't he left a message for Roma? Why hadn't he said where he was going? No one knew about Gardenia Street. No one had any idea where he was. And unless he was very careful, no one would ever know what happened to him. 'You abducted my partner.'

'Yes.'

'Is she all right?'

'You know why I took her?'

Ben played for time. 'I want to see her—'

'I bet you do.'

'I *need* to see her. See she's OK.' He could smell the monkeys outside and hear the soft footfall of someone overhead.

'You know what I want,' Dwappa began. 'The skull's a fake. I want the real one. Then I'll give you back your woman.'

Ben smiled distantly. 'Of course you will. Then you'll just let us walk out of here.' He looked around. 'She *is* here, isn't she?'

'Give me the skull.'

'No, not until I've seen Abigail,' he said, his mouth drying. There was only so long he could stall. Only so long before he had to admit that he didn't have it. 'Let me see her.'

'Have you got the skull with you?'

'I want to see Abigail,' Ben replied, his tone hardening, his eyes fixed on the African's face. 'You killed my brother, didn't you? And Diego Martinez? And Francis Asturias?' He could feel a cold draught blow across his face. Someone had opened a door somewhere. Somewhere close. 'Why did you kill my brother? Why didn't you just take the skull off him?'

Impassive, Dwappa toyed with a dirty coffee cup in front

of him.

'You made him suffer.'

'Not me.'

'Who?'

'Jimmy Shaw.'

'And what happened to him?'

Dwappa's expression didn't alter a jot. 'He died.'

'Who murdered Diego Martinez?'

'Jimmy Shaw.'

'Francis Asturias?'

'Who's Francis Austeris?'

Ben sighed. So his old friend *hadn't* betrayed him. Poor Francis had been just one more piece of collateral damage.

'He was killed—'

'Jimmy Shaw must have done it.' Dwappa sighed, bored already. 'I didn't kill anyone—'

'Yes, you did. Whether you organised the killings or you did them yourself, it's the same thing,' Ben replied as the draught intensified. 'Let me see Abigail.'

To Ben's surprise, Dwappa nodded, gesturing for Ben to follow him.

'Where are we going?'

'You want to see her? I'm taking you to see her,' Dwappa replied, moving past the cages as they approached the stairs. As Ben passed the snakes he felt the draught increase further, smelt the night air, and realised that there was another back entrance. Another way for someone to come up behind him. And corner him.

'Why did you swap the skulls?' Dwappa asked, pausing

halfway up the stairs.

'Show me Abigail and I'll tell you everything.'

'What if I just beat it out of you?'

The words were spoken almost in a whisper, catching Ben off guard. He felt the fear building up in him, mixing with the animal smells and the pungent aroma of herbs, and he knew that if he showed any weakness he – and Abigail – wouldn't get out alive. Guile was his only chance of survival.

'I still wouldn't tell you. And then you'd be left with another body on your hands. And no skull.'

'I could kill your woman.'

Ben tensed, but kept his nerve, bluffing. 'There are always other women. There's only one skull.'

'I didn't realise *you* wanted it,' Dwappa replied, amused.

Turning away, he continued his ascent, Ben taking in a slow, relieved breath as he followed him. At the top of the stairs an old woman sat outside a locked door. She made no eye contact with Dwappa, just moved aside to let him enter.

Abigail was lying on a mattress on the floor, the bandage around her head bloodstained, her eyes closed. Moving over, Ben touched her face, then checked for a pulse.

Dwappa stood watching both of them. 'She's alive.'

'Barely,' Ben replied, trying to keep the anger out of his voice. He had to stay calm, or they were finished. 'Is she drugged?'

'What d'you think?'

'How long before she comes round?'

461

Dwappa checked his watch. 'About an hour. No longer. But that's only if we can do business. Otherwise her next dose might be her last.'

Every threat he uttered was in a soft, almost feminine voice, the meaning of the words taking a moment to register.

'What happened to her?' he asked, gesturing to the bandages. 'Why was she in hospital anyway?'

'She had surgery on her face,' Ben replied, staring at the unconscious Abigail and longing to touch her, to clean her up, wipe the blood off her face. To see her move and speak again. But she lay motionless, her breath hardly discernible, her lips cracked. And beside her the floor scuttled with bugs, a water pitcher left empty by a boarded-up window.

'Well, now you've seen her, let's talk business,' Dwappa said shortly, hustling Ben downstairs and back into the office behind the shop.

Despair welled up in Ben. The moment had come. Now Dwappa would finally discover that he had nothing to bargain with. That he was playing with no court cards, no aces, no hand at all.

'So,' the African whispered, 'where's the fucking skull?'

69

The moment stretched out into infinity. Ben was suddenly
back in Madrid in the country house. He could hear Leon
calling from the study and see the shadow of Detita cross
the black tiled floor. Hot days, longer than weeks, came
back to him, smelling of lemon and hibiscus, accompanying the river, the moon yellow as a church candle – and
the solemn rusty crooning of the weathervane. He could
smell the summer dust, hear the dripping water from an
outside tap as it hit the dry earth, a bunch of spent flowers
closing down their last day.

He was a boy again – before Leon, before Francis, before
Abigail, before loss and confusion. He was young and the
birds flew wide over his head, minnows making their
shifty path down the river. It was the time before all the
church bells rang out for funerals and wakes; before the
dead were closer than the living; before night outlasted
day and before men with blood on their hands talked in
whispers like angels.

'You had it.'

Dwappa blinked slowly. The shop behind him was dimly

lit, the only strong light coming from the street lamp outside the window.

'What?'

'You had it. There was only ever one skull. There was only the skull you gave to Bobbie Feldenchrist. There *is* no real skull.' His mouth was drying, words clinging like reeds to his tongue. 'It was all a fake.'

'*What are you talking about?*' Dwappa gasped as Ben continued.

He was talking from another place. From safety, from the voice of something prompting him, telling him what to say.

'I lied from the start. No one found the skull of Goya. I planted the story for my brother, for Leon. He was very disturbed, very unhappy, desperate to find a meaning to his life . . .'

The birds were winging higher and higher, over the stables, over the first great gobbling of an early moon.

'I wanted to give my brother what he wanted, so I did. I organised the whole thing. Got Diego Martinez to "find" the skull and pass it over to Leon. I got Francis Asturias to say that it was genuine, to write authentication papers for it . . .'

And now here he comes, Goya whistling under his breath, notes that he can't hear. And swinging a block of drawings under his arm. Detita is talking about the old man, and the black horses that come over the bridge at night.

'*There never was a skull of Goya*. Leon never had it. No one

464

ever had it. You were running after an illusion. You all were – you, Bobbie Feldenchrist, the Ortegas. The skull you got is worthless. An old skull that could have belonged to a pauper. I lied to make my brother happy.' He paused. 'I never realised what would happen until it was too late.'

'*You made it all up?*'

Ben nodded, calm, because it was all so very calming in the end. Because he could believe what he was saying, and felt a drowsy removal from a sane world. The lie swung him up higher than a falcon. But soon the air would no longer be able to hold him and he knew he would have to make that long swoop, down into grass, and claws, and prey – and he held his breath.

'There was *no* Goya skull?' Dwappa said hoarsely, standing up.

Ben could feel the draught from the door increase. This time he knew someone was coming up behind him, a shadow shifting across the table from a lighted passage beyond.

'You fucking idiot,' someone said, voice coarse and reproachful.

Slowly, Ben turned his head as a huge woman came into view. Her bulk was commanding, her head swathed in a greasy turban, big hands holding a tray with glasses on it.

'My son! My useless son! Promising to get me out of here. Promising to make money, lots of money.' She slammed down the tray and the glasses tinkled. 'You fucked up. *Again.*'

Pulling up a chair, she sat down, the seat creaking under her weight, her yellowed eyes turning to Ben. Her face was devoid of expression, her tongue flicking out to moisten her lips as she studied him. From the back door came the night air, fluting against the table top as she poured herself a drink and then swallowed it in one.

Filling the three glasses, she pushed one towards Ben. 'No.'

Her eyes were dead, blank, without feeling.

'Drink it.'

'No.'

Shrugging, she pushed a glass over to her son, and then refilled her own, her disgust thick in the air. Dwappa watched his mother drain her glass again. Dry-mouthed, he sipped at his own and then wiped his lips with the back of his hand. His eyes flicked over to her and then looked away, as though he was afraid he might catch her glance. Together they drank, Mama Gala staring at Ben and then turning back to her son.

He shrank. Not physically, but emotionally. Buckled under a lifetime of abuse.

'Fucking moron,' she said, leaning back. The chair creaked as she folded her gigantic arms across the wide girth of her stomach. She smelt sour, unwashed. '"There was no skull, after all,"' she mimicked, then leaned towards Ben. 'This skull – was it supposed to be valuable?'

He nodded, watching the two of them, his back to the door.

'Yes.'

'But it's worthless?'

'Yes.'

'So you've nothing to give us in exchange for the woman?'

The words struck out at Ben. 'I didn't abduct her. Your son did that. He wanted to use her to bargain with me—'

'For something you don't have?'

Ben nodded, Mama Gala laughing like a lunatic. As quickly as she had started, she stopped, turning to her son. Her gaze moved over him slowly, her contempt corrosive.

'You failed.'

'I—'

'*You failed*,' she said again, then emptied her glass, refilling Dwappa's. 'What are we going to do now?' she asked, taking another greedy drink, her eyes watching him over the rim of the glass. 'I've been waiting for you to come good for years,' she went on, putting down her glass and picking at the corner of her left eye. 'Waiting on all your promises. Waiting for the good times. The big time. So many plans and promises you made me. And nothing came of any of them. Such big dreams for such a little runt.'

'I can—'

'No,' she said coldly, 'that's the point, you *can't*. You never could. You aren't able. You sick fuck. You queer . . .'

Watching them, Ben waited. They had believed his story, but what were they going to do next? With him? With Abigail? How likely was it that they would let them go after what had happened? But then again, what would be the point of killing two more people for *nothing*?

In the dim light he watched the couple facing him across the table. A grotesque mother and her murderous son.

'I'll go back to see the woman in New York, blackmail her—'

'Hah! You've been outsmarted, like always. Whatever you try won't come good. People are too clever for you.' She swigged back another drink, the flesh slack under her chin. 'You're no use to me, Emile. No use to me. You disappointed me. I gave you so many chances, but you never came good.' To Ben's surprise, her voice was changing, taking on an odd crooning tone. 'But what does it matter now? It's over. All over.'

A long malicious moment hung between them, Dwappa watching his mother then suddenly beginning to choke, his hands going to his throat, clutching for air.

Slowly Mama Gala leaned towards her son, stroking his face. 'No, just relax. Just be calm, be calm,' she told him, Dwappa's eyes wide, then suddenly drooping. From one moment of bulging terror they had changed into a flat incredulity, his face slackening as he slumped in his seat.

Stunned, Ben watched her. 'What the hell are you doing?'

She turned her great head, the thick neck wrinkling. 'What I should have done a long time ago.'

'You can't kill your own son.'

'I'm not going to,' she replied, loosening Dwappa's collar and placing his slack hands on his thighs.

'Is he poisoned?'

She shrugged, as though the matter was of no interest. *'Have you poisoned him?'*

'Get out!' she said simply. 'Go on, get out!'

Shaken, Ben rose to his feet. He could see Dwappa's eyes following him, imploring him, as he backed away.

'But he's your son—'

'He killed your brother!' she snapped. 'You want him to get away with that? Where are your fucking balls? Why don't you want him dead? I bred him and I can do what I want with him. He'll just be one more animal to keep. Mute, helpless, needing me.' She smiled like a devil, making a kissing sound with her lips as she looked at her son. 'I can keep him with me forever now. You think I don't know what he really wanted? To leave me. To make money and get away from me. Now he'll never leave me.'

She rolled her massive head, loosening her neck muscles as Dwappa stared at her, knowing she had won. Knowing he was locked in, at her mercy, facing interminable imprisonment. Trapped in a useless body, when every day would hold fresh torture. He would beg for death, would long for the end. And Mama Gala would make sure it didn't come quickly.

It was a fitting punishment.

Rising to his feet, Ben moved to the door quickly. He was waiting to be stopped, for Mama Gala to get out of her chair and come after him, for someone – anyone – to prevent him from leaving that terrible room.

'Wait!'

He stopped, turning back to her.

'Remember what I tell you,' she said, her expression lethal. 'Breathe a word of this and you'll regret it. I know you. I know her. I can – *I will* – find you anywhere.' She jerked her head upstairs, to where Abigail was being held. 'I know how to make people suffer. I know deeper and darker then you can imagine. I know tricks to make men mad.' She was talking without emotion, a blank mask of hatred. 'I know a hell within hells. I've been there, and I'll take you with me if you speak a word about this.'

In silent agreement, Ben nodded. Then, taking one last look at his brother's killer, he ran upstairs.

70

Still unconscious and scarcely breathing, Abigail didn't move as Ben drove her back to his house. Although he knew he was taking a chance, he decided that it was too risky to return her to the Whitechapel Hospital. After settling her into bed, he then made a few hurried phone calls and a nurse arrived soon after with the dressings and medication he had requested.

Gently he removed the soiled bandage from around Abigail's head. Wincing as he saw the onset of infection, he bathed the operation site and gave her an antibiotic injection. Abigail never stirred, never woke. He checked her pulse, noting that it was really sluggish, and sat down beside the bed.

Five minutes later he checked her pulse again, but there was no change. He leaned towards her, stroking her face, talking to her.

'Darling, wake up. It's me, Ben. Wake up, sweetheart.'

She shifted in her sleep, sweating, breathing rapidly. Her eyes were puffy from water retention, her hair damp with sweat. Tenderly, he combed it away from her face, sticky tendrils smearing the pillow. Her beauty, marred and scarred, was an ache in his heart.

'Abi, you're safe now.'

Still she didn't wake.

'You're home. With me. You're safe, baby.'

Taking off his shoes, Ben lay down on the bed beside her, holding her to him, her head against his chest. Every breath she took echoed inside his own chest, every flutter of her pulse mirrored his own. He held her and watched the ceiling above them. He watched the darkness deepen, then lift with the first slow-building nudge of dawn, morning coming sleepy on the new day. Once or twice in the early hours he heard an alarm go off, but nothing woke her. Exhausted, he thought he might sleep but remained wakeful, listening, hoping for the first signs that she was going to come round.

He didn't know what toxic substance she had been given, just as he knew the hospital wouldn't be able to help her any more than he could. All he could do was to wait for her. Talk to her, comfort her. Make her hear him.

And come back.

71

Watching from outside Ben's house, Duncan rang the police station. Roma came on to the line immediately.

'Have you found him?'

'Ben Golding's back home,' Duncan replied. 'And I think he brought Abigail Harrop back with him.'

'*You think?*'

'He was carrying a woman. I suppose it was her,' Duncan replied. 'You want me to find out?'

'No, stay there. I'm on my way.'

When he heard the doorbell ring, Ben was tempted to ignore it. But when it kept on ringing he left Abigail and walked downstairs. Through the spyhole he could see Roma Jaffe, and waited a moment longer before opening the door.

Her expression was one of pure annoyance. 'Can I come in?'

'Of course,' Ben replied, stepping back for her to enter. 'I was just going to ring you—'

'I'm sure you were.'

'I've got Abigail back.' He paused, handling his words

473

like rare china, terrified they might chip and shatter even as he said them.

'*Got her back?*' Roma queried, following Ben as he moved into the sitting room. Refusing a seat, she glanced around. 'Can I see her?'

'She's asleep.'

'But she's OK?'

He hesitated. 'I'm not sure. I think she's going to be OK ... I did try to ring you—'

'Who had her?'

'The person who wanted the Goya skull—'

'The skull that's in the Feldenchrist Museum, New York?'

He skirted the question. 'Abigail's home – that's all that matters.'

'Oh, and that's the end of it, is it?' she said. 'Aren't you forgetting something? The deaths of Diego Martinez, your brother, Francis Asturias. You think *that's* done with?'

'I know who killed them.'

Her eyes narrowed. 'Who?'

'Jimmy Shaw.' The name meant something to her, he could tell. 'D'you know him?'

'Shaw's a criminal, a fixer. But he's not a killer—'

'He is now. He killed all three of them.'

'He told you this?'

'I was told, yes.'

'Don't bugger me about, Golding!' she snapped. 'I've been messed around long enough on this case. I need to know what happened.'

Ben hesitated, listening for some movement from above,

something to tell him that Abigail had finally woken.

'Well?' Roma snapped. 'Get on with it!'

'Jimmy Shaw was hired to find the Goya skull. In the process, he killed Diego Martinez, my brother and Francis Asturias—'

'Why?'

'They were in his way.'

'So Shaw's got the skull?' She frowned. 'How can he have it if it's in New York?'

Ben hesitated. 'There are two skulls.'

'Two?'

'One's the genuine skull of Goya, the other's a fake.' He paused, then carried on, the lie prepared. 'The skull I exchanged Abi for is now with the person who hired Jimmy Shaw.'

'And who's that?'

'I can't say.'

Infuriated, she studied him. 'This case involves three murders. You do realise that I could charge you with withholding evidence?'

'I'm not withholding evidence. I don't know anything.'

She paused, unwilling to confide in him, then relented. 'What if I were to tell you that Jimmy Shaw's body was found this morning. He'd drowned – and he had Francis Asturias's blood on his clothes.'

'So that proves it.'

'It only proves he was involved with Francis Asturias's death. What else do you know?'

Ben shrugged, lying deftly. 'I can't tell you anything

else. The exchange was prearranged. I delivered the skull and Abigail was given back to me.'

He was punchy from lack of sleep, willing Abigail to wake, and knowing that to keep them both safe he *had* to stay silent about Emile Dwappa. The police could never know about him or Mama Gala. Because if they did, Ben would spend the rest of his life looking over his shoulder. If he led the police to Gardenia Street he would never sleep safely again. Every day he would be watched. Every night he would wait for the break-in. And constantly he would wonder how, or when, Abigail would be taken from him – this time permanently.

'I saw no one,' Ben insisted.

'Not even Jimmy Shaw?'

'No, no one.'

Roma let out a long, regretful sigh. 'Did you kill him?'

'No.'

'So who did?'

'I have no idea.'

'You can't tell me half a story and I'll back off! People died—'

'My brother included,' Ben interrupted. 'You think I'll ever forget that? I'm telling you, it was Jimmy Shaw who killed them. He did it to get the skull. You've got his body – it's over.'

'But if you had the skull all along . . .' she asked, her tone deadly, 'why didn't you give it to him at the beginning?'

'You want more deaths?' Ben countered. 'Because if you

press me, that's what you'll get. My death and Abigail's death. Two more murders to explain. And you won't be able to stop it. Even if you put a policeman outside that door, the day will come when he's caught off guard. Are you going to watch us day and night? Put someone on duty to trail us? How about at the hospital, Ms Jaffe? Francis was murdered there, Abigail was taken from there. You feel confident you can protect us there?' He shook his head. 'There will always be the one moment, the one street corner, the one night when there's a slip – and then it happens. And you think I'll risk that? You think I'll take that chance when I have the means to keep her safe? Jimmy Shaw committed all three murders, and now Jimmy Shaw is dead. It's over.'

Thoughtful, Roma walked over to the window, staring at Duncan in the car outside. She was trying to weigh up the advantage of arresting Golding, knowing that he would never give her any further information. He would deny knowing anything more than he had told her because she knew he was afraid. Something or *someone* had thrown a scare into him which would ensure his silence . . . But if she left it like this, then what? She fixed her gaze on Duncan intently, relieved that he had not been with her to hear what Ben Golding had said. Relieved that she could – if she *chose* – come up with a version of events which no one would question. Jimmy Shaw was dead. He wasn't going to give his account.

It was her decision to make. If she chose, the case was solved. Jimmy Shaw had killed the three victims and thrown himself in the Thames. It was neat. Tidy. And it would look good on her record.

Expressionless, she stared at Ben. 'Where's the skull now?'

'The real one?'

She nodded. 'Yes, the real one.'

'Missing—'

'That's convenient.'

'It's the truth,' Ben continued. 'The one in New York's a fake. The real one's disappeared. I don't know where it is. I *did* have it, but I don't have it now.'

'What's to stop someone else looking for it?'

'Why would they?' Ben asked, his tone reasonable. 'Bobbie Feldenchrist is hardly going to announce that she has a fake. As far as everyone knows, Goya's skull is in New York. No one looks for something that's already been found.'

'D'you really think it's that easy? D'you really expect me to go along with your story, and lie for you?'

'Yes, I do,' he said, exhausted and desperate. 'I'm hoping Jimmy Shaw's death will be the end of it. You have a solution, an ending. To all intents and purposes, you've solved the case. You've got Shaw's body and the evidence that ties him to Francis Asturias's death. Let it rest. I'm *begging* you to let it rest. Because if you pursue it, if you question me further or charge me, no one will believe I didn't talk and Abigail will be the next victim.' He held her gaze. 'I know what I'm asking, believe me. But I've lost enough. Please don't take anything else.'

72

'We heard that your partner's been found ...' Megan Griffiths said, dropping into step with Ben as he arrived the following morning. He was back at the Whitechapel, taking on his patients and his operations again. Trying to resume normality, although Abigail was still unconscious, a nurse looking after her at the house. 'We're ... I'm so relieved.'

He reached his room and turned to look at her. And then, without a word, he slammed the door in her face.

Having heard nothing further from Roma Jaffe, Ben was hoping that she wasn't going to pursue the case. Not where he was concerned anyway – but there were still unanswered questions. Where *was* Goya's skull? And what was the resolution of Leon's theory? The real meaning of the Black Paintings? Ben had promised himself that he would finish his brother's notes that night. But before he did that, he had something else to do, which was why he had returned to the Whitechapel Hospital.

Thoughtful, Ben recalled every conversation he had ever had with Francis Asturias about the skull. He remembered him describing the reconstruction, how he had hidden it in the box marked CAUTION – ANIMAL REMAINS. He recalled seeing the skull and examining it with Francis and could hear again, in all its blistering clarity, their last phone call.

I swapped skulls. I have the Goya.

I have the Goya ... But where the hell did you put it, Francis? Ben wondered. Where the hell did you hide it? Not at home, not in your workshop, and not in the laboratory. He paused, concentrating. No, that would have been too obvious for a man like you. You would have thought up something clever but whimsical ... Sighing, Ben thought of his old friend and then considered Elizabeth Asturias.

She was smart. Did *she* have it? He didn't doubt for one moment that she had the intelligence to fool him, but then realised that Francis would not have directly endangered his wife. So what *had* happened? Ben wondered. As Francis heard of the deaths of Diego Martinez and Leon he was spooked – he had admitted as much, so unnerved that he had taken it on himself to protect the skull by hiding it.

Ben frowned, thinking of their last conversation. Of how alarmed Francis had become. But what had prompted him to change the skulls? Had someone threatened him? Had the blank email with the ominous address Gortho@3000.com come with a warning? And, most importantly, how long had Francis had to react? Perhaps that was the most important factor. Perhaps time had dictated the hiding place. Think again, Ben willed himself. Suppose Francis had been under threat and had had to act quickly. He would have gone to the storage room and taken Goya's skull, leaving another in its stead. With the real skull in his possession he would have looked for a hiding place in a hurry. Somewhere near. Somewhere accessible. Close by.

Hurrying out, Ben headed for the anatomy theatre. Over 250 years old, it was built in a semicircle so that the medical students could look down on the wooden stage in the centre and watch dissections or examinations. Now only used for lectures, it was still an impressive place.

Ben pushed open the heavy mahogany doors and walked towards the raised dais. At the back of the stage, on the right, was a human skeleton. Having been used for centuries, it stood like a macabre old soldier, baring its teeth at Ben as he moved towards it. His heart pulsing, he touched the collarbone, the skeleton shifting, then reached up and felt the top of the skull.

There were no holes in it.

Exhaling, Ben sat down. He had been sure he was on to something . . . His gaze moved round the anatomy theatre. Where is it, Francis? Why the hell didn't you tell me where you put it? He looked around again, thinking, forcing himself to work it out. Francis knew everything about the structure of the human anatomy. He had studied it for years. No one understood the workings of a body like Francis Asturias.

No one understood the workings of a body like Francis Asturias . . .

In a second Ben was on his feet, leaving the anatomy theatre and moving across the hospital towards the Medical Exhibition Hall. Nodding to the assistant curator, he walked through the entrance doors. For the purpose of study, bodies of all ages had been preserved. There were parts of bodies too, and organs – a whole motley collection of human pieces dried out and wired up, or bobbing for eternity in formalin. But they weren't what Ben had come to see. He was aiming for the far room, where the earliest specimens were held. The bodies of man before he became man. The bodies of their ancestors, the apes.

As he entered he was faced with rows of stuffed chimpanzees and the skulls of assorted monkeys. Torsos which told of the journey from trees to towns surrounded him. But Ben didn't stop to look at any of them – instead he aimed for the exhibit half hidden in the far left-hand corner. Pushing back the obscuring screen in front of the case, he was faced with an antiqued, weathered skeleton, humped over, the wires bending from its years of standing to attention, the bone and teeth yellowed. And crowning the body of the great ape was its skull.

No one would have noticed it. Tucked away in a badly lit corner, one of the least impressive exhibits, it could have remained undiscovered for weeks. But Ben noticed it. Slowly, almost in awe, he approached.

The torso was simian, but the skull was Goya's.

73

It had been a spectacular week for Bobbie Feldenchrist. Not only had the Goya exhibition been phenomenally successful, but the reviews for the Feldenchrist Collection were almost sycophantic. She had, the papers reported, pulled off an amazing coup in obtaining the skull of Goya. Trumping all her rivals, even the Prado, she had managed to secure an artistic legend.

Oh, yes, Bobbie thought, it had been a victory – one of many. She was now a mother, with an heir to carry on the Feldenchrist name. She was more successful than any of her peers. And, most triumphantly, she had Bartolomé Ortega back in her life. The man who had rejected her for Celina had returned. Their affair would soon be public – Bobbie would see to that, and add his head to Goya's in her own personal memento mori.

The reasons for Bartolomé's return did not overly concern her. Bobbie had little belief in love and less in integrity, but she *did* believe in revenge and had been happy to consider Bartolomé's offer. Apparently he had solved the riddle of the Black Paintings and had suggested that it would be in both their interests to join forces. The Ortega Collection working with the Feldenchrist Collection – one with the skull, one with the theory. And so came into existence twin towers of Babel, teetering on the precipice of their own deceit.

Bartolomé's motives were revenge on his wife and brother. He would never divorce Celina – her silence had been bought with the wedding ring – but he would relish humiliating her. He would not disown his son either. Juan was an Ortega, after all. As for Gabino? No, he would not be exiled. Instead Bartolomé would watch Gina's exquisite and prolonged torture of his brother and encourage it. The Ortega fortune with which he had purchased Gabino's private hell would be a constant encouragement to keep Gina as head jailer and his brother under the cosh.

Some of this Bartolomé had told Bobbie. But she wasn't privy to all the details, although worldly enough to know that love had little to do with their relationship. Sex might play a limited role, but ambition was the amyl nitrate which stimulated both of them. But of one thing she *was* certain – Bartolomé Ortega would never know that the skull wasn't genuine. And Ben Golding was never going to expose her – because he couldn't prove it was a fake. Otherwise he would already have done so. From that quarter she was now safe. As for her assistant,

Maurice de la Valle had already forgotten any doubts Bobbie might have had, his memory wiped clean by his ambition.

So it came as quite a shock for Bobbie to receive a call from London. From Ben Golding, no less.

'What d'you want?' she asked, triumphantly rude.

'Are you going to admit the skull's a fake?'

'Don't be ridiculous! If you pursue this, I'll sue you,' Bobbie replied, 'I have the power—'

'And influential friends,' Ben cut in. 'Like Bartolomé Ortega. I believe you two are close again. People gossip so much, don't they?' He paused, but when she didn't answer he continued. 'I know Bartolomé. Only a little, but Leon knew the Ortegas in Madrid. Bartolomé was as obsessed by Goya as my brother was. But he wasn't as clever as Leon—'

'Just get to the point, will you?'

'I heard that Bartolomé has solved the riddle of the Black Paintings.'

The thrill of victory shot through her.

'Yes, he has. And we're going to include it in the exhibition. Bartolomé's writing a book about it too. It's been the work of lifetime.'

'Whose lifetime?'

She flinched. 'What?'

'Leon solved the riddle, not Bartolomé.'

'Oh, for God's sake! You want to claim the skull for your brother and now the theory too – are you out of your fucking mind? Maybe you are. Maybe Leon wasn't the only Golding brother who was mad.' Her triumph made her cruel. 'Bartolomé's solved the Black Paintings. He has a theory—'

'No, he doesn't.'

'What are you talking about?'

Ben smiled down the phone, smiled across the Atlantic – across the sea and the wrecks of ships and aeroplanes, and the bodies of dead mariners. Smiled for all the folly of the world and the greed at the heart of it.

'When Leon died I took all his papers and his computer. And then I found his theory, the solution to the Black Paintings. I deposited a copy with my bank and gave the original to the Prado. They were impressed. So impressed that Leon Golding's theory of Goya's Black Paintings will be published next year to a fanfare of publicity. At last my brother will have what he deserved – his triumph. Albeit posthumously.' Ben paused, his tone contemptuous. 'You should ask your lover how he came by *his* theory. How Bartolomé Ortega got his hands on it.' He relished the injury he was about to inflict. 'You don't know, do you? Of course, he wouldn't tell you the truth.'

'Which is?'

'I didn't trust my brother's girlfriend. And I was right not to, because she stole Leon's theory. She copied it.'

'Jesus . . .'

'But not before I'd already made *my own copy*.'

Bobbie Feldenchrist swallowed painfully. 'What are you saying?'

'Leon's theory is with the Prado, Madrid, and has been

for weeks. *I lodged it with them the day after my brother died.* If Bartolomé Ortega tries to claim that he's the author, he'll be outed for a liar and a fraud.'

There was silence down the line, Bobbie struggling to answer.

'You've got a fake skull and a fake theory. You've got a great big pile of lies and you're sitting on the top of them, holding on for dear life. I wouldn't want to be you. I used to be angry with you for cheating my brother, but not now. I told you that one day you'd regret ever seeing that skull. I warned you.' His voice hardened. 'Bartolomé Ortega lied to you. He used you. But then again, I imagine you used him too. I don't suppose he knows about the skull being a fake—'

She was reeling, but still fighting.

'Do *you* have the real skull?'

'I have nothing, Ms Feldenchrist,' Ben said enigmatically. 'Nothing but right on my side.'

Putting down the phone, Ben paused for a moment, thinking he heard a noise from upstairs and then remembering the nurse who was caring for Abigail. Walking into the hallway, he stood at the base of the stairs and looked up. But it wasn't the nurse who stood there.

It was the very fragile – but resilient – figure of Abigail Harrop.

74

London

Later that night, while Abigail dozed on the sofa in the study, Ben sat down and looked at the skull, now sitting on his desk. Goya's skull – for which three men had died and another had been tortured. Goya's skull – which had been stolen from a corpse and temporarily housed on the shoulders of a great ape.

Thoughtful, Ben kept staring at it. From the day Leon had been given the skull to the poisoning of Emile Dwappa, everything had been permeated with a kind of sickness, a madness of greed. The madness of the art world, who sought to possess the skull at any lengths. The insanity of Leon, driven to the end by his own obsession. And the madness of the Black Paintings themselves. In awe, Ben touched the cool, dead bone of the skull and felt the holes under his fingers, and then he reached into the middle drawer of the desk and pulled out the battered envelope in which were Leon's writings. All his jottings, his scribbled notes, his sketches, and his conclusion. The final and definitive meaning of the Black Paintings.

With the curtains drawn and the lamps turned on, Abi slept on while Ben hesitated, his right hand resting on the papers, preparing himself to read the last entries his brother had made. Now, finally, he was going to understand what had obsessed Leon for so long. The theory for which he had lived and died. The culmination of his brother's life.

It was almost too much to bear. But he began to read.

. . . Coming to the painting later entitled The Reading. The meaning of this has been disputed for many years.

What are this disparate group of men reading? They represent communication. A testimony. Goya's testimony. He is saying 'Look on my works, read them as you would a book. Study what I have painted on these walls and find the message within.' In the image there are three men fixed on reading a book, on the left is a skeleton, and behind them all is a man looking upwards to Heaven. 'Read what I have written, not in ink but in paint,' Goya is saying. 'See death and look to Heaven - as I do - for deliverance.' I believe he was also looking to Heaven to bear witness to what he was suffering. And, if possible, to intervene.

Read what I am telling you. See it.

And now is the time to consider The Cudgel Fight.

For how long have people studied this image without understanding it? But I humbly believe that it represents the most atavistic clash of wills - that of good and evil. A competition, each man fighting for the upper hand, both knee-deep in the mire. For Goya, it represented Spain and France. Light and dark. Life and death. Goya's health against the onslaught of his illness. But most of all I believe that it represents the cause he believed in - the Liberals against the Spanish King. The very reason why Goya, ill and old, was so afraid, hiding within the suffocating walls of the Quinta del Sordo.

We then come to the penultimate image - The Fates. The Daughters of the Night.

These are the three women of allegory who depict the goddesses who determine the fate of man. One spins the thread of life, one determines its length and one severs it. With them is a bound man, whose fate they are determining. But do these creatures really represent the old fable of The Daughters of the Night? Perhaps, instead,

Goya was updating his version and making it peculiar to him.

The three women I believe depict the three women of the greatest importance in Goya's life: his wife Josefa, a gentle soul who spins the thread of life for him by giving him children and hope for a future; the Duchess of Alba, who Goya loved and who controlled him more than any other woman, determining his thread of his life - the thread that bound the painter to her; and lastly, Leocardia.

Ben leaned back in his seat, trying to assimilate what he had just read. Then, after a moment, he continued.

Goya wasn't insane, but he was willing to be believed mad. Why? Because that was his protection. Hiding behind old age, infirmity and deafness - how much less of a threat would the great man seem? But madness wasn't protection enough.

When I examined Goya's skull I saw the small holes in the bone: three of them, of differing sizes. Then I spoke to several specialists who confirmed what I suspected. But I'm hurrying on too fast. I must go back . . . The last picture of the series, entitled The Witchy Brew, depicts an old woman eating, with a skull-headed figure next to her. This was the final painting Goya did in the Black Painting series. It is the conclusion - <u>and it tells us what happened to him</u>.

'Christ!' Ben said softly.

He had been poisoned for a long time, poisoned with lead, the doses of which were increased steadily.

Lead poisoning was common in painters when lead was in the pigments they used - like Flake White, which Goya must have ingested steadily over the years. But suddenly he appeared to have taken in large amounts. When I first obtained the skull I had many tests undertaken. The results were inconclusive because of the age and condition of the skull, but it was agreed that the holes suggested the <u>very real possibility of lead poisoning</u>.

Look at the three holes - these are typical of a long-term ingestion of lead.

Look at the symptoms - sleep disorders, seizures, raised blood pressure, hallucinations, impotence and hearing problems.

Goya was deaf. Sleep disorders were a trouble to him. And hallucinations would explain much of his work. But the fact that the skull has holes in it points to a sudden and drastic intake of the toxin. Not the gradual assimilation which a painter of Goya's time might ingest, but a comprehensive attempt at poisoning.

Of course lead has a half-life of only 20-30 years, so there is no scientific proof which remains in the bone of the skull for scientists to measure. And permission would have to be sought from the Spanish authorities for further tests to be carried out on Goya's body. But the symptoms from which he suffered indi-

cate that Goya had been slowly and summarily poisoned.

The greatest painter Spain had ever produced was being murdered. And he knew it.

'Jesus!' Ben whispered, glancing over at the sleeping Abi.

She was breathing evenly, her hands resting on the blanket which covered her.

Ben thought about what he had just read. *Francisco Goya had been poisoned.* Someone had set out to kill one of the most famous artists who had ever lived. He could imagine the furore Leon's theory would cause when it was published, the consternation which would follow the final, diabolical solution of the Black Paintings.

Breathing in deeply, Ben turned back to his brother's writings.

But then we have to ask, who poisoned Goya? And why?

Goya was a patriot who loved his country, but he was also reckless. I believe that this great artist exiled himself at the Quinta del Sordo when the degenerate Ferdinand VII return to the throne. The King who hated Liberals - of which Goya was one. The King who suspected that Goya had colluded with the French when Napoleon was in power. The King who had tortured and exiled Goya's friends and peers. Ferdinand - who suspected Goya of funding the Liberals in their attempt to form an alternative Government. Ferdinand, the King who lost the throne, and then regained it. And with it, absolute and revengeful power.

Knowing he was under threat, Goya had been in terror of his life.

He wrote his fear in words:

For being a liberal, it's better to die.

He was no longer young, no longer strong, and he was at the mercy of a tyrant bent on revenge.

Ferdinand VII knew that he could not go directly after Goya. The painter was too famous to kill outright. So the artist was killed drip by drip, poisoned steadily. I imagine that the court, with the help of the Inquisition, set Leocardia to kill the old man. They probably pressurised her into the act, using her child as leverage. She had no choice - murder her lover or sacrifice her daughter. So she set about her task, appearing to look after Goya while she was, in fact, slowly poisoning him. Leocardia was his killer-in-waiting.

Look back at the picture of The Fates - the Daughters of the Night. I believe that Leocardia was the goddess who was hired to cut Goya's tie to the world. To sever his lifeline.

If you doubt this theory, more evidence is in Goya's will. After all her years of apparent devotion, Leocardia was left nothing. That would suggest that Goya suspected her, and I believe he did. I also believe that for a time he was too ill and too old to fight for his survival. And so, in an act of creative genius, the dying Goya left the evidence on the walls of the Quinta del Sordo.

He could not write down the names of his persecutors, or their methods - such evidence would have been destroyed immediately. But under the cloak of madness, Goya <u>could</u> leave a trail of oblique images to tell his story.

Look to the paintings - The Witchy Brew, the last work. The feeding of the poison, the figure of death on the left. Goya spells it out for us. It cries out from the wall. It is there for anyone to see. This was no madman, driven by hallucinations and misogyny. This was a man who was dying, knowing that he was being killed. This is not the work of insanity. This was the only way open for Goya to record what was being done to him.

Perhaps he thought he would never leave the Quinta del Sordo and used its walls to depict the images of his tormenters, the poison in the glass, the murderess leaning on his tomb. With the face of Leocardia. How inspired - as his body was slowly poisoned - to leave the truth among the camouflage of insanity! To hide reality among complete and anarchic madness.

Yes, the Black Paintings are dark. They were painted out of darkness, under the threat of death. No works in history were created out of such terror.

I know people will doubt this theory. Of course. I know they will insist that Goya was ill or mad. That there is not - nor was there ever - any cohesive meaning to these images. But I ask you to do him the honour *of thinking again. <u>If there is any doubt I beg you to</u>* *<u>look at the figure of Saturn</u>, the largest and most* *famous picture in the series of the Black Paintings.* *The most urgent, most disturbing and most direct. In* *fact, the very painting which faced anyone entering* *the Quinta del Sordo. The painting which Goya used* *to depict his own murder. Saturn.*

For the word SATURNISM means lead poisoning . . .

'Dear God!' Ben said, staring at the picture then turning back to his brother's words.

Despite everything Goya was a resilient man, mentally and physically. He realised what was happening, and although frail, fought to live. The Quinta del Sordo was not to become his tomb. Rallying what strength remained, Goya applied to visit France for the good of his health.

He wrote:

Six years ago my health broke down completely.

My hearing in particular has suffered and I have grown so deaf that without sign language I cannot understand what people are saying . . .

The King could not refuse. Goya had outsmarted his persecutors. And so, people believed, it was for the good of Goya's health that he left the Quinta del Sordo for Bordeaux. Whereas in reality, he had tricked them into granting his escape.

In France he recovered. Lived a few years more and never returned to the theme of the Black Paintings. Why would he? Goya had left his testimony on the walls of his old home: the history and destruction of Spain, the tyrant Dog of Spain and Saturn, the poison which was meant to kill him . . .

No one in the history of art has ever recorded their own murder. In this, as in so much, Francisco Goya was extraordinary: as courageous as the bulls he had painted so often; as resilient as the Spanish people, as hard and formidable as the dry earth of Madrid. _This is his story, and by this should history judge him._

Taking in a deep breath, Ben leaned back in his seat, glancing over at Abigail again. She was still sleeping, a little nervous colour in her cheeks, her wound hidden under a clean bandage. Her beauty, all the more toxic for its imperfection, pinched at his heart.

And then, slowly and reluctantly, he turned back to the last entries Leon had made.

In recording Goya's death I realise that I am recording my own. There could only be one outcome.

And then a little scrawled after-note.

Ben, See to it that this is read.
See Goya is vindicated.
I am done.
You were the best of brothers.
Leon

I am done . . . I am done . . .

And then Ben knew. He might have denied it repeatedly, insisted that it wasn't true, but in the end he had to accept that Leon *had* killed himself. And then he knew what had happened in that hotel bathroom in Madrid. Knew that all the running, all the fear, the struggle to handle his instability had come to a close. Twice before, Leon had tried to flee a life that was too much for him. Twice before, Ben had saved him.

That night, alone and afraid, Leon Golding had tried for the third time. And succeeded.

75

One year later, Madrid

For the previous month Ben had undertaken numerous press and television interviews, talking about Leon Golding's sensational theory about the Black Paintings. The book had caught the popular imagination and Goya had become a hero again, a would-be murder victim who had cheated his fate. And the dead author had become a celebrity.

Luckily for Leon he had a brother to speak for him, something Ben did willingly. He praised Leon's intellect, his skill, his perception. He remembered him with pride and refused to answer when asked questions about his death. And every critic who had ever belittled Leon Golding's work, or sneered at his eccentricities, felt themselves dimmed by the brilliance of his renown. In death, Leon triumphed. He was no longer uneasy, threatened or afraid. His words had no tremor or uncertainty about them. What he left behind was greater than the struggle of his life. And what the world would remember was that Leon Golding had scored an indelible mark on the history of art.

It was no more than he deserved.

Tired after a press conference at the Prado, Ben walked to his car. The heat of Spain was building. It was hot in the days and at night the air was liquid with moisture. The kind of heat which made a person sweat and leave their windows yawning wide. Arriving at the cemetery, Ben hoped that the massive iron gates would be open and was pleased to see that they were pinned back, almost as though they expected him, even so late at night. Slowly he drove down the main driveway and then parked, taking the box off the passenger seat and moving through the rows of graves. He knew where he was going and without effort he found the headstone.

Staring down at it, Ben could see the name *Detita* written in script, her dates obliterated by the night shadow of an overhanging tree. He thought she would resent being cheated of the sun. Memory, clear as a noon bell, came back to him – of her words, her beliefs. The way she educated the two Jewish brothers in daytime and, at night, taught them about the dark. But not alone. With her accomplice – the ghost of a long-dead man who had once lived near their land. Their neighbour on Spanish soil. The spirit who still haunted them all.

Goya painted murder because he knew all about it. He was obsessed by struggle and the power of evil . . .

Leaving Detita's grave, Ben walked between the headstones till he arrived at the recent burial ground of his brother. The earth had not completely levelled out, the rounded mound catching the moonlight. Gently he rested his hand on the headstone, feeling for an instant the warmth of his brother's flesh as an owl, high in some night tree, hooted sullenly, the moon riding the corner of a passing cloud.

'I love you,' Ben said simply, reaching for the spade he had brought with him.

Under the moonlight he dug, under the moonlight and silence. Deep down into the earth Ben scratched until he reached Leon's coffin. Then he picked up the small square box which held Goya's skull. Gently he placed it on top of his dead brother's coffin, then scrambled out of the grave and began to refill it, the soil echoing as it hit the coffin. Slowly Ben watched the box which contained Francisco Goya's skull disappear under the press of dry earth. Within minutes, there was no trace of the coffin or the skull. And finally, when all the earth was replaced, he stood back and stared at the grave.

He could not have returned the skull to Goya's body. Not without political and bureaucratic wrangling. Not without the risk of its being stolen again. So instead, after much deliberation, he had buried it with the man who was its rightful guardian. It seemed a fitting tribute to his dead brother.

'Rest in peace, Leon,' he said finally. 'Rest in peace.'

As he walked away, a hoarse wind blew some loose soil over the ground and within seconds there was nothing to indicate that the grave had ever been touched.

Heading for the airport, Ben was surprised to find himself taking a detour, turning off on to another road, one which he knew well. The night was very warm, full of insects, traffic and noise, and over the dark water of the Manzanares River steam sprites lingered among reeds and crept under the arc of the bridge. In the distance the lights of Madrid flickered lazily, the sky deepening into purple at the edge of the horizon.

Driving slowly, Ben came back to the worn farmhouse where he had spent so much of his childhood. The place was deserted, silent, a grinning moon riding over the rooftop, the weathervane dancing eerily in a manic breeze. Getting out of the car, Ben moved into the garden, then turned and glanced up at the window of the bedroom he had once shared with his brother. Memories came to him as he walked around the house, the windows looking out at him blankly, all life gone. But as Ben got back into his car he felt some premonition and, startled, looked up in time to see a shape crossing the upper window – the shape of a young man watching him. It moved towards the glass and looked out, resting its hands on the sill.

Calling out for his brother, Ben left the car and ran back to the house – but the ghost had gone. Leon Golding had walked back into the rooms he had loved, back to the library he had studied in, back to the empty corridors and silent walls.

When he drove away Ben kept his eyes fixed on the road. And never looked back.

POSTSCRIPT

Sixteen years after Leon Golding died there was an incident at the cemetery outside Madrid. Vandals had defaced monuments and broken headstones. When Ben was called over to visit Leon's desecrated grave he found the stone smashed and a pentangle scratched into the tablet. Incensed, he asked that his brother's body be removed. He would see to its reburial himself, in an unknown place.

When the earth was removed from over the grave Leon's coffin was found in perfect order – but the box which had been placed on top had disappeared.

The tomb of Francisco Goya, in San Antoine da Florida, Madrid, contains two corpses: those of his mistress, Leocadia, and himself.

Originally Goya was buried in France, but when his body was moved back to Spain in 1899 – seventy years after his death – the head was missing.

Rumour has it that the skull was stolen by a Bordeaux phrenologist, who had wanted to study the skull of a genius. Rumour also intimates that Goya not only painted – but could have been involved – with Satanism.

As an old man he created the Black Paintings, the enigma of which has never been fully explained. Until, perhaps, now.

The head of Francisco Goya has never been found.

BIBLIOGRAPHY

GOYA – Robert Hughes – (Vintage)
GOYA – Enriqueta Harris – (Phaidon)
THE BLACK PAINTINGS OF GOYA – Juan Jose Junquera
– (Scala)
Healthcave.com
Soylent Communications

Spanish Tourist Board
Prado Museum
Dundee University – Reconstructive Department

Copies of the Black Paintings by the author, Alex Connor.

Official works are in the Prado Museum and Art Gallery,
Madrid.

ACKNOWLEDGMENTS

*Research has been extensive and I would like to thank everyone
for their support. The curators of The Prado, Madrid, and The
Louvre, Paris, have given generous assistance. Dr G. Altman has
advised on facial/maxillary surgery, and Dr C. Wilkinson on
facial reconstruction.*

Thanks to you all.